MAR — 2015

SING A WORRIED SONG

THE ARTHUR BEAUCHAMP NOVELS

Trial of Passion
April Fool
Kill All the Judges
Snow Job
I'll See You in My Dreams
Sing a Worried Song

ALSO BY WILLIAM DEVERELL

Fiction

Mind Games
The Laughing Falcon
Slander
Trial of Passion
Street Legal: The Betrayal
Kill All the Lawyers
Mindfield
Platinum Blues
The Dance of Shiva
Mecca
High Crimes
Needles

Non-fiction

A Life on Trial

SING A WORRIED SONG

by William Deverell

ECW Press

To the memory of Josiah Wood, my former law partner, a humanitarian, and a powerful progressive voice as a counsel and as a justice in the British Columbia Supreme Court and Appeal Court. His legacy is enshrined in the MI LELUM S'ULXWEN (Elders Court) Society, which he designed to train elders for the First Nations Court in Duncan, BC, as a means to encourage, in his words, "the reconciliation of cultures made necessary by the imposition of residential schools and the resulting deep-rooted suspicion of our community and its justice system."

Regina v. Skyler. Transcript, p. 453,
December 16, 1986.

DIRECT EXAMINATION OF
MANFRED UNGER (CONT'D)

Q: And when did you return to your hotel?

A: Sometime after midnight. I read for a while, and went to sleep.

Q: And when did you next see the accused?

A: I'm not sure. Mid-morning. Randolph came into the room and I woke up.

Q: Tell the jury what he said.

A: He said, "I really did it this time." I was confused, still half asleep, and I asked him, "Did what?" And he said, "He wouldn't die. I must have stabbed him ten times, and he wouldn't die." I thought he was joking. He said, "It took him forever to die. There was blood all over." He showed me his leg.

Q: And what did you see on his leg?

A: Tooth marks. Blood.

PART ONE
FOR THE FUN OF IT

WEDNESDAY, NOON

"For you, Monsieur Arthur Beauchamp, pâté végétal aux champignons, then coquilles sautées. Baked brie for Monsieur Meyerson, and le coq au vin, which I do not serve Beauchamp, who has sworn off wine in any form."

The year was 1987, in late April; the event was lunch, and the place was Chez Forget, ill-lit and intimate, known for the inspired cuisine of the irascible, despotic Pierre Forget. Arthur had long given up ordering from the menu, having learned it was best to let Pierre have his way.

Arthur was shakily working on a coffee, his fifth that day. With him was Hubbell Meyerson, being supportive — he'd denied himself his favourite Chablis. Hubbell, his friend for thirty years, since college days, headed up domestic law at Tragger, Inglis, a well-established Vancouver firm. Arthur ran the criminal defence side.

Pierre studied Arthur with rare solicitude. "How long are you sober now, Beauchamp?" Pronounced, typically, the wrong way, the French way. *Beechem* was correct, Anglicized over the many centuries since the William the Bastard led his cavalry onto Hastings Field.

"*Dix-huit jours d'enfer.*" One does not keep secrets from the chef de cuisine at Chez Forget.

"*Bonne chance.*" The wiry little man bounded off.

Arthur had been sober since a weekend wassail eighteen days ago at the Gastown office of Pomeroy, Marx, Macarthur, Brovak for a young counsel who'd just been called to the bar. At midnight, the party had spilled onto the street outside the building's ground-floor tavern, the Shillelagh and Shamrock. John Brovak, a brawny, wild barrister, somehow got into a feud with the bouncer, and punches were thrown.

Arthur had been belting out a favourite folk song, "It takes a worried man to sing a worried song," as squad cars pulled up. The officers stuck him, Brovak, and six other raucous, inebriated trial lawyers in the drunk tank for two hours, then had a good laugh as they ordered taxis and let them go. The incident seemed, happily, to have been covered up.

"Taking a little time away from the family this week," Hubbell said. "They're off to Florida with their grandparents. Easter break."

"I'm sure you'll keep your nose clean."

Hubbell looked indignant. "My behaviour will be angelic." This family lawyer had a history of marital misconduct. Arthur couldn't understand that. Hubbell had a perfectly lovely wife, two bright kids. Age had done little damage to this ruddy, handsome man, with his mane of silvery hair and winning smile. He was the one who used to get the girls, back in their college days. Gawky, slat-ribbed Arthur got seconds.

"And Annabelle?" Hubbell asked.

Arthur considered the many possible answers to that roomy question. *She is well*, he wanted to say, *she is true, the marital seas are calm, her days of dalliance are over.* But then he would have to knock on wood. He contented himself with: "Working feverishly on next week's *Tristan*." Arthur's flamboyant spouse was artistic director of the Vancouver Opera. His cup rattled in its saucer as he lowered it.

"You feel you have it under control, Arthur?"

"For the moment. The addiction lurks, though — you always sense it there." Like a crouching predator, ready to spring at the first sign of weakness. Arthur had just survived a long, long Easter weekend. Evenings were the worst, especially when Annabelle worked late and only fifteen-year-old Deborah was there to help him through it. But he tried not to involve her in his struggle, tried to shield her from his pain. Teenagers had better things to do. He'd had to call Bill Webb a few times, his AA sponsor.

"How many days will the trial go?" Hubbell asked. The Skyler case, set for the next day, Thursday, April 23. It would be Arthur's first stint as a prosecutor.

"I'm desperately hoping we'll be done on Monday." Otherwise he'd be about the only lawyer missing from the Tuesday afternoon office party honouring him and Hubbell — a celebration to mark their promotion to partnerships. Arthur might yet find himself uninvited to the event and to the partnership. Managing partner Roy Bullingham made his offer contingent on Arthur "not running afoul of a situation that might grievously embarrass the firm."

Though the debacle in Gastown was known among criminal lawyers, word had yet to reach Bully's forty-third-floor office.

"Different kind of game for you," Hubbell said. "Hitting instead of pitching."

"Far simpler than defending. The entire machinery of the state behind you. Everything presented in a neat package by experienced investigators. And it's been test-run, though abysmally. If I can't do better, I shall retire from the bar."

By test-run, Arthur meant an earlier trial, in December, which ended with a deadlocked jury. A new trial had been ordered. In the face of angry mutterings from the public, the Attorney-General had approached the West Coast's preeminent defence counsel to lead the prosecution.

For Arthur, the prospect was a challenge, something different: a sensational murder case, with its dark irony of a happy-faced clown being bumped off by an alleged thrill killer. It was a chance to see things from the other side, to work with the vaunted Homicide section of the Vancouver police. A chance to demonstrate how a prosecution should be run: transparent and even-handed, without guile or hostility.

The press had dubbed it a thrill killing because the crime seemed otherwise motiveless. The victim, Chumpy the Clown, as he was popularly called, had no enemies or anything worth stealing. He'd been a fixture on downtown streets, from Gastown to Theatre Row, busking with a harmonica, pratfalling, beeping his bright red nose at the kids. He'd been at this for ten years; he was an institution. Tour guides pointed him out. He was named Number One Busker by *Vancouver* magazine.

In his other life he was Joyal (Joe) Chumpy, a beer-bellied alcoholic. A gentle, bubbly fat man with lumpy features he exaggerated under clown makeup. He was fifty-three when, on the morning of Sunday, August 3, 1986, he died in his skid road apartment, hemorrhaging from seven deep knife wounds.

Arthur himself was among Chumpy's many fans, and had regularly dropped him a few bills. But he was resolved not to let his feelings cloud his role as dispassionate agent of the state. Prosecutors were not allowed to show feelings. Properly, they weren't even allowed to *have* feelings.

"I should think you'd be concerned about your image among the criminal class," Hubbell said. "The underworld doesn't much abide turncoats."

"Be realistic, Hubbell. A spoiled brat who killed for pleasure, not profit, gives crime a bad name. The Mob will be cheering me on."

WEDNESDAY AFTERNOON

Arthur spent the rest of that day at the Crown office in the Law Courts, interviewing witnesses and reading transcripts until the words blurred. He puffed for a while on his newly purchased Peterson bent — he'd taken to nicotine to stave off desire for that other, crueller drug — and looked balefully at the array of interviews, the death scene photos, the grisly autopsy report.

None of which much helped Arthur resolve the stickiest puzzle of the case: What made the accused, Randolph Skyler, tick? The handsome, charming twenty-three-year-old seemed an unlikely suspect — studying for a business masters at York University, no previous record, sole offspring of a well-to-do Toronto couple. He was a college athlete — track and field, a sprinter — and a skilled outdoorsman who often joined his dad in Northern Ontario, fishing or bagging ducks and deer.

He'd flown to the West Coast with his best buddy for the August long weekend. That was during Vancouver's acclaimed world fair, Expo 86, a celebration marred slightly on the third day of August by the cruel murder of a jolly busker.

Skyler's pal, a friend since their adolescent years, was Manfred

Unger, a military cadet in Kingston and a key Crown witness whom Arthur had not yet met or interviewed. That distressed Arthur — Unger would be flying in from Ontario late, worryingly late, on the very eve of the trial.

He rang Homicide, reached lugubrious Lars Nordquist at his desk, and asked for the latest on Unger's ETA.

"Half past eleven. Sorry. Witness Services' fault. Some kind of logistical goof." Nordquist promised to meet the plane.

Arthur was determined not to lose sleep over it. Not on the eve of the trial. His debriefing of Unger could wait.

He tamped out his pipe, shrugged into his coat, packed his heavy book bag, and braved the chill damp of an interminably rainy April, summoning the grit to walk past three bars en route to the parking garage and his 1960 Rolls-Royce Phantom V — a fee from a fraudulent stockbroker lacking liquidity. It was an extravagant luxury, that auto, in the shop a lot, but he'd become attached to its timeless nobility.

Two days in court, the weekend off, finish on Monday, God willing. Five more days of drinklessness added to his current eighteen would make it twenty-three. Many years ago he had made it to twenty-six (while recovering from a back injury), so he was striving for a personal best. Counting the days, said Bill Webb, gives a sense of accomplishment, of encouragement. At what point, Arthur wondered, would he be able to say he had overcome his addiction?

It had gotten so bad a few years ago that many believed he was washed up. But flinty, shrewd Roy Bullingham never gave up on him, and chastised him relentlessly for allowing a booze habit to undermine his great skills.

Helping Arthur stay on the wagon was the fact that Annabelle was currently between lovers. Her affairs — *romantic wanderings*, she called them — were rarely discussed, except by their daughter, Deborah, who felt sorry for her dad, with his lack of marital backbone.

Last year, she'd had a dust-up with Annabelle over her fling with a libertine artist. Chastened, Annabelle put her adulterous pursuits on hold, and Arthur's alcohol intake slowed, to the point that he began showing up in court sober, restricting his sprees to weekends.

He'd begun going to AA meetings — sporadically at first, with lapses, but more regularly in the new year, though there was that one spectacular blowout a few weeks ago, which put him in the drunk tank. That had prompted him to take the pledge again, with a determination fortified by the urgent need to arm himself for a sensational murder trial. If only he could get through it on the dry . . .

WEDNESDAY EVENING

In placid, affluent West Point Grey, where the Beauchamps lived, cherry trees were celebrating spring's return with pink bouquets, and daffodils lined the boulevards like dabs of sunshine in the rain. Driving up the lane to his sturdy old brick home, Arthur remembered that his backyard garden needed to be prepared for planting, rain or shine. That, he resolved, was how he would spend the bulk of the weekend — gardening seemed the only soothing pastime he had left.

He pulled into the double garage beside Annabelle's Porsche, picked up his heavy briefcase, and went in, stepping carefully over large sheets of set plans and sketches arrayed across the living room floor: Annabelle's homework. *Tristan and Isolde*. Opening next week, Thursday.

He was pleased to observe that Deborah was also doing her homework — she was in his den, tapping away at a bulky new Wang computer, a device that her parents hadn't quite figured out. "This is so neat," she'd said on first trying it. "It even corrects your spelling."

She broke free to give him a hug. "Can you handle alone, Dad? Mom's dropping me off for skating." She had a figure skater's figure, leggy, limber. Also green hair these days, to go with her green eyes.

"Sure, I can handle alone. I feel terrific. You just worry about your lutzes."

He was feeling soiled by his immersion in Regina v. Skyler and was looking forward to a long, cleansing soak in the bathtub. He found Annabelle upstairs in the master bedroom, dressing for an evening out.

"Don't want to smudge," she said, with a touch of her lips to his. She was thirty-nine, as striking as when he met her eighteen years ago: still svelte, wide mouthed, with large, teasing eyes, and a crop of black hair cut short this month. Eighteen years, and she still gave him palpitations. They used to be just tremors of love, but later, love and hurt.

"I'm sorry, it came up suddenly. The board is insisting I attend the fundraiser at the Media Club. Per Gustavson will be there, signing albums and cassettes."

"Ah, your gifted heldentenor."

"If you won't feel too ill at ease at a cocktail do, darling, you have just enough time to change."

The invitation wasn't emphatic, but Arthur welcomed it nonetheless as a gesture at togetherness. It had been three years since her last extramarital frolic: a thirty-year-old abstract artist, undiscovered and likely forever to be. She preferred younger men. There was only one upside to that: Arthur would have felt even more diminished if her lovers had been his age. But in preparing for her forties, she seemed to have put her restless, reckless years behind her, emboldening Arthur's hopes. He was almost willing to believe.

"I would be poor company. I shall be in my den obsessing over the trial."

"You're holding out okay?"

"It's hard not to feel the pressure." He showed her a story in the day's *Sun*: "Leading Counsel Takes on Thrill Kill Rerun." Pictured was fifty-year-old A.R. Beauchamp, QC, in his robes, tall, gangly, and hawk-beaked, overconfidently snapping his suspenders.

As she read this backgrounder, he undressed in the bathroom and began filling the tub.

"Oh my God, Arthur. Talk about divulging. 'He candidly admitted to having had alcohol problems.'"

"The reporter bluntly put it to me. I'd have looked the fool by equivocating." Prospective jurors would have read that too, but Arthur felt no shame in it. "Tell Mr. Gustavson I look forward to seeing his Tristan and that I have a tape of his Siegfried that I very much like." The tenor was a bull of a man, Swedish, much in demand in Europe. "How old would you say he is?"

"Why?"

"He seems to have just gotten widely known."

"Not yet thirty-five. Most of the great ones don't mature until they're in their forties. Like lawyers, darling. Do me up."

He was down to his underwear when he approached her and began fumbling with a zipper at the back. "You look quite smashing, dear." He felt a touch of Eros as his fingers met her skin, and there came an unexpected erection. She felt it too, and playfully pressed her rump against his loins.

"I love you too, darling. Just hold on to that until I get back."

He forced himself to laugh with her as he returned quickly to the bathroom, flustered. Yet it was a good sign, that brief, humble erection, proof of healing vitality. There'd been a long period when his penis had vastly underperformed, a time of weariness and depression. As the tides are controlled by the moon, his capabilities tended to rise and fall according to current cuckoldry conditions.

As he lay in the tub, soaping himself, images came of Annabelle offering herself, and his cock rose again, unaided, like a periscope. Then came a wave of performance anxiety, and it descended.

§

Wrapped in a terry cloth robe, he went down to his den, selected a tape of Liszt études and settled into his club chair with the Skyler file. He pulled out the photographs first. Mug shots rarely flatter, but in his, Randolph Skyler looked handsome, if defiant. A morgue shot showed Joyal Chumpy's blanched, pudgy body, drained of blood through seven stab wounds. Photos from the crime scene were even more repellent: a room that announced impoverishment and alcoholism and savage, senseless murder. Chumpy was sprawled on a ratty, blood-soaked single bed, a litter of empty beer bottles beside it. The scene inspired Arthur to double down on his pledge.

He gathered up the several volumes of transcripts of the previous trial, and began making notes for a cross-examination that might never happen unless he could force Skyler into the witness box. The Crown hadn't been able to do so last time.

He would have to deal with the miscounted beer bottles — the bumbling over them in the first trial had enabled the defence to hang the jury. Arthur opened the last transcript to the summing-up by defence counsel Brian Pomeroy:

"Okay, so we have one of the crime scene guys telling you he collected twelve empties from that room. And they found an empty twelve-pack. Then after they remove all the exhibits to the lab, they find a thirteenth beer. It's half-empty, same brand, Coors, and it's supposedly sitting on a window ledge behind a curtain. And when did they find it? Nobody could remember. It's missing from their notes. Conveniently, it's the only bottle that has not been wiped clean by the real murderer, and even more conveniently it's got a partial print on it that they say matches the right thumb of the accused. Let's call him the wrongly accused. Or more accurately, the falsely accused. Ask yourself, each of you: Are you willing to take a chance on convicting this young graduate student of this unspeakable crime over something that smells as bad as this?"

Bravo, Brian.

This gifted young counsel had cleverly wangled a mid-December date for Randolph Skyler's first trial by agreeing to waive a preliminary hearing "so we can get him out for Christmas." He knew jurors were at their most merciful just before holiday season.

Pomeroy had done his utmost to discredit the Crown's star witness — tonight's late-arriving Manfred Unger — then gambled by electing to call no evidence. The case went to the jury after two days, and after three more they were unable to bring in a unanimous verdict.

Arthur had shared several courtrooms with Brian Pomeroy and admired the young sharpshooter's skills, although he found him somewhat neurotic — though not in any damaging way. An edgy, cynical chatterbox.

Arthur looked out the window at the empty street. Annabelle would likely be late, but Deborah was usually home by now, nine-thirty.

Back to his cross. Would Skyler come across as a spoiled brat? That was Arthur's sense of him. How did an only child of well-to-do parents decide to kill a total stranger for no reason? A virile young man, attractive to women, according to police interviews, but faithless. There'd been a string of broken hearts and one broken engagement.

It was nearing a quarter to ten, and Deborah's lateness was making him lose focus. He finally relaxed when a familiar Dodge pickup pulled into the driveway, driven by Nels Jensen, her coach, a former pairs champion at some level or other. The engine was stilled and lights turned off, and his anxiety swelled as the minutes dragged past. Jensen was probably just offering her some final pointers on her inside edge spirals. *The upper leg must be extended just so*, he was saying. Running his hand up that leg. Stroking it . . . If she wasn't out of that truck in two seconds . . .

She jumped out, laughing. Arthur felt foolish; obviously Jensen had needed time to finish a joke or anecdote. Arthur hurried back to his club chair before Deborah could catch him at the window.

"G'night, Dad," she said at his doorway. "Don't work too hard, it sets a bad example."

He took that to heart and unfolded a half-completed *New York Times* Sunday crossword.

§

At around midnight, Arthur woke to find himself slumped in his chair, still clutching pencil and puzzle. He rubbed his eyes and rose to go to bed. Without thinking, reacting from habit, he first opened the liquor cabinet, but of course it was bare.

Their bed was empty, unrumpled, sans Annabelle, and he was unable to sleep for nearly two hours, until she returned. He lay still, his eyes closed, as she took a protracted shower. When she slipped between the sheets, he could smell soap and liquor. Maybe something else, something like spent heat. She didn't try to arouse him. He fought for sleep and finally found it.

THURSDAY MORNING

It was Arthur's almost inviolable tradition to drop into Bob's Barber Shop on the morning of a major trial, a tradition that had morphed into near-superstition after an ineffectual attempted-murder defence that was not preceded by a shave and a cut.

So that's where he found himself at nine a.m., the sole customer in a Davie Street storefront a couple of blocks from the courthouse. It had a proper barber pole and catered to a clientele who, like Arthur, couldn't abide salons that proclaimed themselves "unisex."

"Such lovely hair," said Bob, fluffing it up for his scissors. "The lion of the courtroom. I think I prefer it longish for this one. We don't want to look like a gendarme even though we are prosecuting."

Arthur felt less distressed that morning, despite having slept only five hours. Over morning coffee, Annabelle had explained what had held her up. One of her costumers was having "relationship problems," and vented till all hours.

"The prosecutorial look is what we must aim for. *Distingué*. Polished. But not vain or distant. He has the common touch. Shares the jury's repulsion. A thrill killing, the papers say. Was this Randolph Skyler gay, do you think?"

"Indications are very much otherwise." Bob was gay himself, uncloseted, devotedly partnered. "Why? Do you think he might be?"

"Joyal Chumpy was."

"Truly? That's not widely known in the community."

"Oh, it's quite well known in my community, Mr. Beauchamp. He cruised. At night, of course, when he was not in clown costume. He liked to be called Joy then, not Joe."

That wasn't mentioned in the police reports. "I suppose cruising can be a dangerous sport."

"Indeed. One never knows when one might encounter a psychopath with a severe case of homophobia."

§

The Crown had its own dressing room at the Law Courts, but Arthur preferred to use his firm's locker in the gentlemen's robing room. "Turncoat," someone called as he entered from the barristers' lounge. "Quisling," another yelled, to laughter. Even Quentin Russell, the smooth, erudite mob lawyer, joined in, calling, "Collaborationist."

Arthur could handle it. His late, great hero, Cyrus Smythe-Baldwin, QC, had prosecuted once. Arthur was a professional, and he would proudly accept the retainer of any desperate client, even one as notorious as the Attorney-General, especially at five hundred dollars an hour.

He was sliding into his striped trousers when Brian Pomeroy appeared, bright and perky, several lockers away. He called: "Arthur, if you think we're going to finish this ring-dang-do in three days, you'd better ask your shrink for a reality check."

Arthur buttoned his vest, tied his dickie, slung his gown over his shoulder, and strolled over to join him. "I want you to have mercy on me, Brian. I haven't had a drink since . . ." He lowered his voice. "Since we were tossed so ignominiously into the drunk tank."

"We, monsieur?" Pomeroy smoothed his thicket of a moustache.

"Were you not apprehended with the rest of us?" Arthur glanced about to ensure no one was listening.

"You must have been totalled, man. No, I wasn't in the tank with you. I was on the fire escape smoking weed with Mandy Pearl, allegedly trying to put the make on her, or so she claimed. I was too wiped to remember. More likely she was coming on to me. Vamping unavailable men is her favourite leisure-time activity."

The party that night was to celebrate Augustina Sage's joining Pomeroy, Marx, Macarthur, Brovak, and Arthur recalled seeing Mandy there. A small package of dimples, blond tresses, and bold breasts. What those of limited vocabulary called "hot." Recently divorced. She and Augustina were tight friends.

"Anyway, Mandy threatened to tell Caroline I had my hand down her pants if I didn't hire her to junior me. I decided not to take a chance she was only kidding. She'll add some glam to the proceedings. Heartfelt commiserations to you, though: you're stuck with that toadying, anal-compulsive nitpicker . . ."

He bit his tongue just in time, as Jack Boynton, Arthur's junior, came around the far corner into their aisle, charging toward them, harried. A young man with a face creased by a constant frown and decorated with a neatly trimmed beard. "It's four and a half minutes to ten, gentlemen. Had we not best bustle on up to Court 53?"

"Jack, why do you always sound like a badly written line?" Pomeroy, doing up his vest, mocked: "Pray do not tarry, gentlemen. His Lordship awaits within." To Arthur: "Selden Horowitz. Lucky draw."

They strolled out, Boynton waving the two laggards forward into the Grand Hall of the modern, cantilevered courthouse. Its oblique-angled glass roof was supported by spiderwebs of aluminum tubing, its several dozen courtrooms hidden behind vine-covered concrete railings. The three men ascended the sweeping curves of wide stairways.

"Hope you guys found a fix for the inexplicable late discovery of that unlucky thirteenth beer bottle."

"Having spent untold hours on that critical issue," Boynton said, "all is well in hand."

Pomeroy took another shot at him: "Jack, why do your modifying clauses never agree with the subject?"

Boynton, who to his credit had not been involved in the first trial, would lead the fingerprint evidence. Arthur had decided the job demanded an obsessive zeal for detail.

On the fifth level, Pomeroy brought them to a halt. "Pray, let us forbear from befouling the minds of the jurors with frightful displays of photographs of the dearly departed." He switched to plain English: "Don't force me to take it up with Horowitz. I'll admit cause of death. Loss of blood after multiple stab wounds."

"I believe," Boynton said, "we have already responded to that with a firm negative."

Pomeroy ignored him. "And we don't have to spend an hour with the pathologist giving a painstaking analysis of the seven cuts. I'll admit his report."

"Let us think about it." What Arthur was thinking about was getting this over in three days. He sighed on seeing Boynton's mouth purse with reproach.

Mandy Pearl was waiting for them at the door to Room 53. She didn't wait for introductions and grabbed Arthur's hand. "We almost met at Augustina's call party."

"I thought of seeking acquaintance, Ms. Pearl, but couldn't find a way to break through the barricade of men surrounding you."

She turned to Pomeroy. "He *is* a great lawyer."

She offered a milder greeting to Boynton, and all entered the room. It was more than half full and would be at capacity after a day or two. Its chroniclers were in the press box to the left. The jury box, to the right, was waiting to be filled from the panel of sixty citizens the sheriffs had summoned to court. The witness stand stood near the judge's bench, but the prisoner's dock, with its shield of bulletproof glass, was the room's centrepiece.

Pomeroy brought forward a young blond man and placed him there: Randolph Skyler in a dark suit, off-white shirt, conservative tie. As Arthur passed by, their eyes met and Skyler allowed a glimmer of a smile. Maybe he meant to be friendly, but Arthur sensed arrogance. Bold, alert, he was hiding whatever discomfort he felt.

Brian had got him out on interim release after the mistrial, the conditions of which were that Skyler remain in Vancouver and sign in twice weekly at 312 Main Street, the police station. Skyler found a centrally located apartment for which his well-off parents — both working in finance — footed the bill.

While counsel arrayed their papers at either end of a long table, the clerk ordered all to stand for the arrival of Justice Selden Horowitz, a robust man with a ruddy face and the crinkles of one who smiles easily. Arthur suspected he would prefer the English tradition of wearing wigs — he hadn't much on top.

He urged everyone to be seated, greeted counsel, praised the jury panel for performing its historic duty to democracy, then addressed Arthur.

"Mr. Prosecutor, you have set this down for three days. Are you comfortable with that?"

"I will do my utmost to speed it along, M'lord."

Horowitz turned to Pomeroy, who hedged cleverly: "We're working out some admissions."

"Good. The jury will be able to plan accordingly."

Arthur would have to capitulate to Pomeroy by agreeing to those admissions, otherwise his chances of finishing on Monday would fizzle.

Skyler stood, and the charge of murder in the first degree was read to him. "I am not guilty, sir." Polite, emphatic.

§

Within an hour all jury seats but one were filled. Arthur watched as Pomeroy, down to his last challenge, pondered whether to accept a stern-looking male retiree or a comely store clerk. There was little doubt whom he would choose — the dapper young lawyer, with his woolly, roguish moustache, played to women jurors well.

"Challenge," said Pomeroy, and went on to consider the store clerk, as the two case detectives entered: Inspector Honcho Harrison, a barrel-chested old bull, and Lars Nordquist, known as Bones, thin and laconic. Sorely aggrieved after the first trial failed, they'd pressed the Attorney-General to retain a special prosecutor for the retrial. Arthur had been their first choice.

Honcho came up the aisle, looking distressed. "Something is afoot," Boynton said, rising to meet him. Arthur got up too. Randy Skyler was watching with his worry-free expression.

Harrison talked low: "Manfred Unger has been gotten to." Unger had flown in at midnight, exhausted, not saying much to Nordquist. He was now in a courthouse witness room.

Arthur was startled. "Gotten to? How?" The young officer cadet had been back East since the previous trial. A student at the Royal Military College in Kingston, he got only middling grades, but he starred on the intercollegiate rugby team.

"Suddenly, he's suffering terminal memory deficit. You're going to have to sit down with him and talk some serious shit."

The store clerk returned Pomeroy's smile. "Content," he said. "I'm very content, M'lord, with these twelve fine citizens of Greater Vancouver."

While this grandstanding was going on, Arthur was aching to have a drink to help him grapple with the prospect of a reluctant witness sinking the Crown's case.

§

A sheriff led the jurors in — seven women, five men, a few of middle age, most younger. They seemed relaxed enough, resigned to their fate: sequestration in a fine hotel. Horowitz had ordered they be kept in sterile surroundings — limited TV, no newspapers — because of the wide media attention.

"Mr. Beauchamp, you may open to the jury."

Arthur rose, feeling unready, his confidence on the wane. He had spent a few minutes with Manfred Unger while the jurors put their affairs in order for the next several days. Unger was composed, polite but stubbornly uncooperative.

"Ladies and gentlemen, it is my task now to summarize the Crown's evidence so you may have a sense of what is to come."

That, he realized, sounded lecturish. This relatively young jury would better respond to an avuncular approach. Get close to them. Lighten up. "I feel I ought to tell you I've never done this before, prosecute. Handled a few defences, so I know my way about, but otherwise I'm going to bumble along as best I can." That got a few grins — they would have seen the photo in the *Sun*: leading counsel A.R. Beauchamp, QC, snapping his suspenders.

He heard the sound of two hands clapping, and turned to see Pomeroy grinning too, applauding Arthur's humble act. That prompted laughter from the public, the jury box, and even the bench. The brazen defence counsel had neatly turned the tables, exposing Arthur as a folksy snake oil salesman.

Arthur felt a flush rising, but carried on doughtily. "Before Mr. Pomeroy's diverting interruption, I was about to offer a reason why I may seem to be having difficulties as we go along. Those of you who read a recent newspaper will know I had an alcohol problem. This is my eighteenth day without a drop." There came a scatter of applause from the public seats.

Arthur had stooped low with that one, but he was desperate to get the jury onside. The sympathetic looks from the jurors told him it had worked. So did the pained grin from Pomeroy. Mandy Pearl gave him a laudatory wink.

Arthur segued from his own drinking problem to Chumpy's, briefly recreating the lonely, liquor-crippled life of a street clown, describing the dreadful scene in his suite, reviewing the police evidence, the fingerprints, the forensics, the arrest of the accused, and concluded with some words about the jury's role and his own as an unimpassioned presenter of evidence who, though he shouldered the burden of proving guilt beyond a reasonable doubt, sought only that justice be done. Arthur was determined to be a model prosecutor, not one of those belligerent conviction-seekers who infested the Attorney-General's department.

He let Boynton lead the first few witnesses. The photos that had so distressed the defence were pared down; the pathologist's report was admitted as truth, as was the blood analyst's. Net gain of time, maybe three hours.

Boynton meticulously led the crime scene team leader on a tour of Chumpy's apartment — one of three small suites in a 1930s-vintage house on Powell Street, all sharing a front door. Chumpy's was Suite B, comprising a bedroom, kitchenette, washroom, and a closet full of clothes and clown gear.

His body had been found on the afternoon of Sunday, August 3, only slightly warm. Among the exhibits entered was a thin, sharp paring knife, found on a kitchen counter. When analysed, the knife showed traces of human blood, although it appeared to have been washed.

The jurors didn't blanch much on looking at the crime scene photos. The forewoman even lingered over them, maybe out of professional interest — she was an interior decorator. Skyler had on a serious face throughout and occasionally made notes.

Arthur took the next witness: Marcel Fontaine, sixty-one, wan and cadaverous and appearing mightily hungover as he approached the stand. This unemployable alcoholic was the only person the police could find to provide background on Joyal Chumpy. He answered Arthur's questions with a ragged voice as if from frayed vocal cords.

Arthur brought out that Fontaine and Chumpy came from the same dying Quebec mining town. Both were from broken homes, neither with more than a grade-school education. Twelve years ago they began making their way across the continent, doing odd jobs, day labouring, begging, stealing, serving a little time here and there. The witness didn't shy away from these admissions; Arthur had instructed him to be candid.

"I understand you fellows spent some time working at country fairs."

"Yes, sir, one summer him and me got on with a travelling carnival for a few months. That's where he got the idea of being a clown for a living."

Chumpy bought a clown outfit soon after they arrived in Vancouver, where for a couple of years the two men shared a flat, subsisting on social assistance, panhandling, or clowning for spare change. They parted ways when Fontaine found a place for himself.

So far, a not-so-laudable history of Chumpy the Clown. Nothing villainous, few highlights. But Arthur wanted more. *He cruised. At night, of course, when he was not in costume. He liked to be called Joy then, not Joe.* Arthur's traditional haircut had paid off. Bob the Barber's insinuation that Skyler was a homophobic psychopath had the ring of truth.

"Was Joe Chumpy ever married?"

"Not him. I had a wife once, but it didn't last."

"And you were close pals?"

"Yeah, sort of. We didn't know nobody else."

"Why did you move out of that shared apartment?"

"Well, he had his thing going on, and it wasn't my thing, and I . . . eventually I met a lady and moved in with her."

"What was his thing?"

"Sometimes he'd have guests."

"What kind of guests?"

"Young men. Mostly prostitutes, I guess, given he weren't no prize-winning beauty. Once or twice a month, after work, if he had a good day, he'd say, 'I'm taking a cruise,' and he'd go out and, like, do that. He had his own room, but . . . we never talked about it much. Like I say, it was his thing."

"Did you ever warn him about doing that, cruising?"

"I didn't see it was my business."

Arthur was surprised that Pomeroy bothered to rise to cross-examine.

"Tell me, Mr. Fontaine, was Chumpy bringing home a fair bit of cash from his street performances?"

"Maybe on a good night, a weekend. Around Christmas he'd do pretty good. Coins mostly, some small bills. He always shared."

"He did pretty well in the summer too, right? Lots of action downtown. Tourist season."

"Summer was pretty good, yeah. Fifty, sixty bucks on a good weekend."

"And the day he died, August third, that was during a long weekend, after one of the busiest nights of summer, and the town was jammed for Expo 86, right?"

"Maybe, I guess so, yeah."

"So he probably had a lot of money to pay for sex that night, and lots left over."

"Objection. Grossly speculative."

"No more questions."

Arthur's useless, knee-jerk objection had, he feared, merely excited the jury's interest in the scenario hinted at: a robbery gone awry. Chumpy picking up a tramp who'd grabbed his weekend take. A fight escalating to murder.

THURSDAY, NOON

When they broke for lunch, Arthur hurried to a witness room at the end of the hall. Boynton tagged along, fretting about Manfred Unger's defection. "Who do you suppose is behind his little game? Perhaps our learned, sarcastic friend?"

"Brian would hardly suborn perjury. Pick up a couple of sandwiches, would you, and meet me in the library. Evidence Act, Section 9, adverse witnesses. Look in *Tremeear's* and pull the leading case — it's Milgaard, 1971, I think — and anything more recent."

"What kind?"

"What kind of what?"

"Sandwich."

"Use your imagination."

"Shall I presume whole wheat?"

"Yes. Just go."

A hearing to declare the witness hostile to the Crown would tack on at least two extra hours. Arthur's addiction was acting up. He felt shaky for a few moments, then steadied himself.

§

Harrison and Nordquist were outside the witness room. "He's totally clammed up now," Honcho said.

Arthur hoped Harrison hadn't reverted to style and bullied Unger. "I'd like you fellows to find out if he's been anywhere near Skyler, if he's made any trips out to Vancouver. Have they talked long-distance, is there correspondence? Get the police in Ontario on it. His parents, girlfriend, teachers, pals, rugby teammates."

"His parents flew in last night," Nordquist said. "Edmund and Florence Unger. He's a full colonel, former sub-commandant at Canadian Forces College in Toronto, now serving at CFB Gagetown, New Brunswick. She's active in the Presbyterian church there, runs the children's program. They're staying with their daughter, Susan, who's in second year at Simon Fraser University."

"And Skyler's parents?"

Nordquist shrugged. "Came to the trial in December, haven't shown up this time. Too busy, maybe. Not a lot of warmth there."

Arthur entered the room, closed the door. Unger was sitting back from the table with his arms folded, legs crossed, defensive. His light brown hair had a military cut. He was built like a footballer, wide in the shoulders. Round-faced, he lacked Skyler's chiselled looks. A day pack beside him, a newspaper, a *Sports Illustrated*.

"You're feeling okay, Manfred? You've been treated all right?"

"Please remind Detective Harrison he's not my commanding officer."

Arthur smiled. "You're in officer training yourself."

"I've been in officer training since I got out of diapers. But yes, I'm in the program at RMC, sir. Completing my bachelor of science. Examinations are a month away, so thank you for the subpoena."

"Regrettable. This will soon be over. Couple of days. Okay, you've had some chance to think this over."

"I'm not saying anything about the case, sir. I'm sorry."

"Why?" Arthur sat down near him.

"I've been instructed that I don't have to."

"By whom?"'

"A military lawyer said I don't have to talk to persons in authority."

"That's only if you're suspected of a crime."

"Detective Harrison thinks I'm guilty of obstructing justice. I'd like to leave it at that, sir."

"If you remain silent in court, you will be found guilty of contempt and probably jailed."

"I'll deal with it then."

"One would think part of a young soldier's training is to obey persons in legitimate authority."

"This is a civil matter. Civil rules apply." ·

"Your lawyer told you that?"

"Yes, sir."

This was no easy nut to crack. "From all accounts, you appear to be an upstanding young man. Good home. Sterling background. A fine military career ahead of you. Why would you want to throw all that away?"

Unger looked past him at the wall. No sound emitted from his pursed lips.

"I understand your parents are here."

"I asked them not to come."

"They're obviously concerned about you."

Unger turned away, his face tight with the effort to stifle his emotions.

"You don't want to hurt them, do you, Manfred? Something is obviously bothering you, and this is the time to tell me what it is. Once I begin to cross-examine you, it's too late."

He stood abruptly.

"Has Randy been in touch with you?" asked Arthur. No response. "Have you been promised something? Were you threatened?"

Unger clenched his fists, but Arthur didn't detect any anger, just frustration.

"I'm going to leave you alone for a while. I want to you to consider the crime of perjury. Fourteen years."

In the corridor, Arthur told the officers to let him stew for a while. Then, finally, he vented his anger in a loud profanity.

"Well put," said Harrison.

§

Boynton's imagination had produced a ham-and-tomato sandwich and a pickle. His research had yielded a list of mostly irrelevant authorities. The pertinent ones would have to be studied before Unger took the stand the next day. Which meant an evening in the office library.

Arthur would be flying blind in cross-examining him, and could well be in for an unsafe landing. He felt at serious risk of losing this trial. But he must remain the unimpassioned prosecutor. If Skyler got off through lack of proof, that would be the system at work. Easy to say, but he knew, in his heart, it would be a bitter pill.

Before returning to court, he checked in with Unger again. The sheriffs had fed him — on a tray was an empty salad container, McDonald's wrappings, a milkshake. Arthur settled into a chair.

"I'm going to save you for tomorrow, Manfred. I want you to have more time to think about this."

"Thank you, sir," he said blandly. Rather than stewing, he seemed to have recovered his composure. "It's not going to make any difference."

Arthur gave in to impatience. "If you refuse to answer my questions tomorrow, His Lordship will order you jailed until you make full amends. Whether you answer me or not, I intend to come after you without remorse — and maybe even some pleasure after suffering through this feckless mute act of yours. It will backfire. The jury will see it as an obvious setup between two clever college boys."

Unger looked straight back at him, calmly. The tough talk wasn't working. Arthur spoke softly: "Manfred, it's not going to help Randy."

"Randolph. He hates 'Randy.'"

"Why?"

He finished his milkshake, sat back with a grimace, as if regretting he'd opened his mouth and now felt compelled to continue. "It has a connotation he dislikes."

Arthur glanced through Unger's interviews from last year. "Ah, yes, you told the investigators that the girls teased him in high school. 'Randy, randy Randolph.' He scored with the beauty queens, you said. I guess that made all the other fluttering hearts a bit jealous."

"He was popular. You can't fault him for that."

"Well, you're a good-looking fellow too; you obviously don't lack for girlfriends." Arthur scanned the earlier interview. "You're still seeing Ms. Andrews?"

"Janet. We're engaged."

"Good for you. Congratulations. Set a date?"

"We're waiting till we graduate."

"Janet . . . she's in college?"

"Trinity Christian. Health sciences."

"Your dad's a colonel in the army. You must be proud of him."

"Yes, sir. I am."

"I expect you also want him to be proud of you."

Unger's smile clicked off. After a few moments of silence, Arthur patted him on the shoulder and promised he'd be back.

To the detectives waiting outside, he said, "Make sure Colonel and Mrs. Unger have ringside seats."

THURSDAY AFTERNOON

From the fifth-floor railing, Arthur saw Susan Unger coming up the stairs with her parents. The tall, heavy-set colonel was in a suit, and his spindly wife in a dress that one might wear to a church social, ruffles below the neck. He was wincing, holding his back; she was evidently recovering from distress: there were smudges of makeup around her teary eyes.

Arthur corralled them, introduced himself, asked about their trip, and expressed the hope that Susan's student apartment wasn't too cramped. Observing Edmund Unger's grimace, he added, "I'm sure the Attorney-General would be happy to have you as his guest — in the same hotel as your son, if you'd like."

"Bless you," said Florence. "I think a firm bed might be the thing for it, dear."

"Go for it, Dad."

"Thank you, I will. Wrenched it grappling with a suitcase."

"I'll contact Witness Services. But I have to pass on some awkward news. Your son is declining to cooperate with us, I'm afraid. That could have serious consequences for him." The Ungers exchanged surprised, anxious looks.

A sheriff interrupted, calling from the courtroom door. "We'll have time to talk about it later," Arthur said. "Meantime, we'll find seats for you in court. Susan, I regret, must stay outside until she testifies."

The Ungers' seats were not ringside, but in the third row, not far from the dock. Skyler was already in it, and as the jury filed in, he made a show of standing and waving to the Ungers, who looked embarrassed, acknowledging him only with nods. The jury, of course, would assume these were his parents. Arthur found it curious that his real parents had skipped the opening of the trial.

Skyler sat down and reassumed his serious, attentive look. The kind of demeanour to be expected of someone who knew his one-time best friend planned to blow a hole in the Crown's case. *Scored with the beauty queens.* Arthur found himself, with his own challenged libido, resenting him for the largesse of his love life.

From the other end of the table, Mandy rewarded him with another sultry look. He was twenty-five years her senior; surely he wasn't being vamped. Maybe the come-hither was meant for Boynton, because he returned a little finger-wave. Her response was to roll her eyes, still smiling, and turn away.

Boynton whispered: "Do you think it's possible Mandy could have a little crush on me?"

"I can't see why not, Jack." Arthur stood. "The Crown calls Jimmy Gillies."

A Nova Scotian, retired and a widower, this spindly, grizzled senior occupied Suite A of the house on Powell Street, which shared a wall with Chumpy's Suite B. Gillies had been a handful for Arthur to prepare, an old coot, a nosy neighbour. Pomeroy had had good rounds with him at the first trial, when Gillies had come across as too eager to help the prosecution.

Arthur brought out that he and his neighbour's relationship was amicable but not close, not much more than an occasional front-stoop sharing of a beer or a coffee. "He'd play his mouth organ, he was pretty good at that. Everybody in the neighbourhood liked him, but he didn't have no real friends. I'd have to say he was kind of ugly. I hope that don't sound cruel."

Chumpy's irregular routine was to don his clown suit "whenever he got up, usually around three," then head off downtown, sometimes returning after four or five hours, sometimes later, "after the movie pictures let out." Occasionally, he would leave again, in the late hours, uncostumed.

Arthur had him point out their common wall on a floor plan. "What kind of wall is that, Mr. Gillies? Describe it."

"Real thin partition, you can punch a nail right through and the hammer would go with it, and believe me that almost happened. And we had bathrooms back to back, and there's a hole in the wall there. If you stoop you can look through. Not that I ever done it."

"Can you hear sounds from within Suite B?"

"Sometimes more than you want to. You can't hear all the words all the time, unless they're loud, but you can always tell if it's different voices. I can always tell, anyway. Yep."

"Okay. Let me take you to the morning of Sunday, August third, 1986. Tell us what you did and heard."

"Well, I got up, and I was making some oatmeal, and that was just after the nine o'clock news — that's when Rafe Mair comes on CKNW. And anyways, that's when I heard something. It was Chumpy. He said, 'Holy mother, save me, I done wrong.' And he repeated, 'Don't do it, don't do it,' and then there was some, like, sounds, muffled sounds, but no more voices, and then I heard the tap in the bathroom come on, and after a while I heard the door close real quiet."

Real quiet. Arthur didn't like real quiet. Even with an ear to the wall, Gillies was unlikely to be sure what he heard. "Which door?"

"The building's front door, I think. Maybe I heard both doors."

"And did you see something?"

"From the window, I seen a man walking away from the house. I only seen him from the back and the side because the angle's not so good, and he was walking away. He had a denim jacket, jeans, and I remember he had cowboy boots. Sandy hair, pretty well built, I'd say. Young. And I remember he had black gloves on, which I thought was strange on a nice summer day. That's what I remember. Yep."

"Do you see that man in the courtroom?"

"I would say that's there's the man." Pointing at Skyler. "Yep."

I would say. That, Arthur knew, was as good as it was going to get. The jurors seemed to be enjoying this witness, though they likely felt he was overreaching. There was a skeptical look or two.

"Now, I understand you checked on Suite B later that day."

"Yes, sir. Around four. Hadn't heard a peep from in there the whole day. You expect to hear some shuffling, or a toilet flush, or the TV, but it was dead silent. So I decided I should knock on the door, and that's what I did, yep. And there was no answer, and I was surprised because it wasn't locked, so I just went in, and there he was, Joe Chumpy, all naked, lying half on the bed, dead, blood everywhere."

Arthur's throat was dry. He looked balefully at the water pitcher on his table, poured himself a glass. He used to dose his courtroom water with gin in the old days. It still seemed unnatural to take his water straight. He looked to the third row, to make sure the Ungers were still there. Solid citizens, loving parents, they'd be the ones to make that young man see reason. "Your witness."

Horowitz gave Pomeroy the nod, and he rose, shaking his head with disbelief even before asking a question. "Tell me, Mr. Gillies, do you keep an ear to the neighbour's wall the whole day long?" That got laughter from the public, smiles from the jury.

"As I been explaining, it's hard not to hear through them walls."

"Even with your ear to the wall, you can't hear low conversation, can you?"

"Maybe not."

"Did you hear anyone enter Suite B earlier that morning or during the night?"

"Not really. I guess I must've been sleeping."

"How old are you, Mr. Gillies?"

"Going on seventy-eight."

Pomeroy strolled away from him, toward the jury. "You'll agree your hearing isn't as sharp as when you were in the prime of youth?"

"When I was where?"

Louder: "I'm suggesting you've lost a little hearing over the years. It happens, it's normal."

"Maybe so."

"And yet at the trial in December you claimed you heard a . . . let's see." Pomeroy quoted from a transcript. "'A gurgle, and a gutty sound like a death rattle.' Now be honest with us, Mr. Gillies, you didn't hear that at all — you just imagined that, didn't you?"

"It was some time ago, so . . . maybe I thought I heard that."

"That's what it sounds like on TV police shows. Right?"

"Maybe, I guess."

"You didn't hear any screams?"

"No, sir."

"If a man was being stabbed, you'd think he'd be screaming his head off."

"Maybe." Gillies looked deflated already.

Boynton whispered, "How do you think this is going?"

Was he deaf? "Like the RMS *Titanic*."

"How's your vision, Mr. Gillies?" Pomeroy asked.

"Well, as you see I wear specs, and it's pretty good with the specs."

"When did you last have your eyes checked?"

"Just three months ago, January, yep."

"Get a new prescription?"

"I couldn't afford it right then. I figured these will do."

Pomeroy didn't spoil that admission by trying to exploit it — the jury was uncomfortable enough, feeling sorry for the old fellow. Skyler seemed to appreciate his counsel's work, nodding or smiling whenever he scored a point.

Pomeroy went on to exploit the holes in Gillies's identification. He couldn't remember seeing any blood on the man walking from the house. He'd attended a six-man lineup after Skyler's arrest but had been undecided between two of them, though he inclined toward Skyler. A lineup photo showed the other four had dark hair.

"And you've studied that lineup photo many times, haven't you, Mr. Gillies, and so it's not much wonder you picked out the same man in court, a man who just happens to be the only person sitting in the dock."

"I object," Arthur said. "That's not a question, it's a dissertation."

"I withdraw the dissertation."

The jurors loved this, and they were loving Pomeroy. Handsome Brian with his hot sidekick. In the opposite corner was a jumpy junkie on withdrawal supported by a fusspot. Boynton kept nudging him, offering *sotto voce* concerns about the prosecution's fast-vanishing chances.

"At the first trial, Mr. Gillies, you told me Chumpy had visitors from time to time, and one was a regular, a big man." Pomeroy read from the transcript of Gillies's previous testimony: "heavy, swarthy, six feet tall, late thirties, usually wore a windbreaker and toque."

"Well, yep, I guess I seen that feller a few times."

Arthur had no idea who he might be, other than one of Pomeroy's red herrings.

"I understand you went out for a walk on that Sunday."

"About noon, yep."

"So someone could have slipped out of Suite B after the noon hour, and left the building, and you wouldn't have known he'd been in there."

"He'd have to be awful quiet while he was there."

"You'd expect him to be quiet, wouldn't you, if he'd just murdered poor Chumpy."

Gillies couldn't argue with that. Pomeroy sat, and Horowitz ordered a ten-minute recess. Boynton tugged Arthur's gown. "Holy Toledo, what do we do now?"

Arthur scrambled to find his copy of the autopsy report, Exhibit One. There was no mention of the time of death. "Call the morgue, get Dr. Wu down here."

Pomeroy heard that. "Hey, we admitted the pathologist's report."

"Nice try, Brian."

§

Dr. Wu was dissecting a cadaver when the summons got to him, so the trial was slow to resume. Twenty precious, added-on minutes.

Arthur used the time to confer with the Ungers, letting them know he was stumped by their son's sudden, stubborn defiance. They could offer no reasons for it — Manfred rarely talked about the case. But lately he'd seemed, Florence said, "very stressed, very moody." She added, "He's a good Christian boy."

"We're taking him for dinner," Edmund said, still wincing. "We'll tell him to grow up."

After the pathologist finally trotted in and court was recalled, Arthur went directly to the bedevilling issue of time of death.

"We deduced from the rate of fall of body temperature," Dr. Wu said, "that loss of life would likely have occurred between eight-thirty and ten a.m. that day."

"Your witness, Mr. Pomeroy."

"Doctor, you'll agree, I take it, that estimating time of death through temperature loss is pretty rough science."

"There are many variables."

"Could have been a few hours either way?"

"I would find that hard to say."

"Thank you."

There was just enough time to get the fingerprint evidence in, and that task went to Boynton, who went about it more adeptly than Arthur had expected. The print examiner had studied the empties scattered about the suite and determined that all had been wiped clean of prints. The number of bottles examined was eleven, not the dozen that a young member of the ID squad had mistakenly counted, and the analyst had notes to verify that.

The twelfth bottle had been found behind a window curtain, and proof of it was a photograph that hadn't been developed for the first trial: another slip-up by the ID team. That bottle had not been wiped, and blowups of the partial print of Skyler's right thumb provided nine points of identification, sufficient for the examiner to state an unequivocal opinion that the print matched.

A meticulous repair job. Arthur had underestimated his junior — he'd kept the attention of the jurors, whose shrugs and forgiving smiles showed their sympathy for the math-impaired ID officer.

Skyler wore a puzzled look for the occasion — though when Arthur caught his eye, he saw something tighter, something vaguely menacing. Skyler was not shy about these visual exchanges. It was as if he was challenging Arthur.

Pomeroy could do little to resurrect his damaged fingerprint defence, and ultimately lost enthusiasm trying to trip up the combat-readied witnesses. He sat, and Horowitz adjourned until Friday.

"Surprisingly good job, Jack," Pomeroy called.

Mandy followed that up with an air kiss. Boynton beamed. "I do believe, Arthur, something is happening here."

Arthur told him not to harbour any immediate expectations beyond a long evening in the Tragger, Inglis library. He was to get there ASAP, order in some Chinese food, and ask wise old Riley, the research gnome, to work overtime. Boynton's hurt look told Arthur he'd been officious and ungenerous. "Excellent work, by the way. You left no hole unplugged."

Mollified, Boynton sped off, and Arthur slung off his robe and strolled out with Mandy and Pomeroy, who lamented: "I was losing the jury — no one likes a bully." He didn't seem that unhappy. Arthur assumed he was aware there was trouble with the Crown's principal witness.

Arthur turned to Mandy. "And when do you take on your starring role, my dear?" Arthur had a sense that sounded patronizing, but he'd lost track over the last decade of what people — particularly the oldfangled — were allowed to say.

"I hope you don't think I'm just window-dressing."

"I'm quite sure that's not your primary role, though you've performed it admirably."

He couldn't help it, he was old school, he'd practically been born that way, of conservative, over-intellectual academics.

But Mandy took the compliment like, he supposed, a lady, and playfully put an arm around his waist as they made for the stairs. "Day Twenty coming up, Arthur. You're doing great. You're my hero."

§

In the locker room, Arthur mentioned Boynton's amorous fantasies to Pomeroy.

"Mandy thinks he's creepy. It's you she's after, Arthur. She likes the married ones. They're more challenging, but also, she feels, more rewarding."

Arthur hurried into his street clothes and returned to the fifth-floor witness room. Both case officers were waiting for him outside the door.

"Manfred is antsy to split," Harrison said. "We'll keep a tail on him, same with Skyler."

"I need to find some common ground with this fellow, and it won't be intercollegiate rugby. Other interests? Movies, books, games of chance?"

"Detective novels," Nordquist said. "He's reading one now. He was into another one back in August."

Harrison frowned. "You got a photogenic memory, Bones?"

"It registered because I'd read it. Book called *For the Fun of It*."

"Odd title for a mystery," Arthur said, then opened the door.

Unger bent the page of a paperback and slid it into his pack. "I presume I can go now."

"Soon. What are you reading?"

"A crime thriller, sir. *The First Deadly Sin.*"

"Lust. Number one on that ancient list. But it had a different sense two millennia ago: *luxus, luxuria,* with its element of debauched living. These days, we admire the lusty if not the lustful. Lusty lads like yourself. I understand you fellows met some girls on the Expo grounds back in August."

"If you're asking if we got laid, sorry to disappoint. I would not have done that to Janet, Mr. Beauchamp. They were merely a couple of girls we hung with for a few hours."

"Of course, pardon me. Anyway, there's a kind of lust that was accepted in Roman times but that we have trouble with in this century — it involves attraction that many consider atypical. Homosexuality . . ."

"You can stop right there, sir. I'm not interested."

"Meaning you're not particularly fond of gays?"

Unger seemed to measure his words. "I have nothing against them. I don't approve of their lifestyle. I feel it's . . . profane."

"Unchristian."

"Maybe so. I believe in the Word."

"I understand Randolph has some forceful views on the subject of homosexuality."

Silence. Finally, Unger stood. "I'm not playing this game. I'm out of here!"

He grabbed his pack and strode out, past the startled detectives, down the steps.

THURSDAY EVENING

Arthur had kept his mind off drink with work, but the longing came back as soon as he set foot into his house at half past ten. Only a hall light on, Deborah abed, a note from Annabelle: "Last-minute revamp of stage left. Not sure when."

Arthur hoped Hubbell Meyerson wasn't out gallivanting, given his family was away. Arthur suspected the old roué had an affair going somewhere. It took several rings before he picked up.

"This trial has gotten a little messy," Arthur said, "so I could be socked in on Tuesday." The party to celebrate their elevation to the forty-third floor, the partners' floor. "You may have to say a few words on my behalf."

"Bummer, as my youngest might put it. I'll tell them you are trapped behind enemy lines. Setback?"

"A witness gone bad. I thought you'd be out tearing up the town."

"I am in the throes of self-denial, a monk. Pity me as you make love to Annabelle tonight."

Arthur felt troubled as he disconnected. He'd not been blind to the flirting between them, the touches, the eye messages exchanged that they thought he was too distracted to notice. But each knew the other was off-limits, the risks disastrously high.

He readied himself for bed, but he couldn't stop pacing. He tried to ignore the empty liquor cabinet. *Not sure when.* That could mean anything. But late nights were common during the frenzy of rehearsals. He took the phone to the back door and sat on the steps, his hand shaking as he lit his Peterson bent.

He finally settled down enough to ring the Hyatt and ask to be put through to Colonel Unger, to whom he apologized for the lateness of the hour. Though they were still on Eastern Time, the Ungers hadn't been able to sleep. "Our dinner with Manfred was . . . very difficult," Edmund said. "He walked out and left his plate untouched." A groan. "I may have handled it badly."

Arthur expressed his regrets, and dialled Bill Webb.

"How's it going, Arthur?"

"I think I need a little morale boost."

FRIDAY MORNING

Arthur slept poorly and was slow getting to court. In the elevator he fuelled himself from a Thermos of coffee. Harrison and Nordquist were waiting for him on the fifth floor.

Honcho was gruff. "You gonna take another go at him or not?"

"Not. Until he takes the stand." Arthur had given up catering to Unger — he was not the misguided young man's grovelling supplicant. He had no choice but to have him declared hostile, and to whale away in cross-examination.

"Okay, good luck, but Bones and me are of the indisputable view that Skyler has got some kind of hold over that obstinate fuck, and somehow they cooked up a bullshit story for the jury."

"Only one problem," Nordquist said. "We can't figure out how or where they conspired."

He handed Arthur a two-page report. Nordquist had painstakingly traced Unger's movements since the December trial. His only trip away from Ontario was to Gagetown, N.B. — Christmas with the family. Skyler, of course, remained in Vancouver, reporting twice weekly to 312 Main Street.

Arthur wondered what other means of communication might

have been used. Her Majesty's mail? The telephone?

Court 53 was filling up. Arthur finished his coffee. Withdrawal pain was severe this morning. "What about last night?"

"Zilch," Harrison said. "Randy foots it home to his apartment, on West Tenth. At a little before eighteen hours, he orders in a pizza. He watches the tail end of a hockey game: Leafs win big, seven–two. Then lights out. Also around nineteen hours, we have Manfred exploding in the Hyatt restaurant, telling his loving parents to get out of his effing face."

"Effing?" says Arthur.

"His word, effing. He's a good boy, he don't swear. So then he marches off just as the waitress is bringing his medium rare ribs. Straight up to his room. Watches the same hockey game. They're Leaf fans, them cheesy pricks. After the game, Manfred starts wishing he hadn't abandoned his ribs, and goes out and gets himself a burger and a side, which he consumes in his room, watching *First Blood*."

§

The gallery was full, and Arthur felt the heavy air of anticipation. It was Manfred Unger day, but not until the afternoon. Meanwhile, Jack Boynton would try to clean up the witness list.

"Calling Susan Unger," said Boynton. Manfred's sister nervously looked about on taking the stand, then dropped her eyes.

Boynton proceeded to place her in her apartment with her brother. This was late on the Sunday. There was chit-chat. He seemed strained. They each had a beer.

"And what else?"

"We smoked a little marijuana. Not much." Averting her eyes from her parents. They were back in their reserved seats, looking confused and fretful. Arthur reminded himself to thank them for trying and to tell them they did their best.

Pot was apparently not on pious Manfred Unger's list of immoral pastimes. It loosened his tongue, and he confided to Susan that his buddy had claimed that morning to have murdered a tramp. However, she was not permitted by law to relate that hearsay to the jury.

Pomeroy looked ready to spring up should the rule against hearsay be offended, but Boynton forestalled him. "You can't tell us what he said, but how did this conversation end?"

"Well, I told him he'd better call the police."

Unger slept on that suggestion, while staying at his sister's overnight.

Boynton then called Inspector Harrison, who, remembering his training, carried on in careful police-speak.

"Mr. Unger attended at police headquarters at nine-fifteen hours on Monday, August fourth, and voluntarily signed a statement which is . . ."

"Hearsay," Brian said, not rising.

Harrison looked annoyed — he knew the rules. "At ten-thirty-five, myself and Detective Nordquist attended at Room 308 of the Holiday Inn. We knocked, and the accused, who I identify sitting there in the dock, opened the door wearing a pair of jeans and pulling on a sweatshirt. This was a standard room with twin beds. One was mussed, the other made up. Some clothes strewn here and there. Some Expo souvenirs. We proceeded to have a conversation with the accused."

After excusing the jury for a voir dire, Horowitz had little trouble declaring that conversation admissible. A proper caution had been given, no threats or favours advanced, and though the accused had been asleep when the detectives showed up, he seemed alert and responsive and was polite throughout.

Harrison then related to the jury Skyler's problematic denials: he had never met the deceased and was never in his home. "I asked what he knew of this homicide. He said, 'That's awful, no, I don't know anything about it.'"

These proclamations of innocence had been a boon to the

defence at the first trial, given the questionable fingerprint evidence and Mr. Gillies's uncertainty at the lineup. But now, with the print evidence repaired, they could be condemned as patently false.

Pomeroy rose to paint a picture of a cooperative but confused and apprehensive young man.

"You told him he was a suspect in a grisly murder?"

"Don't know if I used those words. It was obvious why we were there." Harrison tended to loosen up with defence counsel, enjoying the combat.

"Two large men come by, rouse him from bed, start firing questions about a murder. He was obviously scared out of his skin."

"Well, I can't say what the condition of his skin was."

"Not surprising, under those circumstances, that he'd say the first thing that came to mind?"

"He said what he said, Mr. Pomeroy."

Brian sighed deeply for the jury, letting them know there was no point wasting more time with this obdurate fellow.

The jury was then excused for a hearing to decide if Unger was a hostile witness and therefore subject to cross-examination by the Crown. Horowitz ruled he was indeed adverse to the Crown. The process took up the entire morning.

FRIDAY AFTERNOON

The jury settled in. The judge smiled benignly at counsel. Skyler hunched forward in the dock with an expression of innocent confusion, as if unsure how he'd got himself into this awkward pickle.

Unger was rigid in the stand, staring fixedly at the Bible he was holding, as the clerk invited him to swear to tell nothing but the truth.

"I swear." He cleared his throat.

"I didn't hear that," Arthur said from his seat.

Unger looked up, saw Arthur glowering at him, then looked down again at the Good Book, and repeated, "I swear."

As Arthur rose, defence counsel shifted in their chairs to watch him, to better enjoy this. Arthur was still unsure how to handle Manfred. He'd given up on the notion of a three-day trial, or any prospect of making it to Tuesday's office festivity, so he wasn't going to rush it. He would have to play it by experience and instinct.

He began by drawing from Unger some background — his Toronto roots, his friendship with Skyler through their high school years and beyond — seeking to portray him as overprotective, willing to alter his evidence out of old loyalty, mysteriously renewed.

Unger didn't look at Skyler once during that backgrounder. Nor did he look at his parents, who were seeming more distressed as the day wore on. His gaze was fixed on the opposite wall.

"This was your first trip to Vancouver?"

"Yes, sir."

"Okay, let's talk about how you spent your time here. You arrived Thursday afternoon. And then?"

"We checked into the Holiday Inn. We took in a few sights, Stanley Park and English Bay. We spent Friday and Saturday at Expo."

"Please do the courtesy of looking at me." Unger instead looked at the judge, got no reprieve, and finally turned his eyes to Arthur. "Let's go back to Thursday night. According to your earlier evidence, you did a little bar-hopping."

"Yes, sir, we did."

"One of those bars was the Gandydancer?" A couple of customers had identified the two of them from photos.

Unger stalled. "I don't remember that name — Gandy . . ."

"The Gandydancer on Hamilton Street. Remember how they were all staring at you?" One of the identifiers had referred to the two handsome young men as "dishes."

"We only had one drink, sir. It was a homosexual bar."

"A homo bar, isn't that what Randy called it?"

"He might have used that expression."

"And he used other expressions. Faggots, fairies, queers, freaks, right?"

"I can't remember."

"He often used such expressions. Come, now. Be straightforward with me."

"I wouldn't say he's particularly attracted to gays. I don't think that's a crime."

"Yes, but the crime we're dealing with here is the likely homophobic murder of a gay man."

That was for the jury, but Arthur also wanted to see Skyler's reaction: it was a look of hurt, as if offended. Arthur had hoped to bait Pomeroy to his feet, to object to such rhetoric, but he held his tongue, declining to drive home to the jury the Crown's theory.

Arthur moved Unger quickly through their two days and one evening on the Expo grounds, an unexceptional time. The witness couldn't recall their engaging with anyone except two coeds from Texas whom they met at Science World and lost in the Great Hall of Ramses.

"Let us move on to Saturday evening. Please relate your movements."

"We had something to eat in a pub, and wandered to the old section — the Gastown area. We didn't do much but walk, stopped in at an Irish bar, had a beer. The Shamrock something."

The Shillelagh and Shamrock. It took Arthur a moment to get back on track — he'd been drunk and disorderly outside that place twenty days earlier. "In previous testimony, you said were looking for a striptease club. Tell us about that."

"Randolph wanted to go to a club he'd heard about, but we never found it, and . . ." A shrug. "I wasn't that interested. We'd been on our feet for two days, and I was tired. I left Randolph to carry on and went back to our hotel."

"Directly? Did you stop anywhere, talk to anyone?"

"No, sir, I went straight to my room. I read for a while and went to sleep." That was about two a.m. He said he woke up at ten upon Skyler's return.

They were into the core of the case. The rest, Arthur expected, would be dental work, drilling and pulling.

"And did your friend give an account of his doings that night?"

"In a manner of speaking."

"Well, what did he say?"

"Something about getting someone in trouble."

The first bald fabrication. Arthur decided not to offer him any more open-ended questions. That one had been a lemon, alerting the jury to the third-man theme. He would have to do better; his withdrawal symptoms had made him lose his edge.

"In your earlier statements, you have him saying, 'I really did it this time.'"

"I believe he said that. But I misinterpreted it." Unger was again looking at the wall instead of Arthur, who moved closer to the witness stand.

"He told you he stabbed Chumpy to death."

"That's what I told the police, but on reconsideration, I realized I'd got the wrong impression."

"Wrong impression? After saying otherwise to the police, after testifying under oath at the earlier trial that the defendant admitted to a savage murder, now suddenly it's the wrong impression?"

As Arthur continued to advance, Unger drew back. But there was eye contact now, and Arthur read anxiety and falseness.

"He mentioned a fight. I got the impression he was involved in ... whatever happened."

Arthur opened a bookmarked transcript of the first trial, began quoting: "'He wouldn't die. I must have stabbed him ten times, and he wouldn't die.'"

"I realize now —"

"Please just answer my question."

"My learned friend is cutting off his witness," Pomeroy complained.

"I think you ought to let him complete," said Horowitz.

Annoyed, Arthur listened to Unger relate what he was sure was an over-rehearsed fabrication about how he'd jumped to a wrong conclusion. He'd been awakened, was fuzzy, honestly believed Randolph was referring to himself as the stabber, but later recalled Skyler's mention of a third man in the room.

"May I repeat: 'He wouldn't die. I must have stabbed him ten times. It took him forever to die. There was blood all over.' I put it to you that those words were spoken to you by Randolph Skyler on the morning of August third."

"I . . . I'm not sure why I might have said that. I was reading a detective novel. That might have been in my mind. I was actually quite rattled."

There was a stirring of discomfort in the public seats; they weren't buying this. The jurors were impassive, however. Florence Unger had a tissue to her eyes. Her husband's expression alternated between despair and displeasure.

"What book would that be?"

"An Inspector Grodgins mystery . . . I can't remember the title."

For the Fun of It, according to Nordquist, but Arthur didn't press the issue.

"That morning, the accused also told you he cleaned the murder weapon, the knife, so there would be no fingerprints on it."

"I'd read about the stabbing in a newspaper later, about a knife, so I expect I was confused by that when I talked to the police."

"I can assure you there was nothing in the papers about the knife having been cleaned. That information was withheld."

"Well, I . . . Obviously, I would have assumed that any knife that had been found had been cleaned, and there'd be no prints."

"And on that Sunday morning, you asked the accused why there was no blood on his clothes."

"I asked because I thought he'd been in a fight."

"But you told the police Randolph said he was naked at the time because he didn't want to get blood on his clothes."

"Again, I don't know why I would have said that. I didn't see any blood on his clothes, so I must have imagined that could have happened."

Horowitz was regarding Unger with what seemed restrained · incredulity. The jury was still giving nothing away. No shaking heads, no smirks of disbelief. Deadpan, maybe stunned.

"You also told the police you saw tooth marks on the accused's leg."

"I assumed they were tooth marks, sir. Randolph didn't explain."

"Fresh teeth marks?"

"So I assumed."

"You saw them up close?"

"Not really, no."

"Did you treat the wound?"

"I got him some lotion, and we applied it."

"We? So you helped."

"I guess I . . . Yes."

"Then you did see the tooth marks up close."

"I must have."

"Let me acquaint you with Section 120 of the Criminal Code of Canada. 'Everyone commits perjury who, being a witness in a judicial proceeding, with intent to mislead gives false evidence, knowing that his evidence is false.' Section 121. 'Everyone who commits perjury is guilty of an indictable offence and is liable to imprisonment for fourteen years.' Do you have that firmly in mind?"

A deep breath. "Yes, sir."

Arthur returned to the table to retrieve the witness reports. "On Sunday, August third, you checked out of the Holiday Inn and moved in with your sister, Susan. You told the police you did so because you were scared, did you not?"

"I think I was more confused than scared. I was afraid Randolph might have done something terrible."

"You told Susan that Randolph had admitted killing someone."

"I said I was afraid he might have done that."

"You told her in no uncertain terms, and you repeated it to the police, quoting Randolph's very words: 'I must have stabbed him ten times, and he wouldn't die,' and you repeated it on the witness stand last December while on a solemn oath to tell the truth." A booming challenge: "Will you admit you are lying now? Lying on the Bible?"

Unger dropped his head. "I must have let my imagination take over. I wasn't thinking."

Arthur fingered through several pages of the transcripts from

December. The next stage would involve confronting Unger with every one of his prior sworn statements. Horowitz guessed what was coming, and proposed they take a break. "Witness, while you remain under cross-examination you may not discuss this case with anyone, friends, family, the lawyers of either side. Do you understand that?"

"Yes, sir."

Arthur stayed in his seat, watching the aisles empty. Edmund and Florence left quickly, stiff, expressionless. Their son hurried after them, passing the prisoner's dock without a glance at Skyler, who didn't seem happy with his friend's clumsy equivocating.

Jack Boynton said, "He prepared himself very well, I would say."

Arthur was taken aback. "You thought he did a good job?"

"I meant that he has safeguarded himself from a charge of perjury."

Fair enough. The vagueness, the refurbished recollection, the wild imagination might effectively inoculate him from such a charge.

"The jury will not believe a word he said, of course." Boynton peeked over at Mandy, more particularly her buttocks, as she bent to pick up her briefcase. "But that leaves the field open for what I expect will be a very glib Mr. Skyler."

"I can hardly wait."

Mandy gave Arthur a helpless smile as Boynton hurried up the aisle after her.

Left to himself, Arthur did a check on his current addiction levels. He'd been fairly comfortable while cross-examining. It was only in quieter moments that he felt the yearning, the gnawing. Twenty days. One day at a time. "Believe in yourself," Bill Webb had said.

§

It took almost an hour to take Unger through all his inconsistent statements. Arthur would typically ask: "Why did you say that?" Unger would typically say he'd got a wrong impression. Or he'd assumed. Or may have read it in a book. But he was fading, slipping up in small but telling ways.

"Why did you tell the police Randolph had stabbed and killed Chumpy?"

"We were, uh, my sister and I, we'd smoked some marijuana — it's not something I often do. I guess I was stoned. I wasn't thinking clearly."

"Why did you agree to contact the police?"

"I thought if Randolph had something to do with this, they should know."

Arthur took a moment to survey the public seats, spotted Colonel Unger, but not his wife. Susan was clutching her dad's hand.

"When was the last time you talked to Randolph Skyler?"

Unger was slow to respond to the change of topic. "I haven't talked to him. Not since his arrest."

"Not by phone?"

"No, sir."

"Have you corresponded with him by letter?"

"We haven't had any communication."

"And for what it's worth, you'll swear to that?"

"Yes, sir."

A frown from the bench. Arthur had crossed the line — a fair-minded prosecutor doesn't badger witnesses. But Pomeroy was the contented cat. Boynton had been right: this man's testimony would be entirely disregarded by the jury. Skyler would blame a swarthy man in a toque. He would say he got out of Suite B just in time. That would open wide the gates to a reasonable doubt.

"And this business of another man being involved, let's be plain here. Randy said no such thing, did he? That's something also dreamed up in your imagination, isn't it?"

"All I can say is when the clouds cleared, I remembered him saying that."

"Saying what exactly?"

"That this big, dark guy came by and he got very upset seeing Randolph there."

"You say the accused described him as wearing a toque and windbreaker?"

"As I best recall."

"On a sunny morning in early August, he was wearing a toque?"

"That's what I heard."

"So what was this visitor supposed to have said?"

"Randolph said they spoke French. I don't think he knows much French."

"Mr. Beauchamp, it's nearing the hour."

"Yes, M'lord. I shall wrap up with this witness on Monday morning."

Horowitz reminded Unger he was bound to silence. He was to report to the authorities any instance of anyone seeking to talk to him about the case. The judge then urged the jurors to enjoy the weekend as best they could. Many looked woebegone.

Pomeroy stood. "With respect, My Lord, I see no reason why this jury can't return home for the weekend. Surely these twelve honest citizens understand it's their duty not to discuss the evidence even with their families."

Arthur had no choice but to heartily agree that jurors were entitled to the comfort of home during such a stressful case. But it was Pomeroy whom they favoured with smiles as they pretended to listen to the judge's cautions not to talk about the evidence with friends, foes, or family. Brian was at the top of his game. Arthur was muddling through.

As court recessed, Boynton told Arthur he'd arranged to "share a beverage" with their learned opponents. "I don't suppose you'd care to join us." Arthur took that as a non-invitation. Three was a crowd, four was a throng.

While the junior prosecutor hurried after the two defenders, Lars Nordquist approached Arthur, offering a well-thumbed paperback book.

"I really think you should read this."

For the Fun of It by Horace Widgeon. An Inspector Grodgins mystery.

"The killer can't get it up. Except when he's killing people."

FRIDAY EVENING

Arthur had time on his hands before his AA meeting, so he took a downtown stroll that included a shortcut across the terrace of the Queen Elizabeth Theatre. The box office was closed, but billboards promoted next week's opening of *Tristan and Isolde,* starring Per Gustavson, a hairy gorilla in Nordic regalia, too flat-nosed to be handsome. Plump Bettina Schneiderhoffen got second billing as Isolde. Annabelle would be inside with her carpenters and decorators. He thought of dropping in to see her, but dismissed the idea. It felt a little like stalking.

He found himself gravitating downhill toward the harbour, Gastown, skid road. An area he knew too well, from when he'd run a single practice from a dilapidated storefront. He traded greetings with a pair of street junkies he'd represented and with a young, industrious prostitute whose appeal he'd won. He was pleased to learn she hadn't let her studies lapse and was completing her second year of college.

Arthur recognized the house on Powell Street where Chumpy had lived. Lights were on in Jimmy Gillies's apartment, so he hurried on, not wanting to be seen. Presumably, Chumpy had bought the case of Coors that night — off-sale, maybe, from one of the many nearby taverns, but no witnesses had been found to prove that.

The killer can't get it up. Arthur was familiar with the affliction. The campus stud, however, wasn't similarly disadvantaged. Naked with Chumpy — that could hardly have been natural for him, but of course he'd picked up that Chumpy was gay, and to bring his guard down had likely teased him with the prospect of sex play. And he would hardly have wanted to be seen on Powell Street in bloodied clothes.

There was nothing in the police reports about the bite marks on Skyler's leg, a serious lapse. The likely reason Gillies heard no screams was that the victim's teeth were imbedded in that leg. What he did hear was, "Holy Mother, save me, I done wrong." Why would Chumpy confess to the Blessed Virgin? Why would he blame himself? Maybe that stemmed from religious guilt about his homosexuality.

At Columbia and Hastings, another former client was hurling drunken epithets at passersby. Arthur crossed the street, accelerated his pace.

The Trial Lawyers Chapter of Alcoholics Anonymous met every Friday evening — the hardest time for counsel still wired from the courtroom — and the meeting, uptown, in a United Church lounge, was just getting under way as Arthur strolled in. He counted fifteen participants, all friends, so he felt silly standing there saying, "My name is Arthur, and I'm an alcoholic."

When he added, "I'm on Day Twenty, ladies and gentlemen," they applauded. He thought of the shouting drunk. He'd been that man, as drunk, as loud. He was better than that.

§

"Problems?" said Annabelle, still embracing him. She'd been in bed, reading, when he got home after an eat-out with his AA mates.

"It's the tension of the trial, dear." He lay there rigid, ashamed. "I've been holding back all day, to the point it's become chronic."

"Holding back in court?"

"I think so." Such half-hearted erections typically occurred when trials were going poorly.

She kissed him. "Never mind. Hubbell called to chat. Harriett and the kids won't be back till Monday, so I asked him to dinner tomorrow. We'll celebrate your coming partnerships. Better, we'll celebrate Day Twenty-One. Three weeks, darling! Congratulations."

Five more days to go before equalling his personal best. It was marked on his calendar, Thursday, April 29.

SATURDAY

Arthur spent most of this rare fair day in his garden, with spade and hoe, and for the most part was able to subdue his concerns over the Skyler case, though it seemed to keep bursting forth, like the rhubarb and the spring weeds.

He felt out of his element working the prosecution side, chafing at the role of Her Majesty's humble servant, felt restricted, shackled by his vow to be a non-combatant, the unimpassioned butler serving up fairness and justice to the guests.

He thought he'd been far too easy on Manfred Unger, a witness he would have shredded as a defender, in which role he hadn't always observed the niceties. At some level, he felt sorry for him. The stress he was under. The painful prevarication under the censorious eyes of God.

As for Randy Skyler, Arthur just wanted to nail the punk.

Annabelle was heavily engaged with weekend rehearsals for *Tristan and Isolde* but got home in time to help Arthur with dinner before changing into one of her "little somethings," as she called her clingy cocktail dresses, her uniform of choice when hosting dinner parties at which men were available to be teased, and wives made jealous.

Arthur pulled the lamb roast from the oven just before Hubbell Meyerson arrived with roses and a bottle of Pouilly-Fumé. He and Annabelle exchanged cheek pecks, in the Continental manner that Arthur thought tiresome.

"You look appallingly beautiful tonight, Annabelle." Hubbell handed her the flowers. "Thank you for taking in this poor, starving recluse. I've been pulling out my hair in lonely desolation while Harriett and the kids are away."

"Bullshit," said Annabelle.

Hubbell declined an invitation to relax in the living room, preferring to lean on the kitchen counter and watch Arthur toss the salad. Annabelle went off to lay the table.

"So what do you think of prosecuting now, Arthur?" He'd obviously read the newspaper accounts. The reviews hadn't been favourable.

"I'll need a miracle to pull this one off. Could be at it all week."

"This could use a quick chill." Hubbell got up with the Pouilly-Fumé, but Annabelle returned, barred his way, took the bottle from him. "Arthur's had a monstrous last few days. I'd rather we don't drink in front of him. It's not fair."

"Nonsense, darling. The sight of wine in a glass will not drive me berserk."

"It's Day Twenty-One, we'll celebrate it with coffee."

"Please, Annabelle. Hubbell brought a fine wine. It would be insulting."

Hubbell backed away, his hands up, staying out of it.

"Subject closed." Annabelle put the wine in the back of the fridge and turned to them brightly. "Let's eat. Everyone to the table. Bring the salad, Arthur."

§

Arthur tried not to mope through dinner, tried to be gracious in accepting plaudits for his creation of lamb and steamed baby potatoes and asparagus, but he was chafing at being regarded as such a weak vessel. He supposed Annabelle had acted out of affection — he was sure she loved him, in her way — but her manner was peremptory, unseemly in front of a guest.

Soon after dinner, he apologized, claiming he was fatigued, and went off to bed with the clear though unspoken intention of freeing Annabelle and Hubbell to share the wine.

He turned the bed lamp on and played with a *Times* crossword for a while, then picked up the worn paperback Nordquist gave him. *For the Fun of It.*

He paused, several chapters into it, to listen for sounds. Nothing, no laughter or clink of glass. He wondered if he should put on his robe and think up a pretext. Then he dismissed the idea. How foolish. How abhorrent.

SUNDAY MORNING

Arthur fell asleep midway through the book, and on rising with the dawn he retrieved it and crept from the bedroom while Annabelle remained curled in sleep. He'd briefly awakened when she crawled in beside him, her breath perfumed with wine.

Day Twenty-Two. Four days from a new personal record. Why wasn't he feeling good about it? After showering in the downstairs bathroom, he padded about in his robe with a cup of freshly ground, doing his morning tasks, making toast, picking up. In the living room, he retrieved the empty Pouilly-Fumé and two empty wine glasses, one on a sofa table, the other on a chiffonier. Twenty feet apart. A proper distance.

His coffee refreshed, he sat in the den in his favourite old club chair with *For the Fun of It*.

According to the one-paragraph biography on the last page, the prolific Mr. Widgeon had penned two dozen novels set in the apparently crime-ravaged town of Illings-on-Little Close, featuring the indomitable but stuffy Inspector Grodgins and his wrong-footed sidekick, Constable Marchmont. Seemingly eager to encourage competition, Widgeon had also published several how-tos about the crime genre.

As a result of a bullet wound to the head suffered in a prequel, Grodgins had developed severe agnosia, impairing his ability to recognize familiar faces. Despite the handicap, his finely tuned skills had him closing in on a bad apple, an aristocrat who'd randomly killed several friendless loners.

Three coffees later, after absorbing much forensic and psychological detailing, Arthur reached the climactic final chapter, set in the billiards room of Illings Close Castle, where Grodgins had assembled the various suspects, none of whose faces he could recognize, among them Lord Scarfe-Robbins, whom the agnosiac inspector wasn't able to pinpoint in the crowd.

"In your efforts at normal sexual conjoining," the inspector declaimed at no one in particular, "you were impotent, sir." That caused Arthur a moment of irritation. Picking on the impotent seemed a low blow. He had his set his hopes on the brawny horse trainer who'd regularly bedded the earl's wife.

Grodgins continued to hurl challenges in the general direction of Lord Scarfe-Robbins: "As Donny Millibun underwent his death throes after falling from the roof, you found yourself aroused to the point of orgasm. Then the killings began. In your warped mind, you realized you'd finally found a satisfying form of congress with another — in death. Yes, murder, the only way you could achieve a sexual climax."

"You're dead wrong, you rotter!"

Grodgins sought the source of that frantic voice, and was finally able to locate Lord Scarfe-Robbins in the faceless crowd, whereupon he produced, at the end of a billiard cue, what he hoped was a pair of soiled underwear. "Your Lordship is perhaps unfamiliar with the new science of DNA profiling. The semen on this garment, sir, holds your genetic fingerprints."

As Scarfe-Robbins bolted for the stairs, a man in some kind

of uniform raced off in pursuit, nearly toppling Mrs. Gullweather. Grodgins could only assume the pursuer was Constable Marchmont.

This absorbing tale failed to parallel reality in a couple of obvious ways. Inspector Harrison, unlike Inspector Grodgins, wasn't armed with incriminatory semen. In any case, randy Randolph was anything but impotent. Otherwise, the plot's similarities intrigued Arthur, although he remained confident that the motive stemmed from Skyler's homophobia.

At any rate, it was Unger, not Skyler, who'd been absorbed in *For the Fun of It*. The thought crept into Arthur's mind that Unger had been conning everyone. Maybe Manfred was inspired by that book to kill for a thrill. Maybe, like Inspector Grodgins, Arthur had been unable to recognize the perpetrator — his eyes clouded not by agnosia but tunnel vision.

For what it was worth, Unger's copy of *For the Fun of It* had been retrieved by Kingston police, who'd got permission from RMC brass to toss his dormitory room. The book had been on a shelf of crime novels. No correspondence with Skyler was found, though there were a couple of photos of him, one in track togs, and several family pictures. Janet Andrews, his fiancée, was prominent on the wall, alone in one photo, Manfred's arm around her in another. The copy of *For the Fun of It* was being couriered.

Arthur went to the phone before it woke Annabelle and Deborah. "Good morning, Arthur," said Jack Boynton. "The pleasure of your attendance is requested at 312 Main Street, homicide office. I believe they've come upon some useful information."

"Yes? And what is it?"

"Honcho has imposed telephonic silence."

"Please, Jack, don't be coy." Unger had prayed to Jesus and repented? Confessed to the murder? Maybe Skyler had absconded . . .

"I'll give you a clue. You asked Unger if he'd stopped anywhere or talked to anyone. His answer, and I quote: 'No, sir, I went straight to my room. I read for a while, and went to sleep.'"

Arthur left the Rolls in the garage. Though piqued that Boynton had been so unforthcoming, he was in no rush, and was determined to get into shape as an aid to conquering his alcoholism.

It was a gentle, hazy day, and he chose a route near the water, joining other Sunday strollers on the paths above Locarno and Kitsilano Beaches, down streets lined with sturdy bungalows and cherry trees in full blossom. After descending from the city's graceful art deco Burrard Bridge into the dense West End, he found the views less attractive: skeletal constructions and cranes and hoardings with signs promising luxury living dominated the landscape. Old Vancouver, the low-key, toned-down town, was disappearing behind these shiny monoliths.

Downtown South Granville was livelier, its various salons offering beer, burgers, hash pipes, used books, Cuban cigars. Granville morphed into Theatre Row, where Chumpy the Clown had entertained for the movie lineups with his mouth organ and his Chaplinesque collisions with light standards and waste bins. The archetypal sad and lonely man in clown makeup. A man chosen at random to die, chosen by . . . whom? If not Skyler, then Unger. Or both. Or, as a Widgeon-worthy twist, a swarthy fellow wearing a windbreaker and toque on a sunny summer day.

Arthur's own gleaming office tower lay ahead, but he turned east and walked through Gastown to Chinatown, where he stopped for green tea and a bowl of hot and sour soup at the Ho-Ho, which he drank while perusing a discarded Saturday newspaper. The Chumpy trial was on the front page, under the headline, "He wouldn't die!" It offered an account of Unger's verbal contortions, along with a photo of him looking haunted as he walked alone from the courthouse. Arthur dallied over the crossword puzzle, then headed out.

Two blocks north of Chinatown, conveniently snuggled into Vancouver's high-crime district, was the blocky, charmless Public

Safety Building. Arthur's last visit had been twenty-two days ago. Shock treatment in the drunk tank, the jolt he'd needed — but one that still hovered like a dark cloud over Arthur's prospects for a partnership.

He found Boynton on the third floor, studying a corkboard on which photos of fugitive murderers were pinned. Arthur asked him how his weekend had gone.

"Not well."

"How so?"

A brave shrug. "I fear it's off between Mandy and me. We had an evening out last night. It appears there are certain cultural values and, let us say, feelings we don't share. She was regretful that she was attracted to me only intellectually. I told her I was attracted to her in a much different way, not meaning it as an insult, but I'm afraid it was taken as such. I felt I ought to tell you that, in case you pick up an unusual coldness from the defence side."

"Well, thanks for the warning."

"I'm actually relieved. There are a few qualities not in her favour. She has a bit of a reputation for sleeping around."

"Then you've saved yourself from heartbreak."

Nordquist broke off the maudlin scene by calling them into Honcho's office. The inspector was relaxing behind his desk, feet up, a glowing cigar in his hand. "I have one of these when I'm feeling good. Not supposed to, eh, Bones?"

"It's your body, pal, your lungs."

Harrison swung his feet to the floor and tipped an inch of ash into his wastebasket. "We got lucky." He passed Arthur a transcription of his telephone conversation with one Laurence Wyacki. "Nice young man. Nineteen. From Detroit. Accepted into Wayne State law school next semester. Lives with his parents. Dad's a high school principal, Mom's a mental health worker. Kid has everything going for him, except he's queer."

"Queer?" said Boynton. "For shame, Inspector."

"Help me, Jack. Is it okay to say homo? Anyway, Laurence has a boyfriend, he's candid about it, his parents accept it. Pretty damn liberal for polacks, you ask me." He blew a plume of smoke that had Boynton backing up. "To make it short and sweet, Laurence Wyacki was in Vancouver on Saturday, August second, and spent pretty well the whole night in bed with Manfred Unger."

Harrison grinned on seeing Arthur's face go slack with astonishment. "We bought him a plane ticket and reserved a real nice room for him. He'll be arriving about seven tonight."

"I'm afraid you gentlemen will have to handle it by yourselves." Boynton's parents were hosting a dinner party. He couldn't let them down.

SUNDAY EVENING

The hotel chosen for Laurence Wyacki was away from downtown, on Denman, near Stanley Park, in the gay-friendly West End. From the twenty-first floor, Arthur could see the sun setting beautifully over English Bay as he waited in silence until Harrison and Nordquist wrapped up their interrogation. He then saw them to the door, promising to join them in the lobby after spending time alone with the young man.

Harrison's rough manner had prompted Wyacki to retreat to the balcony, where he was nervously chain-smoking. He was slender, with shoulder-length hair and a well-tended moustache, the kind Arthur had nurtured a few decades ago, probably for the same reason — to make him seem older.

A.R. Beauchamp, QC, widely regarded as an astute judge of people, was still reeling over having misread Unger. None of the signs had been there, nothing in his body or verbal language. He was engaged, no less, to a student at a small Christian college in Eastern Ontario. A virgin, perhaps, her consummation devoutly to be wished.

Manfred Unger was not only deeply closeted, Arthur concluded, but in love with Skyler. Mr. Popularity, who'd scored with the beauty queens.

Was Skyler aware Unger was gay? Skyler, the presumptive homophobe. But any suspicions he held were likely overwhelmed by the glow of the reverence on offer. It must have been a painful struggle for Unger to play the straight companion.

Arthur joined Wyacki outside, pulled out his pipe, packed it. "I'm glad we've been able to grant you a rare April sunset." Orange stripes were traversed by yellow beams as the sun slid behind the green humps of Vancouver Island. "I want to thank you for extending yourself in this way."

Wyacki hadn't heard about Skyler's first trial and had learned about the current one only because he and his boyfriend had been clicking through channels while waiting for a Saturday night movie. They'd paused at a Canadian news program, and Wyacki immediately recognized the man running a gauntlet of reporters. Wyacki became, as he put it, "seriously uneasy" on learning Unger claimed to have been alone on the night of August 2. He consulted with his boyfriend, then his parents, and called Vancouver homicide the next morning.

"I'd like to say I did it out of a sense of duty, Mr. Beauchamp. But I was freaking about getting implicated."

"Your name didn't come out, but it might have."

"It wasn't just about saving my ass, as Mr. Harrison obviously thinks."

"You'll have to forgive him, Laurence. Old bull, breaks a lot of china."

That got a smile. Arthur lit his pipe, the smoke drifting straight up in the still air. The sun winked out behind the island hills, and lights winked on below. Wyacki tapped out another cigarette.

"I hope you managed to finish your exams."

"I just have two papers to write. No sweat."

They talked for a while about law school — he was a scholarship student — about his career plans: civil rights, maybe some counsel work. Arthur commended him for that, talked of his own early career working pro bono for the poor. He didn't have to play at being avuncular. It came naturally.

"Laurence, would you mind doing another run-through? You were in Vancouver last summer for Expo. How did that come about?"

"Well, my parents bought me a ticket. I was going to come with my boyfriend, but we'd had a squabble over something . . . not important, delete. And I was in a kind of third-rate hotel, it's all I could afford. I had about a week, did the tourist whirl, around the park, up the mountains, a harbour cruise, and three nights of Expo concerts, did the whole extravaganza."

Arthur tamped his pipe, and they went inside to escape a sudden night chill. Wyacki kept talking, pacing the while. "Saturday night — it was my last night, a lovely night. I guess it was pretty late, around midnight, and I had a flight in the morning — and frankly I was lonely, and, uh, I'm walking around Gastown, and the bars are all open, full of happy people, and I don't know what got into me — I don't do that sort of thing — but anyway, there was this guy coming toward me, giving me a long look, and he said he was sure he'd seen me on the fairgrounds, and . . . I gave him a cigarette. We talked. I'm from Detroit. He's from Ontario. Isn't this a great town? How'd you like Expo? That sort of thing."

And they ended up in that third-rate hotel, not getting much sleep from midnight to seven a.m., when Wyacki had to check out and catch his airport bus.

"We exchanged phone numbers. I kept his." Wyacki had given it to the detectives. "I don't know why. I liked him. We had great sex. It was a holiday romance sort of thing."

"But he didn't call you."

"No, and I didn't call him. I knew his situation. The officer training thing. The super-straight parents. He poured it all out — I had the impression he'd never opened up like that with anyone, it was like a catharsis. I was totally uncomfortable about maintaining contact with him, given his circumstances. It all looked pretty gruesome to me, and anyway I had something else going."

§

"Well, gentlemen," Arthur said, "I guess that rules out Manfred as the perp." A comment that was met with silence from the front seat of the cruiser.

Nordquist, at the wheel, clicked his seatbelt on, but Honcho let go of his and craned around — an effort for the bull-necked cop — to frown at Arthur. "Nobody told me we were thinking along those lines," he said.

"A wild speculation," Arthur said, embarrassed that he'd mentioned it. "But what does Mr. Wyacki add to the case but embroidery? We've already proved Unger is an unremittingly bad liar." Arthur was anxious not to expose the law student to the clamour and notoriety he would endure by testifying.

"Bones and me think this is a situation that calls for a little killer instinct, Arthur." Honcho was clearly frustrated by what he saw as Arthur's limp prosecutorial instinct. "What we got fucking us around on the witness stand right now is a highly closeted homosexual, so the way we're thinking, we use the kid as a jimmy."

"A jimmy?" Arthur said.

"A lever," Nordquist said. He was driving Arthur home, up Beach Avenue, by English Bay, grey and sombre in the late twilight.

"A lever," Arthur repeated, finally awake to the possibilities, aware that he hadn't been thinking like a prosecutor, or a cop. Manfred Unger with his super-straight parents watching from their third-row seats. His entire world imploding, the world he'd struggled so hard to adjust to, the rugby team's locker room, the halls and dorms of RMC. His army career shattered in disgrace. That doesn't have to be, they would tell him, if he cooperated, told the truth. Laurence Wyacki wouldn't have to testify; he could be put on the next plane home.

"Manfred may need to consult counsel," Arthur said.

Honcho groaned. "We're supposed to hire him a mouthpiece? Maybe we could wait until he asks for one. Arthur, you got to stop stewing over all the little wrongs and rights. We got a savage murderer on the loose here. He's a piece of shit, he deserves a lifetime bounce — you told us that yourself."

"Let's do it."

§

Before going off to a sleepover at a girlfriend's, Deborah had confided to Arthur that she wanted to escape her mother's loud friends and their "obnoxious tittle-tattling." Arthur retreated too, early, to his bedroom, to a small lamp-lit desk, while Annabelle shared wine and gossip in the front room with a costume designer and an aging, foul-mouthed contralto.

Their laughter kept intruding on his strategizing for Operation Wyacki. In broad outline, it involved acquainting Manfred Unger with the new situation and offering to recall him to the stand on the promise that he would not be outed or face perjury charges. Unger could then apologize sorrowfully to the jury and claim he'd only been trying to help out his long-time buddy.

But there was a slight technical problem: Unger remained under Horowitz's diktat not to discuss the case with anyone while under cross, including counsel. To be enabled to speak with him, Arthur would have to abort his cross-examination as the first item of business on Monday.

Freshly showered and in his bathrobe, he was drafting his pitch to Unger. He would keep Wyacki nearby, in case he was needed as graphic proof.

Again, Arthur was distracted by a peal of laughter from downstairs. They were talking about men, of course, and their multitudinous excesses and deficiencies. Arthur had overheard a partial anecdote while sneaking into the kitchen for a slice of their pizza. Something about a lewd basso taking liberties with a contralto.

An ethics issue was bothering Arthur. Was he bound to alert the defence to the surprise witness? But then it wouldn't be a surprise, would it? Why should the Crown be handicapped by giving away every little secret to the enemy, allowing them to repair breached defences?

At any rate, Randy Skyler ought not to be entitled to any disclosure that rendered the Crown more naked than transparent. Even his parents — notably absent from this trial — seemed to doubt him. According to a memo from Toronto police, the Skylers were troubled that their son hadn't testified at his first trial, that he hadn't proclaimed his innocence on oath.

Other useful reports were just coming in from the Ontario police. A retired Toronto high school principal remembered Skyler as "slick and quick" and Unger as his loyal sidekick. Skyler's former girlfriends were being sought out.

"In your efforts at normal sexual conjoining," the inspector declaimed *at no one in particular, "you were impotent, sir."* Arthur had begun to wonder whether he'd trapped himself in a false paradigm. Maybe Skyler's problem was not satyriasis. Maybe the opposite.

Randy, randy, Randolph. Had those taunters been mocking his ineffectiveness?

Sounds of partying below became sounds of parting, and from his window Arthur watched a taxi bear away Annabelle's guests. Moments later, she came into the bedroom, and began undressing, laughing to herself, tipsy. "Did we disturb you, darling?" From behind, she slipped his robe from his shoulders, kneaded them. She smelled of gin, vermouth, and lemon slices, prompting a swell of double-barrelled desire: alcohol and sex.

He tried to clear his throat. "Not at all."

"Can I disturb you now?" Her hands slid down his chest, his abdomen, the robe falling loose around him. Her tongue tickled his ear, and when he swivelled to meet her mouth, he was engulfed by the hot taste of gin. Her fingers circled his stiffening member, teasing it into a rare, glorious, rampant erection.

"What a lovely surprise, Arthur."

She lowered her head, nuzzled his genitals, then drew his cock into her mouth, bringing him arching from his seat.

MONDAY MORNING

"You seem in oddly high spirits," Jack Boynton said as Arthur jauntily slung his briefcase onto the counsel table.

"Feeling in the pink."

"I don't quite share that rosy feeling."

"I'd be surprised if you did."

A puzzled frown. "It's my view that though we may be better armed now, with Mr. Wyacki, we haven't convicted anyone yet, and there is no guarantee we will."

"I suggest we keep Wyacki in our pocket for now." A peek at defence table, where Pomeroy and Mandy were conferring, readying themselves for Arthur's continuing dissection of Unger.

"We'll have to disclose to them, of course," Boynton said.

"I think not. One only discloses witnesses one expects to call. Wyacki is just a lure, to get Manfred to open up. We have the weapons to turn him around." The note on which he'd left his phone number for Wyacki, his outpouring in their shared bed about his straight parents and the complex masquerade of his closeted life.

Boynton looked shocked. "Arthur, not six months ago, the

Appeal Court reversed a conviction for lack of disclosure of a material witness."

The public galleries were filling. The sheriff called: "Ready, Mr. Beauchamp?" He was eager to fetch the jury.

"A few minutes please." Arthur felt he needed to settle Boynton down — he looked rattled.

"Why is Wyacki material? He merely slept with a witness. He had nothing to do with Skyler." Arthur realized he was getting loud, toned it down. "There's no reason to expose him to the public glare."

"I presume, then, you will start the day by dealing Unger a final crushing blow."

"I shall be suspending my cross so we can talk to the fellow."

"Arthur, I hate to say, but it seems a *very* risky gamble to cut your cross short."

"Jack, trust me." He called: "Bring in the jury, Mr. Sheriff."

Skyler stepped briskly into the dock, resuming his pose of earnest innocence. He'd been watched all weekend, covertly, and had spent much of it in a track suit keeping fit: two complete circuits of the Stanley Park Seawall, swimming, lifting weights in a gym. A long Saturday session in Mandy Pearl's office.

Unger was already on the witness chair, looking wan and depressed. His parents were a few rows behind him, his father perched stiffly, at a slight angle, his mother with the dulled look of the sedated.

The jurors looked refreshed from their weekend leave, as did Justice Horowitz, who entered on the dot of ten, alert and businesslike. "Proceed, Mr. Prosecutor."

"M'lord, I have concluded my examination of Mr. Unger, subject to one issue we'd like to canvass with him, and to that end I ask the indulgence of the court for a recess."

Pomeroy may have been daydreaming, or at best fixated on Juror Number Twelve, the pretty store clerk, who was showing alarming signs of developing a crush on him. But Arthur's words finally registered, and he rose to express puzzlement, then astonishment, and, finally, outrage at what he described as Arthur's effrontery.

"This is unheard of. He's either closed his examination or he hasn't. He isn't entitled to sit down again with his witness, and help him out of his fuddle, then plunk him back on the stand with his memory conveniently refreshed. How dare he plead something as ambiguous as 'an issue we'd like to canvass with him.' I'm ready to go. This witness is under cross-examination, and unless I was suffering an auditory delusion, I heard Your Lordship distinctly forbid him from talking to anyone, including counsel . . ."

Arthur interjected, trying to make the best of a plan gone wrong. "Okay, he's no longer under cross-examination. I am concluding my cross-examination."

Pomeroy whirled to the witness. "Mr. Unger, do you understand that you are still under oath?"

"Yes, sir."

"He's under cross-examination now," Pomeroy announced.

Horowitz sat through this with the majestic serenity of a ship's captain waiting for the squall to pass. Finally, he asked: "Is this your final witness, Mr. Beauchamp?"

Arthur wasn't prepared for that question. "I . . . as of this moment, he is."

The judge looked oddly at Arthur, who, unaccustomed to his role, had forgotten that prosecutors were rarely given the leeway extended to defenders, especially in Horowitz's court. "After Mr. Pomeroy concludes his cross-examination, Mr. Beauchamp, you can decide if your case is closed."

Arthur assessed the implications. A full frontal assault by Pomeroy could bury Unger so deeply in his lies that he might balk at backtracking. Arthur might then be forced to put Wyacki into the mix. He finally sat, gritting his teeth in anticipation of an I-told-you-so from Boynton — who had the decency to hold off.

While Arthur flagellated himself for his miscalculation, Pomeroy began his cross by being excruciatingly helpful to the witness. "You were fuzzy with sleep when Randy woke you that morning." "Randy was so animated, talking so quickly, that you simply misheard much of what he was saying." "You'd gone to bed reading a murder mystery and woke up with that plot spinning in your head." "You had trouble assimilating fact and fiction."

Statements, not questions, but to each Unger responded with a quiet and obedient yes.

"And you were stoned on marijuana when the police fired all those questions at you, and you gave an account that you felt obliged to repeat at the trial last December." "And on reconsideration you realized you'd wronged Randy terribly, and you have shown up here out of a sincere duty to set the matter straight."

"That's right, sir." Or, "That's what happened, sir." Unger seemed to grow more composed under this pampering, returning Pomeroy's kindness by declining to reprimand him for calling Randolph "Randy." Occasionally he glanced at Arthur, as if wondering why he'd been spared a further trouncing.

Pomeroy sifted through his notes. "I'm not sure if you told us how Randy met the deceased."

Unger hadn't, and now repeated, almost word for word, his testimony of December: "He told me he bumped into him while he was looking for a strip club and Mr. Chumpy offered to show him the best stripper bar in town. He was an interesting character, a kind of professional clown, so Randolph accepted his offer to have a beer at his place."

"You never saw him with Chumpy?"

"No, sir, I'd gone straight back to our hotel."

A nudge from Boynton, in case Arthur had missed that palpable falsehood.

Having bandaged Unger's credibility as best he could, Pomeroy focussed on the core of the defence case, the third-man theme — Chumpy's occasional visitor, whom Jimmy Gillies had so helpfully and explicitly described.

Pomeroy embellished the scenario. "You got the impression, as I understand, that this tough-looking fellow in a toque burst into Mr. Chumpy's room." Unger agreed. "And from what Randy said, you assumed this man had a close relationship with Chumpy." "That he was his boyfriend, in fact." "And that's why Randy got the heck out of there when the man erupted in a jealous rage." "Which is why Randy told you he could have got someone killed."

Yes, sir. Exactly, sir.

Arthur couldn't find the energy to object, to stand and fight; he was being beaten into submission by this blatant puppeteering. So he sat back with a wry smile, pretending to be amused.

Pomeroy finally consulted with Mandy, a sign he was out of ammunition. For the first time in his seven hours of testifying, Unger glanced at his parents — a glimpse, no more, at the frowning colonel with his bad back and the decent, upright lady who ran the children's program at the Gagetown Presbyterian Church.

"No more questions." Pomeroy sat, obviously pleased with his morning's work. The jealous, swarthy boyfriend was his reasonable doubt, and his glib client would be well-rehearsed to enhance it.

"Any questions in redirect?" Horowitz asked Arthur.

Arthur was still focussed on Unger, who had suddenly gone open-mouthed, a jolting expression of shock, which he tried to blink away as if it were a dream. He was staring at the back of the court, at the slender, sandy-haired young man who had just entered. And who nodded to him familiarly as he took a seat.

"Any redirect, Mr. Beauchamp?"

Arthur leaned to Boynton. "Get Wyacki out of here." To the court: "No, sorry, My Lord, I was distracted."

"The witness is excused for now. Mr. Sheriff, you may take the jury for an early lunch. I'd like to see counsel in my chambers."

The gallery emptied, led by Boynton towing Wyacki. Unger stepped zombie-like from the stand, watching them, then passed within inches of his parents without seeming to notice them, though his mother reached out to touch his arm.

Pomeroy had been too busy receiving kudos from his junior to notice either Unger's startled look or Wyacki being escorted out by Boynton, in his obvious role as guest of the Crown. He descended on Arthur, bumptious, jovial. "Horowitz is going to tell you to close your case and quit dicking around. Shit or get off the pot."

§

Arthur was expecting an in-chambers spanking — various judges had railed at him many times before, out of view of press and public — but Horowitz was more affable than censorious, and didn't ask why the Crown wished to recall Unger to the stand. Nor did he inquire why Jack Boynton was not present for this discussion. Arthur wasn't about to explain that he was squirrelling Wyacki away somewhere.

Arthur's plea was unadorned. He simply asked to be allowed to sit down with Unger before the Crown formally closed its case. "You saw the strain he was under, Selden. Surely he's entitled to one last chance to set the record straight."

"Beyond that, do you have a further witness?"

"No." Arthur had firmed up his intention to keep Wyacki out of it.

"So what's the problem?" Pomeroy said. "We're ready to go."

Horowitz asked, "You're electing to call evidence, Brian?"

"I can't disappoint my friend by saying no."

The clerk opened the door to Boynton, who looked anxious.

"It's about eleven-thirty," Horowitz said. "I expect everyone to be in place at precisely two p.m. But in the interim I can't see how I can prohibit Crown counsel from talking to their witness."

"That might be a problem," Boynton said. "We can't seem to locate him."

MONDAY AFTERNOON

Arthur didn't bother changing into street clothes, choosing to eat lunch in the Law Courts restaurant, where he anxiously waited for Boynton to report in. Pomeroy and Mandy were at a table not far away, looking too smug. He was kicking himself now about hiding Wyacki from them, but he didn't know how to backtrack and worried that he was digging himself a deeper hole.

It was twelve-thirty, and Arthur was halfway through his ravioli when Boynton, looking frazzled, finally joined him, still in courtroom gear.

"Arthur, we seem to be looking at a bit of a problem, I'm afraid."

"I know there's a problem. Where's Manfred? Where's Laurence Wyacki?"

"He's having a sandwich in the Crown counsel interview room. I was a little curt with him, though obviously he'd meant no harm by wandering into court. Not to cast blame, but I don't believe anyone warned him not to."

Arthur heard that as reproof, and bristled. It was Boynton's role to tend to the witnesses, and he'd blown the simple task of keeping Wyacki away from view.

"And Manfred?"

Boynton glanced at Pomeroy, who blew him a mock kiss. Mandy merely offered a smile, but Boynton rejected it, frowning, averting his eyes. He lowered his voice. "Manfred . . . well, he's disappeared."

Apparently into the dense thicket of West End apartment buildings. A sheriff's officer was the last to see him, exiting the courts by the Nelson Street entrance and walking north. He had not since returned to his hotel room or checked out of it.

"Colonel and Mrs. Unger are distraught. I tried to reassure them he's likely gone off to enjoy a sunny day, believing his courtroom duties were done."

A waiter summoned Arthur to the phone. "A Mr. Harrison, sir."

"Take a deep breath," Honcho said, "and grab a cab. Meet me on the Granville Bridge."

§

Leaning over the concrete railing of the massive bridge, Arthur stared in a dumfounded daze at a metal-sheeted shed roof on Granville Island, a hundred feet below. Emergency vehicles were down there, their lights flashing. A ladder had been thrown up, and officers were bent over the broken, lifeless body of Manfred Unger.

Boynton was sitting on the curb, breathing deeply. He'd taken one peek below and turned white.

"Can we free up the lane, sir?" a traffic officer asked Harrison.

"Soon." The curb lane, southbound, was ribboned off, causing a traffic snarl on this major artery. Gawkers were gathering, whispering their speculations about death and the presence of two gowned men.

"We figured he went walkabout for a while," Harrison said, "getting up courage. Driver of a passing car saw him take flight at twelve-fifteen hours."

"Now what?" said Boynton.

Before court resumed, counsel met in an emergency session in Justice Horowitz's chambers. The mood was sombre, respectful; there were no wisecracks from Pomeroy. Briskly, the two lead lawyers composed a brief joint statement about Unger's death, and signed it.

At two p.m., it was read to the jury. Arthur then announced that the Crown had concluded its case. Horowitz said a few gentle words about the tragedy, and suggested the trial be recessed until Tuesday morning. Counsel concurred.

Arthur observed that when the last juror left, Randy Skyler stopped looking anguished. He strode purposefully toward his lawyers, with an expression of some urgency, and brought them close. Not seeking advice, it looked like, but giving it.

Colonel and Mrs. Unger were not present. They'd been at the morgue, where, Arthur learned, Florence Unger collapsed and was given medical treatment, and they were now on their way to the airport with their daughter. Susan would accompany them home, to await the arrival of their son's body, and arrange his funeral.

How tragic for them. How tragic for the doubtless pleasant and pious young woman he planned to marry.

Arthur might have used the rest of the day to hone his attack on Skyler, but was in such a low mood that just thinking about the case, about its ghastly turn, caused a welling of nausea. It was a task for him to escape from the courthouse, from the media, from Jack Boynton and his hyperactive speculation about what impact the suicide would have on the jury.

"Not to be macabre, but it helps us, doesn't it? They'll conclude Unger jumped because he couldn't live with his false testimony, won't they?" He'd dogged Arthur to the gowning room, to the stairs, and finally to the exit. "But now the defence can say anything about Unger without fear of contradiction. They could even say Manfred did it, couldn't they?"

Arthur had to remind him of Skyler's thumbprint at the crime scene. The defence had invested too much time and energy on their swarthy nameless hulk to change course. Pomeroy had made no bones about the thrust of his case, even chiding the detectives after adjournment: "Why aren't you guys out looking for the jealous lover?" Overly loud, within hearing of a few jurors waiting for an elevator.

There was no point now in telling Pomeroy about Wyacki — the plan to confront Unger about his sleepover, to recall him to the stand, truthful, chastened, and begging forgiveness, had vaporized. There was little to gain by defaming the dead and exposing Wyacki to public embarrassment. Where was the harm in keeping the defence in the dark about him? How could the non-mention of a one-night stand in a second-rate hotel possibly cause the defence the least injustice?

Arthur went straightaway to his office, where he kept casual clothing to change into. He was pulling on a rumpled pair of slacks as Hubbell Meyerson came in jauntily. "First recorded case of someone literally being murdered in cross-examination."

"Damn it, Hubbell, I'm feeling too wretched to find that humorous."

"Sorry, a bit callous, that. Main topic around the water cooler. Hey, the missus and the kids are back, and we're expecting you and yours to come by for a little nosh-up this weekend."

"I'll speak to Annabelle." He laced up his walking shoes, resolved to walk around Stanley Park, the entire Seawall.

"Done already. We're on. Saturday."

Roy Bullingham paused in his rounds and stopped at the open door. "A suicide, I hear. No appeal from that, is there, Beauchamp? What can one say? Brilliant work, sad result, a witness driven to despair."

Arthur didn't have the energy to set Bully straight. Unger had recovered well under Pomeroy's gentle questioning. He'd be alive had Wyacki been warned to stay out of sight . . . That nausea again.

It was Day Twenty-Three, the need gnawing at him, the worst he'd felt for at least a week. Twenty-three. Unger's age.

Bully looked hard at Hubbell, then Arthur. "I suppose this delay puts finis to our little celebration tomorrow. It's awkward, people made plans, the entire staff granted the freedom of the day. Several cases of champagne on order."

"Nonsense, Bully, you're to go full steam ahead. I will be there in spirit if not spirits. Annabelle has promised to pop in to show the family flag, and Hubbell has agreed not to slander me too grievously while saying a few words on my behalf."

"I shall indulge only in fulsome praise," said Hubble.

"Pessimus inimicorum genus, laudantes." Arthur put an arm around his friend, walked him from the room. "The worst kind of scoundrels, those who can praise."

§

Arthur skirted the Stanley Park Zoo and its sulking, pacing prisoners, taking a path past the totems, Brockton Oval, Lumberman's Arch, the eastern side of the dense forest that protects the bustling seaport from the ocean. The Seawall was busy with fellow walkers, joggers, cyclists, the sky clear but for clouds gathering to the west. Rain tomorrow, a system poised to invade. Tomorrow, when he would be locked in combat with a glib liar.

In your warped mind, you realized you'd finally found a sexually satisfying form of congress with another.

You're dead wrong, you rotter!

Maybe dead right. Ontario police had tracked down a couple of his conquests. "It was like he was making love to himself," said a one-time girlfriend. "I got bored," said another.

Jack Boynton had insisted on delivering a sheaf of those and similar interviews to Pomeroy's office. Arthur had balked at giving such disclosure, a forewarning of his cross-examination strategy. But again he reminded himself not to give in to the impulse to win at any cost. That was expected from defenders but unacceptable, even dishonourable, for the Crown.

He continued to stew over the growing possibility that Skyler would cockwalk from the courthouse, smiling his victory smile for the press. No one remained alive who could counter his version; no honest jury could be satisfied to a moral certainty that Chumpy the Clown hadn't been offed by a swarthy, toque-topped man. Arthur felt hollow, hopeless, with victory slipping away, his proofs of guilt feeling more flabby by the minute, all of them controvertible.

It was pleasanter to think of Annabelle, who last night had so magnanimously and proficiently and shockingly fellated him in a reprise of that lovely, lascivious practice after a lapse of many years. And there'd been closeness beyond that, remembrances of happy times, whisperings of love. Fresh evidence to dismiss a lingering unreasonable doubt about her fidelity, strong circumstantial proof that she had come back to him. He was glad he wouldn't be tormenting her tonight with his sour mood — she had a full dress rehearsal.

She had freed up tomorrow afternoon, though, and would be at the office do, vivacious and perky, teasing the senior partners, getting their pulse rates up, feeding their fantasies. Hubbell had promised Arthur he'd be her loyal guard dog.

The other woman in his life had figure skating after school. Arthur didn't want to be alone, so he would try to find a meeting somewhere; a group gathered Mondays at St. James Anglican in West Point Grey.

He paused at the lookout at Prospect Point, with its view of Lions Gate and its sweeping, graceful bridge. Then he headed south, only a couple of miles to go, soaking in the rays at the shank of day. He stuck to the seaward rim, by the stone palisade, to let the speed walkers and joggers huff by.

He took a pass on visiting the Hollow Tree and was just coming upon the crescent of golden sand known as Third Beach when a familiar form rushed past him — not jogging, almost sprinting. Randy Skyler. Who turned and ran backwards for a moment, while he shot a penetrating, venomous look at the man who'd caused his devoted sidekick to take his own life. Then he swivelled and sped away.

TUESDAY MORNING

Half an hour into his testimony, Skyler remained composed and deliberate, polite, earnest, forthcoming. Overdoing it, Arthur felt, given the tragedy of the previous day. Still, the jury was attentive, evidently withholding judgement. He worried they were warming to Skyler, unable to penetrate his mask of normalcy.

Mandy Pearl was finally doing her star turn, slowly and somewhat stiffly leading the witness through his upbringing, his education, his aspirations, his social life — while Pomeroy sat, nodding, occasionally acknowledging dimpled smiles from Juror Twelve. He'd waived his opening to the jury, saving his gunpowder for his summing-up.

The junior defence counsel was not the brazen, confident woman Arthur had come to know. She appeared hesitant, nervous: Unger's death had clearly affected her. A pall had settled on the entire room, and it seemed intensified by the foul weather buffeting the city, a rare lightning storm at dawn, umbrella-tugging winds, slantwise rain. Harrison and Nordquist had just arrived, dripping.

On the first mention of Manfred Unger, Skyler reacted with constricted throat and quivering lip. The jury learned that Unger had been among the closest of his many friends, they'd known each other since grade nine, and had been constant companions, both of them avid sportsmen, deer hunters. They saw each other less regularly after Unger enrolled at RMC. "To be honest, our friendship had become a little too one-sided, and I was trying to back off."

"I know this is difficult for you given the awful event of yesterday, but did he ever show any emotional problems?"

"He had what I'd call extreme bouts of wild imagination. There were definite mental issues. He'd been seen by psychiatrists in high school, he told me, and was often on medication."

This unexpected pronouncement prompted a gratuitous exclamation point from Boynton, by means of a sharp elbow. Arthur glanced behind, at row three: then remembered the Ungers had gone home. They were not available to counter such calumnies.

"I really felt sorry for him, and I hate to say it, but that was the basis of our friendship, his emotional problems. I was trying to help him. He was always calling up, coming by, sticking to me like glue, but . . . he needed a friend. He didn't have many others, and he pretty well dumped everything on . . . I'm sorry, that sounds harsh. He confided in me."

As Mandy prodded, he heaped it on. Unger suffered from disorders that seemed pulled from a psychology textbook: feelings of insecurity, delusions of grandeur, voices, mystic experiences. It got so bad, said Skyler, that he cancelled their hunting trip two years ago, and took away and hid his friend's rifle.

"He was at his worst when he was drinking, or doing drugs. I don't pretend I didn't share them occasionally — marijuana mostly — but he got me to try LSD once, and it was frankly pretty freaky — he was going on about death and orgasms, weird stuff . . ."

Mandy had a quick tête-à-tête with her senior. Again, Arthur got a strong sense of her discomfort. Muffled sounds of disagreement between her and Skyler had been overheard from behind the closed door of a witness room. Pomeroy had been elsewhere; he seemed to have placed his client entirely in Mandy's care.

Skyler carried on unaided. "I should add that as we were preparing for our trip here, Manfred was engrossed in a crime novel called *For the Fun of It*. He talked incessantly about it, even read me passages during our flight. It was about a serial killer who got a sexual thrill by choosing victims at random and then murdering them in cold blood."

It was a palpable effort to explain how Unger might have confused fact with fiction during their exchange on Sunday morning. Mandy seemed content not to pursue it further, but Arthur had the niggling sense Skyler was about to take a few steps too far. He saw in him a potentially rogue witness, prone to ill-advised detours.

Mandy finally got Skyler to Vancouver. "Please give us an account of your stay here, from your arrival."

He began a travelogue: "Beautiful city . . . great beaches . . . friendly bars, friendly people . . . really beats Toronto." An upbeat tone, his feelings of bereavement apparently mastered. "There was an evening concert by, I think they called themselves Doug and the Slugs, and we were too exhausted to do anything that night, and we went back to Expo the next morning, that would be the Saturday, and I remember we did the gondola and Skytrain, and whatever we could . . . The Scream Machine, that was pretty scary."

To Arthur, that rang hollow, but it brought a smile to a few jurors, who may have ridden that twisty roller coaster.

"Okay, let's take you to Saturday evening, after you returned from the fair. Please trace your movements for us. I understand you and Manfred went somewhere to eat."

Again, Skyler digressed. "I forgot to mention that just before that, back in the hotel, Manfred was still into his novel, and he insisted on talking about it. He kept saying things like, 'Do you think it could be like that? Could you get an orgasm killing someone?' He actually said 'get your rocks off,' but I got his meaning." Skyler shrugged and held his hands apart in a gesture of dismay.

From Mandy's reaction — she looked like she'd been side-swiped

— Arthur deduced that Skyler had gone off script. Pomeroy went still as stone.

Unchecked, Skyler continued, turning to the jury, talking excitedly:"I didn't take him seriously, I honestly didn't. I was kidding when I made him a dare. It was something offhand, like 'I bet you can't,' or, pardon my French, 'You don't have the balls.'"

Arthur caught Harrison's unblinking eye. Bones was equally deadpan. Boynton, with his small fixed smile, seemed unsure what was transpiring — it was as if he were struggling to enjoy a badly crafted play.

Mandy huddled again with Pomeroy, intensely this time. Arthur was sure from their strained expressions that their decoy of a jealous, toqued lover was being edited out. Unger was being written in as Chumpy's killer. Skyler was arrogant enough to believe he could outsmart his lawyers.

Pomeroy wasn't leaping to his feet to call for a recess — that would only tempt the jury to suspect that the defence's plan had gone askew. Arthur guessed they were letting this risky detour run its course, gambling it might end safely.

"Go ahead," Mandy said finally, faintly.

"Anyway, that evening we had dinner in a pub somewhere downtown, and then went for a walk in old Gastown, stopped off at a bar or two. Manfred was all set on finding a stripper bar he'd been told about, but the thought of sitting around with a bunch of leering old . . . Check that. Anyway, Manfred seemed determined to party it up on our last night; he even bought a case of Coors, but I was ready to pack it in."

Mandy ventured a safe question:"Where did he buy the beer?"

"From one of the pubs. The Abbott? I can't remember. We stopped in a little park by a cenotaph, and I cracked one open — I think Manfred may have too, I'm not sure — but anyway a patrol car went by and I slipped it back in the case unfinished."

Even as Skyler had been racing around Stanley Park on his free afternoon, his mind had been racing just as vigorously, creating and rehearsing this theoretically plausible scenario.

"By then it was well after midnight, and I was ready to pack it in, and we were walking down . . . I think it was Cordova Street. It was deserted except for a fat little guy who seemed drunk, and Manfred asked him if there was a strip club still open. He said he was Chumpy the Clown, which didn't mean anything to me, but he seemed like a character. He said he could take us to the best strip club in town, but I told Manfred I couldn't hack it anymore, and I went back to our hotel, and they went . . . I don't know."

"Carry on," said Mandy, as Skyler frowned, as if in reflection.

"Oh, yeah, I remember asking them what they were going to do with that case of Coors — they were taking off with it — and Manfred kind of checked the street, up and down, and it was still deserted, and he gave me this big wink, and said, 'Don't have the balls, eh?' and . . ." Suddenly Skyler slumped, downcast. "I did my friend a terrible disservice. I thought he was joking. I just didn't believe he would do it."

An emotional struggle, feigned or otherwise, persuaded Horowitz to order a ten-minute break.

Arthur clamped his hand on Boynton's arm to still his trembling and didn't release it until the gallery emptied, until Pomeroy and Mandy hurried up the aisle after their client.

"What I don't want to hear from you, Jack, is that Wyacki has caught an early flight home."

"I'll check."

"Keep him hidden. Report back."

There was no choice now. Laurence Wyacki would have to testify. Boynton conferred with the two detectives and they hurried off.

Arthur stayed pat, looked over his cross-examination notes, excising several pages, recording fresh thoughts.

§

The ten minutes stretched to nearly twenty, the sheriffs growing restless, eager to fetch the jury, but finally the defence showed up. Skyler, his features firmly set, walked quickly to the stand. Mandy followed with a smile and a confident stride that seemed put on. Pomeroy, lagging behind, grimaced on seeing Arthur's sad smile: a message of compassion for his plight over a runaway witness.

When court was called to order, Juror Five tucked away a crossword puzzle — Arthur had seen her working at a few of those. He approved. It was a sign of intelligence.

On rising, Pomeroy apologized for the delay. "Our client was in some distress."

"I'm okay now," Skyler said, smiling ruefully. A chameleon. But was the jury seeing that? Arthur would have felt more comfortable if he'd seen some rolling of eyes or at least a frown.

Mandy kept her questions short and open, giving Skyler free rein. From her perspective, it wasn't going badly: Skyler was assured and steady, with occasional self-effacing touches.

Arthur listened with bemusement as Skyler turned every relevant detail backwards. It was Unger who roused Skyler from sleep at ten o'clock on Sunday, August 3. It was Unger who said, "I really did it this time" and "I must have stabbed him ten times, and he wouldn't die." It was Unger who'd wiped the prints from the knife; Unger who'd taken off his clothes to avoid staining them with his victim's blood. It was Unger's leg that had been bitten.

Arthur was spared Boynton's repeated nudges because he'd yet to show up. But Nordquist was back and had sent up a note saying Wyacki was safely in his hotel room, Harrison with him.

"What was your reaction to Mr. Unger's disclosures?" Mandy asked.

"I was horrified. I blamed myself, of course, but I . . . I mean, I just lit into Manfred. I was so angry, I even grabbed him by the shoulders, pushed him against the wall. He kept saying, 'He was only a drunken old fag,' things like that, 'a worthless bum,' as if that was a valid excuse. I told him to turn himself in before it was too late. Get help, get a lawyer. 'Tell them you went insane.' 'If you don't do the right thing,' I said, 'I'll call the police myself.'"

A sip of water. The stagy quality of his narrative was not so excessive that it could be easily and unanimously dismissed by twelve jurors. They were watching him intently.

"I was swearing at him, I used some really gross words, obscenities that I don't care to repeat here, and an expression came over his face that I can only describe as complete rage and hostility. I remember thinking, God, he's going through one of his really sick, delusional phases. I felt threatened, but he just turned and roared out of there with his bag packed. I assume that's when he went to his sister's." A woeful look. "And you've heard about the lies he told her. She persuaded him to go to the police, and of course he did, figuring he had to get to them before I did. And now he is dead and I am charged with a murder I did not commit. My best friend . . ."

He trailed off, and gripped the railing of the witness stand to steady himself.

Boynton finally settled in beside Arthur. "How's it going?"

"Oh, just lovely."

"Seriously?"

"No."

"Okay, Wyacki is fine, he's working on a school paper, and he's okay with testifying. I think the guys tossed Skyler's apartment."

"Why?"

"Looking for his script."

Arthur would have to pursue that later. Mandy was asking Skyler if he'd followed up his threat to call the police.

"I fully intended to. I was going to wait until he had a chance to cool down and get real. So when the police came by the next morning, I was in complete shock. I just handled things terribly. I was scared. I don't remember saying I never met Chumpy, but I was so discombobulated I probably did. I did tell them I'd never been in his suite."

Mandy checked her notes. "You were quoted: 'That's awful, I don't know anything about it.'"

"Well, I guess I was just . . . I couldn't bring myself to accuse Manfred of murder . . . I was trying to cover up for him. I was a fool."

As to Jimmy Gillies's sighting of a light-haired young man walking from the building at around breakfast time: "That had to have been Manfred, because he was wearing denim and cowboy boots, just like Mr. Gillies said. I can't explain the black gloves, unless he took them from Mr. Chumpy's suite. I honestly can't remember them. But on God's word, it definitely wasn't me. I'm not a crazy person. I'm not a killer. I'm *not* a killer."

"No more questions."

"Mr. Beauchamp, you have about twenty minutes left — would you like to get started?"

A nudge. "Get him under cross before lunch. Honcho has something for you." Harrison had showed up, peeling out of a rain poncho.

Arthur rose to a hum of anticipation. He looked at his many pages of scribbled notes, then swept them into his briefcase. His usual practice was to circle his prey awhile, especially with a clever character like Skyler, to play cat and mouse, hoping to win on points. But this time, he was hoping for a knockout in an early round.

"Manfred stuck to you like glue, you said. Didn't you ever want to peel him off?"

Hesitation. "Maybe, occasionally . . . I just couldn't bring myself to desert the poor guy. Like I say, he needed help."

"Didn't his clinginess strike you as odd?"

"Clingy . . . I may have exaggerated that. We shared a lot of good times together too."

"You were his hero. He idolized you."

"I guess."

"Must have felt good. Gave you a little glow?"

"I don't believe I ever thought of it that way. I may have felt honoured that he was . . ." A struggle over word choice.

"Attracted to you."

"In the sense of two good pals, yes. I don't know what you're getting at, Mr. Beauchamp. He had a steady girlfriend. I was dating, too. A lot."

"With, for instance, Miss Jean Eubacher."

He was caught short. "Eubach — Yes, I was seeing her."

Arthur was set on exposing the lie of Skyler's vaunted virility. Nothing personal, of course, but it was his best shot at a win. "Would it bother you to know she told an investigator you were a dud in bed?"

That yanked Pomeroy to his feet, and Horowitz spoke sharply. "Mr. Beauchamp, you know better than to sneak hearsay in by the back door."

"I apologize, M'lord. It's a bad habit I learned from Mr. Pomeroy." Even Brian's admirer, Juror Twelve, smiled at this.

Arthur moved to safer ground. "You met a couple of young women on the Expo grounds. Did you get their names?"

"I guess we did, but I can't remember. They were nice."

"Coeds from Texas. You said you lost track of them. Do you think they were trying to give you the slip?"

Skyler was abrupt, as if offended: "Definitely not. If anything, they were coming on to us."

"They were attracted to you?"

"I guess, sure."

"Did you make any effort to track them down before you went on the Scream Machine?" Watch that snide tone, he reminded himself.

"We looked, believe me. We didn't get lucky. *Que sera sera.*" A try for jauntiness that clunked. Frowns from Jurors Three, Five, and Nine.

"Do you find men attracted to you too?"

"What do you mean by that?"

An affronted tone. Arthur was getting under his skin earlier than expected. "Gay men, I mean. Surely a handsome, virile, athletic male like yourself attracts many looks from homosexual men."

"How would I know?"

"Tell us why you really think Manfred was glued to you."

Red-faced, he blurted: "Manfred was totally straight! The last guy who approached me got one on the side of his head."

Arthur heard a few gasps behind him.

"Would this be a good time to break for lunch, Mr. Beauchamp?"

"Yes, indeed, M'lord." Timed to perfection.

TUESDAY AFTERNOON

Harrison managed to look both stubborn and sheepish as he and Nordquist joined the prosecutors in the Crown counsel offices. "I ain't saying I was in there and I seen it. Don't ask, because I won't tell. A confidential informant told me."

Arthur understood this was code for *We entered illegally*. He was shocked. Harrison had a reputation for skirting the rules, but this warrantless search seemed blatant. Nevertheless, he held his tongue.

What Honcho — or his alleged source — had seen in Skyler's apartment that morning was an actors' manual, *On Stage: Tips and Techniques*. A well-overdue library book.

Arthur finished his salami on rye, then examined the records the detectives had got from the Vancouver Public Library, West Broadway branch: a copy of Skyler's library card. A lending card showing Skyler took out the manual three months ago. Arthur wondered, guiltily, if he could somehow get these documents past those sticklers for the rules, Pomeroy and Horowitz, without their learning of the illegal entry. Fat chance. Clear grounds for a mistrial.

The storm outside continued unabated, and Honcho's clothes were still wet from his morning excursion. Had he got into Skyler's apartment through a back window? No, because it was on a second floor. A fire escape maybe, an unsecured window or a picked lock. Arthur asked, "And were any written notes lying about?"

"I'm given to understand there was a transcript of the first trial, but no notes. There was an empty trash basket. Also a computer, which my source knew dick about, even how to start it."

Nordquist looked on passively. Boynton seemed to be making an effort to play the game, pretending to believe in the informant fairy. Arthur was feeling somewhat corrupted.

He was more interested in another book anyway: Unger's copy of *For the Fun of It* had just been couriered from RMC. It was a hardcover, a first edition, Cheltenham Press, London. The author, Horace Widgeon, had signed the title page. And dated it: May 24, 1986. And under that he'd written, "Toronto, Canada." Above that, in impeccably neat handwriting: "Happy birthday, Manfred, from Randolph and Yours Truly!" There may have been a sparse turnout at the signing, because Widgeon had had time to add: "Don't sneak a peek at the last page!"

On that forbidden page, Lord Scarfe-Robbins is marched off to the nick swearing vengeance against the protagonist. "I'll get you one day, Grodgins! I'll cut out your gizzard, you stinking, squint-eyed bastard!" In a brief denouement, Inspector Grodgins arrives home, his agnosia still in full bloom, to find a female foursome playing bridge in the parlour, and he can't tell which is his wife.

"Is the sequel out yet?" he asked Nordquist.

"He has a new one every spring."

"Do we know exactly where this book was signed?"

"A Toronto mystery bookstore," Boynton said. "Owner is one J.D. Singh. He said the author stopped by on a book tour."

Arthur flipped through the book. Throughout were marginalia scribbled in red ink, comments like "Nice!" or "Totally evil, man!"

"Manfred wrote these?" Arthur asked.

Nordquist shook his head. "Our handwriting guy says Skyler."

Arthur tilted a Thermos, refilled his coffee mug. The lawyers and staff of Tragger, Inglis would be gathering now to honour him in absentia, with canapés and bubbly. There would be roasts as well as toasts, he supposed. On the whole, Arthur preferred to be in Court 53, doing his own roasting.

No more mister nice guy. He was in this to win.

§

On stepping into the stand, Skyler seemed to have regained his equanimity. His counsellors, however, seemed harried: they'd been in deep dialogue with their client, and had probably missed lunch. The tension in court was palpable. A sheriff was calling for quiet.

Most of the jurors trooping in were expressionless, intently focussed on taking their seats, but the foreperson, the interior designer, seemed to be suppressing a smile, as if she'd just been joking with someone. She glanced at Arthur, then away. He hoped the joke wasn't on him.

"Proceed, Mr. Prosecutor."

Arthur barely opened his mouth before Skyler interrupted. "May I explain something, Your Lordship. I mentioned I clipped a guy who was coming on to me, but he was drunk and persistent, and I regret having done that. I want to make it clear that I don't have any hangups about homosexuals, if that's what Mr. Beauchamp was implying. My attitude is that's their business, but I happen to prefer women. And I resent the insinuation that Manfred was gay."

"You resent it?" said Arthur.

"I reject it, sir. Manfred not only had a girlfriend, they were engaged. Janet. I'm heartbroken for her. And before Janet, he and I had lots of double dates. I can assure you he had a healthy appetite for the ladies."

"And did his appetite match yours?"

"I also resent the insinuation I was some kind of dud in bed, sir."

The strategy of sticking needles in the soft underbelly of Skyler's vanity was showing promise. "How many women would you say you've bedded?"

Mandy rose. "This is almost indecent. M'lord, how can any of this be relevant?"

"I'll give you some latitude, Mr. Beauchamp."

"Give me a rough count, Mr. Skyler. How many?"

"I haven't kept records. It wasn't my whole life or anything. But it was always normal sex and totally consensual."

"The right girl never came along?"

"I had some fairly long spells with different women. I got pretty serious with one, we moved in together."

"For how long?"

A shrug. "A few months."

Arthur flipped through the Ontario interviews. "Was that the apartment in Etobicoke? Martina Jacobs?"

Skyler looked at him sharply. "Yes. You've obviously done some research."

"You signed a six-month lease, then left her after two months. What happened?"

"That . . . it fizzled . . . it didn't work out."

"Fizzled. Not much electricity, I guess."

Mandy jumped up again. "I object to the baiting of the witness."

"It's cross-examination, Ms. Pearl." Horowitz evidently approved of this new line of questioning.

"Your last relationship was eighteen months ago, with Hennie Forbes, and it lasted about a month, correct?"

"Whatever Hennie said isn't true. Sometimes there's just no magic."

"Another young woman, Lynn West, said she got bored after a week. With Margot Allen you lasted ten days. When it gets right down to it, Mr. Skyler, you were not the hottest item on the auction block."

Mandy bounced up like a rubber ball. "I object on all sorts of grounds."

"Mr. Beauchamp, please refrain from that kind of rhetoric. I don't want to have to cut you short."

"So again, how many women have you slept with, Mr. Skyler?"

"Dozens, more than that — how would I know, I don't carve notches. I can't remember all their names."

"I put it to you that you consistently had trouble rising to the occasion with these women."

"I don't know what you mean."

"You know exactly what I mean. You are without sexual drive. You are undersexed, frigid."

With that provocation resonating about the room, Skyler muttered an apparent obscenity, inaudible to most, and rose a few inches from his seat as if about to spring upon his persecutor. Sheriffs on either side of him rose too, and all three held themselves for a few seconds like racers at a starting line, then sat simultaneously.

"That's a damn lie," Skyler said through clenched teeth. He looked at his lawyers for support, but, to Arthur's surprise, they restrained themselves from accusing him of baiting the witness, though that was his unvarnished intent. And the witness was rising to the bait.

A softer tone: "Let's talk about the book you gave Manfred last year, *For the Fun of It.*"

"Who said I gave it to him?"

"I think you'll recognize it." Arthur retrieved the copy from Unger's bookshelf, held it up before Skyler in the manner of a priest brandishing his Bible at a sinner.

This time it was Pomeroy who rose. "My friend doesn't seem to have any compunction about hiding material evidence from the defence."

"The Crown can prove, if put to it — and that will involve flying in witnesses from his military college — that it was found among Manfred Unger's effects only yesterday. I first saw it a little over an hour ago."

Pomeroy and Horowitz took turns with the book, the judge

perusing the title page, the inscription: "Happy birthday, Manfred, from Randolph and Yours Truly!"

"It might have been more promptly disclosed, Mr. Beauchamp. But you may proceed."

The book was marked as an exhibit and returned to the witness. Arthur showed him the inscription page.

"Okay, I remember now, I bought this book as a birthday present for Manfred, signed by the author. He was a fan of the Inspector Grodgins series."

"Yes, Inspector Grodgins, with his perception problems. What is the disability called?"

"Agnosia. Where you can't recognize people's faces."

"He'd had a brain injury in . . . what was the book just before that?"

"*The Revenge of Dr. Sartorius.*"

"Which you read, didn't you?"

"Yes, I did."

"And you also read *For the Fun of It* cover to cover, yes? You read it before giving it to Manfred."

"All right, it's coming back. His birthday wasn't for a couple of months . . . I teased him and wouldn't give it up until I read it."

"And you teased him by reading passages aloud."

"I guess, maybe."

"And I suggest it was you, Mr. Skyler, not Manfred Unger, who was engrossed in this book. It was you who talked incessantly about it, who read him passages while flying to Vancouver — isn't that so?"

"I already told you we discussed the book."

"Here's one of the selections you regaled him with: 'He could feel it mounting. He could feel it coming. Then, as he watched Tom the Poacher's ruddy face turn blue, there came an accelerating procession of orgasmic jolts, more powerful than with Donny Millibun, more powerful than in his most intense fantasies.

There followed an explosion of pure, rich, volcanic pleasure that coursed hotly through every gland and organ and muscle, and that thickened and hardened his phallus until it felt like a pulsing stretch of tempered steel, and that found such shuddering, ecstatic release through that orifice that he fought to stifle a roar of rapture.' Good Lord. How lurid. The jury must forgive me, I didn't have time to read this over."

Arthur's sudden shift in tone to surprise and contrition after his rich, sonorous reading of the sizzling prose prompted laughter from the public seats, while the jury and Horowitz struggled to maintain straight faces. But Boynton was visibly squirming with embarrassment. Arthur glanced at Mandy, expecting her to be appalled, but she was smiling at him in an almost beguiling way.

Arthur had trouble getting steam up again. To gather himself, he spent a few moments flipping the pages of the hardcover book.

"You read that purple paragraph to Manfred, didn't you?"

"I can't recall what I read to him."

"Let me show you. The entire paragraph is bracketed in red ink. Beside it, also in red ink, is written: 'Ultra, man!' Your handwriting, Mr. Skyler. You may deny it at your peril."

"It was . . . I was being sardonic."

"Allow me to quote the justifications of the nameless killer: 'No one would miss the alcoholic old courtesan. Her time was past. He was doing the world a service.' Your red-inked notation: 'One less loser.' Don't deny you wrote that."

Skyler had gone stiff, his neck muscles tight, his facial nerves throbbing. "One less loser . . . I believe I was trying to convey what the author was trying . . . or what his character was thinking."

"And then this character goes on to strangle another homeless drunk. Again he achieves impressive release. Your marginal note: 'You'd think his hands would be tired! Nice!'"

"I was having fun, I was teasing Manfred."

"You were fascinated by the premise of the book, that the taking of innocent life promised the ultimate sexual thrill."

"I told you already I dared him. I was kidding. He took it seriously. I never did."

"Murder was the only way you could achieve a sexual climax."

"That's not true."

"Witness, in this book, Inspector Grodgins rightly accuses the perpetrator of being impotent." Arthur began turning up the volume. "You found in this story a possible solution for your own impotence. You couldn't find satisfaction in your relationships with women, yet you hungered for release, and you sought sexual fulfilment in the grisly murder of an innocent street entertainer —"

Both defence counsel erupted, Mandy entreating the court, "Make him stop yelling, browbeating . . ." Brian talking over her, "Totally, utterly improper . . ."

"Order."

"Did you enjoy yourself with Joe Chumpy, Skyler?"

"Order!"

"Did you enjoy your explosion of pure, rich, volcanic pleasure?"

Horowitz cut him off by rising. "We'll take the morning adjournment."

Arthur was so focussed, so zeroed in on Skyler, that he was barely aware of the commotion, the shouting, and was startled to look up and see Horowitz striding out in a temper and the jury being led away. He felt a tug at his gown, Boynton trying to break his fierce concentration.

Skyler ignored his lawyers and made his way out with some urgency, maybe a bathroom break.

Pomeroy waited until the room cleared, then accosted Arthur. "Man, I've seen prosecutors go hell-bent for conviction, but this is a new low. I ought to bring unprofessional conduct charges." Boynton tried to get between them. "Yeah, and against you too, Boynton, for being his cloying sycophant."

Arthur left the room, strode outside for a breath of calming air among the blossoms of the tiered gardens of Robson Square. After a while, Mandy joined him, with a cigarette.

"Your testosterone was working overtime in there, sweetie. I almost came."

TUESDAY MID-AFTERNOON

Arthur returned bearing gifts of penitence and self-abasement for having got so egregiously carried away, but when he began offering them, Justice Horowitz waved him off wearily and told him to proceed.

He retrenched a little, pecking away at inconsistencies and absurdities in Skyler's version of what had happened on the Sunday morning. Skyler managed well enough, but he was subdued, shaken. No self-serving speeches or excursions.

Arthur had decided not to raise the issue of the library book detected in Skyler's flat: *On Stage: Tips and Techniques*. Were the defence to catch a whiff of illegality, of Honcho's illegal entry, the Crown's case would be in peril.

So he carried on with twenty minutes of non-threatening questions, until he felt Skyler had been lulled enough, and, maintaining the same tone and rhythm, asked, "The swarthy visitor, Chumpy's boyfriend, did you get a good look at him?"

"I was avoiding eye contact, I didn't want to get . . . No, not me. Manfred said that. I'm just quoting Manfred."

"It is said a liar needs a good memory. *Mendacem memorem esse oportet.* The jealous lover — that was Plan A, wasn't it? That's the story you originally concocted for the jury."

"No, sir."

"But you knew that wouldn't wash, and when you saw an opportunity to heap blame on a young man whose tongue was forever silenced, you changed course, you started paddling to a different shore."

"I'm not sure what you're implying, I'm sorry."

"After Manfred testified against you at the first trial, how did you persuade him to change his mind?"

"I never talked to him once. Not in person, not on the phone."

"So you wish us to believe. But you're not blind, Mr. Skyler, and you're not stupid. You knew Manfred was homosexual. That was your hold on him."

Skyler glanced at his lawyers, as if seeking their intercession, but they were fixed on Arthur, almost hypnotically, as he pressed on.

"He would lose everything were he forced to come out of the closet. Career, the respect of his parents, the love of a young woman. He'd be a laughingstock or worse among his former friends on the sports field. You knew that, and you threatened him with exposure unless he changed his testimony."

"That's a lie!"

"The jury will judge who is lying in this courtroom."

Only about half the jurors met Arthur's eye. He was confident that all reticence, all doubt, would evaporate when Laurence Wyacki took the stand.

"No more questions."

§

Arthur sat back, trying not to look too smug, while Mandy Pearl took her client through redirect examination, applying Band-Aids to her client's cuts. Arthur was content to wait her out, because soon he would announce, "I call Mr. Laurence Wyacki," and the roof would fall in on her prevaricating client.

Annoyingly, Mandy was doing a superb job of resurrection. The reason for Skyler's inability to remain attached: he'd known love, was hurt when Martina Jacobs broke up with him, and was taking pains not to commit himself. As a result, there was a certain amount of disappointment, jealousy, and ("I hate to say it") spitefulness on the part of some ex-lovers.

With Mandy leading him outrageously, he agreed that the prosecution had "cherry-picked" a disgruntled few women. There were many others with whom he kept friendly contact.

He was appalled and sickened by Mr. Beauchamp's slanders. He had never had any issues with his emotional or sexual health, and had medical records to prove it. He'd never been in trouble with the law; there was never a complaint laid against him until the August long weekend last year.

Moreover, he was a supporter of gay rights: everyone should be allowed to follow his own heart. His dentist was gay. A cousin was gay.

"And what do you say about Mr. Beauchamp's imputation that Manfred Unger was gay?"

"Well, I thought that was pretty awful, coming just the day after he . . . he died." Skyler was struggling with emotion, swallowing hard. Arthur had encountered too many artful deceivers in the courts to find this display remotely credible, but feared the jurors — those twelve unreadable faces — might not share his skepticism.

"Would it make any difference to you if Manfred were homosexual?"

"No way he was, I'd known him forever. But . . ."

"Yes?"

"Well, if he was that deep in the closet, I guess it's possible that was why he had all those emotional problems. The drugs, the shrinks, the freaking out. The anger. Taking it out on poor old Chumpy that way, both of them naked."

Mandy seemed uncertain whether to continue that tricky line, then sat. "Thank you."

"We'll take the afternoon break."

As the court cleared, Pomeroy strolled over to Arthur and asked if he planned any evidence in rebuttal. Arthur casually rendered up a copy of Laurence Wyacki's statement. Brian glanced through it, and almost gagged.

"What the fuck . . . Son of a bitch!" Sputtering. "When did you get this?"

Boynton backed away from the spittle, hiding behind Mandy.

Arthur calmly explained. Wyacki came out of the blue, late on Sunday. He'd decided against calling him — and then Skyler changed the script, crossing up even his lawyers, by glibly fingering his best buddy.

Pomeroy stared at him dumbly, then at Boynton. "Did you countenance this? Never mind." To the clerk: "Tell His Lordship I've got a mistrial application. Goddamnit!"

§

Pomeroy continued in high dudgeon in Horowitz's chambers, while the court report transcribed everything, including one or two not-so-mild obscenities. "I can't fucking believe . . . strike that, sorry, I'm frazzled. But they finally cough up this witness after sitting on him over the weekend and the whole of yesterday."

"Let's all calm down here," Horowitz said. "Mr. Clerk, I want the jury dismissed for the day while we hammer this out."

That was when Arthur realized he was heading for a crash landing. Pomeroy's complaint was one that would normally be argued in open court, with the press present, but the judge clearly felt issues of reputation were at play, in particular the reputation of an eminent barrister.

He implied as much during a wrangle that extended through

the day's waning hours. Arthur was dismayed that the judge was lending a sympathetic ear to Pomeroy's denunciations, to his claims that the prosecution had set a diabolic trap, that the defence was being denied the right to a fair answer. In any event, Pomeroy said, Wyacki's testimony was not proper rebuttal evidence, and therefore inadmissible.

Arthur tried to gain Horowitz's sympathy by recounting how a young law student of impeccable background came forward — a mere two days ago — bravely prepared to endure great public embarrassment in order that justice might be done. He'd initially decided the young man's testimony wasn't vital to the Crown's case, but it became so when the jury heard Skyler's wholly unanticipated alibi.

It was rock-solid evidence in any event, complete with corroborating hotel records and Unger's scribbled note to Wyacki with his phone number. The Crown, he argued, was under no obligation to disclose to the defence evidence that had seemed of speculative value.

Justice Horowitz took half an hour to prepare a written judgement that he read in open court, the jury absent, the gallery almost empty, only a few reporters present.

"The Crown may call evidence in rebuttal only if the defence has raised some new matter which the Crown could not have reasonably anticipated. Rebuttal is not permitted for matters which the Crown could have raised before the defence was entered upon. I find that the Crown ought reasonably to have anticipated the alibi relied on by the accused. The testimony of Mr. Beauchamp's too-well-hidden witness will not be heard."

The trial was put over until the morning, for final speeches and judge's instructions. The matter would then go to the jury.

Arthur strode out fuming.

TUESDAY EVENING

Arthur spent a long while outside, shaky, desperate for a shot of strong alcohol, puffing at his feeble substitute, his Peterson bent. He couldn't bear the thought of Pomeroy descending on him again, this time solicitous, masking triumph with ill-meant words of consolation.

The Law Courts had closed for business by the time he returned to the robing room. He was stepping from his striped pants as Boynton dashed in, panting, extending the heavy briefcase with the papers that his boss had abandoned in court.

"Don't disappear like that! What do we do now? He's handed it to them on a platter. You have to ask for a mistrial. We can't go with what we've got."

"We'll go with what we've got." Arthur had to adjust the elastic of his shorts — he was so angry that his testicles hurt. He knew he would soon descend into depression and self-reproach, but for the time being he needed anger, he needed its strength. Strength to fight the tantalizing but dreaded short-term solution to his unhappiness. But how bracing a properly made martini would be right now.

Boynton continued to natter away about their plight, but to give him credit he did not cast blame or utter an I-told-you-so.

Suspenders, suit jacket, loosely knotted tie, and Arthur was off.

"Your file," Boynton called. "Your transcripts. Your summing-up notes for tomorrow." Arthur kept walking.

§

The rain had dwindled to drizzle as the afternoon waned. It was rush hour: crawling cars, hurrying pedestrians, long lines for the buses. Arthur hadn't brought his Rolls that day, and thought of taking a taxi to some isolated spot where he would not have to see people. The Mountain View Cemetery. The CPR Pier, easy to jump off.

But habit took him downtown toward the bank towers, toward Tragger, Inglis. He arrived as a tide of weary, happy humankind poured from his building, heading for tavern or home. His office on the forty-second floor offered the privacy he needed. He would lock himself inside and get it out of his system. He would rant to the shelves of *Criminal Reports* and *Western Weeklies* until he was exhausted.

He arrived on his floor to the sounds of revelry, weary and hoarse, the denouement of an office saturnalia that had spilled into the reception area from the lounge. It came to him only then, as he listened to a mutilated chorus of "You Are My Sunshine" from a circle of lawyers holding each other up, that this was the tail end of the party honouring the two new partners. It had been crowded from his mind.

The very air in the lounge was intoxicating, a potpourri of alluring scents, wines and whiskies, gin and rum. He had to step by Jurgenhoff, financial trusts, who was asleep on a chair, tightly clutching a rye and ginger, his toupee askew. McCowan, commercial contracts, had rolled up his pants and was hovering over a golf ball with a putter. Arthur had played the fool at many similar office festivities, and this spectacle kept temptation at bay.

All the secretarial staff seemed to have fled for safety. Annabelle had promised to pop in, but had probably popped right out again. There was a final dress rehearsal tonight for *Tristan*. He knew he ought to go home to be with his daughter. But he couldn't bear the thought of crying in front of her.

He made himself small en route to his corridor, escaping notice. From behind a nearby office door came the sounds of grunting, puffing, moaning — a couple locked in ecstasy.

All this distracted Arthur from his pain, but it came back as he got to his own office, his cold, lonely sanctuary. He had bungled it. The one and only prosecution he would ever do. A massive blot on his career. The jokes and backbiting. Poor Beauchamp, the old fellow deserved what he got. Tried a shady tactic and it backfired.

He shut the door, and roared: "Shit! Shit!"

He caught a movement, a spindly figure standing at his window, staring into the evening gloom. Roy Bullingham's croaking voice: "You won't mind if we wait until the weekend to move you upstairs? Sorry you'll lose the mountains, but you'll have the ocean and the sunset." He raised a glass of something, probably the Laphroaig he preferred. "Welcome to the starry heights." The old boy seemed a little tipsy.

Arthur slumped into an armchair, fighting another withdrawal spasm. "How was the function, Bully?"

"Meyerson gave you a vigorous roasting. Your charming and vivacious spouse responded on your behalf with grace and wit. After the champagne ran out, I made the mistake of opening the bar in the lounge. The hangers-on are there, looting it. But all work, as they say." He thumbed through a pile of transcripts on the desk. "Bad day, Beauchamp?"

"Horowitz pulled the rug from under me."

"I was so advised by a rather stiff young man who insisted on dropping off your file. He said you have a heavy night of preparation. I shall leave you to it."

Arthur looked balefully at the stack of papers Boynton had delivered. Bully paused at the door. "Damn good thing your arrest for drunk and disorderly didn't sour the occasion. Never quite made the news, did it?"

Arthur opened his mouth, but couldn't find words.

"Be thankful that I play golf with the publisher of the *Sun*. Good luck tomorrow."

Arthur should have known never to underestimate this sharp-witted sole surviving founder of the firm. The old boy not only had powerful antennae, but impressive connections and great discretion.

He opened the file to the rough draft of his jury address and intoned, "Ladies and gentlemen, the onus is on the Crown to defeat the presumption of innocence and to prove this lying scoundrel is guilty beyond a reasonable doubt." He let the summing-up slide into the wastebasket.

He phoned Deborah, found her allegedly doing homework. She'd had a "totally catastrophic" day, having forgotten her English assignment and been upbraided by Mr. Lynch, then getting into a fight with her girlfriend "over some ridiculous triviality," and then being stalked by a pimply-faced ghoul who shared a table with her in lab.

Arthur told her to finish her homework and that he would pick up some Chinese food on the way home. "Then, darling Deborah, I want to hear all about your bad day."

WEDNESDAY MORNING

Arthur tried mightily to present a calm, untroubled face as he arrived at the Law Courts on this drizzling, mournful morning. Apart from greeting the sheriffs and court staff, he kept to himself, taking his place at the counsel table to resume working on a crossword puzzle, which he went at ferociously, with pencil and eraser.

No one approached him but Mandy. She touched his arm briefly, gently, as she passed by to take her place beside Pomeroy, who was intensely engaged with the speech he would shortly give.

The room was packed and buzzing. Skyler, in a blazer, sat stiff and straight, a wounded but brave warrior. He looked hard at Arthur, his lips curling into a little message of a smile conveying the merest hint of triumph, of awareness that the tide had turned in his favour.

Pomeroy rose and scanned the jury with his best, winning, boyish grin. He began by offering solicitous words about Joe Chumpy, whom all of Vancouver loved, and Manfred Unger, a tragic figure driven to take his own life, driven by guilt over his murderous act.

"My client was severely tested by Mr. Beauchamp, who — and let's make no bones about it — is one of the best anywhere at his craft. But Mr. Skyler not only survived the shelling, but stood up very well indeed. Some of you ladies and gentlemen might be troubled by some aspects of this young man, but he's a bright graduate student with a future, and he deserves a scrupulously fair trial."

Brian then walked around the counsel table and stood beside Arthur, who carried on with his crossword, occasionally chewing his pencil end.

"Now, I'm not going to pretend I'm any kind of match for Mr. Beauchamp here; I'm just a simple journeyman. You ladies and gentlemen can expect a vigorous and eloquent address from my learned friend, who I see is so absorbed in his crossword puzzle that the cynical among us might think he's trying to distract attention from me."

Several jurors laughed. And there was more mirth when Pomeroy stood in front of Arthur, blocking the jury's view of him. Arthur, caught out, smiled sheepishly, and put his puzzle away.

"The jury can expect my learned friend to attack Mr. Skyler's testimony with great gusto, but he'll be grabbing at air, because there's absolutely nothing in the Crown's case to rebut a single word he spoke. In the end this is about reasonable doubt. There's ample reason to doubt Mr. Gillies's shaky identification, to explain the thumbprint on the Coors, to justify my client's lack of frankness with the police, to conclude that Manfred Unger was morbidly inspired by the thrill-killing villain from a popular mystery novel."

"'You don't have the balls' — that was the challenge hurled at poor Manfred, who hero-worshipped my client, who took that dare seriously and did a horrendous act to win his approval. Out of loyalty to Unger, the accused kept his awful secret until it drove his friend to suicide."

After canvassing the evidence, drawing from it every exculpatory crumb and particle it afforded, he exhorted the jury in the revered words of Viscount Sankey: "Throughout the web of the English criminal law one golden thread is always to be seen" — the prosecution must always prove guilt beyond a reasonable doubt.

"As you deliberate, ladies and gentlemen, please spare a thought for the many cases where persons have been wrongly convicted, and how shattering and soul-destroying that must be, a lifetime sentence for a crime done by another.

"So I urge you to return this young man to his family and his studies. Has he not suffered enough? Must he live out his life within the cruel walls of a cold, dank, and merciless prison?" With trembling voice he recited a verse from Oscar Wilde's remembrance of Reading Gaol: "'All that we know who lie in gaol is that the wall is strong; and that each day is like a year, a year whose days are long.'

"In closing, I remind you your verdict must be unanimous. There will be debate, but to those of you not convinced, not morally certain, that this young man did this horrible deed, I call upon you to stand firm, stand tall for justice, and return a verdict of not guilty."

There was a single handclap as he sat, and it came from Juror Twelve, in the back row. She was red-faced as she joined the rest of the jury for the morning break.

§

Pomeroy had considerably raised the jury's expectations for Arthur, to the point that anything less than a roof-rattler might seem a letdown. So, rather than allowing his opponent to dictate the rules of the game, he abstained from any histrionics when he stood to address the jury. There would be no drama in his voice, no anger, no fustian arm-waving. No notes. More like a fireside chat with folks from the neighbourhood.

"Let me start off, my friends, by offering my apology for having been absorbed in my crossword. Frankly, I was bedevilled by one stubborn clue: 'Whose nose grows.' Thirteen letters, so it couldn't be Pinocchio. Starts with a *B* and an *A*. Should have known better than to start the darn thing — I get obsessed. I actually got into serious trouble one time when I missed about six bus stops working on one, and got home to a cold dinner and a colder wife." Juror Five, the crossword fan, led the laughter.

"'Whose nose grows.' I don't know why that clue bothers me so much. Maybe because my own oversized sniffer is one of my more distracting features. Anyway, let's get to work."

With the jury warmed up and relaxed, Arthur began by praising Pomeroy: "Such a charming and adroit lawyer. Such a well-wrought speech." Turning to Brian with a broad smile. "Hell of a job, Brian, given the obvious difficulties of your case." To the jury: "Let's face it, he made some of his most awkward arguments seem almost rational." Pomeroy had no choice but to grin and bear it.

"But at the end of the day, the issue here is a simple one, isn't it? Either Mr. Skyler was telling the truth or he was lying. No middle way. If his story is false, there's only one verdict open. It's as simple as that, isn't it, ladies and gentlemen?" A couple of jurors nodded. A good start.

For the next half hour, he methodically picked away at Skyler's many slips and fibs, adding subtle brush strokes intended to portray a bigoted, arrogant, posturing narcissist. "*Falsus in uno,* it is said, *falsus in omnibus.* Untrue in one thing, untrue in everything.

"So are we to believe Mr. Skyler, or are we to believe Manfred Unger, who saw the teeth marks, who attended to that wound, who heard his bosom friend say, 'I really did it this time. He wouldn't die'?"

So began the process of resurrecting Manfred Unger from his previous role of stumbling, self-contradicting witness. Arthur raised him on a pedestal, shone a sympathetic light on him, reminded the jury of the terrible pressure the sensitive young cadet must have been under, with his military dad and pious mother.

"Add to that, the poor fellow was in love with a man who held a metaphorical pistol to his head, who could out him, shame him, destroy him, if he didn't reshape his evidence. And who did indeed destroy him. Manfred Unger had failed his idol with his too-obvious cover story, and Manfred knew that. He was wretched and desolate with self-reproach, and so he jumped from Granville Bridge.

"Having observed poor Manfred, having heard him, having felt his pain, did he seem to you, my friends, to be a man capable of savage, cold-hearted murder? Yet that is what Randy Skyler begs you to believe. The 'baboon-in-the-toque' theory wasn't going to fool you — he finally figured out that you folks were too smart for that, so he came up with this last-gasp effort to blame his dead best friend."

Arthur saw that Skyler was looking at him with a smirk of disbelief, and he took an impulsive shot at him: "And no one's buying this one either, Randy." There was a massive intake of breath in the courtroom. Taking a swat like that was simply not done in a summing-up. But no one issued a challenge.

Skyler's smile did not go away, though it was stiff and fixed as Arthur carried on calmly, reminding the jury what Skyler had scribbled in the margins of *For the Fun of It*: "'You'd think his hands would be tired! Nice!' 'One less loser!' Well, folks, that's pretty much how the smiling gentleman over there regarded Joe Chumpy. 'One less loser.'" All eyes were on Skyler as his smile slowly faded.

Arthur gathered together a few loose ends, spoke of the jury's high responsibility, and asked them to listen attentively to the judge's instructions. He returned to his chair, glanced at the crossword lying there. "'Whose nose grows.' Thirteen letters. Aha!" He looked in triumph to the jury, then to Skyler, and spelled it out: "B-A-R-E-F-A-C-E-D-L-I-A-R."

That caused some laughter in the back. Mandy Pearl stifled a smile, as did Justice Horowitz, who covered up by briskly ordering the noon break.

Arthur slipped outside. He had no appetite for lunch, nor for the reviews, the polite, lukewarm praise that would tell him he hadn't quite pulled it off. Composing himself, like an athlete returning from the field of play, he strolled about the gardens of Robson Square, puffing on his Peterson, occasional raindrops spitting on him from the leaden sky.

WEDNESDAY AFTERNOON

Concluding his instructions, Horowitz finally turned the case over to the jury, with what Arthur felt were superfluous reminders about the presumption of innocence. They could not convict, the judge emphasized, unless they were convinced Skyler was lying.

Skyler's expression — an innocent wronged, being crucified — relaxed when the jurors disappeared but tightened when Horowitz ordered him confined to await the verdict: a standard practice in murder trials. Arthur doubted Skyler would have absconded, given he likely believed he'd won over the jury, or at least had earned his reasonable doubt.

Boynton spoke low as they changed in the barristers' room, a sour harangue. "We know he's lying. Brian and Mandy know he's lying. Justice Horowitz knows he's lying. Everybody who was in chambers knows he's lying, and that includes the court clerk and the court reporter. Everybody but the jury knows about Laurence Wyacki. And the jury may think Skyler's lying, but that's not enough, is it?"

After several more minutes of his morose company, Arthur fled outside, by the Robson Square exit, and filled his pipe. He was soon joined by Mandy, who he guessed had followed him. As he lit her cigarette, she squeezed his hand.

"How long, do you think?" she asked.

"It will not be tonight. Tomorrow. Late tomorrow. Even longer if they're divided."

"We'll be grabbing dinner at the El Beau Room, Brian and I. Join us?"

"Thank you, Mandy, but I'm off to home to shower and change. Annabelle and I have an opera opening to attend, and we've reserved a late table at Pierre's."

This mention of wife and itinerary failed to deter Mandy. She touched his cheek, then jotted a number on a business card. "My home phone. Call whenever."

§

It was five o'clock when Arthur hung up his wet raincoat and wearily trudged upstairs to the main bedroom. Its bathroom door was ajar, the shower rumbling. Annabelle had laid out his old tux, ill-fitting now as he grappled with the added weight of middle age. He suspected he was not going to enjoy Wagner's tale of noble, wounded, death-seeking lovers. He was not in the mood for tragedy.

He kicked off his shoes as Annabelle swept into the room, naked but for towel-wrapped hair, and she started on seeing him. "My God, Arthur, announce yourself. You could have been anyone." She sat at her high-mirrored vanity. A glass of red wine was on it. "Please get a move on, dear. We have to be there an hour before."

Undoing his buttons, shouting over her hair dryer, he unloaded his day, trying to be jaunty and offering his assurance that he would not be dragged away to court in the middle of the second act. "It's beyond all possibility that the jury could come back with an early verdict. Too much for them to mull over. They don't have time, what with two hours off for dinner."

It would only upset her were he to mention he'd planned for the extreme unlikelihood of a quick verdict. Jack Boynton had insisted on knowing his seat number at the Queen Elizabeth Theatre: H17, near the aisle. There was always a chance the jury could pop in to ask questions of the judge, but typically such questions were easily dealt with, and Boynton would amply cover for him.

Annabelle caught him in the mirror staring at her shapely naked form, a vision by Renoir. She raised her glass to his reflection. "Am I making you uncomfortable?" As if to lower any expectations, she quickly put on underclothes and a slip. "When are our reservations at Pierre's?"

"I told him ten-thirty."

"I can't imagine we'll be out of the theatre much before eleven. Depending on ovations." She sat to paint her toenails ruby-red. "I really had hoped to go backstage for a celebratory drink with the cast and crew."

"Pierre knows we're coming and will wait for us. We'll likely have the place to ourselves."

"Sounds wonderfully romantic, darling. Eating like starving wolves under candlelight at midnight."

He paused while stepping out of his pants. "I could whip something up now."

"No time. Let's take your car, Arthur. It shows us better."

"To whom do you want to show off?"

"Darling, it's opening night." She rose, approached, startled him with a luscious hot-tongued kiss. "Congratulations on a trial well fought. You'll win. You always win."

Once again, that electrifying touch of her skin. His trousers were now around his ankles, his blood flowing.

"Oh, wow, excuse me." Deborah was standing in the doorway, her skates slung over her shoulder. "Sorry, I didn't think you guys would be making out at half past five in the afternoon."

Arthur whipped a robe on, embarrassed, hoping she hadn't seen his erection — which had receded like a breaking wave. Annabelle didn't have such qualms and would often parade about naked in the house. She was justly proud of her thirty-nine-year-old body.

"Guilty or not guilty?" Deborah asked.

"We're not guilty, darling," Annabelle said, laying out her makeup.

"I mean your trial, Dad."

"We won't know until tomorrow. Tonight your mother and I are going to relax."

"Hmm. You didn't look too relaxed just a moment ago." Deborah was a modern girl, sexually educated, at ease with such matters. Maybe too at ease — Arthur wondered if she was a virgin. He picked up his tux, and went to the bathroom.

"Wash your hands, my sweet, and do my fingernails."

When Arthur returned, showered, shaved, pulling up his braces, Deborah was still bent over those nails, painting them ruby-red. They were talking about Tristan and Isolde, the legend.

"But why does she die?"

"She wills herself to die, to be with Tristan in heaven. Don't smear!"

"I can do it, Mom."

Arthur finally won a struggle with his bow tie. "An Arthurian legend, I'm proud to say."

"You look so splendid in black tie," Annabelle said. "Poor Per. His costume weighs a ton and he's supposed to lift Bettina in the second act, and he twisted his back in rehearsal. She must weigh in about one-eighty. But we needed her big voice, anyone else would be diminished by Per."

She blew on her fingernails as Deborah helped her into an off-the-shoulder gown, also ruby-red. She looked luminous.

WEDNESDAY NIGHT

By the third act, Arthur was bored. He was no great admirer of
Wagner, all the pomp, the breastplates, the thundering orchestral
themes. And he didn't like it that Per Gustavson was taking so long
to die. *Poor Per. I really had hoped to go backstage.* Was she hinting that
he might wish to go to Chez Forget alone, while she dallied at the
opera after-party?

She was definitely in party mood. Two glasses of red at each
intermission. Gay and witty with their friends, flirting with the
husbands while Arthur stood by smiling like an idiot. It bothered him
that Annabelle was so eager to be seen and admired. And so successful
at it. He'd never understood vanity; it wasn't part of his character.

Tristan was dying, and only Isolde's magic touch could save
him. Surely it was the longest death in opera history, the entire
third act, with Gustavson limping around with what turned out to
be more than a slightly wrenched back. He hadn't even tried to lift
Bettina in the second act. Still, Gustavson, a vibrant, dramatic tenor,
was saving this production. The sets were brilliant, of course: stately
structures and colourful tents by the Irish Sea. Arthur had praised
Annabelle lavishly during the breaks.

But he had trouble focussing on the stage — the tension of the trial had not abated, and he could not forget that look of sheer hatred from Skyler during his cross. *Vultus est index animi.* The face is the index of the soul. Arthur's insinuations about Skyler's limited and morbid form of impotence, about his many failures with women, had enraged the young man, whose strutting machismo was enhanced by a vanity that dwarfed Annabelle's.

The jury could be out for days, for a week, then return in deadlock. Skyler would surely be home free if he got another hung jury. The Attorney-General's office wouldn't have the tenacity to try him a third time, because they'd thrown everything into this one, including Arthur, who had buggered up a sure win.

Someone would have to lock him in a room and bar the windows if Skyler walked. After he lost Turk McGrew's revenge shooting a decade ago, he went on a bender that ended with him penniless on a beach in Mexico, calling Bullingham collect to beg for air fare and forgiveness.

He remembered that the next day, Thursday, would be an historic marker. If he could make it through the next thirty hours, he would equal his personal best — though he'd been laid up in hospital for many of those twenty-six days in 1983. This time, he'd been fighting a taxing, touch-and-go murder trial.

Twenty-six days. The goal was in reach, tantalizing. He could make it.

Win or lose, he ought to take Annabelle to an ancient, romantic place this summer. Florence and Venice would be overrun. Maybe Greece, his other spiritual motherland. A cozy hilltop hotel on the Peloponnese, overlooking the Aegean Sea. Or the islands so loved by Byron. *The isles of Greece, the isles of Greece! Where burning Sappho loved and sung . . .*

His reputation, even his career, would be damaged if he lost. All the more reason to take a holiday. A long one.

"*Die Leuchte, ha!*" Gustavson bellowed, dying. "*Die Leuchte verlischt!*" The torch goes out!

It was as Isolde rushed in, too late to save her beloved, that the summons came, an usher with a dimmed flashlight crouching at the end of the aisle, a hoarse whisper: "You're needed, sir."

Annabelle, loudly: "Damn it, Arthur."

A muttered, "Sorry, darling," then a grunt of pain as Arthur stepped on a toe, and another "Sorry." People were half-rising, craning to see. Gustavson went majestically off-key, a strident high note as he died at last in Bettina's bounteous arms.

The phantom of the opera, his mischief performed, crouched his way to the nearest exit in a frenzied state of embarrassment.

§

Arthur raced from taxi to courthouse, coatless, in his tux. A verdict had been arrived at. No time to gown up.

In Room 53, everyone but the judge and jury was waiting for him, and the clerk was petulant over the delay as he went to fetch Horowitz. Boynton fidgeted anxiously, but had the good grace not to natter as Arthur joined him. Mandy and Pomeroy were tense, and Skyler more so, coiled tighter than a sailor's knot, his face clenched in a rictal smile.

Horowitz looked Arthur over in his formal wear, but managed to maintain a straight face. "Bring in the jury."

Even before they were seated, Arthur read the verdict from their expressions and body language. A few jurors boldly smiled at him. These were the ones who'd prevailed on the others to pass up a sleepover at the Hyatt. They all seemed at peace, unanimously content.

Pomeroy read the obvious portents too and sagged a little. Not too much, because he held no affection for his client. Boynton, however, was eating a pencil.

The anti-climactic verdict was delivered calmly by the forewoman: "Guilty as charged, My Lord."

Skyler went white, rose like a launched missile, calling out loudly and raggedly: "This is wrong! I am not guilty." Then, turning on Arthur: "I'll see you hell!"

The sheriffs were about to jump into action, but Pomeroy was already at Skyler's side, cooling him out, doubtless offering assurances about their substantial grounds of appeal.

Horowitz ignored the outburst, though he gave Arthur a sympathetic look. He appeared relieved by the verdict — he'd probably been concerned that the Crown would appeal his decision to bar its prime and final witness.

He wasted no time in sentencing. "Mr. Skyler, you have been convicted of a murder committed in a most brutal and sadistic way. The Criminal Code requires that you be sentenced to life imprisonment with no eligibility for parole for twenty-five years. I so order. Take the prisoner away."

§

Arthur was too distracted to relish victory. He was in a fever to join Annabelle at the after-party at the Queen E, so after freeing himself from Boynton's jubilant bear hug and accepting Pomeroy's perfunctory handshake, he barrelled through the press scrum outside the court, offering only a cliché about being a mere toiler for justice, the demands of which had clearly been answered. Skyler's threat to see him in hell was a mindless outburst best ignored. He left them to ponder Horace's enduring wisdom, *Culpam poena premit comes.* Punishment follows closely on crime's heels.

Jurors are forbidden by law from disclosing the whys and hows of their decisions, so Arthur was concerned, outside the Law Courts, when Number Eight, a construction foreman, approached and shook his hand with the grip of an ironmonger. But all he said was, "Good job. Good riddance."

§

It was nearing midnight when Arthur's cab dropped him back at the theatre. The doors were locked, but some lights were on, maybe for the cleaners. Or for the after-partiers, somewhere backstage. He wasn't able to get anyone's attention, and finally hurried off to retrieve his Rolls from the parkade and get on his way to Chez Forget — Annabelle could be waiting for him there.

The garage had almost emptied out, with only a few vehicles left in the staff area. But one of them was the Phantom V, backed into a dark corner, just as he'd left it. Approaching, he heard a moan as if someone were in pain or distress. Then a cry, resonant, familiar.

He peered through the windshield, but could see nothing. Then a car came by toward the exit, and its passing headlights briefly illuminated undulating shapes in the Phantom's back seat, and a bare, ruby-toenailed foot braced against the frame. Again, Arthur heard that rich tenor cry, rising to an octave above middle C, in key, a perfect high note.

§

Pierre shrugged off Arthur's apology. "Chez Forget is never closed for Monsieur Beauchamp." He held the door for his doleful guest. "We are waiting for madam?"

"Madam is not coming." In black tie, no overcoat, he had walked directly from the parkade, down the rough part of Granville, ignoring the fawning attention of the many panhandlers. Chez Forget had only ten tables but a kitchen large enough to accommodate the temperamental chef's ego. His waiter and sous-chef had left.

"I will not inquire. It is not my business." Pierre led Arthur to his usual table in a nook near the kitchen door, past two couples dawdling over cognacs and liqueurs. Tony d'Anglio and a *compagno* with their tipsy, young *compagne di gioco*. D'Anglio barely acknowledged his sometime lawyer, who had recently prevailed for him — twice: an illegal sports book; bribery of a bylaw officer.

"You will have the escargots to start, and *un petit morceau de paté Forget*, then the poulet paprika, hearty for to cheer you up. Something liquid, I leave that problem up to you."

"A martini, Pierre."

The chef hovered uncertainly, then bent, his voice lowered. "I promised not to tell you, but now I tell you. Not because you are *un client merveilleux* who understands the arts of tipping, but because of loyalty to my fellow man. She was in here with him three, four nights ago."

"Thank you, Pierre. A martini. The usual. Two pearl onions."

"Maybe this is not wise, if . . . How long are you sober now, Monsieur Beauchamp?"

"It's Day Twenty-Five. It's time."

"Just one, maybe, yes?"

"Just one."

After that just one, it would be too late to call Bill Webb. At any event, it wouldn't be right to rouse him from his bed. He wasn't going to get drunk. Just one martini to lighten the mood.

The first teasing drops rolled across his tongue and caused an agreeable jolt of recognition: the taste of juniper and dry vermouth and freedom from care. Welcome back, old friend. Another sip, and he could feel the desolation and bleakness start to fade.

Tony d'Anglio tossed a wad of bills on the table, and his party rose to leave. He paused at Arthur's nook as he slid into the sleeves of his coat. "Gonna miss using your services, Mr. Beauchamp."

"Why so, Tony?"

"Now that you're working for the heat."

Emboldened by gin, Arthur defended himself with the famous last words of the Moor of Venice. "'I have done the state some service, and they know't. No more of that.'" But d'Anglio had already turned his back and walked away.

Arthur held out his tongue to catch the last drops of his martini, then, holding to his pledge to have just one, ordered a glass of Pouilly-Fumé instead, to go with his escargots, and it tasted so fine that he had another. When the poulet paprika arrived he switched to a robust Tuscan red. With Pierre standing by, he was about to take a sip when his wrist was grasped by one hand and the glass removed by another. He was too startled to resist.

"That's all for you, Mr. B.," said Mandy, setting the glass on a table behind her, then gripping his two reaching hands. Pierre fled to the kitchen. "Did she jilt you again?"

"Who, my dear?"

"Mandy Pearl may look like a dumb broad to you, but it happens that she, along with the entire BC Bar Association, knows that you're in a long-term abusive relationship, and you're the abusee. I have come to free you from her, Arthur."

"How?"

She let go his wrists. "There are other possibilities. Than her. Than this." Gesturing at the Chianti beyond his reach. She hollered: "Pierre, please get me the bill and a doggy bag."

He erupted from the kitchen. "A doggy bag? What is this doggy bag? Chez Forget does not have doggy bags. This is not the Burger King."

"And two double espressos. This man has just won the trial of the decade, and I'm going to take him home and fuck him." She was high; Arthur caught scents of beer and pot.

"Another glass of the same, Pierre," he said. "You may as well bring the bottle."

"Sorry, Arthur, the jig is up. I'm with the Alcoholics Anonymous Enforcement Unit, empowered by law to arrest you." She frowned at Pierre: "I'm charging you with aiding and abetting."

Pierre grumpily set the espressos in front of them and wrapped the poulet paprika in silver foil, plate and all. Arthur kept wanting to reach for that glass of wine, but Mandy hovered over him, passing him the demitasse, forcing him to sip his caffeine, straightening his tie, signing Pierre's chit.

Although past the tipping point and in thrall to a powerful thirst, Arthur found himself unable to resist her, but didn't know why. He even allowed himself to be led out to her car as she cradled his plate of food. He wondered if he'd been half-hoping someone would come along to save him. And why shouldn't it be this busty, lovely young woman who had shown him so much teasing affection?

Be careful. *She likes the married ones. They're more challenging.*

Yet he was titillated by the prospect of giving in to her advances. Dare he do so? Tit for tat, my darling. That flat-nosed tenor with his out-of-whack back. Arthur hoped that he'd wrenched it so badly tupping Annabelle in the Rolls that he'd be out of commission for the rest of the run.

He found himself in a late-model Buick, with the top up, into which she strapped him as one would a child, and kissed his cheek. "Relax, I'm not going to eat you." She took the Granville Bridge to Fairview, talking gaily about the trial. "Brian honestly thought he might pull this sucker out — the underdog beats superdog. Might have had a chance if that narcissistic shit hadn't changed course on us. They'd be coming back late tomorrow, you said, but the jury saw right through him."

"I underestimated their wisdom."

"Please, take credit. You were fucking brilliant. 'A liar needs a good memory.' And that speech — who wrote it, Shakespeare? She mimicked: 'I come not, friends, to steal away your hearts.'"

Arthur surprised himself by laughing. "'I am no orator, as Brutus is, but as you know me all, a plain, blunt man.'"

"Let's hope poor Randy doesn't get gang-raped in the BC Pen, because he'd probably enjoy it. Enough shop talk. What happened with your wife?"

Although he was already worrying about where his next drink was coming from, Arthur was feeling well lit, and found himself letting go, describing, with full-throated indignation, the parkade, the Rolls, the ruby toenails, the climactic cry of the heldentenor with the bad back. He stalled, confused by Mandy's laughter, then realized he'd been depicting the scene as farce, and he had to smile.

She took over then, telling him about her own bad marriage to a man who ran off with "a brainless, late-blooming flower child." She was carrying on about that betrayal even as she led him by the hand into her modern townhouse on the Fairview Slopes, depositing him on a sofa and relieving him of his tuxedo jacket. "All men are pricks, Arthur. Except you, for some reason. You're just a teddy bear."

She went behind him, flicked off his suspenders, and began massaging his shoulders and spine muscles. Strong, expert fingers. "Man, you're stiff."

She finally left him for the kitchen, and he looked about, the wall art, the coffee-table books, a few scholastic and athletic trophies. No liquor cabinet. A coffee grinder started up. He stood up, trying to still his anxiety, went to the kitchen and took in the fearful sight of a bottle of vodka upturned in the sink, as if newly emptied. Two washed and rinsed wine bottles lay nearby.

He studied the scene with great wistfulness. "You've done this before."

She set the coffee maker going. "Sometimes I go to meetings. Sometimes I just drink. My dad was AA too. So was my mom. How about something else instead? A heightened experience?" She produced a joint.

"I did that only once, when I was twenty-five. It was not a night to remember."

She shrugged, moved close to him. "Something different then. Something to get you through the night. You're a lovely man, Arthur. You're going to waste."

Her kiss was gentle at first, and he responded nervously. He didn't know where to put his hands, but she solved that by placing them under her blouse and pulling up her bra. They were beautiful breasts, but he wanted a drink very badly.

"Let's take our coffee upstairs," she said.

She tugged him. He stayed rooted. She kissed him again, open-mouthed, and her hands went between his legs. He was shy, not used to this, its brazen suddenness, and was overcome with performance anxiety and with his gnawing other need. She couldn't tease up much of an erection, and he blushed with embarrassment.

PART TWO
WORRYWART

THRILL KILLER EARNS PAROLE

By Canadian Press

Randolph Skyler, convicted in 1987 of the apparent thrill killing of a popular Vancouver busker, will be allowed to spend the remainder of his life sentence out of prison.

The Canadian Parole Service confirmed on Thursday that Mr. Skyler, 48, has been released from Collins Bay Institution in Kingston, Ont., where he has been completing an MBA degree by correspondence. The Service provided no other details, citing privacy rules.

The young Toronto student was visiting Expo 86 in Vancouver when he was charged with the apparently motiveless stabbing death of Joyal Chumpy, known as Chumpy the Clown, in his small downtown flat.

A first trial ended with a hung jury. During the second trial, Manfred Unger, a long-time friend of the accused, committed suicide after being declared a hostile witness.

In cross-examination at that trial, Mr. Skyler was accused of seeking sexual pleasure from the act of murder. He reacted to the guilty verdict by loudly protesting his innocence.

SUNDAY, SEPTEMBER 16, 2012

"Strike! Miss Menzies sure got fooled on that one." Play-by-play announcer Scotty Phillips is sitting on a folding chair near first base. A microphone transmits his voice through coils of wire to speakers on his car roof. "Strike three, and Tildy has retired the side."

Tildy Sears is the star chucker for the home team, the Nine Easy Pieces. They are playing the San Juan Islanders for the championship of the Inter-Island Women's Baseball League. It's an international event, little Garibaldi Island against a powerhouse American team.

"Our Tildy has got a great arm, eh, folks?" A smattering of applause. "Great legs, too."

Spectators shout light-hearted taunts at Scotty for his sexist excursus. From the beer garden, Margaret Blake calls out an offer to objectify *his* parts.

"Nobody ever accused me of being politically correct." Scotty ignores the boos. A corpulent land developer, red braces, red of neck, he has been quaffing a few between innings. "Up next is the Islanders' dishy third-basewoman — any objection to that, ladies?"

More boos. Laughter. Catcalls. Everyone is having a good time on this sunny September Sunday, except perhaps Arthur Ramsgate

Beauchamp, QC, who is toiling in the beer garden. Almost half of Garibaldi Island is at the game, by Arthur's rough count — some two hundred lolling on the grassy slopes above the diamond, fifty more on benches in this roped-off square of meadow, which is unwisely situated too close to the third-base line. Arthur has already had to duck one foul ball. He worries about injuries, accidental death, a massive suit against the Garibaldi Recreation Committee. Arthur is a worrier. It is what he does best.

Right now, what most worries him relates to a scary bit of hearsay conveyed to him this morning, just after church, by island postmaster Abraham Makepeace: "Looks like one of your unhappy clients wants to kill you." The reference was to the contents of a fax waiting for Arthur at the General Store, which provides that service for techno-duffers. Despite the postmaster's penchant for reading others' faxes and unsealed mail, he adheres to strict business practices, so more cannot be revealed to Arthur until he picks up the fax on Monday. "I already said too much," Makepeace whispered, then hurried off to his van to join his family.

An unhappy client wants to kill him? The postmaster's idea of a jest? No sense of humour has yet been divined in dour Abraham Makepeace. More likely, the nosy postmaster misinterpreted the message, which he obviously puzzled over.

But it isn't that easy to lightly toss away the death-threat fax, because Arthur got a call yesterday from a colleague at his old law office — Tragger, Inglis — asking if he'd seen the news item about the paroling of Randy Skyler. No, Arthur had not.

After some effort, using his primitive Internet skills, he retrieved the piece, which was succinct and accurate, though it neglected to mention that, while "loudly protesting his innocence," Skyler had directed a postscript to the prosecutor: "I'll see you in hell!" The threat has always stuck with Arthur. Twenty-five years since that trial, and it hasn't much dulled in memory.

Arthur shakes his head. He must focus on his volunteer role here:

to accept blue tickets in exchange for a serving of beer or cider, or white tickets for wine. It's not a task that requires any intellectual effort, yet Arthur is discomforted by the seductive perfume of hops and grapes. But it's for a good cause, a fundraiser for the island's athletic program.

Beside him, Margaret Blake, also a conscripted volunteer, is running the till, selling those tickets. Margaret is the Member of Parliament for Cowichan and the Islands (usually called Cow Islands), and leader of Canada's Green Party. She used to be Arthur's wife. Until — this was several months ago — she decided he ought to call her his life companion, a phrase she claims implies equality as opposed to possession. Arthur can barely get his tongue around it. He doesn't like the brave new words of the twenty-first century.

Arthur hasn't mentioned the mysterious fax to her, or anything about Skyler. She'd only fret. He's tried to convince himself there is a humorous twist to this: Makepeace had likely misread a common colloquialism. "I'm going to kill you for not writing." Something like that. The sort of thing his blunt daughter in Australia might write. Deborah, a high school principal in Melbourne, is eight years divorced, but, according to her last phone call, has met "someone authentic" on an Internet mating site, and they are seeing each other. Arthur doesn't know how to respond to that. Nor to Deborah's revelation about one of her mother's least notorious affairs from decades ago. "You didn't know?" she said, shocked.

A crack of the bat. "And Felicity Jones beats the throw," Scotty announces. "I don't have to remind everyone she got picked off stealing last time."

Felicity gives him the finger, then takes off after the next pitch and slides unsafely into second. Inning over.

It's a tight game, one to nil for the Easy Pieces in the eighth inning. Everyone knows but dares not say that Tildy Sears is one inning away from a no-hitter. Arthur has followed baseball enough to be aware of its most celebrated superstition: merely mouthing the word *no-hitter* puts a curse on the pitcher's chances of completing it. Nor are obvious synonyms permitted. The superstition is widely embraced by players and fans. Even major league announcers tiptoe around the word during live broadcasts.

Scotty Phillips, who has returned to the beer garden to refresh himself for the bottom of the eighth, is also a strong believer in this aphonic ritual. "Don't say it, Arthur," he commands on accepting his refill. "Don't even think about it."

He chugs back his ale, returns to his post, lowers himself carefully into his folding chair. "Okay, folks, this here's the ninth inning. Tildy takes the mound again. It's still a one-run ball game, and there's other stuff going on here that I better not talk about, but you all know what I'm talking about."

Arthur watches Tildy Sears stroll confidently to the mound. A comely, raw-boned gal, twenty-five, six-foot-two, with a lightning fastball, she runs a home security business. She has almost single-handedly got the Pieces to this final playoff game.

Arthur's attention is drawn by Ernie Priposki, who's waving a ticket at him, demanding yet another pint. Arthur wants to cut him off but isn't sure if he has the authority.

"I think you've had your last one, Ernie."

"No way, I got two more tickets. Two tickets, two beer, we got a binding contract — ain't that the first thing you learn in law school?" Shouting: "It's the law!"

Fortunately the real law is here in force, and, smelling trouble, they are fast approaching: gloomy Ernst Pound of the Mounties and his scowling sidekick, Auxiliary Constable Kurt Zoller. Arthur toys with mentioning to them — as if in passing — the fax with the supposed death threat.

Scotty calls, "Our Tildy has one more out to go, folks. History is about to get made."

A foul ball whacks a plastic beer glass, and Constable Pound scuttles from the spray before planting himself in front of Priposki, who glares back stubbornly. "Ernie, you're gonna take your beer and sit down and finish it, and then you're gonna walk home." Pound brandishes the keys he's removed from Priposki's truck.

"That evens the count at two and two, folks. Come on, Tildy, baby, you can do it."

Everyone is fixed on the game except Kurt Zoller, who is sniffing the air. "I smell marijuana." He exits the licensed area, takes several steps, then seems to lose the scent, and wanders over to his car, to caress it. His latest toy, a second-hand, bright orange Hummer.

Scotty Phillip booms: "What do you say, folks, was that a bad call or what?" This stirs the crowd to boo the umpire. "Another swing, and she's out! No ... No, the ball got away! Safe on first! Relax, folks, Tildy can still win that no-hitter ..."

All players, all spectators, everyone in the beer garden, join in a mass sucking-in of breath. That is followed by utter silence. Even the birds dare not sing, or the crickets. In his folding chair, Scotty is frozen in shock at what he has done, his microphone dangling between his legs.

Tildy Sears pulls herself together, checks the runner, rears back, throws. Her looping curveball is met with a clunk of the aluminum bat, and arcs just over the reach of the shortstop. A cheap hit, but a hit, and there are runners at first and second.

Tildy asks the umpire for a time out. She lays her glove on the mound and walks toward Scotty. It slowly dawns on him he is in peril, and he struggles from his chair, but finds his feet tangled in the coils of microphone cable. The chair collapses from his exertions, and he is propelled face forward into the grass, his ample rear raised.

Tildy is impassive as she approaches this inviting target. No one makes a move to intercede, not the players on either team, not the umpire, not Pound or Zoller, not Reverend Al Noggins, and not the Member for Cow Islands, who mutters, "Get him."

In his struggle to free himself, Scotty has fallen out of his suspenders, and Tildy takes advantage of that by shoving the microphone down the back of his pants and into his nether regions. Her proud bearing as she returns to the mound says she might have gone further were she not capable of mercy.

She strikes out the next batter on three pitches. The crowd erupts. People are jumping and dancing perilously on the grassy slope. It's a stirring sight to see Tildy mobbed not only by her own teammates but also the opposing players, united in their celebration of the sister who stuck it to the boorish pig who broke up her no-hitter.

Arthur is inspired to recite Byron's line: "Where the virgins are soft as the roses they twine."

"I don't think you'll find any rose-twining virgins there," Margaret has taken on a cynical way since becoming a politician. There's been a coolness about her lately, though one she doesn't show to others. Arthur wonders if she's become a little bored with her stuffy partner. Another worry. Add it to the list. Along with: *Looks like one of your unhappy clients wants to kill you.* Maybe not a client. After all, would newly paroled Skyler dare, even anonymously, to send a threatening fax? He'd be back inside in a wink. The idea is ludicrous.

Cars and pickups are pulling out. Priposki is sullenly working the parking area, soliciting a ride to the bar, where the party will continue. Zoller has a handkerchief out and is daubing away at something on the roof of his orange chariot, maybe a bird dropping.

Arthur hopes to pick up his own obsessed-over beauty tomorrow — his classic 1969 Fargo is in Garibaldi's small service station, where he dropped it off this morning for a tune-up. He has vowed never again to surrender the Fargo to the haphazard care of his former mechanic, Robert Stonewell, alias Stoney, who is more adept in the fine arts of loafing and stalling than auto mechanics. Five months it took for a carburetor job.

Ignored, alone at third base, Scotty Phillips is having problems retrieving his microphone, which has fallen down his pant leg. It is time to close up, clean up.

Margaret pulls off at the West Bay lookout so they can watch the sun kissing the breasts of distant islands before descending behind the white mounds of the Olympic Mountains. Silvery Diana rises plumply in the east, smiling at the mortals below: Arthur and Margaret, in her green, hybrid constituency car. This is the vehicle she uses to tour her domain, from Salish Sea to Pacific Ocean. She'll return it to her riding office tomorrow before flying out — Parliament is about to go into session.

"Lovely." The sunset, she means, and its long, September afterglow. "This is what I miss most."

Arthur wonders where her life companion ranks on her missed-most list of West Coast attractions. He will miss her more than any sunset, but he can't bring himself to say that: it sounds corny. He ought to count himself lucky that they were able to share her long summer recess, even though it was interrupted with country fairs, ribbon-cuttings (how she abhors those), baptisms, weddings, anniversaries, funerals, the entire life sequence.

Tomorrow she will be gone, likely until Thanksgiving. When lives aren't shared to the full, bonds are weakened: separate experiences, different interests, diversions, friends. Happy moments aren't enjoyed, tribulations aren't shared. Without the glue of day-by-day communion, there is a coming-apart, a distancing — that's what Arthur fears is happening.

Or maybe there has always been a distance, unrecognized by Arthur. Sometimes he wonders if he really knows her, if he has access to her heart. She's not open about herself, finds it awkward to express intimate feelings. Arthur has to assume she is less in love with him than she was with her first husband, a pioneer organic farmer who died in a tractor accident.

He is as much in love with Margaret as on the day he proposed, fifteen years ago, after his tumultuous first marriage finally failed.

But he wonders whether absence has made her heart less fond. Does that account for her detached ways with him, the little messages of disapproval, the casual frictions over morning coffee?

Surely she's hugely distracted by politics, that's what is filling her mind, the impending grind of Parliament, trying to get her voice heard amid all the noise and bombast, fighting for her green agenda. To stay in top form, she must keep some space between her and dreary Arthur. He understands that, must somehow accept it. He must stop continually seeking reasons to be unhappy. Maybe there's a group. My name is Arthur, and I am a worrywart.

His other addiction has long been conquered. He hasn't had a sip since 1987, twenty-five years and five months ago, on the day — coincidentally? — that Skyler was sentenced to life.

It's late, he's hungry and looking forward to getting back to Blunder Bay. Arthur is never at ease being away from the farm all day, though he has full confidence in Yoki and Niko, his energetic Woofers (they're enrolled in a global organization, World Wide Opportunities on Organic Farms, full board for a half day's work).

Yoki and Niko are in their early twenties, and thus must be referred to as women, but Arthur can't help it, and calls them girls. They are soon to return to Japan to complete their schooling. Computer virtuosos.

The two share Margaret's former house, which is in shouting distance from the larger one Arthur bought sixteen years ago — to escape from Vancouver, from the law, from a cheating wife. Annabelle left him for Bayreuth and a flamboyant conductor, and very quickly Arthur fell spectacularly in love with his attractive agronomist neighbour, a widow a decade and a half younger than he. He had known, when pursuing her, that she was immersed in politics — she'd twice been elected Island Trustee — but hardly expected this: a marriage divided by three thousand miles.

And now he is again about to become the lone and lonely master of Blunder Bay, their forty consolidated acres, their goats, sheep, horse, cow, dog, cats, and chickens, plus a couple of bossy geese.

They are soon rolling by their darkening pastures and down a dirt driveway bordered by snake fences. Their houses are on either side, both charming and old, with gingerbread, leaded glass. The Woofers' house was built by homesteader Jeremiah Blunder in 1894, shortly before he failed to appreciate the potency of his own moonshine and fell into his well.

Homer barks a welcome and leads them to their front door. As Arthur switches on the house lights, the death-threat fax, which has been circling around his subconscious like a shark, breaks the surface. Should he tell Margaret about it? Not now. Anyway, she is already at her BlackBerry, checking messages, dialling Pierrette, her chief of staff in Ottawa. It's the only phone she uses, avoiding cranks and time-wasters. Arthur faithfully vets her incoming calls on the house line.

That phone rings, from the kitchen extension, as Arthur pulls the remains of a potato salad from the fridge.

"Wonders never cease, I finally got through. How's it hanging, old stick?"

Perpendicularly down, Arthur wants to say. It's Hubbell Meyerson, his former best friend. He insists on calling a few times a year, usually from Barbados, apparently unaware that Arthur knows of his treachery.

"I'm well, Hubbell. Just sitting down to dinner, I'm afraid." Arthur hopes that sounds icy enough.

He can hear lively African music, drumbeats. There's a party going on. Hubbell seems to be into the sauce. Now retired from Tragger, Inglis, he was recently named High Commissioner to Barbados, a plum from friends in Ottawa. He enjoys inherited wealth and has been a generous political donor.

"Short and sweet, then. I shall be flying up to Ottawa for the royal visit next month, and I'm thinking of a detour out your way, business to attend to. Chance for a little nosh-up, talk over old times. If we can remember them." He chuckles.

Arthur hedges. "Let's both check our calendars and see if that's possible." He could pretend he promised to visit Deborah in Melbourne. But maybe this is the proper time to confront the adulterous blackguard. Yes, but not on the phone. Next month. Over lunch.

"Give my love to Margaret . . . Damn fine of her to show up for my swearing-in, by the way. Okay, I'm being called upon to help a black beauty pop a cork. Might just get lucky tonight. It's my birthday, did you know?"

"Happy birthday."

Arthur returns to his potato salad, feeling insipid, glum. *Give my love to Margaret*. He can't remember her mention that swearing-in. Or Hubbell at all.

"You didn't know?" Deborah had said on her long, teary, tale-telling call. What Arthur hadn't known was that Annabelle and Hubbell were lovers in the 1980s. A time when Arthur was convinced that she had abandoned her adulterous ways and was being true to those long-ago vows.

Annabelle has been living in Lucerne, in a chalet, part of the spoils of her latest divorce, but flew down to Australia several weeks ago, got very tipsy, and confessed all to her daughter. The bad abstract painter, the flat-nosed Swedish tenor Per Gustavson, who was merely a little treat, a quickie in the back seat of the Rolls. Meyerson was the main course. Right through 1987. Sneaking Annabelle down to his yacht or up to his Grouse Mountain chalet.

It's history, Arthur tells himself. Bury it. He has been renewed, he is at last and forever happily married. Life companions.

Why didn't she mention she was at Hubbell's swearing-in?

MONDAY, SEPTEMBER 17

The filmy light of early dawn is spreading over Ferryboat Cove as the *Queen of Prince George* approaches. She's a battered old tub popularly known as the *Queen George* or, commonly, the *Trannie*. She has a vending machine that spits out a dung-coloured liquid advertised as coffee, and another with chips, Cheezies, and chocolate bars, so one has to board her already fortified. Which is why Arthur and Margaret are at the ferry slip's burger stand, a converted Winnebago, and are sharing the house specialty, Winnebagels.

"Thank you for seeing me off. You didn't have to."

"I'm not one to sleep with a woman then slough her off in the morning. Also it gets me halfway to the service station."

"Poor Stoney, he'll be hurt that you're not using him."

"It's a simple oil and lube that would take him half a week." Stoney, a jack-of-all-trades (mechanics, carpentry, landscaping) and a leading island entrepreneur (taxi, vehicle rentals, pot) has been a fixture in Arthur's life since he first set foot on these otherwise benign shores. His own personal gremlin.

Margaret orders a coffee to go. "Do try to come out for a few days."

Arthur wonders if she means that. She's had an apartment to herself in Ottawa ever since her roommate moved away. But Arthur abhors the national capital as much as he loves Blunder Bay. There is always stiffness between them there. It's the political intensity. The clubbiness of the town. But also the shallowness.

The *Trannie* clangs into the dock. Arthur shoulders his pack and escorts her to her car, midway up the boarding lane. He holds the door for her. "I'll miss you deeply." He pulls down his slouch hat, embarrassed that others might see this display of feelings. *"L'absence est à l'amour ce qu'est au feu le vent."*

"Absence is to love what wind is to fire."

He smiles approvingly. "Your French has vastly improved."

They kiss and say adieu.

§

The parting was bittersweet but mostly sweet, and Arthur feels buoyed as he begins his hike, lifted by her loving smile and gentle kiss. His worries over her seem silly now. He has got to stop creating these bizarre scenarios. Margaret loves him. Randy Skyler doesn't. So what? Who cares? Ancient enmities fade with time.

Such silliness. He laughs at himself, then sings off-key: "It takes a worried man to sing a worried song," a tune he can't get out of his head. "I'm worried now, but I won't be worried long." It's a sunny day for a healthy, heart-pounding climb from Ferryboat Cove to the gas station: up Centre Road to a high, rocky plateau that offers fine distant views. Arthur rests at the brow of the hill, taking in the grand tableau of the islands of the Salish Sea, the Coast Range, the Olympic Mountains.

Sadly, the view is marred by its foreground: the greasy, gravelled frontage of the two-pump garage at the entrance to Evergreen Estates, the island's sole subdivision, a mélange of box-like homes on small lots with septic and potable water issues. It should be called Nevergreen Estates, Margaret often jokes, for, although all its roads and byways are named after trees, too many lots are bare of them.

In closer view is what Garibaldians call "Downtown." The garage and a thrift store are across from the lumberyard and the recycling depot and beside two storefronts occupied by Doc Dooley's clinic and Wholeness and Wellness Health Foods and Vitamins, with a pair of realtors and an insurance agent upstairs.

The garage used to be called the No-Service Station until a couple from rural Alberta bought it, retired farmers whose welfare once depended on keeping their trucks, tractors, and harvesters running. Brad and Barb, salt of the earth.

Barb is at a gas pump and waves as Arthur strolls into the garage. A pickup is on the hoist and Brad is underneath it. But it's not Arthur's pickup. His Fargo is nowhere to be seen.

Brad crawls out, wiping grease from his hands. "Didn't he tell you, Mr. Beauchamp?"

Arthur's worry meter gives a reading somewhat above its base level of Moderate Fusspot.

"He said you changed your mind, wanted him to do the tune-up. Close friend of yours. Stonewall, or . . ."

"Stonewell."

"Yup, Rob Stonewell. He's a great talker, ain't he? I hope there aren't no problems. He said he was your best friend, and he'd do it for nothing. He actually knew that old truck pretty good, the way he talked about it. He even had his own keys to it."

§

Arthur waves down yet another offer of a ride — he isn't capable of being pleasant to anyone right now — and continues his trudge back down Centre Road, contemplating the filing of a criminal complaint. His dark suspicion is that Stoney, who recently wrecked his Ford F-150, needs a vehicle to haul his cannabis crop to the annual growers' fair this week.

For the last fifteen years, ever since Stoney sold him the Fargo, the trickster has enjoyed a guaranteed annual income from it. Mysteriously, the old high-riding truck tends to break down whenever Stoney has cash flow problems. But the time of playing patsy to this pirate is over; Arthur will listen with wry amusement to Stoney's honeyed pleas and will fearlessly spurn them.

When he reaches the Centre Road ridge, Arthur pauses to take in the narrow valley's vastly contrasting visions of rural landscaping. In the lee of the hill is the Shewfelts' cozy ranch house with its meticulously tended lawns and flowerbeds, and plaster elves and Disney dwarfs cavorting among neat rows of apple trees.

Beyond that is Stoney's cluttered three acres. The Shewfelts have filed innumerable bylaw complaints against him for keeping unsightly premises, but have had to settle for a ten-foot cedar fence that doesn't quite hide the charnel yard of abandoned cars and trucks, their parts skeletonized, their bodies left to rust. In plain view, atop a rise, are Stoney's tumbledown house and garage, his beat-up dump truck and flatbed trailer, a couple of rental vehicles, and Arthur's Fargo. Arthur assumes those are Stoney's legs sticking out from under the chassis.

He makes his way up there by stealth, finding him still under the truck, either working noiselessly or sleeping or passed out. Or maybe he thinks he's hiding.

"I just saved your life, man."

Arthur's chocolate-brown walkers have given him away.

"The brake fluid tubes are shot, eh. That clod at the gas station woulda let you drive off with barely half a inch of leaking hydraulic fluid, and you'd've gone flying down Breadloaf Hill, and I'd be at your funeral instead of fixing your truck, making a eulogy about how you were this icon, man, a prince, my mentor, and how much I trusted and respected you, and all the time I'd be hiding the pain, the betrayal."

By the end of this, Stoney has wiggled out, slippery from what indeed could be brake fluid. Arthur will let him say his piece. He will not be bamboozled this time.

"For the first time in my life, I'm going to be truly honest and let my emotions show. I was hurt, man, hurt that my long-time confidant, my mouthpiece, my hero, would go sneaking around behind my back to some Alberta wheat farmer who probably ain't even certified."

Arthur sees no point in reminding Stoney that neither is he.

"Me and you and this here old girl are a tradition, we're an important part of island history. We been through too much together to end it over a simple tune-up. This here vehicle was my gift to you."

"No, it wasn't."

"It would've been except I was a little hard up at the time. The point is you love this here Fargo, and it loves you, and I feel I've almost got like a God-given duty to keep her running for you for as long as you both shall live. I was hauling on the emergency all the way down the last hill, man, so that's another thing I've got to look at."

Arthur can't find words, doesn't even know where to start looking. All he can do is stand and stare at Stoney, who shows no signs of offering the expected cringing apology, and instead has raised his scrawny form to full height, chin up but trembling with emotion, like a cheated lover fighting his pain.

"Yeah, and I'm also hurt because I got pride. I'm like family, man, to you and Margaret, I'm like the son you never had. I've always been there when needed. All of Garibaldi has got to know you took the Fargo elsewhere for a tune-up. What does that do to my stature in the community, man? I spent years building up my reputation, and then the island's foremost, respected dignitary brings it crashing down like the temples of Rome."

Arthur sighs. Yes, maybe he was too rash in going to the service station. But let it be a lesson to Stoney. "How long will this take you?"

"Not to worry, it's job one. I have to get some hydraulic lines. Couple of days?"

A week at least. "Sure." Arthur is staggered by the scale of his defeat. He has to sit down, chooses a tattered car seat over by the dump truck.

Speedily recovered from his outpouring of emotion, Stoney perches on the Fargo's running board and rolls a cigarette. "In honour of restoring our friendship, sire, may I extend a personal invite, as executive director of the Growers Association, to our annual Potlatch this Thursday." Though they're alone, he drops his voice: "This year it's at the old quarry. Starts at noon and continues until everyone's flat on their ass."

By Potlatch he means the Marijuana Growers Fall Fair, where produce from Garibaldi's major export competes for the McCoy Cup, named after a local sculptor caught green-handed with a heroic half-ton of cannabis. The event is usually attended by a dozen or more island growers, plus several mainland wholesalers. A Thursday was presumably chosen because the local constable regularly takes that day off.

"You could come as our official mouthpiece."

Arthur wishes people would accept once and for all that he doesn't act for dopers anymore, that he's well and truly retired. "A Potlatch is an honoured aboriginal ceremony of giving, not a pothead bacchanal. I will not attend." Arthur is still smarting over his unconditional surrender.

"We invited Doc Dooley to be on our distinguished panel of judges."

Arthur scoffs. "That's ridiculous. Why would he be so unguarded as to take part?"

"It's widely unknown, but he grows a few plants for medicinal purposes."

That is true — to Arthur's shock, Dooley has confided as much to him. They are fierce rivals, the lawyer and the doctor, regularly the top two contenders for Most Points in Fruits and Vegetables at the Fall Fair. This year again, Dooley bested Arthur, winning his seventh straight Mabel Orfmeister Trophy. Arthur was crushed.

Dooley, almost ninety, has shown no symptoms of senility, so it's ridiculous to think he's agreed to take part in this lawless event. Major movers of marijuana will be there, from Vancouver, maybe even Seattle.

Arthur gets impatient with the careless flaunting of criminal statutes on this island. His view, however stuffy and old-fashioned, is that a well-ordered society obeys the rule of law. Some, including the local Member of Parliament, want the cannabis law changed, but Arthur can't get around his distaste at the thought of the government being in the business of getting its citizens stoned.

The Growers Association has been dangerously open about its annual affair. It has escaped detection over the years, but Constable Ernst Pound has been increasingly relentless since his marriage fell apart. Meanly, Arthur flirts with the thought of joining the war on drugs, dropping the dime on these fellows.

"Can I give you a ride somewhere, chief? On the house."

"I shall walk." Arthur doesn't want to admit his feet are aching. He rises, shoulders his pack.

"Hey, I got an old Pinto I can give you. Courtesy car." He points at it, a rust-red death machine that has obviously done a roll in the ditch.

"Don't bother."

"I'll do better, the Pinto's an insult to the great man." There's alarm in Stoney's voice as he watches his best customer stalk off. "I just scored a beaut for my fleet, man, the Kozonskys' old family Caddie, I just gotta do the papers with them and I'll run it up to you."

"I'd prefer that you focus on my Fargo."

"Cross my heart."

§

Arthur is still licking his wounds from that encounter, and is much put out with himself, as he detours from his way home, limping into Hopeless Bay. Why is he stopping here? There was some urgent mission . . .

The fax! Age is causing his mind to slip. Yesterday the fax was Worry One. He's preoccupied — it's about Margaret, it's Sudden Departure Syndrome. He's battled it all the way from ferry to gas station to Stoney's to here. It will take a few days, maybe weeks, for the ache to lose its grip. "I'm worried now," he sings, "but I won't be worried long."

He hobbles on to the hundred-year-old General Store and Post Office. A designated heritage site, it's awkwardly joined at the hip with a recent addition, an out-of-plumb licensed lounge that overlooks the public wharf. Its risky, sloping deck hovers over rocks and tidal pools. It has been named the Brig, in honour of a local pub that burned down many years ago.

Parked on a bench outside it is Nelson Forbish, editor of the local newsweekly, the *Bleat*, who is feeding from a super-economy bag of corn chips. He is super-sized himself, at nearly a hundred and fifty kilos, and Arthur winces as he tests the bench to ensure it will hold them. He removes his shoes and massages his feet. It is ten-thirty: he has walked for three hours since seeing Margaret off.

"How's the weight program, Nelson?"

"I'm giving it a break. It's too taxing on the body." He looks around, as if to confirm they're alone. "Marijuana Growers Potlatch, Thursday at noon, the abandoned quarry. Not for publication. Mum's the word." He gestures at Ernst Pound's RCMP van, sitting among the beaters and rusting pickups parked out front. Auxiliary cop Kurt Zoller's vivid orange Hummer is there too.

"Do me a favour, Arthur, I'm not good at stairs, can you go up there and see if it's something newsworthy?"

Forbish indicates the second-floor deck of the bar, where Pound and Zoller are questioning the island idlers, probably having caught them flouting the no-smoking law. Pound has been known to turn a blind eye to this infraction, bartering leniency for information. Since his wife ran off, he has been increasingly sulky and snappish — he hates his Garibaldi posting. He doesn't much like Zoller either, a nitpicker who loves parading about in a clean, ironed uniform. The Hummer H1, recently bought second-hand, is presumably intended to enhance the jackboot image he relishes. In real life, Zoller runs a water taxi business.

Pressed into service as a news gatherer, but curious just the same, Arthur wiggles his swollen feet back into his shoes, heads up the stairs to the deck, and takes up a position quietly behind the two officers. They are questioning four of Garibaldi's more prankish rogues, all of whom have pints on their shared table but are hiding their cigarettes. Ernie Priposki gives Arthur a conspiratorial wink.

"I'm thinking of giving you a pass on these smoking violations, boys." Pound glares at Zoller, who is trying to draw his attention to a full ashtray on a railing post. "Stow it, Kurt. In fact, gentlemen, I don't think we need to hand out any traffic tickets either today. And maybe not until the weekend. No hassling, no breath tests unless you run someone down. And you can smoke your frigging faces off out here."

"What's the catch?" says Gomer Goulet.

"Just help us out about the Potlatch."

"Potlatch?" says Ernie Priposki. "What Potlatch?"

There's a chorus of similar queries, an exchange of puzzled looks.

"I can do it the easy way and nip it in the bud, or I can bring in the whole Vancouver Island drug squad." Pound's voice is rising. "And bust everyone! And bust you for withholding state's evidence!"

Arthur has never heard of such a charge, except perhaps in movies. He's embarrassed for the officers.

"Kurt, I want you to go down to where their vehicles are illegally parked, and I want you to ticket every frigging bald tire, loose muffler, and expired plate. Everything!"

Zoller seems unsure whether Pound truly means it, and stalls. "Just do it!"

Zoller gets out his ticket pad and moves smartly down the stairs.

Honk Gilmore, a sly, thick-waisted, sixty-year-old, has been silent, but can't resist. "Withholding state's evidence — what's the law on that, Mr. Beauchamp?"

Pound whirls and, on seeing Arthur, visibly deflates. The boys erupt in knee-slapping mirth.

"You seen it, counsellor," Gomer says. "Police brutality."

"No story here," Arthur hollers down to Nelson Forbish. He puts a hand on Pound's shoulder and leads him inside.

Pound makes a soft sound, a moan or a groan, as he seats himself at a table in a windowless corner. Even in the dim light, he looks haggard. "I'm doomed here. I don't have any credibility on this frigging . . . It's the island of the damned."

Arthur nods in apparent agreement. He's anxious to see that fax, but Ernst must be allowed to let off steam.

"I've done two consecutive tours on this rock. I'm supposed to get reassigned this fall, but they're never going to let me off it. Everyone else gets shuffled around but me. In my paranoid moments, which is most of the time, I feel like there's a conspiracy to drive me frigging insane. A medical experiment, like they do in the CIA, to see how much it takes to break a serving officer. Gentlemen, the first thing we do is destroy his marriage. Then let's make him the laughingstock of some tight, twisted, little hellhole of an island."

Edwina's affair with the local telephone man was open, notorious. Ultimately, she moved in with her lover, pregnant by him. That is the main reason Pound is desperate to get off the rock. Arthur gets it. The public shame he himself endured as a cuckold propelled him into exile.

Voluptuous Emily LeMay, the ageless siren, sets two coffees on the table. "Goddamnit, Ernst, tell Zoller to stop dicking around with the cars down there, he's killing my business." To Arthur: "Heard your sweetie left on the morning ferry." Lips to his ear. "Emily's open for business anytime for you, big guy." She enjoys teasing him, sometimes gets him to blush.

As she sways off, Pound resumes his dirge. "Seriously, Arthur, they've got it in for me at division headquarters. I heard it from someone up the line. They think I've done piss-all in this shithole. They're going to stick me with another two years here if I don't nab someone soon. Someone big."

He looks at Arthur in a needy way, as if seeking deliverance. Arthur sips his coffee.

"It's my only chance, Arthur. My only chance to escape from this Alcatraz." He takes a deep breath. "It's this weekend, isn't it? The Potlatch." He is unnerved by Arthur's steely gaze, and stammers: "I . . . I saw you up at Stoney's. We all know he's one of the ringleaders." He takes a gulp of coffee, chokes. "I don't care about the little guys, the Stoneys, the small growers. But big-city dope dealers are due in, heavies, racketeers. I just want to collar one of them. Just give me one of them."

He sags, wipes perspiration from his forehead, and raises a hand in surrender. "Forget it. That was insulting to you, I'm sorry. I'm pretty messed up."

Kurt Zoller has been hovering by, and announces himself now by jingling his keys and handcuffs, one of the compulsive acts he's prone to.

Pound swivels to him. "What is it, Kurt?"

Zoller is holding a nearly depleted ticket pad. "I got Johannsen for six, including no emergency, broken tail light, and I got Gilmore for exhaust pipes and muddy plate and . . ."

"Give me those tickets." Pound gets up, snatches the pad, drops it into the trash bin, then heads down to his cruiser. Zoller follows, red-faced.

Arthur carries on to the store, finds the mailroom unattended, picks up a frozen pizza for tonight and some fruit to eat on the way home. Gaunt, spindly Abraham Makepeace pauses from stacking onions and holds up a finger to say he'll be a minute. Arthur wanders down the aisles of pots and mops and stationery and books, cheerlessly examines the little stack of autographed copies of *A Thirst for Justice: The Trials of Arthur Beauchamp*. The covers are dominated by his long nose in profile. "Now half-price!" a sign shrieks.

It's a second edition, revised, in paperback. Wentworth Chance, its author, revelled in the Hogarthian details: the gin-spiked pitcher on the counsel table, the drunken quarrels with judges, the lonely horror of the skid road years. He held little back, including Arthur's futile and hilarious relationships with the other sex. Despite all, the putative hero comes off as a reasonably lovable old coot.

Makepeace finally passes him his mail: a Hydro bill, two magazines, and a postcard from California. The postmaster saves Arthur the bother of reading it. "It's from your grandson, Nick. He's doing advanced computer electronics at Stanford, on a scholarship. Getting settled in. Sends his love. You'd think he'd email you, but he must know you haven't got a clue about computers."

"I am not computer-illiterate. The fax, please, Abraham."

He fetches it from the Blunder Bay box. "Let me just check this is the right one." He takes a few moments to peruse it. "Yep, that's what it says, someone wants to take you down. It means bump you off. Maybe you overcharged him."

He withdraws it from Arthur's reach. "Glad to see your correspondent shares my complaint about you not having an answering machine. You're never home when he calls, and you don't answer his emails neither. That's why he had to resort to this fax. All the way from the rainforests of Haida Gwaii, which I like better than when we used to call it the Queen Charlotte Islands, it's more poetical. Two pages, two dollars."

Arthur digs in his pockets, places two loonies in Makepeace's left hand, and tugs the pages from his right.

"It's pretty darn confusing about why someone wants to kill you.

Guess he'll explain it, he's coming down to see you. Pomeroy. Brian Pomeroy. "

Alarms are ringing in Arthur's head. Brian Pomeroy, against whom he had done sweaty battle over Randolph Skyler's fate. *Someone wants to kill you.*

"Weren't you in the same law office or something? Fast talker, if he's the same fella used to come over for visits. Kind of jumpy and wrought up was my impression."

Brian Pomeroy, the inventive, crazed, substance-abusing counsel with whom Arthur shared many trials. Different law offices but similar practices: the vigorous defence of criminals and, occasionally, the innocent. They've remained friends since the Skyler case, but have rarely talked about it, and whenever they have Arthur has sensed a bitterness, the resentment of the sore loser.

Pomeroy had been on his way to becoming one of the top young guns of the courts, but then came a series of crashes: his marriage breaking down, drugs, more drugs, then a cocaine-induced psychosis that had him trying to write mystery novels. He fought and lost his wife's divorce action, went broke, tried a gold mining scheme that didn't pan out, tried being a full-time beach bum in Costa Rica, failing even at that, then began a small practice in the islands of Haida Gwaii, in the remote North Pacific.

The fax's first page is just a cover, with Brian's name, an address in Port Clements, and his fax number. Arthur folds it for now, tucks it into his shirt pocket. Makepeace leans toward him. "Don't spread it around, but the Potlatch kicks off Thursday noon at the old quarry."

"I shall not whisper a word."

Arthur pays for his pizza and pears, slings on his pack, walks out, contemplates the long trudge to Blunder Bay, then settles his aching joints on the bench that Nelson Forbish has deserted, pulls out the fax.

"Dear Arthur, I have to assume you have (accidentally?) put your phone on mute, because it rings endlessly, chillingly. Each unanswered peal causes my spine to spasm. Has my god and mentor been murdered in his sleep?"

Makepeace is not alone in finding that pretty darn confusing.

"So I checked Tragger, Inglis's website, which trumpets the fact that although ostensibly retired you remain a partner. I got the receptionist to give me your email and this fax number. Claimed not to know if you had a cell phone."

Arthur had given her instructions to say just that. The number of his little Nokia is known to only Margaret and a handful of discreet friends. That is partly because his life companion, in a waggish moment, changed the ring tone to "Twinkle, twinkle, little star," and he doesn't know how to change it back.

The fax continues: "My emails don't bounce back, so I must ask: is it too much bother to look at your inbox? Or have you created a filter to junk all messages from any sender named Pomeroy? — Pause for a return to reality. — Beauchamp create a message filter? Does he even know how to open his mail program?"

Arthur does know how to read his emails, but he can't remember when he last did so. Perhaps a week ago.

"I can't afford Air Canada's monopoly rip-off fares, so I'm coming down there by ferry and bus. Here's the gist: a certain fellow whom you grievously offended is back in freeside and he's out to take you down. Nuff said. Brian."

For a moment, Arthur's anxiety neurosis is in full bloom, then he swallows hard, struggling to recover. And he does so with some success, by remembering that the conveyor of this deadly message is a master of the wild theory, full of preposterous, paranoid scenarios. Drug-addled half the time. Yes, this has to be typical Pomeroy malarkey.

Baldy Johannsen walks from the Brig with the overly prudent gait of the impaired, then takes a misstep near his pickup upon spotting the clutter of tickets on his windshield. He decides he needs a lawyer. "Hey, Arthur, old buddy, old pal, lemme give you a liff home."

"Thanks, Baldy, but I need the exercise." He heaves himself to his feet and slogs up the road.

§

On his homeward hike, Arthur continues to buoy himself by putting Pomeroy in proper context. He's an infamous practical joker, whose multiple offences range from sabotaging a prosecutor's briefcase, from which, in front of a jury, she pulled out a dildo, to forging a love note from a judge to an attractive juror, a note that somehow made its way into the exhibit box, resulting in a mistrial.

Brian's post-divorce mythic spectacle involved no mere breakdown. Arthur believes he actually went mad. Drug-induced or otherwise, the illness was of an intensity that wins insanity verdicts. On one occasion he bolted from a courtroom and ran down the rainy streets of Vancouver in his gown, flapping like a chicken. Later, in a hospice for recovering junkies, he tried to hang himself. He quit a hectic practice as senior partner of Pomeroy, Macarthur, Brovak, Sage, and ran away as far as he could, and Vancouver lost one of its ablest trial lawyers.

Satisfied that Pomeroy is either experiencing another delusionary episode or, at best, is playing a prank, Arthur softly sings that he won't be worried long, and limps along Potters Road to his cedar-canopied driveway. He is reminded that the snake fence has to be rebuilt where Stoney's aide-de-camp, Dog, recently backed into it. So many chores to be done. Today he walked almost the length of Garibaldi Island, stubbornly refusing all offers of rides. Pride has its price, and his is exhaustion and hunger, which he will alleviate presently with a hot shower and a hotter pizza.

Among the trees, Arthur glimpses a gleaming black sedan parked near his porch. It's the Kozonskys' 1982 Cadillac. Stoney has honoured the offer that Arthur turned down, the discourtesy car. Also parked there, at a picnic table, are Stoney and Dog. The well-filled ashtray and many beer cans testify that they likely pulled in while Arthur was at the store and have been enjoying a late afternoon break from their labours. From fifty feet away, he can smell pot.

Stoney spots Arthur advancing, and calls: "Yo, padrone, we were worried, man. We were just about to go look for you. Right, Dog?"

His laconic, snockered sidekick merely smiles in agreement. This genial, broad-shouldered runt earned his nickname because of his devotion to his master. His real name is a Polish one, unpronounceable and unspellable. He's an island favourite, though, always volunteering to help out the ill and old when weeds need whacking or wood needs stacking.

"Sorry to have caused you fellows so much inconvenience."

"No damage done. We were only hoping we wouldn't run out of liquid refreshment before you got here to drive us back. We'd've walked but we got to save our energy for the Potlatch." Stoney takes a final drag, pinches the roach and flips it away. A finger to his lips. "It's at the quarry on Thursday."

"Yes, at noon. Everyone on the island seems to know."

He looks shocked. "We only told some trusted confidants who guaranteed they wouldn't say nothing. Not to rub salt in any wounds, but did I tell you we'll be celebrating the life and achievements of the seven-time Orfmeister winner?"

"Doc Dooley would not dream of coming within a thousand light years of your function."

"Maybe he ain't as stuffy as you think. He's young at heart."

Arthur wonders how he has allowed this conversation to deteriorate into a debate about the Potlatch. He is hungry; he has other things to do, including holding at bay a worry monster threatening to rise from its too-shallow grave. He will waste no more breath warning Stoney about the risks he's taking on this island of idle tongues. A stiff fine and a lengthy spell of probation might just smarten him up.

"Okay, about this here vintage DeVille. She's been sitting in Joe

Kozonsky's garage for the last ten years, just needed gas and oil and she fired right up. One of the last great V8s, eh, so there'll be a fuel issue. Right fender needs straightening, and Joe says that spiderweb on the windshield was from a pebble, not a bullet, though it looks like it. Sometimes she don't gear down going up a steep incline, so you gotta give her some pedal or put her in low. I hope you can drive an automatic." He clicks open the tab of another beer. "Oh, hey, I ain't being a good host — you want to share this last one?"

"Thank you, no." Arthur has been proudly AA for almost twenty-five years, yet he still gets offers, usually out of misplaced courtesy.

"Otherwise, you got this here luxomobile for as long as the Fargo takes, not a bad deal, eh?" He opens the doors, shows the spacious interior. "Lots of room to take your produce to the Saturday market. You could put ten big pumpkins in the trunk."

The sales job is working. Arthur hasn't had a comfortable vehicle since he retired his Rolls-Royce.

"We'd linger awhile, sahib, but we got a little Potlatch preview party going. You know how it is, eh, you got to build up slowly for the main event. So if you can just drop us at Hamish's studio, Dog and me would be mighty grateful. Right, Dog?"

"Absolooley." A valiant effort from the squat sidekick, who clambers dutifully into the back of the sedan.

Arthur takes off his pack, lowers his weary body into the front seat, and is promptly seduced by its unFargoish comfort. This is Stoney's offer of penance for nicking his truck. Arthur will reinforce such good behaviour by taking them to their Potlatch preview, a test drive.

§

Back home, he sinks wearily into a swivel chair behind his old desktop computer, and devours a mushroom salami pizza while reading Brian's emails. The two most recent were urgent demands that he respond. The first was chattier.

"To catch you up, Arturo, I am surviving on notarizing documents (twenty clams a pop) and by trading advice for halibut steaks, fresh-laid eggs, and psilocybin shrooms, supplemented by the occasional legal aid fee, while pooling resources with the exotic woman who currently shares my bed, a Haida artist.

"Having papered an entire wall with rejection slips, I've given up on mysteries. I'm trying out a couple of screenplays instead. I am cool; I am together. I like to think I have recovered from the spectacle I made of myself after Caroline's breathtakingly successful divorce suit and her court-sanctioned theft of all I owned but my shoelaces.

"But this is not about my continuing struggle for survival but yours. You're in danger. The Web is infested with police spies, they have access to all our emails, and for reasons only they know, they're watching me in particular. We need to talk privately. I'm heading down there *au plus vite*."

He added, "Say nothing, rien, nada," and ended his note with: "Be wary, don't worry." Don't worry? It's like asking Arthur not to breathe. He shakes his head, to clear its cobwebs. Psilocybin! Magic mushrooms! Clearly, this death threat scenario is a drug-induced Pomeroidal delusion. Arthur is in as much danger from Skyler as Brian is from some fantastical, vast spying apparatus of international police agencies. He worries that Brian has gotten so heavily into his shrooms that he's developed a paranoid psychosis, and will arrive at Blunder Bay babbling about cabals and conspiracies that somehow involve Arthur.

If he's not mad, he's simply putting Arthur on, having fun with the renowned worrywart. But would a prank be worth the pain of a thousand-mile journey from the misty, mystic islands of the Haida nation? Probably, in Brian's case.

Arthur emails him back, explains he rarely answers the house phone because he's under siege by telemarketers, and lets him know — calmly, humouring him — that he would be delighted to host him and share some good conversation.

There is little else of note in his inbox. Yet another invitation to join Facebook. A reminder about Thanksgiving at Al's and Zoë's, bring the Woofers. A function being planned in Vancouver in late October to honour and roast a retiring judge and his replacement. Justice Thomas McDougall, whom the Chief Justice persuaded was too senile to carry on, is leaving the bench. Mandy Pearl will take a seat on it.

Comely, eager Mandy Pearl. Clumsy, tipsy Arthur Beauchamp. He hadn't been able to get it up for her the first night, but — wonders will never cease — he'd achieved success on the second night, and the fourth. Mandy had introduced him to tai chi and taught him some basic moves. Somehow, that had lessened his thirst, his need.

It was Mandy who'd weaned him from the bottle, Mandy with her loving, her expert massaging, her counselling. She'd locked him in her townhouse from Thursday to Sunday, she ministering, he talking. It was the alcohol that had disempowered him, she said. Stay off it and they would make love night after night like this.

He stayed off it, but went back to Annabelle, helplessly, unable to break the bonds of masochistic love. She assumed he'd been in a dry-out centre. Everyone did. No one knew about him and Mandy.

Arthur is about to close up when a message from Pomeroy appears, expressing relief that they'd connected, detailing his travel schedule, and warning that "they" were watching. "Special Agent Harry Hacker studiously reads my outgoing traffic, so we have to be surreptitious. You may have to look that word up, Harry."

WEDNESDAY, SEPTEMBER 19

Arthur has been trying for the last two days to get through to Margaret, badgering her staff. He has not been wholly able to still his jitters about Pomeroy's hazy, weird warning; he needs someone to share it with, a sympathetic ear. But when he finally gets her on the line this evening, he clutches when he is about to divulge why he called.

"I ought to mention, dear . . . ah, pass on that."

"What?"

"Oh, I guess . . ." He has caught himself just in time. He won't burden Margaret with an unsubstantiated death threat. She would only worry. That's Arthur's job. "Well, I was wondering how to tell you about the Fargo, Stoney claims he saved my life. Its brakes were going."

"What are you talking about, Arthur?" He detects that new, impatient tone again.

Arthur backs up, fills in the gaps, and then continues like a wind-up toy, robotically, with more tales from home, the courtesy Cadillac, the demoralized Ernst Pound and his lust to bust tomorrow's not-so-covert Potlatch, the nonsense about Doc Dooley showing up at a marijuana bacchanal.

"Please slow down, Arthur. You'd better make sure the doc doesn't get caught standing in the middle of a ton of export-quality Garibaldi Gold."

"It's Stoney's joke. His way of needling me because I lost the Orfmeister again."

His tales all told, Arthur gives her a livestock report. A garden report. A weather report. Not even hinted at are the bad tidings Pomeroy may relay when he arrives in a few days. Only the prying postmaster knows anything. Otherwise Arthur has obeyed Pomeroy's emailed caution: *Say nothing, rien, nada.*

"Are you well, Arthur? You sound a little hysterical."

"Everything's fine. Tip-top."

He apologizes for monopolizing the conversation, and asks what's up in the nation's capital. Her list is challenging: a Throne Speech that gave less than lip service to the environment, botched inquiries into the vast atrocity of exploiting the Alberta tar sands, another draconian crime bill on its way, creeping fascism in the Prime Minister's Office.

She's venting. Margaret regularly finds relief from doing that, though she does it too often in public. Not all her sound bites win applause; sometimes her barbed tongue causes too stinging a wound. But that is our sharp-tempered Margaret Blake. She has been threatened with slander suits and occasionally has had to apologize.

Pierrette is on call-waiting, and they have to wrap up. "I love you," he says.

"I love you too, of course."

That sounds to him mechanical, passion-free. Again, he feels a sense of not knowing Margaret. So different from Annabelle, the vivid, playful temptress. In contrast, Margaret is narcissism-free, focussed on the world around her, this threatened planet. And he is proud of her, honoured to be her life companion, even though she has been, of late, very much . . . elsewhere. In physical distance, yes, but emotionally too. But that's okay with him. Way down on his worry list.

He lights his pipe and rocks slowly on the squeaking chair as he reads today's *Bleat*, hot off Nelson Forbish's printer.

A photo of Tildy Sears and her teammates graces the front page under the banner headline, "Congratulations, gals!" and the subhead, "Easy Pieces Win Ladies' Inter-Island." A sidebar is headed, "Scotty Phillips Blooper Fouls No-Hitter."

Lower on the page, Forbish bangs the drum for a coming event at the community hall: Tildy will be given the keys to the island by its elected trustees. Then a dinner in her honour sponsored by the Chamber of Commerce, followed by a dance. In his page-two editorial, Forbish demands she be awarded the Garibaldian-of-the-Year trophy, a traditional island honour haphazardly determined by a mysterious series of petitions, polls, and ballots. Arthur has won it once, lost another on a close recount.

Arthur retreats to his old form-fitting club chair, picks up an interpretation of Euripides's extant plays, of which he's writing a review, works at it awhile. Then Pomeroy's paranoid voice intrudes, whispering, "Be wary, don't worry."

THURSDAY, SEPTEMBER 20

Cooler air has arrived, and it is grey and misty on the last official day of summer. Here on the north side of the island, the wet side, dew is heavy on the pastures even at noon. Arthur is on his way to Mary's Landing in the gas-gobbling guilt machine with the spiderwebbed windshield. Reverend Al Noggins has summoned him to a tête-à-tête at the graveyard behind St. Mary's Church. He claimed to be facing a moral dilemma, but wouldn't divulge more.

"Now what?" Arthur mumbles. Every day, it seems, brings him something fresh to stew over. Surely Al is not about to confide he's having an affair with a parishioner, one of those alluring widows in his flock. That would be intolerable. Some legal issue? No, a moral dilemma, he said.

Perhaps it had to do with today's signal event, the Marijuana Growers Fall Fair and Potlatch. Arthur doesn't give a hoot about it, frankly. He wouldn't care if all the crops on show got confiscated — that would smarten them up. Should there be a major bust, no amount of cajolery will see him involved in the defence of a bunch of losing stoners. He has sworn — loudly, in public, during interviews — that he will never undertake another trial; he is *hors de combat*, a gentleman farmer now.

Mary's Landing is in a quiet, mist-thick nook: a public dock, a pebble beach, a small wooden church and annex, and, on a knoll beyond the parking lot, Garibaldi's graveyard, whose two hundred dead are sheltered by a giant big-leaf maple now changing into yellow autumn dress. The church lot is empty when Arthur rolls in and proceeds, as directed, up the path to the little cemetery, with its clutter of crosses and tilting, weather-worn gravestones.

He is in a dark suit, something he almost compulsively wears when visiting a cemetery. An inbred formalism, probably inherited from his starchy father and enhanced by attending too many funerals. A breeze soughs through the branches of the maple, sending leaves spinning and conjuring filmy shapes from the patches of fog. He shivers, looking about for malefactors. *Be wary*.

There is an order of precedence in this graveyard: pioneers near the front, with the ocean view, long-timers down the hill, newcomers in the misty bottom, with the flashier stones one expects from parvenus. Arthur intends eventually to be buried in this graveyard, hopefully among the long-timers. Epitaph: Here lies a fusspot.

Out of the fog comes Reverend Al on a scooter. He chugs into the lot, parks by the Cadillac, doffs his helmet.

"What's with the Mafia getaway car," he says, coming up the trail.

"Stoney's loaner," Arthur shrugs. "Why are we meeting among the dead?"

"Because people respect one's privacy in a graveyard." They are startled by a sound — a squirrel scooting up the maple's trunk. "You've heard about the Potlatch, of course."

"At the old quarry." Arthur checks his watch. "As of fifteen minutes ago."

"The worst-kept secret in the history of humankind. I have a moral issue: To whom do I owe the greater duty, to the law or to local growers, many of whom I've counselled? They may be dopers and stoners, but they're *our* dopers and stoners . . ."

"Okay, so what?" Arthur doesn't want to sound impatient, but Al becomes prolix when excited.

"A parishioner phoned me this morning. He has a place on Tatter Inlet just a few lots from Kurt Zoller's water taxi dock. He was up just before dawn, taking a piss off his deck when a launch pulled in, and he saw Kurt hustle outside to help tie it up. A bunch of characters with fishing gear disembarked. He said it looked fishy. I told him I'd investigate."

"I advise you to stay right out of it."

"Okay, but the dilemma is compounded by something else I heard. The other day. From Honk Gilmore. I assumed he was joking —"

"Yes, yes? Heard what?"

"That Doc Dooley would be dropping by, as a political statement. He wants to challenge the marijuana laws. I thought he was kidding, but I phoned the doc anyway this morning, and he wasn't home."

Arthur is overwhelmed by a vision of Dooley being cuffed and led away for prints and mug shots. What if the good doctor, in a moment of caprice, were actually to show up to judge the annual fall harvest?

He looks at his watch: it's half past twelve. He orders Al to go home. "I will handle this."

§

As Stoney warned, the automatic transmission is disobedient on steep inclines, but Arthur makes it up to Evergreen Estates without stalling. He parks and jogs to the crest of the hill and into Doc Dooley's terraced acre of gardens, berry bushes, and orchard, and finally to the steps of his vine-covered bungalow.

"The doctor's out," the housekeeper announces, looking suspiciously at the panting visitor, in his dark suit.

"But his van is here."

"He took his bicycle. Said he'll be gone awhile, wouldn't say where."

Arthur carries on to Dooley's little medical clinic in Evergreen Estates' micro-mall, but the door is locked. He tries the emergency pager number, and is told that only an off-island physician is on call. He'll try to intercept Dooley on the road.

Garibaldi's primary artery, Centre Road, bisects the island, so Arthur chooses it first, driving slowly, peeking up and down its unpaved dead ends. But he comes across no cyclists in the sparse weekday traffic. At a T-intersection he turns up Gwendolyn Valley Road, a potholed lane that climbs steeply to the quarry before petering out as a trail to the national park. It's not often used off-season.

The Cadillac again threatens to stall on the uphill until Arthur shifts down manually. He can barely conceive of the doctor, in his ninetieth year, pumping his way up this most mountainous of the island's byways. But maybe nothing is beyond the Orfmeister multi-winner.

The old Caddie finally lurches onto the quarry's white, dusty entrance road. A limestone seam, thrust from the ocean floor in eons past, was well worked and the pits abandoned half a century ago, leaving steep-sided gulleys in the hill. There are alleyways and cul-de-sacs not easily accessed, and caves as well, and it is in one of these that Arthur suspects the pot partiers have gathered.

In the parking lot, he sees only the old, rolled Pinto that Stoney tried to foist on him. Doubtless the less reckless members of the Growers Association have parked elsewhere, to avoid attention, and hiked up here, or, maybe like Dooley, pedalled.

He pulls in beside the Pinto, finds a broken tree limb to use as a walking stick, then climbs a circuitous path around the rim of the quarry, hoping to gain a vantage point. He hears muffled conversation below but can't see anyone until, finally, he mounts a rocky ledge with a panoramic view. In a narrow defile is a single makeshift table with a meagre display of offerings: half a dozen small brown-paper bags. There seem to be only two attendees at this annual gala: Dog and a long-haired, bearded tough in a biker's jacket. No bicycle, no Doc Dooley. It's one-thirty, the event should be well under way.

The biker, whose leather club jacket proclaims him to be a Devil's High-Rider, is poking his nose into one of the paper bags, apparently newly bought. Meanwhile Dog, presumably the vendor, is wandering about in an apparent woozy insensibility, clutching a half-empty beer bottle.

When Arthur twists around, he catches glimpses in the second-growth fir at the base of the quarry of several men and women moving about with the swaggering gait peculiar to the unmounted members of the RCMP's narcotics division. Radios, binoculars, and gun-sized bulges. The snout of Zoller's orange Hummer pokes from the undergrowth.

When Arthur swivels another eighty degrees, he sees two officers in the parking lot combing through his Cadillac. A broad-shouldered woman is reaching under the driver's seat, and her male associate is cleaning out the glove compartment.

Arthur hurriedly retraces his steps, anxious to set matters right and avoid having to sue the federal government for its servants' trespasses. As he reaches the parking area, he sees the male officer dump the contents of the car's ashtray into an exhibit bag.

Before Arthur can protest, he is grabbed in a bear-like grip by the female officer, and is shoved forward over the trunk of the car.

"Spread 'em!"

Arthur is too winded even to curse as her hands sweep down his spread-eagled body and up his thighs, expertly, muscularly, indelicately.

"Looks like we got number one, anyway. Let's see some ID, pal."

Her partner is examining the cracked windshield. "Nice old buggy. Ask Al Capone over there if somebody took a shot at him."

Arthur is wondering if Brian Pomeroy is psychic and this is the forewarned danger. He can sputter only a couple of intelligible words: "appalling" and "ridiculous."

"Heard it before," says his captor. She handcuffs him, swings him around, goes through his pockets, and fishes out his wallet.

"Who's the suit?" This third voice is familiar, and when Arthur is able to focus he sees, coming from a channel cut into limestone walls, the head of the Vancouver Island Coordinated Drug Enforcement Unit, a combatant in trials past. As Inspector Eugene Klostert closes in on them, his smile wavers, fades, and is replaced by grimacing dismay. "Mr. Beauchamp?" he says pleadingly, as if begging him to deny it, hoping this is his doppelganger, impresario of the soft-drug Mafia.

The woman officer backs away, uncertainly. Ernst Pound emerges from the passageway, stops suddenly, backs up a step. He seems to be looking for a place to hide.

"Take those goddamn bracelets off him, and give him back his wallet," Klostert commands, and while she does so, he joins the other officer for a huddle.

Arthur rubs his wrists and shakes the dust from his suit. "I take it, madam, you're a master of some form of martial arts."

"Just a little judo, sir." She looks shaken, maybe by the prospect of a massive claim in damages for assault and false arrest.

Klostert draws him aside, clearing his throat. "I'm hoping you'll let this one go, Mr. Beauchamp. Owens found a roach and some doings in your car's front ashtray."

"It's a loaner, Inspector."

"I'm not going to doubt that. Maybe they didn't have cause, but they're frustrated. This whole operation has gone to shit."

The circumstances would have inflamed the suspicions of any normal, over-anxious cop, and Arthur has suffered no lasting injury. "I will forgive."

Any explanation of why he's here would require mention of Doc Dooley, so he's content to let Klostert assume that a client facing arrest summoned him — by cell phone or maybe smoke signals. To maintain that fiction, he sets off to look for a handy client.

The inspector overtakes him, bellowing at Ernst Pound, who has found no place to hide and stands paralyzed near a limestone wall. "Operation Pot-Snatch? Is that what you call this, Constable? I call it Operation CFU, Completely Fucked Up." Arthur feels badly for the stressed-out local cop who has capped off his dismal career by helping engineer a law-enforcement disaster.

Klostert rejoins Arthur, puffing, his voice cracking. "Damn nincompoop. We've been conned." A trail of empty beer cans leads them to the clearing with Dog's skimpy display: the several paper bags. Dog is no longer upright, but stretched out on an air mattress, passed out or asleep, beside an empty case of Blue.

Standing over him, like a proud huntsman with his kill, is Garibaldi's auxiliary constable, still in his biker's jacket with the Devil's High-Riders insignia, though he has removed his dark glasses, ill-fitting beard, and hairpiece. He's still holding his bag of marijuana, presumably his evidence of trafficking. Zoller looks confused on seeing Arthur and Klostert approach.

"Sir, the suspect is one Dogmar Zbrinjkowitz, alias Dog." Arthur is astonished at how faultlessly the surname flowed from Zoller's tongue. "He didn't make me, Inspector. It was easy as a pie, except I had to wake him up to do the buy." He opens the paper bag and peers into it. "I think we can safely assume this will analyze as high-grade cannabis sativa."

A scrawled sign on the table reads: "$30 an oz, prime organic."

Klostert asks, "Did you ask him where they moved the Potlatch to?"

"Couldn't get him to spill, sir." Zoller glares at Arthur. "I guess it's too late now that he's lawyered up."

Klostert looks down on the supine form, now snoring. "You know this man, Mr. Beauchamp?"

"A long-time upstanding member of this community. Until now."

The inspector shakes his head. "I had better things to do today. I was going to get off early, take the boys fishing."

"What do you want me to do with him, sir?" Zoller asks.

"He's your collar." Klostert walks off, muttering, still shaking his head.

Pound remains immobile, but offers Arthur a wincing smile. Zoller is left with the task of bringing the drug lord to justice. He shakes Dog, who opens his eyes and stares at him with the rheumy-eyed contemplation of an aging spaniel.

Zoller speed-reads the caution: "Dogmar Zbrinjkowitz, you have the right to remain silent, but anything you say will be used as evidence. Where are your confederates?"

Arthur feels he ought to tell Dog to say nothing, but that would imply a lawyer-client relationship, and Arthur does not want to get mixed up in this. His firm vow never to do another trial has now been buttressed by the new fear of being embarrassed in a public courtroom, made the butt of jokes in barristers' rooms over the intimate search by the judo expert: *"Heard she gave his dick a real good squeeze." "Enough to give the old boy a hard-on."*

Zoller persists. "It will go easier for you if you cough up your co-conspirators."

Arthur is fascinated by the look of concentration on Dog's face. This humble young man of few words seems to be turning red with the effort to remain silent. Finally a loud noise erupts, recalling to Arthur one of the Bard's best-loved lines: *A man may break a word with you, sir, and words are but wind.*

SATURDAY, SEPTEMBER 22

When the phone rings at breakfast time, it's usually an offer to
consolidate loans or get in on the ground floor of something, but
this time the seller has a folksy approach: "Good morning, Mr.
Beauchamp, this is old Jake from down here at Jiffy Electronics, and
today we're offering a special on answering machines."

"Have a nice day, Jake . . ."

Pomeroy shouts: "Don't hang up! I'm down to my last loonie
and my cell is out of juice."

"Where are you?"

"The bus is taking a shit stop in Campbell River. Unless
omnipotent God has devised yet another way to fuck me, I'll make
the seven o'clock ferry. I hope Garibaldi is rocking on a Saturday
night. I'm going to need to unwind my ass after this noxious ride.
I'm wedged beside an inept mother from whose womb has emerged,
as if in *Aliens*, an incessantly screaming monster."

"As a matter of fact, there's a dance at the hall. Celebrating an
international baseball championship by our Nine Easy Pieces."

"Ask them to save a piece for me."

"Sadly, you'll miss the afternoon parade. I'll meet you at eight-forty. I've had Mop'n'Chop over to spruce things up and make a bed for you."

"Hope it's no trouble."

"Don't worry."

Arthur reflects on how odd it is to hear his own voice saying that. Pomeroy's ebullient manner has encouraged him to believe the news about Skyler will not be too devastating. More likely a joke. His jauntiness, though, might only mean he's high. Arthur hopes it's not cocaine again.

§

Arthur wishes he'd brought an umbrella. He and a substantial contingent of fellow islanders are still waiting for the parade to show up, and it has started to shower. The four-float cavalcade was supposed to have marshalled at the back end of Evergreen Estates half an hour ago, and the folks waiting along the parade route, Garibaldi's one-block downtown, are growing impatient.

He finds shelter under the canopy of Wholeness and Wellness Health Foods and Vitamins, whose proprietors, a middle-aged lesbian couple, are inside, dealing out nut bars to parents with wheedling children. The storekeepers also sell, and usually wear, T-shirts respectively labelled "Wholeness" and "Wellness," and they don't mind being addressed as such.

He is pretending not to be aware that Doc Dooley is standing nearby, outside the adjoining storefront, his clinic. Arthur is still embarrassed by Thursday's imbroglio — the indecent assault, the handcuffs — and fears having to explain to Dooley what he was doing up Gwendolyn Valley Road on Potlatch day. Arthur was just coming off that road when Dooley pedalled past, returning from the General Store, saddle packs filled with groceries.

A sound of bagpipes in the distance. The dreaded but never avoidable Garibaldi Highland Pipers, who rise to every island occasion. But at least the parade is under way. Those without rain gear or umbrellas have fled to their cars to wait out the Pacific squall.

There is no escaping Dooley, who is making his way toward him. Arthur expresses delight at seeing him on this august occasion.

"Couldn't figure what you were doing the other day, Arthur, coming off Gwendolyn Road in that gas guzzler."

"Hurray, I believe the rain has stopped. Just in time. This parade had better be worth the wait."

"Heard you had some doings with the tactical police squad they brought over, at that bogus Potlatch up by the quarry."

Word is out. Is that why locals have been suppressing smiles as they stare at him? Maybe Ernst Pound blabbed or, more probably, Zoller, boasting that he did what a whole drug squad couldn't: make an arrest on Pot-Snatch Day. *I wasn't there to exactly see it, but a certain local lawyer got worked over pretty good in the you-know-where* . . .

Dooley has spotted Stoney. "That fellow Stonewell — can you imagine, he actually invited me to that damn fool event."

Stoney is at the lumberyard across the road, climbing a stack of two-by-fours to get a view. Arthur walks briskly over to join him, just as the Garibaldi fire truck, all lights flashing, comes around the bend with a bleat of siren. A listless cheer goes up.

"Man, I been looking all over for you, counsellor."

"For how long?"

"At least since I woke. I been mostly laid up for two days. I'm ashamed to admit, but the Potlatch was a down scene on account of Dog getting busted, plus I got into some real morbid reefer." Stoney slides off the pile of lumber and digs into a pack of roll-your-own tobacco.

"I rather had the impression Dog was being used as a decoy, to lure them to the wrong spot."

The shock seems almost genuine; Stoney spills some tobacco. "Put Dog in danger? No way, man. Dog and me are like one, we're attached in deep supernatural ways. Somehow, he must've got sucked in by our own propaganda. I told him, Honk's barn. I told him three weeks ago, I even wrote it down for him."

"Can he read?"

"Jeez, I never asked him."

The fire truck is followed by Ernst Pound in the RCMP van. He looks even more desolate than usual, staring straight ahead, earning only a reluctant smattering of applause. From somewhere comes a catcall, a boo. Everyone on the island knows about the fiasco that was Operation Pot-Snatch.

"Honk Gilmore's barn, you say."

A one-handed roll, a lick of the tongue, and the cigarette is lit. "Yeah, they need a warrant to come on private property. Best advice you ever gave me."

The Highlanders' skirling discourages conversation for a while. The band is wet but game, playing "Scotland the Brave." Three pipers, two drummers, and, bizarrely, an accordionist: none other than Kurt Zoller, who looks as ill fit out in a kilt as in his police uniform. Zoller glances quickly at Arthur and Stoney, then away.

Arthur hears the words "Nazi Dognapper," but the rest of Stoney's shouted expletive is drowned in the triumphant squeals of the pipe band. Stoney is still carrying on about Zoller when that abates. "I'm gonna get his wormy ass, man."

Arthur has his own agenda. "The Fargo."

"What?"

"The Fargo. Should I assume not a lot of work has gone into it?"

Stoney expels a billow of smoke. "Well, with one thing and another, I ain't been able to get to the city for them brake linings."

"You said it was leaking brake fluid."

"That too."

The Business Owners Association's float is dominated by a giant papier-mâché baseball bat that has drooped in the rain and now resembles a penis struggling to sustain an erection. There are poster-sized photos of the Easy Pieces and a banner: "If you believe, they will come." The display gets a cheer.

"I don't want that truck used to move marijuana."

"I am pained to hear you infer such a thing, sire."

The next float features the Fensom Family Singers, and their overly spirited rendition of "Take Me Out to the Ball Game." Then comes a truck-pulled trailer with the Easy Pieces in team uniforms, throwing candy kisses to the several dozen people lining the route.

"Anyway, I seen you been enjoying that luxury craft over there." The Cadillac, parked by the thrift store. "Suits you, counsellor. Nobody wants to see Dog's attorney driving to court in a junk pile. What kind of alibi do you figure we can come up with for him?" He smokes, waiting for a response. "I mean, man, he's been in the lockup on Saltspring for two days, eh?"

Arthur has done what he can for Dog; he has urged the Legal Aid Society to retain experienced counsel. Arthur doesn't do drug cases. He is retired. He has more immediate things on his mind. Like Brian Pomeroy, due at eight-forty on a milk run.

Here comes Tildy Sears, seated in the back of an open convertible, waving like an imperial monarch to her loving subjects. Garibaldi has been thirsting for a hero and is pulling out the stops for her. Her business, Garibaldi Home Security, is booming.

Stoney keeps pressing. "He's spending the weekend in a cell, probably full of perverts, man. He ain't going before a judge until Monday. Dog don't know how to ask for bail. He's naive, he could plead guilty because he thinks it's the right thing to do."

"Be assured, Stoney, that I shall not be undertaking the defence of your sidekick. He'll likely be released on his own recognizance on Monday. In the meantime, he has the rest of the weekend to dry out from a drug-and-alcohol spree." Arthur raises his hand to check the expected protest. "As a witness to his arrest, I cannot act for him."

Stoney looks at him bug-eyed, unbelieving. "That ain't the Arthur Beauchamp we all know, relying on a technicality. I thought you'd leap at the chance. This island's gonna be in a uproar; Dog is loved by all. He helps the old folks, chops their wood, mows their lawns, fixes things. This is an uplifting human drama, the generous, hard-working little midget up against the hulking monsters of the state, and only one superhero can save him." A pause to catch his breath. "You're our vehicle of revenge against Kurt Zoller, man. He's spreading rumours a lady cop felt you up during a search. It's time to topple him, like they did to them Arab dictators."

"Well, I must get back. I have an important review to write. Then an old friend is coming by for a stay." The parade over, people are dispersing, cars pulling out. Arthur strolls across the road to courtesy Caddie.

§

Saturday evening loads are generally light, so the *Queen of Prince George* is only a few minutes late, sliding into the dock with a jarring bump. It is growing dark and is drizzling again, so Arthur waits in his car while the ramp is lowered and the foot passengers disembark.

Brian Pomeroy has lost weight since Arthur last saw him — about three years ago — but looks wiry and strong, unbowed by his weighty rucksack. He's greying handsomely, still has his Mark Twain moustache but now wears glasses, wire rims. Long coat and bush hat, unlit cigarette in his hand.

He scans the vehicles in the picking-up line, zeroes in on the Cadillac DeVille, sets his pack in the back seat, and joins Arthur in the front. A gaunt, haunted look, one that has appealed to the nurturing needs of his many seducees. Intense eyes and clear, rapid-fire speech.

"I am here to save you, brother."

"From Randy Skyler? I'm dying to find out why." Arthur merges the Cadillac into the line of home-going traffic, glances at Brian, his sardonic smile. Arthur's hands are tight on the wheel as the traffic line crawls up Ferryboat Knoll.

"I'm not going to talk about it in a car that conjures images of Ronald Reagan and Maggie Thatcher. I need the right rustic ambience — a roaring fire with a hot toddy for me, a soothing cuppa for you. I calculate you've been sober twenty-five years. Let's hear it for 1987. I gave odds in the barristers' room you wouldn't last a month. I actually got action from a couple of your undying fans who believed faith trumps logic and reason. They took fifteen hundred skins off me."

A tale Brian has told before. His memory may not be sharp, but so far, Arthur has picked up no hint of the feared psychosis. Brian is just being as logorrheic as ever, a city version of the long-winded Fargo-napper. And likely just as high.

"I tried AA, but there were too many drunks," Brian says. "Confession does not come easily for me — I never know where to start. So for penance I am doing shit work for poor people, making barely enough jack to pay for a shack and a kayak, just sliding along in Haida Gwaii. It's depressingly beautiful up there. The rain is so constant it's irrelevant. Mind if I smoke?"

"Go ahead. And what are you seeking up there?"

"Peace. Oneness."

"You won't find it on Garibaldi Island."

§

While Pomeroy unpacks in the back bedroom, Arthur builds a pyramid of kindling in the living room fireplace. The day's rain has left a chill in the air. On his return, Pomeroy pours himself a Scotch from the guest bar, then stares out the window at Niko and Yoki sitting around a fire, roasting wieners. "I don't imagine they'd be much use in a crisis," he says. "How's Margaret?"

"Excellent, but feeling embattled."

"Swimming with sharks does that to you. Brave woman. Saw her in a dot-com journal, she was looking hot. Some cocktail do. She was with your buddy Meyerson."

Hubbell's swearing-in as High Commissioner to Barbados. Arthur feels his stomach tighten. He fetches his tea from the kitchen and returns to find Brian flipping through the collection of CDs. He chooses something dense, the massive Mahler Seventh, then squats across from Arthur, who is having trouble getting the kindling going.

"Okay, I am about to repeat to you the words of a former client, said under the umbrella of solicitor-client privilege, about yet another former client who allegedly — if I may paraphrase the great A.R. Beauchamp, QC — sought orgiastic joy in the grisly murder of an innocent street clown." He suddenly gets up. "Oh, the book. Before I forget."

As Arthur waits for Pomeroy to return, he turns down a table lamp so he can better spy any furtive figures lurking outside. Just Niko and Yoki.

Pomeroy returns with a copy of *A Thirst for Justice*. "Wentworth gave me a moment in the spotlight in chapter eighteen, but I'm eclipsed by your gargantuan shadow." He hands Arthur a pen. "Just your signature, in case I have to sell it to keep from starving. Wentworth didn't pull any punches, did he? Good thing he didn't know about you and Mandy."

"Know what?"

He just smiles.

Mandy Pearl is also mentioned in chapter eighteen — "Death of a Stranger" is its title — as well as elsewhere in the book, as counsel against him on a couple of trials. Arthur hopes Brian isn't spreading base rumours about her — she's a distinguished barrister, en route to the bench.

Arthur scrawls his name on the title page, almost furiously. Brian is spinning out matters in the most annoying fashion, obviously relishing the drama, the slow drip, drip, drip of hints. It's as if he's acting out his own screenplay, deliberately ratcheting up the suspense.

"Mind if I smoke?" Brian perches by the fire, which is blazing at last, and lights up. "This isn't easy for me, Arthur, sharing a privileged communication. Rather unethical, don't you know?" He takes a sip of Scotch neat, makes a face. "Yeah, you're thinking: Pomeroy has the ethics of a pickpocket at a charity auction. Okay, but only outside working hours. In professional matters, I take some pride in my ethics. Also, if the Law Society gets wind of one more breach, I'll have earned enough points to lose my ticket."

"This is worse than water torture, Brian." Arthur's worry meter is spiking.

"To the point. You pissed Skyler off, and he swore that once he was out of the freezer he was going to track you down, and slit your throat. His words."

"Spoken when?"

"A few years ago. To a fellow inmate at Collins Bay, a professional recidivist who tested his luck out here on the coast after his release and had the bad fortune of getting nicked for a heist but the good fortune of hiring me as a lawyer. He walked. Paul 'Pig-Eyes' Burch, noted jewel thief."

Arthur vaguely remembers the name, from some news story or other. A mob hit?

"We had a beer after. He was in a good mood. The name of a common acquaintance came up. Back around 2008, he shared a cell with randy Randy, who, after twenty years in stir was still very emotional about things. Burch said he kept going on about how that fucking prick Beauchamp ruined his life by pulling a fast one in court. Once he was out, he'd track you down and kill you. The last thing you would see would be his smiling face. Stuff like that."

Arthur lets out a slow breath. The news is disturbing, but how serious could Skyler have been? Jailhouse chatter is often all about anger, complaints of injustice, vows of vengeance. Hyperbolic bravura. Venting. "You're suggesting I take this seriously?"

Brian shrugs. "Yeah, because Randy said much the same to me after he went down. I wanted to talk about the appeal. He wanted to talk about how he was going to carve out your gizzard to eat on toast."

Arthur feels his throat constrict. "And why did you never tell me this?"

"Solicitor-client privilege."

Mahler congests the parlour with orchestral gloom as Arthur tends to the fire, adding split alder, while Brian refills his whisky glass, lights another cigarette, and glances out the window at the flickering bonfire, Yoki and Niko with their wiener sticks. "Those gals look lonely." He checks his watch. "Nine-thirty. You mentioned a dance at the hall."

"I am not in a dancing mood."

"How can we not celebrate such an epic sporting triumph?" Brian has picked up the *Bleat* with its front-page photo of Tildy Sears being mobbed by her teammates. "Says here that Ms. Sears, more commonly described as 'our Tildy,' runs a home security business. Voila, our stars are aligned."

Arthur isn't listening, he's thumbing through Brian's copy of *Thirst*, chapter eighteen, "Death of a Stranger," jogging his memory with the details. Chumpy's sad dying declaration: *Holy mother, I done wrong.* The seven knife wounds. Manfred Unger's leap to his death. The surprise witness, young Wyacki, who never got to testify. No mention, thank God, of Inspector Honch Harrison's illegal entry into Skyler's apartment.

"A condition of Randy's parole is that his lawyer be kept advised, so this dweeb of a parole officer called. He doesn't seem much on top of it. He'll phone again Monday with details, but apparently Skyler hasn't had any lucrative job offers — surprise, surprise — and has elected outdoor work as a transition job, caretaking a park in Northern Ontario."

"And where is your jailhouse informant now, this Paul 'Pig-Eyes' Burch?"

"Enjoying everlasting peace. The competition took him out about sixteen months ago. It was in the papers. Hey, he honestly believed Skyler was serious about taking you down. He spent two months listening to his tirades from the bunk below."

"Twenty-five years is a long time to hold a grudge, Brian."

"Explicable, however, if it's become an obsession, nursed over the last quarter century into a classifiable disorder. A psychopathic obsessive-compulsive may soon be stalking Garibaldi Island while the object of his obsession relaxes by his cozy fire reading about the glory days of Rome."

"What exactly did Skyler say to you after his sentencing?"

"While you were being hustled by Mandy Pearl in Chez Forget — don't deny it, there were witnesses — randy Randy was ranting over how that pompous prick of a prosecutor had set a trap for him, had conned the jury, and if he ever got out you were going to buy it in a very messy way. As I say, your gizzard was mentioned."

Coincidentally, as Arthur leafs through the biography, he finds that avian organ mentioned in a quote from *For the Fun of It.* "I'll get you one day, Grodgins!" Lord Scarfe-Robbins cries. "I'll cut out your gizzard!" Add plagiarism to Skyler's sins. Again, Arthur wonders just how seriously he should take this. Here was a man reeling from a devastating verdict and indulging in a juvenile tantrum. In searching for someone to blame he quickly settled on the prosecutor. It was almost to be expected. But still calling for blood after twenty years? A little unusual.

"You may want to move to safer digs until things shake out. Ottawa is lovely in the fall."

"I shall not be going to Ottawa or anywhere. I'll not be frightened out of my home by some hobgoblin invented by an over-imaginative lawyer who trades his services for psilocybin mushrooms."

"You ever tried them?"

"Never have, nor will."

"Well, there's a bag of them in your freezer."

"I would rather not know that."

"A friend's coming over from Vancouver to pick them up."

How far this once fine lawyer has fallen. Dealing magic mushrooms. Yet he seems buoyant, full of energy and humour. An exotic Haida artist awaits his return. He's having fun writing some kind of screenplay. He is poor, but out of the rat race. Arthur is also out of the rat race but with substantial means. Why shouldn't he be even more at peace than Brian?

"If you're into mystic experiences, add some fungi to your tea. I might take a sample to the dance. By the way, Arthur, did you ever complete the transaction with Mandy?"

"What transaction?" He tries on an expression of bewilderment.

"Getting laid. She was going through men like a tractor mower after her divorce. A.R. Beauchamp was a real catch for her trophy case. Top shelf. Maybe you heard — she's going to the BC Supreme Court."

"She'll be a fine jurist."

"Here's your choice, Arthur, you can come with me to the dance and perform your role as respected island elder, or I'll take the Caddie and you can sit around with your Woofers and roast your weenies. We can get back to all the Skyler shit tomorrow. Maybe I'll invite Tildy over. We can make some plans to keep you alive."

"The keys are in the car."

"Meantime, to the shower, ho!" Brian strikes a mannered, hammy pose. "And thence to arm myself with a manly scent that hopefully will twitch the nostrils of the strikeout queen."

§

Arthur spends an hour in his club chair, reading and rereading the chapter called "Death of a Stranger." He is distracted occasionally by a rustle outside, or a snap of twig, but sees nothing from his window except leaves stirring in the breeze. His yard lights are on, and he wonders if that is wise. Maybe he should shut off all lights — why illuminate an intruder's way?

He has always taken pride in not locking his doors on carefree, innocent Garibaldi, and he'll be damned if he'll do it tonight — he's not going to surrender to his inner worrywart, to give in to irrational fear. Besides, he has his own alarm system: Homer, his border collie, who sleeps light and awakes alert, and two tough, noisy geese, which patrol the farmyard.

But he doesn't have the Woofers. Brian stopped at their bonfire and offered to run them up to the dance. Niko and Yoki hesitated, giggled, succumbed.

The dance will also miss another of the island's iconic figures: Dog, who is in the Saltspring hoosegow. *The little midget up against the hulking monsters of the state.* Arthur refuses to entertain regrets over having rebuffed Stoney's plea.

Maybe he ought to have gone to the dance. Surrounded himself with friends, protectors . . .

As he makes his evening cup of tea, he laughs at himself for being silly. Skyler was released less than a week ago, and from a prison in faraway Ontario. He will not appear on Garibaldi Island out of the blue.

Arthur still can't accept that Skyler's hunger for revenge has not abated. Or that he would take any risks. Skyler might be psychopathic, but he's not stupid.

On the other hand, he might have read *Thirst for Justice* and remembered why he hated Arthur: for exposing the charade of the masculine heartthrob. "You are frigid!" "You sought sexual fulfilment in grisly murder!" Yes, that might have rekindled his enmity.

He decides that the negligible chance of confronting Randy Skyler tonight is taking up too much of his worry quota. He will tuck that one away until he faces present danger — for instance, if Skyler doesn't show up for his park job. A more legitimate source of immediate concern is the presence of psilocybes in his fridge. Brian could drop a loose word at the dance, and some stoner might slip in and nick them. Yes, it is probably wise to lock the house. Just tonight.

SUNDAY, SEPTEMBER 23

Arthur wakes up in a sweat to the smells of coffee and frying bacon. Nine-thirty. The nightmare that is slipping away featured him in clown gear, a bright red nose and long, floppy shoes as he was being pursued by a knife-wielding ogre. As Arthur desperately flapped his way to the Fargo, the truck kept receding into the distance . . .

The dream was the feature event of a fitful night, its deep silence punctuated by the wild whoops of a barred owl, driving him awake at midnight to listen a long while to the creaks and groans of this old house, trying to distinguish the sound of footfalls on the stairs.

He creaks and groans himself as he rises from his bed to look out his dormer window. The courtesy Cadillac is below, in the driveway, but he didn't hear Brian and the girls return from the dance.

He pulls on a robe and goes downstairs to find Brian flipping pancakes. Tousled, still in yesterday's clothes, but looking merry. "Smart move, Arturo, locking the doors, except you left a side window open. He'd have found his way in easily. Then you're trapped upstairs, and you'd have to jump out the window and end up crashing through the veranda roof, injured and helpless as he raises the knife for the final thrust."

Grinning. Why does he take such delight in causing Arthur the creeps? "Have you slept at all, Brian?"

"The Avenger never sleeps." He pours Arthur a coffee. "Hell of a party. Things got kind of psychedelic."

"I'd like you to get rid of those mushrooms in the fridge." He is both repelled by and drawn to them. What magical, mystical experiences do they offer, how safe are they, does one throw up . . . ?

"Soon. Unless my guy doesn't show. If he doesn't, I may ask you — don't be afraid to say no — to front me a few bills for a flight home day after tomorrow. I've got a brainsucker next week: aboriginal issue, fishing rights."

"Happy to pay for your ticket."

"Maybe you should come up there too. Hide out on Haida Gwaii. You sure you want to stick around this lonely outpost?"

Arthur picked up his tabby, who was purring at his legs. "This is our home, isn't it, Underfoot? Our castle. We will defend it against Mr. Pomeroy's phantasmagorical visitants."

"Okay, it's on to Plan B. How competent are the local police?"

"Not very."

"Don't suppose you have a gun."

"Shotgun in the basement."

"Ever use it?"

"No."

"Take a plate, grab some flaps. Hey, don't you look gorgeous in the morning? Six foot two, eyes of blue."

Arthur pauses while filling his plate, and looks oddly at Brian, then turns to see Tildy Sears yawning her way from the back bedroom, in rumpled party clothes — Arthur has never seen her in a dress before. "Morning, Mr. Beauchamp." She touches Brian's handsome, haggard face, kisses him lightly. "Morning, you."

Arthur sits at the kitchen table and eats, feeling as awkward as this unlikely pair seem at ease. He wonders if Brian is aware she has a boyfriend, known as Moose, a seaman far away on the cold North

Pacific. But last night the town fathers gave her the keys to Garibaldi, and she must have assumed they came with the right to mate with whomever she wished on this special night. Apparently she couldn't resist the glib dissolute with the psilocybes.

She and Brian appear to be coming down from a psychedelic high; they're giggling hoarsely about the night's comic interludes. Apparently Zoller was about to drive home when he noticed someone had spray-painted "FREE DOG!" on the Hummer's hood. Leaving the motor running, he charged into the hall, seeking paint-stained culprits, zoning in on Stoney, who welcomed him with a grin and clean hands. When Zoller returned outside, the Hummer was gone.

Tildy sits by Arthur, whispers, "Moose doesn't have to know about this, eh?"

"No, he surely doesn't." Tildy has been known to play about when Moose is at sea. He, however, does not believe in open relationships. Noses have been broken, and eyes blackened, of those who have dared to sample her charms.

She nudges Arthur playfully, attacks her pancakes, talking between mouthfuls. "Brian told me all about it, Mr. Beauchamp. About the killer who's coming to get you. Too weird. I mean, totally."

"Yes, totally." So much for the hallowed solicitor-client privilege.

"So the first thing we're gonna do is rig up an alarm system, with, like, whatever — sensors, motion detectors, cameras, battery backup. I got just the setup, scored it from Mookie Schloss. Remember, her old man kept trying to sneak back into the house? Now that they're reconciled, I got it cheap. It's like beyond cool, the kind movie stars use for their mansions."

"Good, we don't want something hokey." Brian has joined them. "I explained to Tildy you're prepared to shell out for this job. We worked out a security plan with the Woofers. Niko will do the day shift, Yoki will do nights. One of them accompanies you wherever you go."

Arthur stifles his complaints — Pomeroy is fixated on his dubious scenario, a drugaholic's delusion. Installing alarms is overkill. Arthur is not going to be put in quarantine. He has a farm to run, a life to lead. But somehow he can't bring himself to disappoint Tildy, whose typical work, checking absent owners' houses, lacks the excitement offered by a lurking, cold-blooded murderer with revenge on his mind.

Breakfast over, Tildy and Brian do a reconnaissance of the house. Let them have their fun, no harm is being done. And given that the leader of a national party lives here (occasionally) it's quite reasonable that they add some security. Ought to have done it long ago.

Margaret will be home for Thanksgiving. How will he explain having Blunder Bay wired up like the Royal Mint? She abhors the very notion of a security state. Under cross-examination, will he be cornered into telling her about Randy Skyler, about his long-ago threats? Massively exaggerated by Brian, he would say. No, he will not disturb her over something so fanciful. She has more important things to worry about. The future of the planet.

He phoned Margaret yesterday to regale her about the showdown at the old quarry, his abortive arrest as Mr. Big, his groin search by a judo adept — all of which she met not with laughter but anxiety, as if she suspected his mind was starting to falter. She would be convinced of that were he to confide that a convicted thrill killer proposes to carve out his gizzard.

Arthur will tread water until Skyler's parole officer calls on Monday with the full report. Until then, he is not going to worry.

§

On his return from Sunday service, Arthur changes into rough wear to tackle a job over which he's been procrastinating: the reconstruction of one of the split-cedar snake fences that flank his driveway. It has been in disarray since Dog backed into it, a miscalculated U-turn.

Stoney had called out from the sidelines, "You got another few inches," and the fence went down like dominoes.

Arthur never uses nails when he builds a snake fence. It's a form of country art, laying those long, zigzagged cedar rails over uneven ground, using only God-given tools, his hands gloved against slivers. He surveys the task — a giant game of pick-up sticks. But it's a pleasant day: a sky of scattered cloud, and the country air is sweet, and the barn swallows are on the wing, fattening themselves on flies for the winter, and the tree frogs are merrily croaking. He bends to his work, hefting a bottom rail onto a rock base.

Stoney and Dog's failure to honour their pledge to repair the fence has not encouraged Arthur to aid in Dog's defence. But he feels pressure from the community. There were rumblings after the service, on the lawns on St. Mary's, about how poor Dog was being treated, how he wasn't getting any help. He'd done free chores for a lot of those folks, especially the elderly. Stoney spoke the truth: *Dog is loved by all.*

Relax, Arthur had told the congregants. Our beloved Dog will get bail on Monday. Any half-competent counsel will get him acquitted, given Kurt Zoller's clownish undercover skit as a Devil's High-Rider.

The issue has been further complicated by the kidnapping of Zoller's vehicle. It's either a prank or a futile hostage-taking. "Nigh impossible to hide a Day-Glo orange Hummer on this wee island," said Reverend Al.

For a while, Arthur becomes lost in the tasks of resurrecting his rustic fence, but he starts on hearing an engine coughing down Potters Road toward the driveway. A motorcycle appears. The spare, young driver pulls in by the house, removing his helmet, freeing a long ponytail. Brian comes out to greet him.

Arthur returns to his project, but sneaks looks, sees Brian go into the house and return with his bag of mushrooms. It is opened and inspected. Brian pulls out several, eats them, extends the bag to the buyer, who also samples a few. They sit on the steps for half an hour, and Brian extends his headphones. The buyer listens through them, smiling, a foot tapping to the beat as he scans the island-dotted sea. A few minutes later the ceremony is completed by the passing of a wad of bills.

After the stoned biker finally chugs back up the road, Brian strolls over, grinning. "I'm still in Zone One, seeking entry, knocking on the doors of perception. Meanwhile, if I can lend a hand . . ."

"It will be a particularly finicky task for one enduring mystic experiences."

Brian produces a small Ziploc bag. "I kept just enough for us. Teonanacatl, the divine mushroom of the Aztecs, whose horny artisans sculpted shrooms rising like erect schlongs from gods' heads. Our own Northwest golden top, *Psilocybe cubensis,* is also known to be holy, despite its excremental origins: the sacred mushroom of cow dung. Certifiably organic, by the way."

Arthur ignores the offered bag and listens mutely to Brian's chatter, his vaguely coherent assurances that Zone Two would bring novel perceptions of space, motion, time, colour, while Zone Three offers a "deep sense of oneness," whatever that might mean. As Brian rhapsodizes, Arthur restores the fence to its former handsomeness, five split cedars tall; it needs only to be braced at a tricky corner over a rainy-season rivulet.

Brian continues to ramble on, in his bemushroomed state, between draws from a cigarette: Arthur risks missing out on a chance to time-travel to the palaces and theatres of the Rome of Virgil and Cicero.

Finally, Brian wanders off to enjoy his deep sense of oneness on a bench overlooking the bay. He applauds as if at a performance as a pair of sandpipers whirrs by and violet-green swallows chitter and dive and soar. The blue sea, the forested islands, the distant, vast Olympic Range: how could perception of such beauty possibly be enhanced by a fungus that sprouts from cow dung? Or, for that matter, bull shit.

Arthur has to use a posthole digger for his brace pole, and works up a sweat excavating the baked soil of early autumn until Brian returns. Arthur assumes he has graduated to Zone Two or Three by now, but he looks bothered and glum.

"You went too far, old buddy, and you know it."

That seemed bitter, not to mention incomprehensible. "Too far?"

"Firing that shot at Skyler in your jury speech."

No one's buying it, Skyler. Arthur remembers saying something like that.

"You took your job too personally, bub. You violated the prosecutorial code of honour. You were wetting your pants to nail my guy, setting traps, hiding evidence, hiding your Michigan law student. Wyacki. I kept the transcripts. Read through them a few days ago and had a revelation. The bulls did an illegal sweep of Skyler's flat, didn't they? The late, great Honcho Harrison, who broke more laws than he ever enforced."

Arthur recalls the guilt he'd felt just knowing about it. An illegal trespass that, if disclosed, could have caused a mistrial. The shrooms may have altered Brian's mind in some way, but they hadn't dulled it. The jig was up.

"The only useful thing Honcho saw was a book about acting. I didn't use it. And a computer. He didn't even know how to turn it on."

"But you didn't disclose! You withheld material information! I'd have got the case thrown out!" He is shouting, but now he slumps, and his eyes dampen. "Sorry, Arthur, this trial's been with me for the last twenty-five years, I obsess over things like how you used a fucking English parlour mystery — a piece of fiction! — against him." Shouting again, mimicking Arthur: "'You were impotent!' It was all smoke and bluster, an accusation made of cotton candy, and the jury devoured it."

"The jury quickly and unanimously agreed Skyler was a liar. There is nothing you could have done about that."

Arthur picks up his tools and leads Brian back to the house. It's tea time. He wants this conversation to stop. It's about ancient matters. Brian has correctly diagnosed himself as obsessive. He won't let go.

"I kept up hope until I lost the appeal. The only relief I got is when they dumped on you. I was angry at you, angry at the verdict. But maybe I was searching for someone to blame other than myself."

In the Appeal Court, Brian denounced the excesses perpetrated by a rookie prosecutor who hadn't appreciated the historic role demanded of Her Majesty's fair and disinterested counsel. The three appeal judges affirmed that some of Arthur's tactics had been "a shade less than savoury," but found that any harm was minimal, and they unanimously dismissed the appeal.

"That case was the turning point of my life." Brian sits on the steps, still shifting between moods, morose now, staring at his hands. "My career never recovered from it. I got sucked into a downward spiral. All the drinking, drugs, the inconstancy . . . I lost Caroline's respect."

He's still rambling as they mount the steps to the veranda, where Arthur exchanges his workboots for hiking shoes. He shoulders a pack. Afternoon tea will wait.

"And then I lost Caroline totally. I cheated on her, yeah, even gave her the clap once. I deserved getting skinned in court. Couldn't keep up the alimony. I was spending a mint on pain relievers. Mostly, snow, blow, snot grass. Once you starting accepting retainers in kind from Cocaine Bill and Morphine Sue, it's over. Where are you going?"

"I'm about to enjoy a deep sense of oneness."

§

Halfway to Hopeless Bay, near the ferry turnoff, Arthur intuits that he's being followed. For a moment he feels clammy, but the sensation fades when he turns to see Niko a hundred paces away, hurrying toward him on her plump, short legs. He waits.

She's out of breath as she says, "Not to worry," a newly learned expression. "Not to worry, Niko is here." There's a whistle around her neck, a smart phone in her hand, for use in an emergency as a weapon. She seems to be affecting more courage than she feels.

As they walk, he tries to explain — in the basic English they employ — that any alarms rung by his visitor are false. Brian is a comedian, a storyteller, a writer of many failed fictions, and Arthur has decided to let him have his fun.

Niko seems unconvinced and swivels continually, behind, to left and right, like a Secret Service agent. "Very bad man, he say. Cut out . . . what is gizzard, please?"

Arthur tries to explain it's an imaginary organ unless one is a bird, a colloquialism for the stomach. She is all the more confused.

"Not to worry," he says. He hums the Worried Man tune. He can't help it. How does the next stanza go? "Twenty-nine links of chain around my leg . . ."

The General Store and Brig come into view as the road descends. A dozen vehicles are parked out front, including the RCMP van. Arthur gives Niko money for groceries and treats at the store and carries on up to the pub.

Ernst Pound is sitting at the bar. Kurt Zoller is wandering among the patrons, handing out flyers, presumably duplicates of the one tacked to the bulletin board picturing a shiny orange Hummer, its owner smiling from the driver's seat. "HAVE YOU SEEN THIS VEHICLE?"

Despite the heavy police presence, there's an illicit poker game out on the deck. Smoking is open and rampant. No one's afraid of Pound now — the author of Operation Pot-Snatch has no one's respect, including his own. He's off-duty anyway, in jeans and a ball cap, drinking beer. Zoller ventures to the deck with his leaflets, only to find himself getting ribbed by the boys.

Arthur drops some change into an honour box and retrieves a one-page weekend extra of the *Bleat*. A Nelson Forbish exclusive is headlined: "Drug Raid Backfires, Popular Local Busted." There was "widespread concern" that Mr. Dog Zbrinjkowitz was being held without bail "in retaliation for the botched raid." Zbrinjkowitz? A miracle if that was not misspelled. Farther down: "A militant pro-Dog faction is suspected in the mysterious disappearance of local law enforcer Kurt Zoller's Hummer."

Arthur sits on the stool beside Pound and signals to Emily LeMay that he'll have his regular: black tea with one-percent.

"I'm on strike," Pound says. "I'm a wreck. Don't blame me about Dog. He's Kurt's nab. I got nothing to do with it. Klostert is in a rage over that frigging freak show, he's pushing to get me transferred to where the sun don't shine from October to March. At least I'll be out of this festering snakepit."

"I don't know if you've heard, Ernst, but someone wants to kill me."

"It's just a mush-rumour." He tries to smile, but it's more of a grimace. "Get it? Mush-rumour. Mushroom rumour."

"I get it, Ernst. How did you hear?"

"The dance. There was this mouthy off-island dude passing around his produce like after-dinner mints. I'd have collared him, except it would have backfired on me like every frigging thing I've ever done on this island."

Arthur sips his tea, annoyed with Brian. He will make sure he's on that flight to Haida Gwaii on Tuesday.

"Tildy Sears was in thick with the shroom guy, her and her entire infield, all competing for his favours, and then she and her team came over to tell me how to do my job. They were tripping, I couldn't make hide or hair. A disgruntled former client is after you. You overcharged him, cheated him, got him wrongly convicted, drove his brother to suicide. One dame had a theory it's a psycho who escaped from the nut house. Another had you boffing the wife of a jealous husband. A serial killer. A thrill killer! That's a good one."

"That, unfortunately, is the official version of the rumour."

"Great. A thrill killer roaming about. Just what this island deserves.

It's bullshit. I told those girls to shut up and not get folks riled up."

"His name is Randolph Skyler. Call up his record. Better yet, read chapter eighteen of *Thirst for Justice*. I gave you a copy."

Pound shrugs, takes a swig of Alka-Seltzer, grimaces. "Edwina took it. Every frigging thing. She sneaked into the house while I was on Ponsonby. She and that shit from Telus. They must have had a moving van."

"At any rate, the report is highly exaggerated and totally unlikely. Based on a few petulant words spoken a quarter of a century ago, and supposedly repeated to a cell mate, a thief. Nevertheless . . ."

Pound has his own agenda. "Now we got Kurt's Hummer being held hostage. I'm not even going to ask you what you know about it."

Arthur gives up. He will talk business with Pound another time. Zoller is still out on the deck, firing back at his tormentors, rattling his handcuffs, a gesture that scares no one. Arthur, whose own beloved vehicle has been truck-napped multiple times, feels a morsel of empathy for him. But he'll not get dragged into it.

Emily, who is usually sunny but seems grumpy today, sets Pound up with another draft, then pushes the tip jar toward Arthur. "All proceeds to Dog's defence." She strides off. Feeling ridiculous, Arthur slips a twenty into the jar. That seems cheap, and he adds twenty more.

Zoller finally comes back inside, followed by Honk Gilmore, taunting him. "Anything happens, Kurt, we got your back. We may be a little slow getting there, is all."

"You want my opinion, Honk, you fellows are conspiring to obstruct justice. Tell them what the Criminal Code says, Arthur."

"Dog's in the can for what?" Honk yells. "A measly bag of seeds and sticks?"

Pound gets off his stool. "Easy, boys."

Honk rails on. "Kurt here sticks thirty bucks in his pocket and picks up a bag from the table, you call that dealing dope?"

Honk has more than a little expertise in dealing: he's a prosperous retired grower. Arthur surmises that Garibaldi's ragtag unit of law enforcers hasn't learned that he hosted the Potlatch at his farm.

Now Honk directs a cold look at Arthur, one easily read: here sits the great defender, consorting with persecutors of the innocent. "You always been a big hero to Dog. We expected more of you, man."

"I shecond the motion," Baldy Johanssen slurs, passing by on the way to the men's.

Arthur slaps the bar and stands. "I've had enough of this, gentlemen. I am formally and officially retired from the practice of law. I am a *farmer*. Get used to it. Tomorrow morning, Dog will be represented in court by a first-class counsel who will arrange for his release on minimal bail terms. You have my word on that."

The rebellion quelled, Arthur buys a round for the house and goes off to fetch Niko at the store.

§

Arthur whips up a blackberry smoothie before settling into his club chair for Margaret's regular Sunday evening call. Usually, she has unwound from a week in the House by then, but she's worked up tonight. "Things are going crazy here, Arthur. It's just been leaked that they're gutting the Species at Risk Act. This is a government without courage or conscience, sycophants to the energistas." The energy lobby.

He offers to join her on the barricades and spurs her on with occasional exclamations of support. Arthur's concerns pale against the loss of woodland caribou, of burrowing owls. He feels dwarfed by this bold, energetic woman of high conscience and noble causes. No wonder she's cooling on him. If she is. Is he just imagining that?

He realizes that he must not let the mush-rumour find its way to Ottawa. He has to call off Tildy and her security system, call off the Woofer bodyguards. How witless it was of him to have heeded an alarmist with a record of nervous breakdowns.

When Margaret asks how their gentle island fares, Arthur struggles for words. "Amid the usual turmoil, Brian Pomeroy has shown up. He has probably entered Zone Five by now." Arthur's guest is on the veranda, in a hammock, bundled up, with his laptop on his stomach, composing a scene, chuckling to himself.

"Zone Five? I suppose that means he's flying on something." Margaret knows him well — over the years, the Bad News Bear, as she calls him, has achieved Most Frequent Visitor status at Blunder Bay. "You sound a little strained. Have you been taking your supps?"

She has him on health food supplements. Sometimes he forgets and makes tasty smoothies instead. He says he's bursting with health, and tries to prove it with a vigorous account of the Dog and Hummer show, the rebukes suffered from fellow Garibaldians, the antics of Brian Pomeroy, his liaison with Tildy.

"What's the reason for his visit?"

Arthur buys time by loudly draining his smoothie. From the veranda, there's a burst of maniacal laughter. A comedy? Horror, more likely. "Friendly visit. He had some downtime. Leaves Tuesday. We're rehashing some of our old trials."

"Poor you. And poor Dog. He's such a gentle, generous character."

He quickly assures her, as he has assured the entire island, that Dog will be sprung tomorrow in Saltspring Provincial Court.

Since making his dramatic vow in the Brig, Arthur has persuaded the Legal Aid Society to send over a specialist, a drug defender. He has Reverend Al ready to testify to Dog's high standing in the community — Al will be on the early ferry to nearby Saltspring. The public's right to know will be enforced by Nelson Forbish of the *Bleat*.

"Meanwhile," he adds, "the orange monster remains lost."

"Far better for the environment if it stays lost. Don't repeat that."

They laugh, and chat a little more, and at the end, she says, "Thanks, I needed that." Her words make Arthur happy, yet when he hangs up, he feels let down, feels the distance between them. He wants her in bed with him this night. But of course that thought, that desire, makes him feel guilty. She is alone too. A woman of healthy sexual appetite, she may be suffering more than he, with his less active libido. How often has she been tempted?

There he goes again.

It's all due to Annabelle, who made him forever distrustful. He knew there'd been a few men — but eighteen? She must have been babbling drunk when she confessed all to Deborah. Eighteen! As his daughter related this heroic feat on a long-distance call from Melbourne, he sat numbed on a kitchen stool. Her chiropractor. Her accountant. A forensic shrink on Arthur's retainer. A busboy in Barcelona! Hubbell Meyerson . . . recently sworn in as High Commissioner to Barbados, with Margaret Blake as his guest, looking hot.

Arthur goes out into the starry night and does his tai chi.

MONDAY, SEPTEMBER 24

Wet and wild-haired, Brian grimaces as he emerges from bed and shower, finally, at a quarter to ten. "Crashed on re-entry," he says, pouring coffee with a shaky hand. "Revisited my fucked-up life for hours. Couldn't escape."

So much for Zone Five. He even looks like a bad trip. He's been eating poorly, and stands gaunt in cutoffs and a ragged message T-shirt, a Will Rogers saying: "Never slap a man who's chewing tobacco."

Arthur puts some toast on for him, warms the rest of the scrambled eggs, then passes him a note with the phone number of Irwin Jenkinsop, Skyler's parole officer. "I didn't say you were out of it, just out. He asked you to get back to him at your leisure. Lacking in his voice was a note of alarm. I have told Tildy to put matters on hold."

"That must have been a blow. I practically guaranteed her the job."

"Thus was she persuaded to bed with you?"

Brian jumps when the toaster pops. "I'm wrung out. Need to get down." He steps outside and lights a cigarette. Not nicotine but cannabis: Arthur can smell it, presumably an antidote to stressful re-entering.

Saltspring Provincial Court will be in session by now. Reverend

Al has promised to phone when Dog is out of custody. The laconic little man has joined Tildy Sears in the panoply of great Garibaldi heroes. Celebrations are planned. The Highlanders, ever eager for an occasion to perform, will pipe him off the afternoon ferry.

"Primo, gives a nice little uptick," Brian says on his return, snuffing the joint between carbon-stained fingers. "Got it off that Stoney dude, traded him for some fungi." He returns to his coffee, stirs in sugar, sips, plucks the portable phone from its cradle.

He connects quickly. "Yo, Irwin, sorry I was out. Always try to get in three clicks before breakfast. So, you got hold of that Skyler file?"

Arthur can't hear Jenkinsop, but assumes he's asking what has prompted Brian's inquiry.

"Okay, we got a situation. I'm his former lawyer, so ethically I can't say too much, except that he may be targeting the man who prosecuted him. I'm with him now. Arthur Beauchamp, QC." A long pause. "The same."

Brian clicks on the phone's speaker button, fills his plate, and sits and eats.

A sound of papers being shuffled. "Okay, Randolph Skyler. Walked out of Collins Bay on Thursday, September thirteenth. Took a bus to Toronto to see his dad. His parents are separated. She's in a retirement community in Arizona. I can confirm that Skyler is still in Toronto, but not for long — he's due to start his job Wednesday. That's up north, the Abitibi Conservation Area."

His job will be to manage the park over the fall and through the winter, keeping cross-country ski trails open, watching out for poachers. He'll be working from an isolated cabin at the mouth of a river, doing his rounds by foot, canoe, and, during the northland's seven-month winter, snowmobile. Skyler asked for outdoor work, Jenkinsop explains, said he wanted to get back in shape while finishing his master's degree by correspondence. "Then he plans to see what's available in the business world."

Brian spreads jam on his toast, waiting. More doesn't seem to be forthcoming. "Irwin, tell me this guy is not armed. Tell me that the usual terms of parole are in effect, especially the firearms prohibition."

An audible clearing of throat. "Well, uh, no, I think that was waived. Dangerous animals up there, and he has no criminal history involving guns. So, yep, he'll have a hunting rifle. They'll be giving him a safety training course. He did some hunting as a young man, I understand."

"Look, Irwin, I'm going to ask you to put your notes aside and give me your impressions of this guy. You've talked to him at least a few times, right? Did you pick up he might be holding a grudge?"

"He did some hard years in max. Learned to handle himself after some scuffles. Did a long turn in the hole. I'd say he was probably bitter, yeah. But then he underwent some behaviour changes, I gather. And they moved him to medium security, where he mellowed out. At least that's what he told the parole board."

"Did he show himself as angry or bitter?"

"He kept his thoughts to himself. With me, anyway."

"But not with others, maybe?"

"I remember seeing something . . ." Irwin stalls.

"Like what? There are psych reports, right?"

Brian was a skilled hand with reluctant witnesses, and hasn't lost his touch. Arthur hears more papers being shuffled. This parole officer seems pleasant enough, but not totally conversant with the file. Probably overworked, ministering to scores of troubled parolees newly on the street.

"Dr. Arnold Hawthorne. A shrink. Sorry, this is several pages long, tests, interview notes — let me flip through . . ."

Brian turns off the speaker, takes the phone out to the backyard, with Arthur following. Out comes a cigarette, tapped from the pack, caught between his teeth. "Irwin, why don't you just scan it and send it to me?"

Arthur gathers some objection is being taken to that.

"Okay, maybe I can walk you through it . . . Or just fax it, can you manage that? Yeah, just a minute." He covers the mouthpiece. "What's your fax? Shit, you don't have one."

Arthur hesitates, then writes down Abraham Makepeace's fax number.

§

Dutifully but sourly, Brian does the dishes, then lies down on the chesterfield with his laptop, leaving Arthur with the task of driving to the General Store to retrieve the fax. He has to do some shopping too. The bottle of malt whisky won't survive Brian's three-day visit.

The good news is that Skyler is in Ontario and will be staying there. Still, Brian found a way to make Skyler's choice of job — custodian of an empty tract of wilderness — seem sinister. "He could easily grab a flight out here, hop on the ferry, do the dirty deed, and hop back, and no one would notice he'd been gone."

Arthur is more concerned right now with those unremembered lines from Dr. Hawthorne's report. Before heading off to the General Store, he locates Niko in the garden's cucumber patch, and tells her she is relieved of guard duty — the bad guy everyone is worried about is three thousand miles away. She almost seems disappointed that the adventure is over.

As he hoists her basket of pickling cukes, the RCMP van rolls up the driveway, bearing Pound and Zoller, unwanted guests but somehow not unexpected. Zoller alights outside the barn. He is out of uniform, wearing the Day-Glo orange safety vest that he favours — it matches the Hummer. He hauls out a pole with a metal club duct-taped to one end and, armed with this weapon, enters the barn.

By the time Arthur deposits Niko's harvest by the kitchen door, Zoller has returned to the farmyard and is probing some blackberry brambles. Pound remains in the van, morosely watching him. He waves listlessly at Arthur, tilts some Alka-Selzer to his lips.

Now Zoller is orbiting the Cadillac DeVille, bending, examining the tires for tread, his awkward weapon precariously balanced on his shoulder. As Arthur approaches, he rises with a defiant look. "I tried Stoney's Pinto, but it broke down. It's a mute point, because Stoney said I could have this here vehicle for a preferred rate. I hope you got no awkward repercussions over it."

"What is his preferred rate?"

"He said I could have it for nothing."

"The keys are on the dashboard. Put that damn thing down."

"It's a metal detector, this here's a magnet." He lowers it.

"Do I take it my truck is ready?"

"I believe Stoney said words to that effect and that he would try to bring it around hisself."

His vagueness makes Arthur uneasy. "I'm astonished that you two are so chummy. I thought he might be on your list of suspects." Arthur has little doubt as to who is the brains behind Operation Hummer.

"Robert Stonewell isn't a person of interest. The exact time my vehicle got stole, he was inside the hall undergoing interrogation by yours truly, and my further inquiries have determined he neither aided nor abetted in his felony. In fact, he's at my beckon call by agreeing to be of assistance to the state by keeping an ear out and donating this means of transportation."

Zoller has succumbed to Stoney's machinations with staggering ease.

"I'm checking every inch of this island's thirty square miles." Zoller clicks his heels. "Permission to explore your property, sir."

"Make sure you close the gates."

Zoller takes off up the trail to the north pasture, where Yoki is working. Arthur wanders over to Ernst Pound, who apologizes for the intrusion. "I'm dropping him off here. I'm tired of driving the dimwit around."

He's buttoned his regimental shirt askew, and he smells of old sweat and gloom, but he seems relatively sober today, so Arthur offers him a succinct account of the Skyler threat, and the recent lessening of it. Pound listens with weary impatience.

"Just like I said, it's what the bull left in the meadow. That's all I get on this rock. It's game over, Arthur. I'm going to quit the Force. I've done eighteen years. All I ever wanted to be was a cop. It was my only dream." He looks about to cry. "I gave up trying to make corporal long ago."

Arthur quickly looks away so as not to see the poor fellow fumble for his dark glasses and a tissue. Zoller is halfway up the hill, poking his magnet into a thicket of broom, a hostile invader that the Woofers have been commanded to repel. Shy Yoki stands by, with clippers and a spade, as Zoller disappears into the thicket. She can't restrain a giggle when he comes out the other side with a rusted metal bucket dangling from his magnet.

Pound speaks in a croaking voice that builds in intensity. "You got to save me, Arthur. My super just sent me a letter warning it's the last straw, that tank of Kurt's getting boosted, my auxiliary constable's frigging car! Stolen from under our noses! I'm looking at a disciplinary proceeding, a suspension. I'm suicidal, my life's at stake." He sighs with a resonant tremolo. "You know what's going on, Arthur, everyone confides in you. I'm begging you to intervene, help us find his frigging Humvee!"

Arthur is tempted to trot out his old standby: *I want to help but am ethically bound not to.* He knows that's a stretch, but all his instincts tell him that trying to mediate this standoff would be like stepping into quicksand. Yet he pities Ernst Pound. "We'll talk about it on the way to the General Store, all right?"

§

They follow a crew cab into the store's parking lot, and Arthur quickly alights from the RCMP van, relieved to be free of the morose Mountie, regretting that his heart went soft, that he offered to mediate. Ernst wept his thanks.

Felicity Jones, shortstop for the Pieces and a chum of Tildy Sears, is among the work crew climbing out of the truck and heading up to the bar. She returns Arthur's greeting, then gathers her friends in a whispering huddle. Clearly, the story of the stalking killer is spreading, at Garibaldi warp speed. He will have to reveal all to Margaret before she gets a twisted version.

Entering the store, he checks to see if his cell phone is still on. It's nearing noon, and he hasn't heard from Reverend Al. Barring some procedural delay, Dog ought to be out by now, celebrating, hitting up Al to fund a six-pack for the ferry. Maybe the circuit judge was late getting to Saltspring. Maybe Al forgot Arthur's cell number.

Arthur rings Stoney, resignedly listens to his message: "You have reached Loco Motion, vehicle rentals, repairs, and twenty-four-hour taxi service." Arthur demands he pick up, and when ignored he announces, in a voice so loud that heads turn, that he is waiting at Hopeless Bay for his Fargo to be brought to him. "Otherwise I'm contacting an old client, known on the street as Cut-em-up Hymie."

As he picks his way through the grocery section, Wellness and Wholeness converge on him. "We think it's so brave," says Wellness, "that you decided to stay on the island." Wholeness urges him to turn up for their regular healing circle. "Sharing our anxieties with friends can bring peace and strength." Arthur tells them he appreciates their concern.

Shopping done, he lines up at the Canada Post outlet, studies a new flyer on the cork board. It demands to know why Dog has been denied his day in court, and warns that Garibaldi is becoming a police state. Below the text is a photo of the stubby little fellow holding a puppy. For the full story, supporters are asked to go to www.garibaldicommunitybulletinboard.ca/savedog.

Abraham Makepeace is involved in a complex special-delivery transaction. "It costs twice as much as regular and is just as slow, you want the truth."

"Just do it my way, and quit carping," says the combative island ancient, Winnie Gillicuddy. Probably another birthday gift for one of the centenarian's scores of descendants.

Makepeace grumbles, "Okay, make my day difficult," and begins the paperwork.

Winnie turns to Arthur. "Well, what's your excuse for letting Dog stay locked in the hoosegow? He hasn't finished chopping my winter wood, I'll have you know."

"I stand falsely accused, madam. They may be releasing him even as we speak."

"Damn fool government should legalize that shit."

When Arthur takes her place, it's four minutes past twelve, but Makepeace grants him a rare exception to his traditional noon-hour break. "Only because of your dire situation."

"*Fama crescit eundo.* The rumour grows as it goes. I am under no threat."

"That ain't the way I see it." He produces a few envelopes and a magazine, but fondles the fax awhile. "Couldn't help glancing over this when it came in. Appears you're dealing with a psychopathic killer. His rehab didn't take."

"Fine. Thank you. I'll take it now."

"Let me make sure these here pages are in order. Here, on the last page, this is what scares me. 'In brief, the subject' — I guess he'd be the sadistic killer you prosecuted — 'the subject claims that he is no longer angry and embittered, but his assurances do not ring sincere.'"

Arthur wrests the fax away, numbly walks out to the ramp to the Brig, and orders a bottle of malt whisky and a soothing black tea. "You look a little pale," says Emily LeMay. "Feeling guilty?"

About Dog, she means. Arthur bleakly studies the fundraising jar for Dog's defence. He adds another twenty, takes his tea to a table by the oceanside window, and reads Dr. Arnold Hawthorne's fax. Its appendix of qualifications states that he's an experienced doctor

— not of psychiatry, but psychology — who lectures at Queen's and specializes in antisocial personality disorders. He prepared this report for the parole board last year, before Skyler's release. The first few pages describe the standard tests: word association, completing sentences, interpreting images, the Rorschach.

Not unexpectedly, Skyler got straight A's on the Hare psychopathy checklist — for multitudinous traits: superficial charm, grandiosity, lack of remorse and empathy, pathological lying, need for stimulation, failure to accept responsibility for his actions. "Subject continues to deny any involvement in the death of Joyal Chumpy." An antisocial personality disorder of this type, Hawthorne warns, correlates strongly with a high risk of recidivism.

As Arthur is only too aware, Skyler earned his parole nevertheless, a mere six months after he was eligible.

In his concluding paragraphs, Hawthorne comments on a "remark made in passing" by Skyler about "some unfinished business." Arthur takes a deep gulp of his tea, reads on: "When pressed about particulars, he reacted as if confused, then said he'd been joking. However, his words were spoken in the context of his trial and conviction. They suggest he may be prey to an obsession of some kind."

Arthur sees that Tildy Sears has joined Felicity Jones and her beer-quaffing workmates. He catches her eye, and gestures her over — he hasn't the strength to rise himself.

"Ah, Tildy, just the one I wanted to see. I've had some second thoughts about that security system the stars use."

§

Driving him home in her banged-up Jeep, Tildy detours to Evergreen Estates and stops at the Pan-Abode she shares with Moose when he's on shore leave. As she alights, she wags a finger at him.

"You totally ain't going to say nothing, eh?"

She has asked him twice. As if the whole island doesn't know about her dalliance with Brian, who, luckily for him, will be long gone when Moose, a heavily tattooed former amateur boxer, returns from the cold north seas.

"I would not compromise a lady."

"Whatever," she says, a word of a myriad uses. She picks up a few boxes of electronic gear, and when they're under way again Arthur dimly hears, obscured by rattling doors and sonic booms from the exhaust, a familiar, distant tune.

"Too weird," Tildy says, in obvious reference to his ring tone. As he digs into his pack for his phone, she mockingly sings, "Twinkle, twinkle, little star, how I wonder what you are."

He hollers a hello to Reverend Al, hears his strained, doomful voice, only a few words making it through the racket of the Jeep: "idiot," "screwed up," "pissed off."

Tildy pulls into the Shewfelts' driveway. In the quiet shelter of their pruned hedges and under the watch of their garden gnomes Arthur steels himself and says, "Please give me that again, Al. Calmly."

"I'm trying to be calm, damn it! Dog's been screwed by his counsel, some supposed big Vancouver name. He didn't show, didn't call. The judge waited until noon, when word finally came in that this joker missed the ferry because he'd been hauled over for speeding. Then the judge, who's a nincompoop —"

"Careful, Al. Are there any reporters in range?"

"Just Forbish." To whom he calls out a proposed headline: "'Local Do-gooder Framed in Travesty of Justice.' The damn judge wouldn't let me speak."

Provincial Judge Eddie Hayward is better known as Haywire. The good reverend had sought to intervene, to speak up for Dog, but Hayward announced he couldn't "hear" him: a term of art favoured by sticklers of rules.

"He was saying you have no standing in court. Were you a lawyer, he would not have been so deaf."

The judge then told Dog he could speak for himself, and the shy little fellow apparently froze. Hayward was in a cranky mood, and took it out on Dog for his counsel's negligence by remanding him in custody for three more days. That was after the Crown counsel claimed to have information that Dog was part of a major trafficking ring between the islands and the mainland.

Al didn't get the name of this brazen prosecutor, but her wild accusation has Arthur in a sputtering dither. He feels somehow to blame for matters going so awry.

"Anyway, Dog got bumped over to Thursday — on Garibaldi."

The last Thursday of the month: Haywire's regular Garibaldi day, mostly traffic tickets and small claims. Al identifies the defence counsel as B.J. Bingham, whose secretary claimed vaguely he was "currently unavailable."

Arthur knows him. Ballentine J. Bingham, big in name only. A garrulous hairy ape, a stoner, the go-to counsel for the soft drug trade, but hardly a leading light of the defence bar. Maybe he was on speed when he was pulled over. Arthur will have a word with the Legal Aid Society about this.

What else could go wrong today? It's said that bad news comes in triplet.

As if in response, to fill the quota, a vehicle appears over the brow of Shewfelts' Hill. It's Arthur's Fargo, its bed piled high with black dirt or manure. The engine gives off a happy, well-tuned sound and the brakes hold as it slows for the final downhill curve before accelerating on the flat. Stoney is at the wheel of the smoke-filled cab — from what Arthur can make out he looks distracted, upset, so it's likely he heard about Dog's setback. Roaring past, he's oblivious to Arthur's attempt to wave him down.

He considers urging Tildy to take up pursuit, but sighs in defeat. "Let's carry on."

"Twinkle, twinkle," she sings.

§

Brian is in the kitchen, at the sink, cleaning Dungeness crabs so freshly caught their limbs are still trembling.

"Where did those come from?" Arthur doesn't hide his bearish mood as he puts groceries away.

"The planet may be going to shit, but Nature still provides from her pillaged loins. While putting about in your runabout, I retrieved four of these fine fat fellows from your traps. Yoki and Niko will share two of them."

"I haven't set any traps."

"They were out in your bay."

"I don't own the bay."

"My bad. Poached crab would be apropos, but I've already started the barbie."

Heat is shimmering the air above the brick barbecue by the picnic table, on which dishes and cutlery are arrayed. The sun is weakening, and there's a late afternoon chill, so Arthur is glad to see a wood fire in the pit. He must remember to make amends to island crabber Gomer Goulet, an apology and a bottle of rum.

"You don't seem too happy, Arthur. I detect an uncharacteristic testiness."

Arthur passes him the fax, and after dispersing his purchases goes into the living room, where Tildy has spread out her supplies: tools, wiring, cameras, motion detectors, a fearsome-looking siren, like a small tuba. When triggered, Tildy explains, the system will call 911.

She is muttering, trying to decipher a manual. "Warning. Battery must not be exposed to rain. What battery? Okay, forgot the battery." She promises to return with it, and heads off.

Arthur dials and listens again to the recorded message from Stoney's round-the-clock taxi service. He frets about how to get Brian to the morning ferry. He won't be sorry to say goodbye to his caustic guest with his unnerving alarms.

He finds Brian outside, by the barbecue, sampling the newly bought Glenlivet as he squints over the psychologist's report. Finally, he hands it to Arthur.

"No need to grovel in apology for having doubted me." Brian throws the two crabs on the grill. "We'll know the worst on Wednesday if Skyler doesn't turn up for work. But I suspect he'll wait awhile, try to lull you into a state of unguarded passivity."

Arthur again wonders why Brian seems intent on taunting him. Has he held this grudge for twenty-five years? *I was angry at you, angry at the verdict.* Does he honestly blame Arthur for his own law career going downhill? Or is his behaviour just his way of working through the creative process — he has confided he's cranking out a horror script.

Breaking through the fog of his worry comes a familiar engine hum. Arthur's Fargo magically reappears, purring down the driveway, coming home.

"Forgot to mention, Stoney came by earlier. He wants your professional opinion as to whether there's any chance of Dog getting out of jail in his lifetime. You really ought to get off your heinie and do something about that, Arthur."

The truck pulls up close enough for Arthur to confirm that the payload is well-composted manure, dark and rich with a healthy smell. Stoney fishes out a few cans of beer and joins them, looking grumpy, his jacket open over a crude message T-shirt stencilled with "Save Dog."

Stoney takes a peek at the crabs on the grill, accepts a cigarette from Brian, blows a smoke ring into the still air. "Maybe you wanna call off Cut-em-up Hymie."

"A jest."

"What hurts is that I wasn't going to charge you a dime for this life-saving job on them suicide brakes. No strings attached. Perish the thought I'd petition you to be of similar charitable mind by giving services in kind to the Free Dog Coalition."

"Well, let's talk about Dog."

He sniffs. "What's to talk about? Arthur Beauchamp don't

handle two-bit cases where a guy who helps old ladies and wouldn't hurt a mosquito is framed for running an international dope trafficking cartel."

"Where did you hear that?"

"Nelson Forbish. That's what some bloodthirsty lady prosecutor told the judge."

"I am one with the Free Dog Coalition, brother," Brian says. He restrains Stoney from opening a beer, pours him a generous dollop of the Glenlivet.

Stoney salutes the Fargo with his tumbler. "She's all yours, counsellor. You may want to give her a fill-up on account of I drove all over the island looking for you. If it was someone else than Garibaldi's most respected and trusted dignitary, I'd say you been giving me and Dog the old runaround."

Arthur affects nonchalance as he strolls to the Fargo, checks for the key — it's in the ignition, on a ring with a designer roach clip, its pincers like protruding teeth. He retrieves and pockets it. There are two boxes of "Save Dog" T-shirts in the cab.

"Grab a couple of them for you and Mr. Pomeroy here," Stoney calls. "Only twenty-five bucks each, I eat the GST. By the way, that's pure organic manure back there, two yards of it, a little gift the boys chipped in for your gardening pleasure. No obligation."

Arthur hides his irritation at this high-pressure pitch, remaining silent as Brian sets on the table a pot of garlic butter and a tray with the crabs, then fetches an extra plate for Stoney, who sits.

Arthur sighs as he lowers himself onto the bench beside him. "We can get this solved very quickly."

"I ain't dealing with the enemy."

"Stoney, despite my better instincts, I have long served as your legal adviser. And I have never failed you, have I?"

"No way, Arthur, I ain't going to help you find his crummy Hummer. Not till Dog is on the street, man. I got to respect the wishes of the Coalition."

"Pound won't press charges if Zoller gets it back."

"Dog's doing time for doing crap! He didn't even have no weed to sell, he had to borrow some of mine. Thirty a lid, leftover shake, outer leaves, you could smoke it until it's blowing out your ass and you couldn't get high. He was so hammered I bet he don't even remember being at the quarry. Where'd they find that peckerhead lawyer? Never even seen Dog, ain't shown up in court once."

No more trials, Arthur vowed, no courtrooms, nevermore. But his escape routes are closing as fast as his resolve is crumbling.

Brian raises his glass. "To Dog!"

"To Dog!" cries Stoney, raising his.

Arthur, without a glass, raises his hands in surrender. "To Dog!"

THURSDAY, SEPTEMBER 27

"Ten years!" thunders the judge, and Arthur rises to protest as Dog is dragged shackled from the court. But though Arthur's mouth is moving, his larynx straining, his eyeballs bulging, no words flow from his lips. The wild-haired judge breaks the deathly silence. "I can't hear you," he yells. "I can't hear you!"

Arthur almost levitates from bed on being awakened by a deafening clamour from downstairs. Still in the fog of sleep, he tries not to believe that a bomb has gone off in the courtroom of his dream, setting off fire sirens.

He scrambles from the room in his pyjamas, with pillows pressed to his ears, to see, from the stairs, Tildy Sears desperately seeking an off-switch, a wet spill of coffee on her shirt. Shiftless and Underfoot collide in the cat door while trying to escape.

The siren is going through cycles, like a car alarm, with ear-splitting whoops. The Woofers race in just as Tildy finds a solution in her manual, a master code she punches into a small keypad. The silence is spectacular in its suddenness, though broken by clucking and cackling and honking from the fowl outside, and Homer's frightened barking. Arthur finally dares to descend.

Tildy tries to make a joke of it. "That'll scare him off, eh?"

She's been here two days, setting up this supposedly foolproof system. Arthur isn't sure if he'd rather be murdered in his sleep than hear that din again. "Maybe you can find a way to tone it down, Tildy."

"No problem."

Arthur isn't reassured by a phrase invariably used by Garibaldi tradespersons for head-scratching setbacks.

Niko and Yoki wander about, examining the system, shaking their heads, and exchanging telling glances. They'll soon be returning to their electronics college in Japan. The keypad and monitor may seem archaic to them. Everybody seems to be into computer electronics except Arthur, who almost proudly admits he hasn't graduated into the twenty-first century. "Try twentieth," Margaret said.

Tildy screws up her face at the manual. "I don't think this was translated real good from its original Japanese or whatever. Okay, siren can be set for a maximum six K radius hearing distance. Guess the last user must've done that. Whatever."

She answers her cell, then announces that the Free Dog Coalition is planning a rally. She hurries off to her Jeep.

After Niko and Yoki head out to calm the livestock, Arthur sits down to his morning oatmeal. It is nine o'clock. Garibaldi Provincial Court won't get going until the inter-island ferry pulls in around mid-morning. Arthur is thankful he's facing only a bail hearing and an adjournment — he hasn't slept much or well.

His rude awakening has aggravated the tension he's under — he's more unsettled than at any time in the last, worry-rich several days. Did Skyler show up for work yesterday or not? Why hasn't Brian answered his calls? Nary a whisper from him since he left two days ago.

Meanwhile, Arthur must re-earn the respect of his fellow islanders by freeing Dog from the clink.

He is nursing his wounds after a bad start yesterday with the prosecutor, Ms. Renee Vickers. Before calling her, he nosed around for a dossier on her. The consensus: she's young, bright, and tricky. One source, who lost a spousal assault to Vickers, claimed she has a feminist chip on her shoulder. A second informant, who lost a hit-and-run to her, called her a scalp collector, warning Arthur she'll be out to hang his on a long pole.

The Attorney-General recently seconded Vickers to serve with Judge Hayward's travelling circus on the Gulf Islands. Arthur was not able to reach her until yesterday, on her cell, and she was short with him, claiming she was burdened, between trials, and unwilling to confer while B.J. Bingham was on the record.

Arthur persisted, stung by her brisk tone, with a complaint about her preposterous theory that his client was involved in a major trafficking ring.

"For your information, Mr. Beauchamp, and I have very *good* information, an annual event occurs on your island called a Potlatch, at which mainland exporters make bulk buys of prime bud. As such, it is alleged that Mr. Dogmar Zbrink . . . How do you say that?"

"We just call him Dog."

"Well, Mr. Dog was aiding a consortium of high-end drug dealers by luring authorities away from the real Potlatch. Some of these dealers have major international connections. I take this case very seriously."

"Who gave you your very good information?"

"You know very well I can't divulge that."

"As a friendly gesture, Ms. Vickers, let me warn you that Kurt Zoller has a tendency to blow things massively out of proportion. I shall see you tomorrow morning. Thank you for taking my call."

The snip. Did she have no idea whom she was talking to? This was supposed to be a simple case. That officious young know-it-all clearly won't be open to dropping charges; the trial will be a contest for his scalp.

§

After dressing in clothes retrieved from a mothball-reeking wardrobe
— black suit, white shirt, blue tie — Arthur heads for his Fargo
and finds Yoki sitting on a hay bale in the back — the manure was
shovelled out yesterday. Niko climbs in beside him, wearing a Free
Dog T-shirt. She is excited about seeing a Canadian court in action.

"Jury will say not guilty," she confidently predicts.

"I'm afraid we won't have a jury for this piddling case." In
lowly Provincial Court. He's back where he started fifty years ago,
defending junkies, drunks, and hookers. Now, in 2012, it's a beer-
swilling pothead.

"What is piddling? Like making pee?"

"Like making pee."

"Twinkle, Twinkle," goes his cell as he takes the turn up Breadloaf
Hill, and he stops on the narrow shoulder. It's Pomeroy, finally. "Can't
talk long, I'm on the highway to Skidegate, trying to pass a logging
truck. Thought you might be worried, so here's a heads-up. Our
barely competent parole guy finally connected with someone from
that godforsaken tract of park reserve where Skyler's supposed to
start working."

"And?"

"Just a sec while I take that sucker." A sound of accelerating
engine as he launches into song: "Mine eyes have seen the glory of
the coming of the Lord."

"And?"

"You don't want to hear this, Arthur."

"Actually, I do."

"Oh, all right — here's the startling twist — he showed up! On
time. Wednesday morning. For a two-week training course in their
office. Glory, glory, hallelujah! Over and out."

For a moment, Arthur is irked by Brian's typically flip manner
of squeezing out every molecule of suspense, even with good
news. But now his relief is palpable. He can focus on taking on, to
quote Stoney, "the hulking monsters of the state." In particular, the

bloodthirsty Ms. Renee Vickers.

While parked, the Fargo has been overtaken by several battered island vehicles and a big convertible filled with Easy Pieces, including star chucker Tildy Sears. Arthur can't pull back into the traffic until Stoney races by in his flatbed, several protestors in the back. The Free Dog Coalition, most of them habitués of the Brig pub.

Atop the hill is the Community Hall, a once-a-month makeshift courthouse. The washroom is currently out of commission, and there's already a lineup at a portable toilet set up, too prominently — as if for the view — on the ridge overlooking Evergreen Estates and the far fields and forests.

Arthur and his entourage join about sixty Garibaldians milling around the grassy mesa, waiting for the circuit court staff to show up. Stoney is already in action, leafleting and hawking T-shirts, getting resistance. He's dropped the price to twenty.

Nelson Forbish waddles about with a bag of chips and his camera, which he aims at Arthur. "Look confident, please." Picture taken, he discloses he's switching his allegiance from Tildy Sears. The *Bleat* is about to endorse Dog's pro bono counsel for Garibaldian of the Year, a tribute Arthur recoils from — it means being invited to all sorts of community events; he came to Garibaldi seeking peace.

Kurt Zoller is standing by his borrowed Cadillac with a small knot of supporters: a couple of his accordion students, a few members of causes he spearheads, the Crime-Stoppers Club, and Bust the Island Trust.

Though Zoller is only a volunteer in the RCMP auxiliary, he is fully though baggily uniformed for this momentous occasion. He looks up from a much-thumbed statute book, sees Arthur smiling at him, and nods appreciatively, observing that he too is wearing his best. He abandons his support group to shake his hand.

"Before we get going on this trial, Arthur, let's agree it's nothing personal, even though we're on opposite sides."

"You, of course, are on the side of law and order and decency."

"Exactly right."

"Then I must be on the side of crime, chaos, and corruption."

"I wouldn't go that far." He reflects. "Maybe a little bit. Anyway, I been boning up here on the Narcotic Control Act." He opens the book to a marker: "Now as I read this here, anyone convicted of trafficking in marijuana is liable to imprisonment for life."

Arthur won't distress him by explaining he's relying on a statute long repealed in favour of less draconian measures.

Zoller lowers his voice: "Life imprisonment seems a little harsh, so I'm thinking maybe we can nip this in the butt with a plea bargain, and get him out sooner. One condition, of course: I get my Hummer back."

"That's very kind of you, Kurt. I take it you're prepared for trial nonetheless."

"Well, me and the prosecutor lady already had a real good sit-down over this, so she's aware of some explosive international ramifications which maybe you ain't." He squares his shoulders. "I got this case down cold. You don't want to deal, fine. Kurt Zoller is ready when called."

Their attention is diverted to a caravan ascending Breadloaf Hill: an SUV with the judge and court staff; a red compact driven by a young red-headed woman of slight build — presumably Renee Vickers; a police cruiser bearing two officers; and Ernst Pound in his RCMP van with Dog in the back, both looking woeful.

A cheer startles Dog as he's escorted to the hall. He looks about, manages a helpless smile for Nelson Forbish's camera.

A final vehicle sweeps up the hill, a Porsche convertible with Ballentine J. Bingham, Esquire, at the wheel, counsel of record for the accused. Yesterday, Arthur left word with Bingham's secretary that her boss needn't bother appearing — but maybe he is showing up merely to collect his legal aid per diem.

Bingham emerges from his car sporting a cowboy belt and boots, a ponytail, and a whisk broom of a moustache. He greets Arthur by

235

twisting his extended hand into one of those raised, supposedly hip grips that Arthur detests.

"Arthur B., QC, long time. Heard you'd retired to some island paradise, wasn't sure where. Somebody gave me a copy of your bio, maybe I should've got around to reading it." He frowns as he gazes at the milling throng. "Is some kind of happening happening here?"

"The masses are in revolt."

He perks up. "You got some press covering this horseshit case?" He looks to his left, sees Forbish taking a shot of him, returns a broad smile.

"Free Dog T-shirts!" Stoney calls, holding one aloft. "Fifteen loons, get 'em while they last!"

Bingham retrieves his file from the car. "Who's Dog?"

"Your former client."

He peeks in his file. "Dogmar Zed . . . Hey, wait a minute, *former*? I got no notice. I put time into this case, bro. You can't just muscle —"

Ignoring his protests, Arthur leads him around the back, to the annex by the tool shed. Ernst Pound is muttering to himself, careworn, distracted, as he lets them in.

Dog rises wide-eyed from a chair, a hint of hope in his anxious smile. "Praise Jesus," he says, a soft command that startles Arthur — Dog isn't known to be either religious or ironic. He pats him on the shoulder. "Mrs. Gillicuddy wants you to finish splitting her winter wood today."

"Okay, Mr. Beauchamp."

"But we have to clear up a few technicalities first. Mr. Bingham here is on record as your counsel."

"Hey, buddy, sorry I was a little late getting to you. I do an exclusive practice in weed, brother, unlike Mr. Beauchamp here, and I figure we can make this a test case for freedom to smoke, man. Strike a blow for the right to blow one, hey? What do you say?"

"You're fired," Dog says.

By the time Arthur makes it into the hall, it's packed except for a seat reserved for the defence counsel: a rustic wooden chair with a wobbly leg that has him tilting to starboard. It feels ignominious to end his legal career in the lowest of the low courts, waiting in discomfort while a prosecutor young enough to be his granddaughter finishes a trivial trial — a continuation from last year, a hard-partying weekender who drove his car into the Hamiltons' roadside pumpkin stand. He suspects Renee Vickers called this case first as a way of making him cool his heels. A petite, pug-nosed freckle-face, she works quickly, methodically, confidently.

One can never tell what Eddie Hayward is thinking, but he likely mistrusts the defendant's claim that he burped while blowing into the breathalyzer, thus causing the reading of point one five. The judge is known as Haywire partly because he's wont to render decisions that don't make sense and partly because of his appearance: thick hair that repels comb or brush, wraparound glasses framing eyes that constantly dart, as if he were on alert for conspiracies.

He is backed up by his regular sheriff, clerk, and court reporter, all grinning as Vickers recalls the breath test operator to deny he ever saw, heard, or smelled a burp. Expert witness Charlie Jillings then opines that a burp wouldn't alter the result anyway. Arthur knows Corporal Jillings well, a blood-alcohol expert with a degree in pharmacology.

Arthur reviews the Crown particulars that Ballentine J. Bingham grumpily handed over before peeling back down Breadloaf Hill. Scribbled at the bottom of the third page is the figure ".23." Arthur finds himself gearing up, moving into courtroom mode, suppressing the concerns of the past few days.

After the pumpkin-stand terminator has been fined and banned from driving for a year, there's a break in the action. Arthur draws Charlie Jillings aside and asks him to stick around. He's not going anywhere anyway — the next ferry doesn't leave till four p.m.

Vickers, acting as if she has just now become aware of Arthur's presence, introduces herself. "How did you get rid of Bingham?" she asks brightly.

"I let him know that if he were to botch Dog's defence, the locals would hang him from the nearest maple tree. Our townsfolk are in high dudgeon, as you may have observed." There's no place to meet quietly in this busy building, so Arthur says, "Let's go for a stroll."

Outside the hall, they are watched intently by the two dozen Dog lovers who have followed them out, and by those in line at the portable outhouse. He steers her past it, up a hill, a five-minute stroll to a sturdy wooden bench carved with two decades of initials and hearts, and with a barrier-free view of the Salish Sea and beyond to the Olympic Mountains. The cliff face drops a hundred metres to a cluster of jagged rocks.

"We call this Lovers' Leap," Arthur says, "though none have ever been known to do so."

"How charming." Then it's right to business: "Mr. Beauchamp, the accused has no visible means of support, no family here, no roots, is known to drink to excess, so I'm going to oppose his release. Sorry."

Immediately, she has gotten his goat. He waves a sheaf of papers. "Ms Vickers, I have a score of testimonials. But I suggest we set aside the issue of bail. I should think you'd rather talk instead about pulling the plug on this mess. The local citizenry is out in force today in support of a fellow islander who is known for his unstinting dedication to helping those in need."

She seems to be trying not to smile as she stares out at the serene waters of the inlet, Ponsonby Island and its trail of islets.

He clears his throat and continues: "You surely won't want a lot of people, particularly those in high office, wondering why you didn't nail the coffin lid on this stinker before it got into the mainstream media. It's the kind of light-hearted pathos the public loves, a poor, generous soul under siege by the full power of the state."

She tries to smother a laugh, and he realizes he's been at his pompous worst, sounding like a relic from a century ago.

"I guess I can see why you wouldn't want a trial, Mr. Beauchamp. Splashing it all over the media that you got crotched by a female narc at the scene of the crime."

The graphic verb "crotched" is new to Arthur. He feels less embarrassment than irritation at her dig — obviously, the story of his humiliation at the old quarry has gone the rounds of the prosecution offices. This competitive scold is clearly itching to take on Arthur Beauchamp, a major test for the young scalp collector, to be delightedly shared with her comrades over a glass of chilled Pinot Grigio.

"Ms. Vickers, that incident is already a source of ribaldry locally. I don't give a hoot if the rest of the planet shares in the merriment. However, if you think it enhances your case, please run with it — though I suspect you're a better lawyer than that."

"Sorry, I was out of bounds. Or joking. Forget it." A shrug, as if she'd expected a richer sense of humour. "Mr. Beauchamp, I have no recourse but to go full speed ahead. We all know the situation: the arresting officer's vehicle has been stolen. He is determined to give no leeway."

"Madam, your arresting officer is a loose cannon. His claim that Dog was part of some vast international conspiracy is a myth of his own wild imagining, is vexatiously ill-founded, and unprovable to boot. You are wasting the public purse on going after small cheese. It's a picayune case!" His shout is heard by onlookers who have approached too closely. All but Stoney take a few steps back. He's brandishing a placard: "STOP THIS PERVERTION OF JUSTICE!!"

Vickers remains placid. "If your guy is such small cheese, why has he got A.R. Beauchamp as his lawyer?"

Arthur fears he's losing ground. He speaks of the reverberations on Garibaldi, the plea from Constable Pound to settle things down, the certainty that Zoller's Hummer will be restored to him once the charge is dropped.

Vickers takes umbrage. "I'm not going to be accused of bartering a dope trafficker's freedom for a car stolen from a cop. The Crown does not give in to hostage takers. I've prepared this case, I'm ready to go to trial on what I've got."

"Ms. Vickers, in the normal course of business, a trial will be many months away. Doubtless by then a bright and energetic counsel such as yourself will have moved on to greater things. I sense in you an eagerness to test my mettle, so let's see if you're up to it. Let us go to trial today."

Words fail her. She has been put on the spot, and pride will make her reluctant to turn tail and run. "Hey, I'm up for it — except I don't have all my witnesses, the drug analyst, the attending officers . . ."

"I shall admit the analysis of *Cannabis sativa*. I'll admit location, date, and time. None of the other officers witnessed the alleged transaction. Kurt Zoller is your whole case, all the rest is just cake decoration. And to top things off, Zoller is under the apprehension that the trial will be proceeding today. He's eager, and he'll never be better prepared."

She looks down, traces a finger along a carved heart on the seat, looks up, studies the view, gazes expressionlessly at the several dozen watchers, then more intently at Zoller, standing erect and determined among his little coterie of backers. She knows she has little to lose and a chance to fell a giant.

"Long as you can sell it to Haywire, game on."

§

When court resumes, Vickers runs through her remaining list: liquor and traffic violations resolved by guilty pleas, fines meted out, trial dates set, adjournments granted. Hayward is testy and distracted, scanning the crowd as if for troublemakers, regularly glancing out the window. Quite a few are still out there, mostly smokers.

Arthur is down on himself for having got the worst of the battle on Lovers' Leap. The woman is relentless, And now, having bluffed Vickers into agreeing to the quick trial, he feels unprepared. What if he were to lose? This tight little island would never forgive him.

Vickers calls Regina v. Zbrinjkowitz, and the prisoner is led from the back to a supportive murmur from the public seats. Hayward's darting eyes take in all the Free Dog T-shirts.

He acknowledges Arthur, though without apparent pleasure, wary of tricks and traps. When Arthur proposes they proceed directly to trial, Hayward tenses, his face immobile except for his eyes, which flicker brightly like candles in a breeze as he looks from Arthur to Vickers to the buzzing rabble restless in stackable plastic chairs.

"Today?"

"If the court please. Else we shall all be twiddling our thumbs until the late-afternoon ferry."

"I set this for a bail hearing. This is unprecedented."

"Your Honour has a well-earned reputation for not blindly following precedent. Public agitation has arisen over this case, so Your Honour has a splendid opportunity to bring closure and a return to calmness."

"The Crown is in accord?"

"Ready to proceed," says Vickers.

"Me too, Your Honour, sir." Energetically spoken by Zoller from the front row.

"Constable, I can't hear you."

Zoller, looking confused, raises his voice. "I'm the arresting officer, sir. Ready to proceed."

"I can't hear you!"

Zoller yells back: "Auxiliary Constable Zoller! Ready to proceed!"

"Constable, you will stand when you're addressing court."

Zoller stands at attention; "Yes, sir, Your Honour," he shouts. "Can you hear me now, sir?"

"Shut up and sit down!" Hayward looks about wildly, gestures at the scene outside the wide windows, Stoney with his misspelled sign: PERVERTION OF JUSTICE. "Look at that. Crazy people out there. Insult to the courts. How can I run a fair trial?"

"With your usual devotion to justice and fair play," says Arthur, hoping Hayward will not see his truckling as sarcasm. But he knows this man, his high regard for himself.

Hayward looks at his watch, at the ceiling, out the window. "Can this be completed today? I have the annual dinner meeting of the Victoria Pressed Flower Society this evening. I am chairman. There are awards to be given out. I am *not* going to miss the four o'clock to Swartz Bay. Which means we pack up here at three-thirty, not a nanosecond later."

Arthur calculates: the lunch break is almost upon them, leaving maybe ninety minutes for an afternoon trial. "Not a problem," he says.

"I hope to be brief," says Vickers, carefully.

"Take the plea," Hayward says.

Arthur places a hand behind Dog's shoulders and moves him forward two paces, a chess move, a queen's pawn opening. The clerk reads the charge of trafficking in marijuana and asks how he pleads. Dog looks up at Arthur, who whispers the answer.

"Not guilty," Dog croaks.

"Speak up!"

Dog clears his throat, tries with better result, and the case is put over to two o'clock. "Be warned," Haywire hollers as he departs. "If we're not done at three-thirty there'll be a two-month continuance."

§

While the Women's Guild is busy in the communal kitchen, preparing soup and sandwiches for the court staff and lingering locals, Arthur heads off to the Brig for a more private lunch, with his breathalyzer expert.

"Tell me this rig is safe, Arthur," Jillings says, as the Fargo begins the descent down Shewfelts' Hill.

Arthur tests the brakes, and they answer eagerly, without a jolt or squeak. Arthur is disposed to forgive Stoney. *I just saved your life, man.*

Jillings frowns at the designer roach clip dangling from the ignition key, with its tooth-like pincers. Arthur doesn't try to explain its provenance. He is focussed on the trial, the time limits, the need to keep Jillings's testimony succinct.

The Brig has taken on the atmosphere of a small, local fair, attendees bantering with Stoney, who, afraid of taking a bath on the T-shirts, has knocked the price down to ten dollars.

Not unexpectedly, Ballentine J. Bingham is here, presiding at a couple of joined tables bedecked with pitchers of beer and tenanted by an enthralled cluster of Free Doggers.

"Thirty tons of sinsemilla, boys, and those horse's apples lost that coastal tub in the fog. You may recall seeing me on TV, calling it the biggest investigative fuckup of the last decade."

Arthur and Jillings order the lunch specials, then find a table on the deck, private enough, but Bingham's foghorn carries out the open doorway. "Yeah, you're quaffing suds with the guy who got the Rivera gang off. Cost 'em plenty. B.J. Bingham don't come cheap."

Over halibut and chips, Arthur briefs Jillings, asks questions, makes notes. When Stoney wanders by, carting his box of shirts, Arthur excuses himself, catches up to him.

"Tell your troops to stay away from the windows of the hall, and to stow all their signs and antics. The judge may take it out on Dog. Maybe by remanding him in custody until November."

Stoney promises to pull the demonstrators and tries to leave, but Arthur grips his wrist. "We made a deal, Stoney. I am doing my part. Do yours. Release Kurt's Hummer."

"Yeah, but . . . I ain't saying you won't get Dog off, I got utmost faith . . . but first I got to dump these shirts." He hauls a bundle of them across the ramp to the store.

Bingham is passing out cards while giving instructions on how to evade a customs search. "So when they open your bag, you got all your soiled underwear on top, maybe a shit stain on your gonches. They suddenly lose interest in fighting the war on drugs."

He catches Arthur's fierce look. "Hey, Hometown Favourite, how's it going? Get that little fucker out on bail yet?"

Arthur lets that slide, suppressing his ire behind a smile that betrays a lack of confidence. The worrier within has raised its ugly little warty head, warning of things going wrong this afternoon. Especially with a wild card like Hayward presiding, jumpy, distracted, fretting about making the flower pressers' do.

Vickers is sharp, ambitious. Stripped of its excesses, her case would be simple: Dog sold an ounce of marijuana to an undercover cop.

Arthur has to get around that simple fact.

§

Zoller takes the stand looking so flushed and tightly wound that Arthur surmises all did not go smoothly between him and Vickers. She has tried to pare down the Crown's case, but it's soon apparent that her witness is doggedly sticking to his course.

"Tell us what you did in connection with this case."

"Yes, ma'am, being a long-timer resident of this community, I am familiar with an annual ritual known as the Potlatch."

"Let's put that aside for now. Tell us where you went that day."

"I have to explain about the Potlatch first. For all intensive purposes what it involves is local growers meeting with big-time traffickers from the mainland . . ."

Hayward is studying Zoller with distaste, and interrupts. "How do you know this? Have you ever been to one of these Potlatches?"

"They're common knowledge, sir."

"I'll ask again. You ever been to one?"

"No, sir, not personally."

Hayward has realized that this windy witness may become an obstacle to his making the four o'clock. He checks his watch, turns to Vickers. "Can't we get to the point? This is about a single alleged drug sale, isn't it?"

Zoller does not give up. "Well, my theory is this was a ruse . . ."

"This court does not decide issues based on irrelevant hearsay."

Vickers speaks calmly. "Constable Zoller, just tell us what you saw and did that day."

Zoller looks aggrieved, but to give him credit, as Arthur regretfully must, he has been gifted with a never-say-die mindset, a knack for bouncing back. And soon his sad face lifts as he eagerly describes his role-playing as a Devil's High-Rider, front man for Operation Pot-Snatch.

Without prodding, but relishing each detail, he describes the crime scene, the abandoned quarry, the dead end where he encountered the accused. Two-by-eight boards stretched over quarried rock comprised Dog's table, which bore his produce and a simple sign advertising prime organic at thirty dollars a bag.

Dog was prone in a sleeping bag on an air mattress, but he woke up at Zoller's approach, rising to his full five feet, one inch, as Zoller drew two bills from his wallet, a twenty and a ten.

During all this, Hayward constantly checks his watch. His occasional entreaty to hurry it along only wastes more time, as Zoller, who has memorized his many pages of notes, loses his way, and continually has to back up and reload.

"Quickly," says Hayward. "Then what?"

"I handed him the thirty . . . no, that's later. First I smelled a bag and detected a strong smell of marijuana, which I am familiar with through previous incidents though I have never in my life smoked it."

Hayward groans. "Why should I care?"

Zoller doesn't take that as rhetorical. "Well, because my experience in similar drug-related cases has given me insider knowledge, and . . ."

Vickers takes her turn at reining him in. "Did you have a conversation with the accused?"

"Yes, ma'am, and by the way he gave no indication he recognized me. I asked him if this was good marijuana and he replied in the affirmative, and that was the whole conversation. I then proceeded to give him the thirty dollars and pointed to one of the bags, and he handed it to me."

"And is this the bag of marijuana that you bought that day?"

"You can take it for granite, ma'am, because it has my initials on it and the time."

"Exhibit One, Your Honour. And then?"

"Then he went back onto his air mattress."

"No more questions."

"Excuse me? I haven't finished."

Vickers sits, a signal that she, at least, has finished.

"I also questioned him about where his confederates were hiding, and he wouldn't tell me. I had strong reason to believe . . ."

Hayward erupts. "She said no more questions! That's your job, to answer questions, not rattle on." Turning to Arthur. "Cross-examination. And I'm looking at the clock, Mr. Beauchamp." It was nearing three o'clock.

"Then let's get to it. Mr. Zoller, when you asked Dog if this was good marijuana, he replied, as you put it, in the affirmative. But in your arrest notes, you don't have him replying at all."

"I wrote down that he nodded and smiled. I took that as affirmative, sir. He was smiling ear to ear."

"Did you take a count of the beer empties lying about?"

"Yes, sir. Exactly seventeen empty bottles of Lucky Lager were seized in evidence, along with an empty pint bottle of Lamb's Navy Rum. If you'll refer to my notes, on page two, near the bottom, you'll see I concluded that a drinking party had occurred there the night before."

Arthur takes a deep breath. "Now, Kurt, you and I have been

kicking around this island a long time, and both of us know Dog is an avid consumer of alcoholic beverages and prone to bouts of drunkenness during which he tends to smile from ear to ear. I want to suggest to you, Kurt, and I hope you'll agree, that on that Thursday afternoon Dog was completely plastered."

"He looked the same to me as he always does, Mr. Beauchamp."

"He was crocked. Sozzled. Let's not pretend otherwise."

"Well, I never seen him without that smile, so maybe I never seen him sober. Not being a drinking person, I would say I'm not the right one to ask."

"Come now, Kurt. He was dead drunk on your launch when you took him to the RCMP lockup on Saltspring."

"I believe he was sleeping, because he was snoring."

"He was given a breathalyzer test at the Saltspring detachment. Are you aware of that?"

"I believe that's a formality they do when someone is brought in who is intox . . . has been drinking."

"And that was close to two hours after his arrest?"

"One hour and forty-seven and a half minutes."

"And the reading was what?"

"Two point seven millilitres of alcohol per one hundred millilitres of blood."

"At that rate, Kurt, he would be dead."

He seems unsure why. "Can I check my notes?" Permission granted, he studies them for what seems an eternity: "Sorry, it's point two seven."

"More than three times over the driving limit. And that's why he was lights-out drunk when you made your alleged buy."

"Irregardless, he took my thirty dollars and handed me an ounce of marijuana."

This is probably the worst possible note on which to end the cross-examination, but the clock is ticking, and Arthur is aware that trying to reel in this wiggling fish is risky, and he sits.

As the Crown rests its case, Zoller makes a quick exit from the building, in the clenched manner of one who needs to pee urgently.

Arthur calls Corporal Jillings, hurries him through the boilerplate: the science of analyzing blood alcohol readings, alcohol's effects on human behaviour, and finally narrows his focus to the case at bar, to the human beer keg watching from the prisoner's chair, solemn and sober.

Without Zoller to upset him, Hayward restrains himself, though he still keeps glancing at the wall clock, at his watch, at what Arthur guesses is a ferry schedule.

Jillings continues uninterrupted: "It is likely that the reading, if taken at the time of arrest, would have been at least point three zero and perhaps higher. The accused would have been stuporous and barely aware of his surroundings if aware of them at all, and would be subject to mental blackouts even though appearing conscious."

Arthur checks the time. A quarter after three. "Would he be capable of forming an intent to make a drug sale?"

"In my opinion, it is unlikely he knew what he was doing."

Hayward perks up. "Okay, I get it. Your defence is he was so drunk that his mind wasn't going with the act."

"Quite so, Your Honour."

"I had a case like this once . . . never mind. Let me ask the witness: Corporal, just because there was an exchange of drugs for cash doesn't mean the accused knew what he was doing, right?"

"He may well have been acting by rote, unthinkingly."

"It's like the drunk driver who somehow gets home from the bar because he's done it hundreds of times. Right?"

"Yes, Your Honour."

Arthur knows he has won this case — in the nick of time: it is twenty-seven and a half minutes after three.

Renee Vickers looks resigned as she too realizes that Hayward, obsessed with making his four o'clock sailing, has cornered himself into having to acquit. Otherwise, a contested bail hearing would mean he won't be giving out awards at the flower pressers' gala.

With the evidence all in, Hayward checks his watch. "We have two minutes. I don't need to hear from Mr. Beauchamp. As for you, Ms. Vickers, you can argue till you're blue in your face."

"I'm not even going to try." She turns to Arthur, chin up, noble in defeat, failing to suppress a smile.

Eddie Hayward smiles too, for the first time this day. A smile that widens as he recites a quick judgement finding ample reasonable doubt on the issue of drunkenness. That smile makes the judge seem oddly pleasant and normal, Arthur can't help chuckling, and that causes Vickers to laugh openly, and court clerk and court reporter join in while they stuff their bags and briefcases.

Soon, the audience chimes in — the townsfolk and barflies, the Free Doggers, the Woofers — a celebration that grows from infectious to contagious, the entire room laughing, almost uncontrollably, with Tildy Sears and several other Easy Pieces doubled up in the back row. It's one of those exceptional, brilliant moments of mass elation — an exaltation in the Garibaldi Island Community Hall.

"I find the accused not guilty. You are free to go, Mr. Zibber . . ." Hayward is lost in the maze of that name. His poor effort causes another round of laughter from the locals. They all stand and applaud him as he adjourns this session of Garibaldi Provincial Court and heads for the back door with his staff in tow.

"That was fun," Vickers says, pulling on her coat, shaking his hand, darting off. She will have a tale to dine out on. A ferry tale.

Arthur turns to Dog, who shyly takes his hand and struggles to put his gratitude into words while smiling from ear to ear. "Praise the Lord," he says.

§

Outside, pausing to loosen his tie, Arthur watches as the Coalition shepherds Dog to a van, its engine revving for a run to the Brig. But he observes, confusingly, that among the many lingerers laughter has given way to sad, guilty looks. Yoki and Niko are waiting by the Fargo, and they too seem troubled.

"Poor man," says Niko.

"We feel solly for him," says Yoki.

Arthur's attention is directed to the escarpment of Breadloaf Hill. He can just make out, between arbutus boughs, the bench at Lovers' Leap, where Kurt Zoller sits, head bowed, his shoulders pulsing with grief.

His small support group, the Crime-Stoppers and the Trust Busters, has deserted him, but several others are moving toward him — slowly, carefully, so as not to provoke him into a suicidal leap. One of them is Stoney, who has abandoned the Brig-bound van.

Arthur makes to join them, but stops to watch a strange interplay: Stoney buoyantly greets Zoller and joins him on the bench. Zoller utters a few woeful words, and Stoney wraps him in a two-armed hug.

Stoney's unprecedented behaviour, embracing the Nazi Dog-napper, spurs Arthur voyeuristically into hearing range.

He hears an offering of succour: "You'll always have a friend in Bob Stonewell."

"They've made me into an escape goat. I'm never going to see my Hummer again."

"Hear me, old buddy, hear me good. Bob Stonewell will get it back from those bums who lifted it off you. I promise."

FRIDAY, SEPTEMBER 28

"Some kind of plugged fuel line issue," says Reverend Al. "Fixable. They say she'll be back in service this afternoon."

The *she* referred to is the *Queen George*, the *Trannie*. She returned to home port yesterday afternoon when her engines faltered, and never showed up at Ferryboat Cove for the four o'clock sailing.

"Terrible shame," says Arthur, with a straight face. He has just picked up Al in the Fargo, and they're heading up to Centre Road.

"They pressed the *Saturna Princess* into service, but the pokey old tub didn't pull in until after nine. I guess a lot of Winnebagels were sold."

Arthur knows it is mean-hearted to take Haywire's plight lightly. It must have been especially painful to endure five straight hours of Ballentine J. Bingham. Overtime pay will be a bitterly small recompense for the chair of the Victoria Pressed Flower Society.

Meanwhile, Zoller managed to survive the night, well sedated by Doc Dooley. "It's admirable, isn't it," Arthur says, "the way the island has found so much compassion for Kurt. Some of the fellows from the Legion sat up with him all night."

"Kurt may be a stupid jerk, but he's our stupid jerk."

They are en route to bear witness on this sombre day — low-lying clouds, mists in fields, sporadic showers — to the unveiling of the distraught escape goat's hidden Hummer. Stoney's beery, slurred instructions by phone, late last night, were confusing. As best Arthur could make out, he was to show up at half past ten today in front of Stoney's driveway. Arthur relayed that to Pound, then had to repeat it and tell the depressive constable to write it down.

Tildy Sears didn't show up this morning, and is likely working through a hangover, so cables are still strung all over the house. There's no urgency — Randy Skyler is on a two-week course to qualify as a wilderness watchman.

If Skyler remains steadfast in seeking rehabilitation, Arthur may have to give up his pastime of fretting about him. He's not sure how he might fill that gap. How would he handle his daily routines without a crisis to deal with? The alternative, preferred approach is to transform himself, to learn to stop being a worrier and adjust to a carefree state. After all, has he not just won a magnificent courtroom victory? He's the island's latest hero.

Al kids him about that: Arthur is odds-on favourite to win the Garibaldian-of-the-Year trophy. "Tildy has dropped out of favour. Dog's a long shot, but he'll get the recovering alcoholic vote if he can stay away from beer till the election. I heard he didn't take a drop at the Brig and left early."

Where has Dog's new-found piety come from? Arthur guesses that someone from AA got to him in the lockup. Maybe one of the zealots, with their Bibles.

As they make the long descent to the island's central valley, Al cranes around. "Don't look now, but I think that's an anti-tank missile."

Through the rear-view, Arthur sees the Cadillac DeVille, the metal detector pole strapped to the roof. Zoller is alone, wearing dark aviator glasses and an orange life vest. Behind him comes Ernst Pound in his cruiser.

Ahead, in the shelter of Shewfelts' Hill, Stoney can be seen pulling out in his truck, Dog beside him, a backhoe on-board the flatbed. Stoney waves for the procession to follow him, and all must slow while his truck grinds up the hill. Zoller is impatient, tailing the Fargo's bumper.

When Stoney takes the sharp turnoff to Upper Mount Norbert Road, Arthur guesses they might be heading for Alder Valley, a farming area: a couple of market gardens and a community farm.

The road hairpins around Mount Norbert, then descends to a lowland of alder trees and ferns, ten acres of which have been cleared and drained by the Community Farm Society. Arthur can see the deer fence, a few tool sheds, a greenhouse, and rows of raised beds, some harvested and bare, others still offering fall produce. The vehicle gate is closed. A seven-foot hill of manure sits by it, ready to be wheelbarrowed in.

Many residents of Evergreen Estates, where the land is rocky and barren, have plots here, and several of them are in animated conversation about some pumpkins whose fast-spreading vines are threatening a spinach patch. All pause to watch the flatbed, Fargo, Cadillac, and police cruiser park by the gate.

Stoney steps down from his cab, followed by Dog, who seems unusually alert and sober. He does not look at all fatigued, though he reportedly showed up at Winnie Gillicuddy's at seven-thirty this morning and split and stacked two cords of fir.

Stoney looks around. "Okay, these are the rough coordinates they gave me, eh?"

Zoller frowns, leans his magnetized pole against the garden fence. "Who's 'they'?"

"Kurt, you've been around, you know how it works. I had to call in some debts to get the instigators to talk. Can't mention any names for fear of reprisals."

Ernst Pound joins Arthur and Al by the Fargo. "Other than Kurt, is anyone buying this bullshit?" He's wearing an amalgam of RCMP harness and rough wear — jeans and a ball cap — so it's hard to tell if he's on duty. He's chewing mints, but Arthur's trained nose picks up the scent of rum.

Zoller takes a deep breath as he surveys the wide swath of alders and ferns in the wetland outside the deer fence. He tests his pole on the metal gate, which grabs it with a clang. He pulls the heavy magnet away with some effort and the force causes him to swing around. The pole plunges into the manure pile like a heat-seeking missile, almost dragging Kurt with it. Another clang, rather muffled.

"There's something in there, man!" Stoney says excitedly. "You've done it, Kurt. You've done it!"

Zoller retrieves his pole, uses it to hollow out enough of the compost to reveal a thick tarp covering his Hummer. "I want to get a trace on this manure," he says.

Stoney unchains the backhoe. "I'll have it out of there in a heartbeat, man," he calls down to Zoller, who looks wary, disbelieving. "Trust me, eh. Bob Stonewell plays the backhoe like Heifetz plays the piano."

Dog shakes his head. "Ain't a real good idea, is what I think." It's remarkable enough to hear Dog complete a sentence of such complexity, but Arthur has never dreamed he'd hear him publicly admonish his hero and mentor. Stoney is looking oddly at Dog, as if trying to decide whether to feel betrayed.

"I also think it ain't a good idea, Stoney," Reverend Al says.

"Did you boys bring shovels?" Arthur asks.

Dog responds by grabbing one from the flatbed, stripping down to one of the leftover Save Dog shirts, and going to work.

"That's the Dog we love, man." Stoney retrieves a spade from his truck. "Who wants to have a go?"

Zoller complains he has on his clean clothes. No one else comes forward. Between grunts, Dog says to Stoney, "Get on it, boss."

Stoney is taken aback by the blunt command, then forces a big smile to imply he and Dog are sharing a joke. He makes a spirited effort with the spade, occasionally pausing to grimace and hold his back.

Restless with the slow pace, Ernst Pound borrows a shovel from one of the community farmers, all six of whom are now at the gate. More implements are brought from the sheds. Arthur and Al do shifts. The gardeners join in.

But none match Dog in industry. An inspirational force, he takes no breaks, and hums a well-loved tune: "What a friend we have in Jesus."

WEDNESDAY, OCTOBER 24

"The dark themes that resonate throughout ~~comprise concern~~ pertain to the capricious gods and their ~~godforsaken~~ foundering playthings: [members of?] the blighted human race."

Arthur pauses to decipher his messy pencilled edits. It is evening, and he is at his desk trying to come up with erudite commentary on the new translation of Euripides's plays. His review is intended for the *Journal of Ancient Drama*, and he fusses about getting it right and getting it done on time: he is two days from deadline.

And yet he can't focus. It's the camera up there, high on the wall, always on, blinking, a distracting green. There's another in the kitchen, two more outside. They connect to a monitor on his desk. It's eerie, seeing himself on that monitor, in profile, scowling. He's tempted to dismantle Tildy's mazy, over-engineered Rube Goldberg derangement, which he suspects is out of date. It has not lessened his fears, may even have exaggerated them.

It's been a month since that hectic, disturbing visit from Brian Pomeroy, who occasionally makes distress calls — he's broke, his Haida artist has moved out — or to pass on reports from Parole Officer Jenkinsop. The thrill killer remains at the Abitibi Conservation Area, checking in with headquarters regularly by satellite phone. An enforcer of laws, he has already ticketed three poachers. He is well regarded. A model parolee.

Still, Arthur worries. *The subject claims that he is no longer angry and embittered, but his assurances do not ring sincere . . . He may be prey to an obsession of some kind.* Arthur has tried in vain to contact Dr. Hawthorne, who has taken leave to write a paper on sociopathic behaviour patterns. He's somewhere in Ontario cottage country. Arthur intends to track down his cell number — there's been a storm over Georgian Bay, and land lines are down.

Here, on the West Coast, October has been remarkably warm and dry, setting a record. Arthur feels sorry for Margaret, who has missed out on this fine month and had to cancel Thanksgiving at Blunder Bay. She's been working relentlessly, attending rallies when not in the House, constantly on her BlackBerry. The law protecting endangered species is at risk, and the bill will come before Parliament within days.

Yet she has not sounded weary, and on their last weekend call she was vigorous and quick witted, excoriating the fools across the aisle with sound bites too explicit for the press. The late-night sessions, the speeches, the cocktail affairs. Where does she get her energy? Again, Arthur has the sense they live worlds apart, that he does not know this mystery woman.

After her harangue was done, Arthur found the courage to drop Hubbell Meyerson's name. "Did I mention he's coming out here this weekend?" They'd agreed to meet at Arthur's club in Vancouver. Arthur found no way to wiggle out of it. "He's stopping en route to Ottawa. For the royal visit."

"I can hardly wait," Margaret said.

Arthur finds that enigmatic. She could hardly wait for what? For the royal visit? For Hubbell? Arthur's mention of his name doesn't elicit any sudden recall of her attending his swearing-in. Arthur has not yet shared with Margaret his daughter's revelation about Hubbell and Annabelle. He'll not speak of it to anyone until he confronts the scoundrel.

He thought of mentioning Skyler to her, but in an offhand way, an anecdote, a jest. But he couldn't find a way to make it seem funny.

Had she come for Thanksgiving, how would he have explained all this security apparatus? He couldn't have told a lie; he's maintaining one though, by his silence.

He looks balefully up at the camera, then down at the stubby, ugly monitor and keypad. *I got it cheap. It's like beyond cool, the kind movie stars use for their mansions.* Back in the 1980s, maybe. The system even issues recorded warnings, in an irritating male voice. Bright sensor lights flood the yard when the system is triggered, as it was last week. Cameras, lights, and the siren outside the porch are armed or disarmed only by punching codes into a keypad.

Homer won't set it off, or the geese, or even an escaped goat. But last week, Mabel Lewis's mare got loose and wandered into the yard. While the siren blared, Arthur thumbed clumsily through his notebook for the shut-off code, then had trouble punching the five-digit sequence into the keypad. He has since had Tildy change the code to something he can remember.

He returns to the Euripides criticism, jots down a few more phrases, flips through the book, laboriously copies a passage onto his notepad. He has never learned how to compose on a computer, and has stubbornly refused to try. He can barely type anyway.

It's Wednesday. He has to have this done by Friday, the day he ships out to Vancouver to join that venerable and hard-drinking assemblage of criminal lawyers, the Downtown East Side Trial and Error Society, for a toast and roast of outgoing Justice Thomas McDougall and incoming Justice Mandy Pearl.

The estimable Mandy Pearl, who gave herself to Arthur as a substitute for the bottle, who put him on the dry. Arthur still cherishes that brief, empowering week, an *affaire d'amour* he's spoken of to no one, not even Margaret. He sees Mandy occasionally when he's in Vancouver, over tea, or at an AA meeting, but that magic time in 1987 is rarely mentioned — because of awkwardness, he supposes, or delicacy. It annoys him that Pomeroy has guessed it.

He checks the daybook he's been keeping to remind him of events and duties. "Reserve *Trannie* Vancouver and return." Done. "Reserve Confed Club." Must do. He's a life member of the Confederation Club, his stuffy long-time lodgings in Vancouver.

Tomorrow: "AA at St. Mary's Hall, 7 p.m. Bring Dog." Arthur is Dog's sponsor, and is taking him to the meetings. Last week the shy fellow finally found the courage to speak, earning applause and laughter: "My name is Dogmar, and I just found out I'm an alcoholic."

Sunday. Brunch with Hubbell Meyerson. A distasteful date. Arthur intends to be blunt with the aging sexual freebooter. This friendship is over, pal, kaput.

Arthur's daybook also reminds him there's a Halloween party at the hall on the thirty-first, next Wednesday. It's a fundraiser for the Recycling Society. Arthur is on its board and so cannot avoid the loathsome occasion. Tickets at the door, cash bar, prizes for best costumes. The community website has details.

A wave of weariness carries him upstairs to bed.

THURSDAY, OCTOBER 25

Arthur's courtesans are trying to dress him in Japanese ceremonial garb, like an ancient samurai or shogun, but he resists and flees naked into the hall, among dancing ghosts and goblins. "Prize for best costume," Scotty Phillips announces from the stage. "Arthur Beauchamp, please come forward!" A camera captures Arthur under a spotlight as he stands immobile, his hands shielding his private parts. Margaret walks in, fresh from Ottawa, and screams.

The scream increases tremendously in volume, ear-splittingly so, and on achieving consciousness Arthur jumps up and presses pillows over his ears. It is dark, his bed clock says a quarter to five. An exterior spotlight reveals an eight-point buck bounding away. The siren is howling just outside his dormer window, under the overhang, and he would yank it from its wires were it not a foot too far to reach without risking a fall.

"Do not come closer!" commands an amplified, threatening male voice. "You are trespassing! Stay away from the house!"

He scurries downstairs in his pyjamas, stops at the control panel, his fingers hovering above the keypad. What is the password? Changed to something he should easily remember, but he can't.

He's written it down, twice, on yellow stickies. But he can't find either one. Frantically, his eardrums pounding, he checks around the monitor, on the desk, runs out to the coffee maker, where he often leaves notes for the morning. Nothing.

The alarm continues its medley of noxious noise. *Wheep-wheep. Screech. Brap-brap-brap.* "Stay away from the house! Police are on the way!"

Arthur fetches a kitchen knife, desperately tries to cut the cable that runs upstairs to the siren. When that fails, he grabs the kindling hatchet and ferociously chops the line, splintering a section of wainscoting. The emergency lights dim, but the tuba-like abomination under the second-floor overhang remains robust, fuelled by its battery. He risks deafness if he returns upstairs.

The two Woofers, supposing it's another false alarm, take an inordinate time to show up, but when they do, they are wearing headsets. They survey the situation and fetch four water pails, which they fill and haul upstairs.

Hands to his ears, Arthur hustles outside, making for the root cellar, then pauses to watch the girls at the dormer methodically hurl the four pails of water at the siren. A simple technique they learned at their electronics college?

"Do . . . not . . . come . . ." It dies a painful, gasping death.

§

Dawn light glimmers over the wooded hills as Arthur and the Woofers, warming themselves from Thermoses of coffee and tea, move about the grounds, settling the chickens and goats, two of which are still shaking with shell shock.

Arthur hears a vehicle and knows who's coming. He strolls to the driveway, and presently Ernst Pound alights from his cruiser. "I thought you said there wasn't going to be a next time."

"We had to kill it in self-defence. Ridiculous contrivance. Hare-brained idea."

"I wasn't sleeping anyway." Pound has thrown a coat over his pyjamas. He looks like a dead man walking: wan, thin and hungry, hungover. He has yet to follow through on his vow to quit the Force, and has been going about his work, however mechanically, but folks have been worrying about suicide.

Arthur pours him a coffee and explains about the deer and the stubborn siren and the resourceful Woofers and how he finally found the shut-down code on a sticky under a fridge magnet.

"Maybe I haven't been taking this serious enough." Pound groans at the prospect of putting his head to work. "What's up with this Snider character?"

"Skyler." Who, Arthur explains, is apparently doing a stellar job policing a patch of Northern Ontario wilderness. "I'm more and more inclined to feel he was just blowing steam with his threats . . ."

Wheeep, wheep!

Pound jumps. "Jesus frigging Christ!"

The little tuba is indestructible. It has super powers, has risen from the dead. Its disembodied voice seems oddly speeded up, frantic: "Do not come closer! Police are on the way!"

Arthur and Pound jump into the police van and tighten the windows. They watch the Japanese warriors go into action again, fetching a ladder and the garden hose. As they douse the monster, its screams and squawks wane, struggle back, whimper, and finally fade into silence.

§

"Given the originality of Codwaller's symbolic approach to the prophesied transformation of Hecuba into a bitch, he will be forgiven for his lapses into unnecessary euphemism." Arthur stabs a period at the end of that, pleased, and underlines a few examples of the author's euphemistic overkill. It is almost noon, and he has finally been able to unwind, to wrestle this review into shape.

He spent much of the morning with Pound, over servings of bacon and eggs, talking about Skyler. The constable wearily gave up making notes as Arthur read selections from Dr. Hawthorne's report: the anti-social personality disorder, the recidivism, the unfinished business.

Pound was fidgety, and before Arthur could get him out the door, he surrendered to his bad habit of using Arthur as his sounding board for his many woes. Failed marriage, failed career, failed life — these cares, he intimated, dwarfed Arthur's.

"I don't know whether to quit the Force or just kill myself."

That had Arthur spending half an hour desperately trying to build him up. He looked more together on leaving, but Arthur called Reverend Al, asked him to put out an alert.

He tries not to look at the damage done by his hatchet, the butchered wainscoting. A repair job for when he has the energy. Meanwhile he worries whether the siren had been alerting him. Warning him not to succumb to the notion that Skyler was merely blowing steam. "Do not come closer!" it roared in desperation, knowing the end was near.

He returns to his review for an hour and finally completes a reasonable draft. He must now type it into his computer. Input — is that the word? Then output it on the printer and send it off.

Enjoying a moment of accomplishment, he freshens his tea, thinks about taking a nap, but decides against risking another bad dream. Stark naked at the Halloween dance. Courtesans dressing him in hideous Japanese regalia. No symbolism there — Niko and Yoki have been creating costumes for the dance next week. He is to go as a mighty shogun, they as his concubines.

He schemes over how to break that date. A stomach ache, a cold, a twisted ankle. The phone interrupts. He hopes it's Dr. Hawthorne, on whose cell phone service Arthur has left a message.

The voice is whispery, sinister. "I haven't forgotten you. I'm going to get you if it's the last thing I do."

The mimicry sounds eerily authentic. Arthur is not fooled but his blood runs cold.

"I assume, Brian, that you're so focussed on your horror script that you've lost your sense of humour."

"I'm making up for that with a powerful sense of irony. In that I am suddenly far less concerned with the possibility of your ghastly death than my own. A killer is stalking me on Haida Gwaii. Okay, a prospective killer, a wannabe murderer of me."

"How sober are you right now, Brian?"

"I am serious, *mon vieux*. This morning I got a call from a friend who runs a B & B in Masset. One of her guests was trying to locate me. A bodybuilder with tattoos on his tattoos, on a two-day leave from his freighter, which is taking on cargo in Rupert. Gave his address as Garibaldi Island, BC."

"Moose has never actually killed any of Tildy's paramours, so I'm sure he won't do much more than give you a sound beating. Where are you now?"

"Peeking through the curtains of the apartment above my office. I've decided not to hide my shingle out front — everyone knows where I hold court, just past the tsunami warning sign in Port Clements. So I put a notice on the front door. 'Aloha, gone on vacation.' With the number of the Maui Four Seasons. I'm staying holed up here until he catches the midnight ferry to the mainland."

"Assuming you survive, are you still flying down for the East-End Bar function?"

"Can't afford it, but hell yes — not for that nutter McDougall, he's so senile he doesn't know it — but for Mandy Pearl, with whom I used to smoke dope and with whom you enjoyed, to quote the great Horace Widgeon, explosions of pure, rich, volcanic pleasure. Don't deny it."

"I trust you will not be spreading false rumours."

"Dearie, dearie, of course your tawdry secret is safe with me. Anyway, the main reason I got you on the horn is Skyler has done a bunk."

He pauses as if for effect, while Arthur almost spills his tea.

"He didn't call in today. They've been trying to raise him on his satphone. No luck. They think maybe he's had an accident, so they're sending out searchers. By Ski-Doo, float plane, whatever. My theory is he just fast-tracked his ass out of there, and is on his way to these western shores to fulfil his destiny. In case Moose snuffs me, you'll have to call Jenkinsop for more details . . . Jesus, the body Nazi is at the door. He's banging on it, holding a tire iron. Goodbye, Arthur, I love you." He ends the call.

Arthur declines to buy into the script; it smells strongly of confabulation, a comic riff, and at best it is highly exaggerated. However, the truant thrill killer scenario seems chillingly real.

After an hour's effort, unable to reach Jenkinsop, Arthur gets his superior in the Parole Service, a cautious bureaucrat who reluctantly — Arthur is not on the official contact list — confirms Brian's news, but won't add to it or speculate. A search is on. It may be hampered, however, by a storm front moving into the Abitibi Conservation Area.

Arthur is a two-finger typist, and those fingers are unsteady, so the document on the computer screen is marred by typos. These, he has learned, can be corrected by manoeuvring about with the arrow keys, then hitting one that says "delete."

His mind is not on this task, it's doing time-and-motion calculations. Supposing Skyler decamped two nights ago, how would he travel, how would he make his way to the nearest airport? He'd hitchhike, maybe — that's half a day. Another day of difficult flight connections, but conceivably he could have arrived in Vancouver in time to make this morning's ferry. More likely tonight's.

Arthur decides to skip this evening's AA meeting. To skip Garibaldi altogether. He doesn't care to spend the night under the dubious protection of the waterlogged security system of the stars. He cancels his ferry reservation, books a flight on Sid-Air for four o'clock, then reserves a room at the Confederation Club. A safe house. Restricted to members, known faces.

He looks out at a bucolic scene of golden-leaved autumn — nothing threatening out there but Yoki and Niko, approaching with their regalia. Another fitting. What madness caused him to agree to this? Well, he won't be around on Halloween if Skyler is still on the loose that day.

FRIDAY, OCTOBER 26

Ensconced securely in the Confederation Club, Arthur again tries to make contact with Dr. Arnold Hawthorne at his cottage by storm-tossed Georgian Bay. The land line is still down, and his cell phone unresponsive.

Arthur is in the dining salon, picking at his mixed salad, skimming the reviews in the *Times Literary Supplement*, half-listening to several old boys at the next table. Where was Skyler? Not a word from Brian since yesterday. Presuming Moose did not put him in an emergency room, he may be on his flight to Vancouver.

"Don't remember heat like this in late October." One of the retired tycoons, all in their eighties. "Beginning to wonder if the doomsayers are right. The climate change crowd, their scientists."

"Nonsense, Belwuther, they're all crying havoc just to get government funding. We've had severe weather ever since Noah's ark."

Another ancient chimes in. "The earth goes through cycles. Warms up, cools down. Got to learn to live with it, roll with the punches."

"Twinkle, twinkle, little star." Arthur quickly finds his phone, as other diners snicker.

"Been trying your home number all fucking day," Brian complains. "Finally traced your secret cell. Where in God's once-green earth are you?"

"My club, listening to the wisdom of its elders."

"I'd kind of thought my close friend and father figure would be desperately trying to reach *me*. I assumed you'd been made immobile by panic over my imminent demise."

"I assumed, of course, that you were crying wolf."

Arthur hears the sound of a match being lit, smoke being inhaled. "Okay, Moose didn't bang on the door. Lacking healthy skepticism, he took the 'Aloha, I'm on vacation' notice at face value and returned to his rented Hyundai. I also made up the tire-iron part. I thought you might like some drama in your life. By the way, I've stopped jacking off in frustration over my screenplay — I'm having real sex with it, and it's coming, baby. Inspiration has thickened and hardened my phallus until it feels like a pulsing rod of tempered steel."

It takes a moment for Arthur to source that line. *For the Fun of It.* "If you've exhausted all digressions, can we get on to Skyler?"

Another pull on the cigarette. "Okay, he's still AWOL. There's the mother of all snowstorms raging up there, all aircraft grounded, an RCMP rescue team is trying to get in by snow tractor. But . . . I hope you're sitting, Arthur. Are you sitting?"

"Spit it out!"

"They're also looking for a couple, two middle-aged men, who disappeared in that same wilderness area. Gay guys, married. Canoeists, wilderness buffs. Hang on, I got another report coming in. No, don't hang on, hang up, I'll be right back."

It takes him a while to honour that promise, leaving Arthur to stew over the implications. Two gay canoeists. A homophobic psychopath. He summons the server to take away his unfinished salad and bring his tea.

"Class A debentures." One of the old boys. "Two-year renewable.

Reliable. Proven holdings, oil sands."

"Timber and coal. That's what made this province rich. Sticking with them."

Twinkle, twinkle. The refrain continues until Arthur finally finds his phone hiding under the *Times Supplement.* The server smiles indulgently; he's used to dealing with the senile.

Brian speaks rapidly. He's in his car, rushing to make his flight. "The snow tractor got to Skyler's cabin just an hour ago. The joint was clean as a synchronized swimmer's cunt, but no Randy, no fire in the stove. Ski-Doo and dirt bike were in a lean-to, snowed in, untouched. Snow-covered canoe near the shore. A backpack, some survival gear, one pair of snowshoes — all missing. Also missing, the two canoeists."

"What about his rifle?"

"That wasn't mentioned in the cops' last report."

"Do they know who they're dealing with?"

"Not sure, but I hear you, man. Here's a psycho who hasn't had sexual fulfilment since he carved up Chumpy the clown. Got to cut ass to catch that ferry. I'll call with frequent updates."

Naturally, Arthur disbelieves that and spends much of the afternoon foraging for news, finally connecting with a reporter from the *Northern Daily News* who's working on the story. The latest word is that police found Skyler's Remington rifle stowed in his locker. His sole weapon is a hunting knife.

Arthur then manages to reach Dr. Arnold Hawthorne by cell, a howling wind in background. The psychologist is amiable and open, delighted to talk to the notable lawyer profiled in *A Thirst for Justice* — indeed, he'd only recently reread chapter eighteen, "Death of a Stranger."

He remembers Skyler well, and expresses a few Good Lords over his vows of bloody revenge against Arthur, as passed on by "a person in the know." Hawthorne is grateful to him for helping connect the dots; Skyler's claim to unfinished business now has context.

"I must advise you, Mr. Beauchamp, to take utmost care. Those obsessed with revenge tend to have long memories."

Arthur fills him in on the two canoeists.

"That is of concern. I don't have much of a fix on Skyler's sexuality. It's quite abnormal, obviously. Bisexual, maybe, but in denial, if he's sexually inclined at all. And yet there are those strong homophobic undertones."

Before leaving for the East-End Bar toast and roast, Arthur calls Ottawa. Pierrette Litvak, Margaret's perky aide-in-chief, says she's in Committee, opposing "another draconian bill from the Attorney-General."

"Good for her. And how would this bill diminish our fundamental liberties?"

"It'll make it tougher for murderers and rapists to get parole. She's such a softie, your spouse. Everyone deserves a second chance, et cetera."

§

It's seven o'clock, and Arthur is off by taxi to the annual meeting of the Downtown East Side Trial and Error Society, which traditionally gathers in an East Hastings hotel, in the beating heart of working-class Vancouver.

Brian has yet to call in with any further update, but assuming he caught his flight there'll be ample time to confer tonight. There is much to talk about. The survival gear suggests Skyler went off on some insidious adventure. Maybe to track and murder strangers. Maybe to pursue more worthy game. But how could he expect to escape from the Abitibi wilderness with no access to a vehicle or airplane?

Arthur vows to put the matter out of mind as the taxi pulls up at the pillared front doors of the Tropicana, a small hotel remarkable only for its unlovely décor: faux palm trees and fading beachy murals.

These East-End Bar events tend to be drunken and occasionally dissolute affairs, but the invitees — barristers and judges all — are sworn to silence about whatever may transpire. No photos, no recording devices, no gossip.

The evening is well under way in the dining salon, where a buffet is being laid out: dishes, cutlery, dinner selections on warmers. Most of the action is at the cash bar, which is being patronized by counsel who impede Arthur's progress with handshakes, hugs, and, in the case of Madam Justice Mandy Pearl, an almost uncomfortably ardent kiss, with a touch of tongue and a taste of wine.

"Aw, you pried yourself from your dopey little island just for me. How sexy is that?" She grins, sips red wine, a woman off the wagon — but it would not be wise to comment on that. Not tonight. "God, Arthur, you don't age, do you?"

"'Age cannot wither me, nor custom stale my infinite variety.'" He always enjoys the way she laughs, open, unsparing. "I am at your feet, Milady, overcome by the sheer radiance of your glowing countenance."

"You old fraud." She does look lovely, in a tight red dress, not quite décolleté, but cut low, her cleavage veiled by a scarf.

Of the myriad things Arthur has felt guilty about over the years, their fling does not even make the list. He considers it a small compensation for Annabelle's eighteen men. She may have guessed he'd been with another woman, but she never asked and he never told. Just as her affairs were never spoken of.

"Truly, it's a great delight to see you elevated, Mandy. And even a greater delight to see off poor old Tom McDougall."

She hooks arms with him, and they study her fellow honouree, who is standing by one of the beach tableaux, squinting at a toy monkey dangling from a plastic palm frond. "The cerebrally challenged old fart has a dozen decisions on reserve, he can't make enough sense of them to render judgement, and the Chief has assigned me to retry them. It's sort of a rookie hazing. I'll join you later."

She is drawn into a scrum of men. In her fifties, she's still a magnet, still attractive, still available — unmarried since that early divorce. One of her admirers, moustachioed pothead Ballentine J. Bingham, circles an arm about her waist, and is not repulsed. Irritated, Arthur retreats to the coffee urn.

He thinks of tea but opts for coffee, and while pouring a mug he has a moment of discomfort, sensing an undesirable presence approaching — confirmed when, weaving through the crowd, glad hand outstretched, comes Jack Boynton.

"Arthur Ramsgate Beauchamp, QC. Who has forgotten more about life and law than most here will ever learn."

Arthur has seen little of him since 1987, but memories return of his gift for stiff, stock phrases, his bur-like clinging throughout the Skyler trial. His rigid smile seems a mask; his body language betrays discontent. He's fat fellow now, the Deputy Attorney-General.

"I presume you heard I achieved an elevated position on the short list. They interviewed me, of course, had me under the old microscope, searching for blemishes, ghosts in the closet."

Arthur has to work to make sense of what Boynton is nattering on about. He probably angled hard for the open judgeship.

"They liked what they saw, I dare say. One divorce, that was it. Her adultery, not mine. But then Mandy had one too. For some reason, they must have discounted her drinking issues. It was an agonizingly close call, your essential flip of the coin." He pours a hot chocolate. "Well, of course, being a woman helps."

His expression stiffens as he watches Mandy provoke her admirers to laughter. "As you may recall from the Chumpy trial, she and I have a history." He goes to Arthur's ear. "Came close to having a premarital relationship, but . . . she had a past of some, shall we say, profligacy. Under the circumstances, I wasn't ready commit myself to going further."

That isn't quite the story Arthur remembers. Obviously, Boynton still carries a torch after twenty-five years, now wreathed by envy and resentment.

"Well, it's a real old-times get-together, isn't it? Mandy, you, me, and I hear Brian Pomeroy is coming — pity what happened to him, career-wise. All we're missing is Randy Skyler." Boynton laughs, to signal he's being funny. "Seriously, I hear he made parole." He sips his hot chocolate.

So far, Arthur hasn't gotten a word in, though he hasn't been much interested in trying. But now he struggles with his silence. There is so much to relate that the task seems almost futile.

"Well, I'm sure he learned his lesson," Boynton says. "Smart, college-educated, sportsman, good family — not your basic recidivist. Chumpy was a one-off, surely."

"Jack, we need to set aside some time to talk about Mr. Skyler."

"Damn right, let's do that. Over dinner sometime. Funny, it comes back like yesterday, how you trapped Skyler into that one big lie. If you don't mind my saying, Arthur, you cut it close to the line there. 'A shade less than savoury,' isn't that what the appeal bench said? Had it been any lesser counsel, I think they'd have taken his skin off."

Arthur takes another peek at Mandy. Bingham is hovering over her, vulture-like in his Stetson and denim and cowboy boots, loudly relating some rambling anecdote: "So finally I said . . ." Her eyes implore Arthur to save her.

"I do believe," says Boynton, "that Her Ladyship is sending me a message. I am being called upon to rescue her from that lout."

Arthur gallantly lets Boynton be the hero, watches him stride toward Mandy as if on important business, cutting Bingham off just before the punch line, escorting her away, ultimately to the chow line. Mandy pauses at the salad display to send Arthur another imploring look.

He must leave her to her admirers, because others have taken him aside, all with the firm of Macarthur, Brovak, Sage — good friends, sharp counsel, to whom Arthur would regularly refer surplus clients. They are all tipsy, talking over each other, recalling good times, Brovak offers a stirring re-enactment of the aftermath of Augustina Sage's call party in 1987, when he slugged a Gastown bouncer, causing a melee and a mass arrest of counsel.

Missing from this core group, gratifyingly for Arthur, is junior partner Wentworth Chance, his overly diligent biographer, who has spurned the event in favour of the Vancouver Writers Festival. Also missing, so far, is Brian Pomeroy, who, in better days, was their partner. What is holding him up?

Augustina catches him looking at Mandy, and tiptoes to his ear. "She's had a crush on you forever, Arthur."

The two women are best friends, confidantes, but he wonders if she's kidding. "You are well aware, Augustina, that she ought not to be drinking. I presume you'll look after her tonight."

"Why don't you?"

Arthur sighs. He will keep an eye on Mandy. He can do little more than that right now, because there are no empty chairs at the table she's sharing with Boynton, who has just bought another bottle of red and is refilling Mandy's glass. Surely he knows she's AA.

Arthur is late to the buffet table and is hurriedly filling a plate with the remains when Provincial Judge Sophie Marx, a big, commanding woman, takes to a podium and welcomes all to the annual general meeting of the Trial and Error Society. She shouts over the continuing tumult: "Order, order, please!"

"Double rye whisky and a beer chaser," someone yells.

"Motion is denied," says Marx. "Minutes of the last meeting are hereby waived, and we'll go directly to the new business of immolating our two victims. The no-buns rule is in effect."

A dinner bun is thrown at her. Quips and ripostes fly. Arthur takes his tray to a table away from the action, near the door to the lobby.

Sophie Marx scrutinizes retiring Justice McDougall. "Let's find out if Tom is sufficiently *compos mentis* tonight. Judge, do you see me over here?" McDougall waves weakly, trying to smile. "Do you know where you are?"

"In trouble."

"He seems fairly responsive today." Marx catches Mandy reaching for the wine bottle. "Oh, and I see Madam Justice Pearl is into the sauce tonight. Maybe because the Deputy A-G is trying to get his hand between her legs. Okay, who wants to drag them through the mud first?"

Arthur is unable to come to grips with his boiled cauliflower and overdone pork chop, the runt of the litter on the warming tray, and keeps an anxious eye on the door, fighting the temptation to slip outside and call Brian on his cell.

The speeches are spicy and sharp-witted. There's not much original ammunition left when Arthur's turn comes, and he merely thanks McDougall for giving him so many opportunities to successfully appeal his inscrutable decisions, and congratulates Mandy Pearl for earning her crimson sash despite her charm, intelligence, and sterling character, the lack of which has been a long-standing requirement for judicial appointments.

Arthur is followed by Abigail Hitchens, who begins with a manhood-eviscerating joke so lewd that buns fly. Arthur deserts his cold, rubbery chop, finds his phone, and heads through the lobby to the street, busy East Hastings. B.J. Bingham's Porsche is in the hotel parking zone, and he and Pomeroy are lolling brazenly against it, bobbing their heads over something obviously illegal.

Brian is wearing a sports jacket and tie, and looks unaccountably happy, and this makes Arthur anxious. It suggests something has gone awry. His eyes seem to be glowing. Maybe it's just the cocaine.

Bingham twists a finger up a nostril as he waves Arthur over. "Hey, Save Dog, man. Never got a chance to applaud you for your big upset win. Wanna try a little pixie dust to keep the engines revving?" The offering is the gutted shell of a ballpoint pen and a little mound of powder on an iPad screen.

Arthur smothers his irritation as he declines. Bingham fills his nostrils, shows his utter disdain for hygiene by licking the screen, and returns the iPad to Brian. He slips it into a carrying case, bumps fists with his fellow stoner, then lets Arthur lead him off, down the street a ways. He is late, he explains, because he stopped to wholesale a psilocybe crop to pay off his line of credit. Etiquette demanded there be a formal shroom sharing.

Brian takes a few stumbling dance steps. He can't seem to stop smiling. "I love this old barrio. It doesn't screw around, no frills, no bullshit. Proletarian. Fuck the rich." He stops at a junk store window, admires the clutter inside. "Can you see the elegance here, Arthur? The harmony? A canvas. A poem." He takes a photo with his iPad, and as they continue on he chuckles again.

"Let me in on the joke."

"Better tighten your cloacal muscles." Brian taps the iPad, goes online, pulls up a story from the *Toronto Star*, expands the print so that the headline jumps at Arthur:

"Paroled Murderer Defies Blizzard, Saves Lives of Toronto Canoeists"

Arthur feels discombobulated and looks up to orient himself. Hastings Street, a passing 16 trolley bus, a union hall, a 7-Eleven, pedestrians on their cell phones. All is normal, he's not hallucinating. He stares dumbly at the screen again, at a recent photo of Skyler, in park attendant attire. At fifty, he looks fit, thicker than in his youth, big in the chest. He has a week's growth of grey-streaked beard, some loss of hair on top. The same cold eyes.

Arthur collects himself and reads on. The account has Skyler setting out into the storm late yesterday, after the two canoeists failed to check out of the reserve as promised.

A long trek along the riverbank, a flashlight his only aid in the growing, swirling darkness, finally brought Skyler to an overturned canoe snagged in the branches of a fallen tree, and, a hundred metres downstream, on the shoreline, two men in wet clothes, both shaking with cold, one with a broken ankle, the other desperately trying to start a fire with a wet lighter.

Skyler quickly got the fire going, and pitched a small tent nearby, in which the two men — a married couple, the story adds — shared a double sleeping bag while Skyler stayed up through the night, gathering wood, tending the fire.

The storm didn't abate in the morning, but at noon he led them out, carrying the injured man on his back though knee-deep snow. Late in the afternoon, they finally arrived at his lakeside cabin, where the RCMP rescue unit was waiting and provided emergency treatment.

The two survivors had lost all their gear to the river and, according to an outdoors expert, could well have expired if Skyler had not found them. They were being brought out by snow tractor.

Mr. Skyler wasn't yet available to be interviewed by the press, but was reported to have told police he was merely doing the job he had trained for. A senior Mountie was quoted as saying, "This man deserves a medal for heroism."

§

Back in the Tropicana, a strong urge to pee propels Arthur to the men's room, where he braces himself with a hand to the wall, fumbling with zipper and penis. At the washstand, he composes himself, staring at the reflection of an old geezer running a comb through his hair, looking just as he feels: foolish.

He goes back to the hall, where the speeches are winding down. He barely takes them in. Justice McDougall finally rises in response, with a speech so garbled that he earns applause and cheers with every incoherent phrase. Mandy must already have given her rebuttal, for she has liberated herself from Boynton and joined Brian Pomeroy beside a tropical sunset, where they embrace and begin sharing jokes and anecdotes.

Arthur sidesteps the stampede to the bar and joins a group of colleagues from the Trial Lawyers AA Chapter. He pretends to listen to their reminiscences, but he's lost in the Abitibi wilderness.

He's not sure what he ought to be feeling: shock, relief, embarrassment, joy, irritation at himself? He has a vague sense of having been gulled, played the fool, but can't pin down why. The truth is hard to accept: he has misread Randolph Skyler. Arthur Ramsgate Beauchamp, who may be certifiably paranoid, has allowed obsessive, irrational fears to run rampant, feasting on him, a cancer.

He realizes he's being asked a question. "I'm sorry, what did you say?"

"I asked, are you a DD, Arthur?"

Designated driver. Thankfully not, he replies. He's without a car and intends to leave before bedlam erupts. There are signs already. Abigail Hitchens is striding away from one of the tables, where Chuck Grimstover is wiping wine from his face and shirt.

John Brovak is being bellicose, rehashing a manslaughter with its prosecutor, promising to beat his ass on appeal. Both are drunk. Insults are traded. Traditionally, East-End Bar events aren't complete without a black eye or swollen lip. It is time to go. But first he owes a duty to Mandy Pearl.

She's in double trouble — the stalking Deputy A-G is plying her with another wine while she weathers the dreadful Waylis Rhodes — Endless Rhodes, they call him — who is forever recounting his life's spiritual journey.

This time, Arthur will not fail her. Her expression on seeing him approach is of unrestrained relief, and she quickly slips an arm into his, says, "Ta-ta, gentlemen," and leads him away. "Time to get out of Dodge."

They go out by a back door, where the smokers are gathered in the darkness. She clings to his arm, needing his support to keep her balance while still holding a not-quite-empty wine glass. "Okay, I'm an alcoholic," she says. "But only when I drink."

They arrive at a side street, where she proves herself sober enough to point out her car: a sleek sedan of a certain age. She fumbles in her bag for the keys and hands them to him. "Let me unfreshen your wine," he says, spilling it into the gutter.

"Actually, I wasn't going to. Then I saw you walk in, and decided, okay, just one, to slow my palpations."

"Palpitations, Mandy. Let's find some coffee."

"I have my beans flown in from Costa Rica."

Arthur can call a taxi from her home, but he wonders if a stop-off there might prove tricky, given the signals he's receiving. But he can't deny he's flattered and that he enjoys her playful company.

She lives at the far end of Kitsilano, near Jericho Beach. Arthur and Margaret were there once, several years ago, at a dinner party that made his life companion uncomfortable. Bad vibes, she said later. But tonight, he will keep Mandy company for as long as it takes. It's the AA code of honour.

The car has a front bench seat, and despite his urgings Mandy won't put on her belt. Instead she moves close to him, too close, to his ear, teasing him with the scents of light cologne and red wine. He suppresses wrong thoughts, his hands tightening like vices on the steering wheel.

Keeping his tone light, he rattles on about Skyler: the empty threats, his own ludicrous concerns, Skyler's release on parole, the headline rescue. "Oh, my God," she says, repeatedly, absorbed now, withdrawing to a safe distance, occasionally laughing, maybe at him, at the absurd neurotic hole he's dug for himself.

Arthur finally persuades Mandy to belt up, but he continues to pour words, a venting, a release. He summarizes Hawthorne's harsh dissection of Skyler, the glibness and grandiosity, the pathological lying, the need for stimulation. This from an expert in sociopathy who warned that the obsessively vengeful have long memories.

Mandy has desisted from her kittenish ways by the time they arrive at her sturdy little bungalow, and she manages to make her way from garage to kitchen door without assistance. While she grapples with a complex coffee maker, Arthur checks for liquor stashes, in cupboards, on shelves.

She catches him prowling in the living room. "Relax, the joint is clean." She hands him a latte, seats him on a long couch, and stands over him, sipping from a steaming mug, studying him. She has said nothing about Skyler, and he can't guess what she's thinking.

She seems more sober, even businesslike, as she instructs him to remove his suit jacket, which he does, leaving on shirt and braces. She takes strength from her coffee mug, puts it down, moves behind him, lowers his braces, and digs strong fingers into his shoulders. He remembers her massages from 1987. They are life-giving.

"Randy was definitely not a member of your fan club, Arthur. He decided you had it in for him. Which you did. Accused you of tricking him. Which you did." She's still tipsy, but coherent. "But I got the sense it was more about your calling him impotent — beyond impotent, erotically fucked up. Either way, he's not crazy enough to kill you for it."

He leans forward as she moves down his back, the upper spine. Those muscles were rigid but are loosening up. "Still doing tai chi?" she asks.

"When I can scrounge the time. That feels very good."

"You've had no lapses?"

"Not since you dragged me out of Chez Forget with my meal in a doggie bag."

"I'm surprised Brian hasn't driven you back to drink. He's a world-class bullshitter. He's probably made up half that stuff. 'Carve out your gizzard to eat with his toast' — that's typical Pomeroy-speak."

"Dr. Hawthorne is not a bullshitter."

"He's writing a book about psychopaths, Arthur. He wants psychopaths. He needs psychopaths. Maybe he creates them."

Arthur is buoyed that she's so sanguine about the matter. It helps him relax; he feels muscles relax in his lower back.

"Why did you run away from me and go back to Annabelle?"

Those lumbar muscles tighten again. Inhibitions loosened, she has broken their unwritten agreement not to talk intimately of that intimate time.

He struggles to respond and to do so honestly. "That was a mistake . . . as events have shown. Regrettably, I was too much in love with her."

Still behind the couch, she continues to work on him, silently. He's at a loss to guess what she's thinking. He was a prisoner of love in those terrible '80s, a victim of his own masochism. Mandy should not have felt rejected.

She bends toward his back, her arms around his neck, puts her lips to his left ear. "Please sleep with me tonight," she whispers.

He is speechless with confusion and desire. Her hands slide under his shirt, down the fur of his chest, inducing an unwelcome swelling below, a message she cannot and does not miss. Suddenly she is on his lap, her dress and bra straps loose, a bounteous breast being offered in the cup of her hand.

He is mesmerized by it, this Rubenesque whiteness, that succulent brown gumdrop at its hub. He has made politeness a virtue all his life. Would it be bad manners to spurn her gift? Does he owe it to her to act on the honest urgings of his libido? *Throw caution to the winds,* a small voice says.

He gently clasps the points of her shoulders, and pushes her away from him. "Let's have another coffee."

Stillness for a moment, then she slides away, off his lap. "Margaret?"

"I'm sorry."

SATURDAY, OCTOBER 27

A taxi returns Arthur to his club at a woefully late hour — he dares not look at his watch. But it will be Sunday evening in Melbourne, and Deborah should be home. With her one fledgling flown to Stanford, she is alone.

Before phoning, he takes off his rumpled suit and starts a tub. Deborah answers right away. "Wow, Dad. So great to hear your voice. I'm just making dinner. How are you?"

She suddenly draws away from the receiver, laughing. "Hands to yourself! I'm talking to my father."

"My goodness," Arthur says. It's dinner for two. Is her companion the "someone authentic" she met over the Internet?

Deborah explains: "He tried to take advantage of me as I was marinating." Lower, confiding: "God, Dad, he is so cool, so un-Australian and non-sexist. Smart, funny, not bad to look at when he combs his hair."

His name is Grant Shanahan, she says. He's some kind of ocean scientist, several years divorced, like her. He's been staying over on weekends. There are plans to merge more closely, now that Nick is in California.

A prize plucked from an Internet dating site? Arthur finds that amazing. He always thought those outfits were bogus, a scheme to profit from the lonely. Like those sexy singles his computer offers up. But he's happy for his daughter. Her ex, a stockbroker, was a bit of a bore.

"My God, Dad, it must be late back there. Why are you still up?"

An AA emergency, he says. Deborah would remember those late-night calls. "Sweetie, I'm incredibly happy for you. But take it easy, it's never wise to move too fast with these things." He's an expert.

He explains he needs some quick advice about how to handle Hubbell Meyerson, who will be joining him for brunch in seven hours.

"You'll handle him in your usual way, Dad. You won't make a scene. You won't confront him. Beauchamps just don't *do* that sort of thing."

Arthur takes umbrage at this accusation of cowardice. "Just wait and see. I intend to let him have both barrels. Out of curiosity, how many times was Annabelle with him, did she tell you? In her inebriated unbosoming."

"I didn't ask. It was a purging. She actually felt better afterward. Hey, Dad, let it go. I wish I hadn't told you. You've got a different life. A terrific life. With a terrific woman. How is everything with her?"

"Fine, I believe. Sometimes I'm not too sure, but that's just me."

"Oh, God, now you're worried about Margaret. Mom really left her scars. Dad, this sort of neurotic thinking has got to stop."

Arthur crawls into the tub, feeling spanked by his own child.

§

It is getting on to a quarter to twelve, Arthur has a flight out of the harbour in forty-five minutes, and he's trying not to show impatience as Hubbell, over a second martini, regales him about the hedonistic amenities of his diplomatic posting: the nubile girls who run papers in to him to sign, the private pool at his adjoining residence, which he encourages them to share, the beaches, the tropical sunsets, the carnivals.

He has a deep tan and has grown a curly beard as amends for his baldness, and has fattened his face with chipmunk cheeks but somehow retains a robust handsomeness.

The server comes to take their plates. Arthur's poached eggs are sitting poorly in his stomach. He wonders if Meyerson suspects that Arthur knows. He's being very jaunty. There's no hint of embarrassment or guilt.

"Sorry we couldn't do this up proper," Hubbell says, "but I'm expected tonight at a reception for Their Royal Highnesses' advance guard." This seems meant to impress the old boys at a nearby table, who are watching the news on a big-screen TV.

"Oh, by the way, I'll be renting a suite at the Château next month, inviting some players, investors, not green but greenish. I'm going to ask Margaret to say a few words, and we'll see if we can't raise a little moolah for her, for those by-elections."

Hubbell is waving for the chit, doesn't notice Arthur choking on his tea.

"Twinkle, twinkle, little star." Arthur is too flustered to remember in which pocket he put the phone. His fellow diners are grinning. Hubbell sings, "How I wonder what you are."

Arthur finally flips open his cell. Almost noon, it says. He's had maybe five hours' sleep.

It's Mandy. "Just wanted to thank you for not busting me for attempted rape. How long did you stay?"

Arthur hesitates. What should he reply in front of Hubbell? "Until I could hear your gentle snores," he says. They talked until half past midnight, when he persuaded her to drink lots of water, take Aspirin, and head for bed. He stayed for another hour, doing crossword puzzles, feeling over-caffeinated.

"Stop obsessing over Skyler, Arthur," Mandy says. "He doesn't give a shit about you. He's too full of himself."

"Yes, I heard him on the radio." Skyler earnestly going on about his new life mission. He made a "mistake" many years ago — an admission of guilt, finally? — and wants to give back, to reach out, help kids. The story was also on the inside pages of morning editions, the 1987 trial only lightly touched on: A street beggar. A lot of drinking. Numerous knife wounds. The name of prosecuting counsel was not mentioned.

"I'm off to do Pilates. That's how we lonely middle-aged women relieve our sexual frustration."

"If truth be told, I was tantalized."

"I know. Ciao."

Meyerson dabs his lips with his serviette. "Gentle snores? Tantalized? Sounds like you got laid."

Arthur's expression is flinty, unmerciful. "I would never do that to Margaret, to my marriage. She is not just my loving partner but my best friend."

Hubbell can't hold eye contact and is rescued by the server with the bill. Arthur now knows that Hubbell knows that Arthur knows. About Annabelle.

You'll handle him in your usual way, Dad. To which Arthur responded weakly: *We shall see.* He and Hubbell come from proper backgrounds, the best families, private schools, and are indoctrinated with good manners and discretion. Among men so programmed, there is no known outlet for personal feelings, especially over such awkward and intimate matters as fornicating with your best friend's wife.

Arthur loses this train of thought, distracted by images on the TV screen: Skyler talking about his sudden conversion to humanitarian causes.

One of the ancients at the next table remarks, "He carved up that street person, that clown, remember him? One of those Granville panhandlers."

"Repaid his debt, I'd say, rescuing those gay boys. This country needs heroes."

Arthur and Hubbell listen to this in silence without looking at each other.

Hubbell rises. "I'll get you to your plane."

Arthur stays seated. "I've ordered a cab. It's only ten minutes."

Hubbell seems about to offer his hand, then puts it to a substitute use, tightening his tie. Jocular in parting: "*Hasta la vista*, old boy."

"Goodbye, Hubbell."

SUNDAY, OCTOBER 28

Arthur takes a break from mulching his beds this sunny afternoon, and sits down on a garden bench with the *Bleat*. He's been keeping out of the way of the workers in the house. Tildy Sears is removing the remains of her alarm system, and Fred the Fix-It Man is repairing the wainscoting.

Both are earning overtime, but Arthur just wants the work done, wants all reminders of his former state of high anxiety to disappear. He has taken an oath, in the manner of the true teetotaller: he is going to beat his worry affliction.

It's working. All he had to do was change his mind-set, to respond to his many inner questions rationally and sanely. Nobody is trying to kill you, Arthur. Your life companion is not having an affair. It is ludicrous to think she might be any more attracted to Hubbell Meyerson than, say, to Nelson Forbish. Good on you, Beauchamp, you've handled the stress as best you can, and have come out of it smiling, and it's a lovely autumn day. Be happy. Repeat that mantra. *Be happy.*

Relaxed by that exercise, he opens the *Bleat*, which reminds readers on the second page, in oversized type, of the island's traditional

Monster Ball on Wednesday. "Your chance to strut your stuff to the hot tunes of the Red Tide Blues Band." A popular Gulf Island crew of grizzled rockers, none of them under sixty. "All funds to recycling. Prominent local businesses (see ads on back page) are giving away $100 prizes for best individual costume and best ensemble, for groups of at least two." That's what the Woofers are aiming for, with their version of *The Mikado*. "Not to worry," he told them. He's going to get right into the spirit of things.

The good news is that Arthur will escape being named Garibaldian of the Year. According to the *Bleat*, the latest poll has Dog with an insurmountable lead. "In an exclusive interview, our local hero would only say, 'Praise Jesus.'"

Buried in Forbish's "This 'n' That" column, is this item: "We're happy to confirm that rumours a former client of a certain local lawyer has been stalking him on the island are unfounded in fact." Arthur hasn't heard that version: a stalker.

Oddly, though, he has had the sense of someone following him on hikes, once yesterday, once this morning. A codger in shoddy attire, slouching along a few hundred metres behind. Whoever he was, he couldn't keep up either time. No worries there. No worries anywhere.

Tildy calls him from the open kitchen window, then continues talking on a portable phone. Arthur makes his way there, waits for her conversation to end. "Awesome. I never been in Haida Gwaii. Maybe the long weekend, if I can save enough bread from this job. Here's Arthur."

She presents him the phone. "He's kinda crocked."

Brian is loud and slurring. "Yo, Arthur, I looked all over for you last night . . . No, that would be Friday night . . . Anyway someone said you dinked off with Mandy. Hey, man, I won't ask, and that way you won't have to lie. I've been too fucked up to contact you — I'm just emerging. Got so shit-faced I missed my flight. I'm still in Vancouver, somewhere up high, man, it's a penthouse, Brovak's, I think, and I'm with a small group of survivalists . . . survivors, and we've been going since Friday night . . . It's Sunday, isn't it?"

"Yes, Brian. Why don't you call back when you've fully emerged?"

"I've been thinking of you, man, I can't get you out of my head. In case you're still worried about Skyler."

"I'm not."

"Jenkinslop . . . sop . . . the parole guy, I got this email from him. He's okayed Skyler taking a leave in Toronto for a week, with his dad. But he's got to show up every other day at . . . somewhere, it's in my iPad, some police station."

"I see. That will afford him a chance to give his interviews from the nation's media capital."

"Should be on *He's Got Talent*. Has that 'Aw, shucks' shit down pat."

Skyler has been getting undeservedly favourable press — the media hasn't dug hard into their morgues, reporting only the motiveless killing of Chumpy and the five-day trial leading to conviction, while burying Justice Horowitz's comments in sentencing: "a murder committed in a most brutal and sadistic way."

"Well, thanks for calling, Brian. You had better find some place to lie down."

"Hang on, Arturo, and let me say something here. Not easy, but I owe it to you. Because when I think about it, I'm not sure I wasn't trying to lay a trip on you. Skyler's threats seemed real at the time, twenty-five years ago, and . . . okay, maybe there was a hidden motive — an unconscious motive — a vengeance thing over the way you side-swiped me at that trial. Still smarts. I never got back on track."

"Brian —"

"It's okay. I'm okay. I just want to say I may have exaggerated some things. No question he wanted to do you in, but I added a little colour. The quote about eating your gizzard with his toast. I'm not exactly sure where that came from."

"Horace Widgeon?"

"I blew it, man. Took some crippling blows, couldn't help it, I blew it."

Arthur tells him to sober up and call back when he can make sense.

§

Margaret's Sunday evening chat is what she calls a "quickie." No fleshly symbolism intended, though it's rapidly spoken, this account of an exhausting weekend of protests and rallies to save the Species at Risk Act. She has a spot tomorrow in question period. The government front bench will be well rehearsed for the issue. She will surprise them, take on the justice minister "over that pervasive war-on-crime bill" instead. The Green leader is not a one-trick pony.

Presumably she's referring to the bill that would lengthen the terms of parole. Arthur doesn't ask for details; he's unwilling to admit he can't keep up with all her political battles. In general, the art of politics, which this sound-bite artiste revels in, is a mystery to Arthur, who regards routine affairs of state as insignificant within the great sweep of history.

Allotted two minutes of speaking time, Arthur restricts himself to a synopsis of the East-End Bar event. He doesn't mention the aftermath, with Mandy Pearl. He doesn't know why. Nothing happened.

Margaret is being pulled away. "Ciao," she says. And adds something else, maybe an expression of her affection. Maybe not.

"I love you," he says into a dead line.

TUESDAY, OCTOBER 30

He runs sluggishly from the masked ball, burdened by his regalia, tripping over the hem of his kimono, and the pursuing beggar is closing the gap. He stumbles through a doorway into a familiar room, it's his old living room in Point Grey, his old sofa. Black-masked Aphrodite is supine on it, her legs spread high, Silenus the satyr thrusting between them.

"Hasta la vista!" the half-goat cries, discharging into the goddess, her mask slipping as she arches.

Arthur wrenches himself awake before she can take it off.

For a while he lies sweating and trembling under his heavy quilt, then raises himself up on his elbows to watch the thick morning mists of autumn creep across the pastures of Blunder Bay. It was Annabelle, surely. Hadn't he seen crimson toenails? Or was that from another nightmare? It was the same sofa, though, the one on which she and Hubbell rutted after he went to bed early with *For the Fun of It*. He has long repressed all thoughts of that evening.

He didn't recognize those legs, though, as Annabelle's. He lurches to a sitting position, trying to bring back a fading dream memory of those limbs: thinner, tauter, tanned, familiar.

Freud warned of this sort of thing. Arthur's solemn vow of abstinence from worry has only dumped all the crap into his unconscious, where it smouldered and erupted in an ugly dream.

He must try harder. It is totally laughable that Margaret would find that lubricious old gasbag of any interest. Except as a source of campaign funds. Surely she wouldn't sell herself for that.

He curses himself for even thinking the last thought, heads for the shower, a cold, punishing one. Yes, he fell off the worry wagon briefly, but you fall and you get up again, and again. No doubt there'll be further tests of his equanimity. Coming up, after chores: a full dress rehearsal for Halloween. He can take it.

He improvises the lyrics and sings: "I was worried then, but I'm not worried now."

§

Arthur has been summoned by his Japanese harem to the Woofer house, where these courtesans to the shogun are costuming him. He shows good humour and massive patience. It's for a good cause, for the recycling depot, and Yoki and Niko want so much to win a prize tomorrow night.

They are in flowered kimonos, both armed with fans. Niko, who has powdered her chubby face white, is studying herself in the tall hallway mirror. Yoki is dressing him in heavy dark robes, a breastplate of flattened tin cans, a helmet with a conical top. In a curved cardboard scabbard is a blunt-edged sickle pretending to be the blade of a ceremonial sword. He's wearing a tin loin plate too, presumably to defy any attempt at emasculation. As a final flourish Yoki pastes on a lecherous moustache. A glance at his reflection proves what he fears: he looks like an idiot.

Niko takes a picture of him on her smart phone. "Now you walk." Arthur takes a few steps. "Not like 'fraidy cat, please. What is word? Swagger."

Homer wanders in, takes a look at him, and barks in protest. "Please, ladies, enough. I have important duties." He's due at the Hall to help set up.

The girls start to unpin, unhook, unzip, untie. He finds himself in his boxer shorts, covering up with the leather breastplate, as the girls make jokes in Japanese, apparently bawdy.

Twinkle, twinkle. He quickly pulls on his pants, and retrieves his phone. It's Margaret, and she's unusually buoyant. "We beat them up over Bill 94, they're going to pull it back. It was the most amazing thing."

"Bill 94. What one was that?"

"The tough-on-crime bill. No second chance. Arbitrary terms of parole."

"Of course. For murder and rape." A softie, Pierrette called her boss.

Margaret explains why it was the most amazing thing: a paroled murderer embarrassed the government by performing an epic rescue in Northern Ontario. "What an amazing, timely example of the power of rehabilitation. A man named Skyler. After something like twenty-five years behind bars. Why does that name seem familiar?"

"I prosecuted him."

"Oh, my God."

"It's in my biography, which may be getting a plug in the *Toronto Star*." An enterprising reporter was on the phone to him this morning about "Death of a Stranger," buttering him up over his incendiary cross-examination of an impotent thrill killer, asking for comment on Skyler's heroic deed. Arthur regretted that he had no thoughts to share.

Margaret has rushed off to find and flip through her copy of *A Thirst for Justice*, giving Arthur time to figure out how to avoid opening up the whole quagmire. One day soon, not now, he will find the courage to tell his life companion about his near-paranoid illness, the threats, tracking Skyler by phone, scanning the bushes for strangers, the relentless ear-splitting siren.

Margaret finds it "fascinating" that he put away a supposedly psychopathic monster who ultimately, as an epic twist, showed such bravery and selflessness. Arthur has little to say. He does not want to recall that difficult trial and the trauma attending it, his struggle to stay clean, Annabelle and the heldentenor. And Hubbell.

He remembers his vow not to worry. Happily, Niko gets them off-topic by borrowing the phone while Arthur ties his shoelaces. "Niko here. How is life? All happy here. Please look at BlackBerry for excellent photo."

Margaret laughs on retrieving an image of Arthur as shogun of all Japan. Arthur is pleased that she's in such bright humour and he presses on, entertainingly, about how he has turned over a new leaf, is worry-free, is actually looking forward to Halloween.

"Oh, by the way, I forgot to mention I had that lunch with Hubbell on the weekend." Now he's done it, impulsively, blindly. "He mentioned something about doing a funder for your by-elections."

"Yes, he did say something like that. In passing."

"In passing?" How often do they pass? The old goat seems to spend more time in Ottawa than Barbados.

"I think he came up to me after a press conference. I told him, fine, work on it, we're broke, we're beating the bushes for money."

She was looking hot. Stop it, he tells himself. Remember your vow.

"Well, let's hope he can come through for you." There seems nothing more to say. "I miss you, darling."

"Me too," she simply says.

He wants to tell her how much he loves her but somehow that would seem pushy, forcing a rote response.

The sense that he doesn't truly know her comes on as he disconnects. Who is the woman behind the politician's mask?

He kicks himself. He can do better than this.

Be happy.

§

Arthur doesn't want to be late — there are witches and goblins to be displayed, pumpkins to be carved — so he speeds his pace, takes a shortcut through the north pasture to Potters Road, being happy as promised, happy to be outside on this blissful afternoon, the sun boiling the mists away, not a whisper of wind, maples in yellow dress, dogwoods in red, the fall song of a white-crowned sparrow.

As he passes Maud Miller's roadside stand, he senses a movement, a deer, maybe, or a loitering dog. He turns but sees only pumpkins, cucumbers, and apples.

He is cautious now, and where the road makes a sharp bend, he detours off it, behind a hedge. Soon he makes out, once again, the old codger in a ragged cloth coat and felt hat, apparently trying to shadow him. It takes a few moments for him to recognize that woeful face beneath the week's growth of beard.

Arthur emerges to confront him. "What are you up to, Ernst? Are you following me?"

"I'm on undercover duty. Someone out there wants to bump you off. You said so yourself. A thrill killer."

"It's over. Didn't you read about it? Skyler is a hero."

"Don't believe what you see in the newspapers. He's here. I know it. He stole my frigging gun."

"What do you mean? You lost your gun?"

"It's not anywhere. I had it last weekend, I think. I was playing with it . . ."

"*Playing* with it?"

"Never mind. I think he took it. Skyler."

Arthur suspects Pound is suffering a full-blown psychosis. "Let's walk together. We'll go up to the Community Hall." Maybe Doc Dooley will be there, or Reverend Al, someone to offer help.

"No, we can't be seen together." Pound falls back. Arthur carries on, slowly, letting him follow, but when he begins the ascent of Breadloaf Hill, the poor fellow has vanished like a ghost.

Be happy.

WEDNESDAY, OCTOBER 31

Niko and Yoki fidget impatiently until Arthur's Fargo finally pulls in to the Hall grounds, the dance well under way. Arrive late, leave early — that is his plan. If the girls want to linger, they can hitch a ride back. He finds a quick-getaway spot not far from the outdoor biffy, where a witch and a scarecrow wait in line.

As they enter the hall, Arthur pulls his helmet down over his ears to mute the shrieking guitars and the howling of ragged, aging voices. The Red Tide Blues Band, made up of retirees from touring bands, prefers heavy metal, a genre that Arthur doesn't quite get, but deign to play old rock-and-roll favourites.

Arthur has yielded to his courtesans' demands they make a staged arrival, so as they follow along, bowing and fanning, he swaggers ahead in his thick robes and tin armour and conical hat, awkward, ill at ease, embarrassed beyond measure.

Dancers and drinkers — in costumes that are hokey but entertaining — make way for them. Tildy and the Pieces are gunslingers, with Stetsons, toy guns in holsters. Emily LeMay is a credible hooker and is being escorted by Abraham Makepeace, her bejewelled pimp. Baldy Johannsen wears a dress, as usual. There's a pregnant nun, a standard.

Mookie Schloss, a Playboy bunny, comes by with a tray of cookies for sale, proceeds for the recycling depot. Niko buys one and playfully sticks it into Arthur's mouth. Chocolate chip, not bad.

Dominating this lavish masquerade is Nelson Forbish, a sumo wrestler, folds of fat pouring lava-like over his skimpy thong. As he snaps pictures of Arthur and his fluttering escorts, the lead guitarist plays a riff from *The Mikado*: "Three little maids from school are we." This ends their set.

Scotty Phillips, dressed appropriately as a carnival barker, jumps up to the stage. "Okay, he's finally showed, so let's hear it for good old Arthur Beauchamp, first runner-up as Garibaldian of the Year." Applause. Arthur will finish his cookie with a coffee while plotting his early exit. "And it looks like we got a new top contender for group entry — look at them geisha girls fanning his butt. Twenty-minute break, folks, while our panel of judges meets in the kitchen."

Arthur leads his entourage to the back, where pastries are for sale, as well as tea and coffee, a mug of which he takes to a table by the rear exit, where the Nogginses sit with their beers. Bored with him, Niko and Yoki depart with their cameras.

Zoë is Mary Poppins. Reverend Al has again hauled out his old long johns, dyed red, and tail and horns. "Quite a few boys enjoying their feminine side," he says. "The year's one big chance to indulge in a favourite fetish."

Arthur has seen at least five men dressed as women. A few women have also come as men. Three clowns. Two Elvises. A Mickey, a Minnie, and a Mighty Mouse. The lazy wear masks of the prominent, some scary, a Vladimir Putin, a Stephen Harper, a Donald Trump. There are characters from a popular cartoon series. "That's Homer," Zoë explains. "That's Krusty the Clown. Over there is Sideshow Bob." She's a fan of *The Simpsons*, has sat Arthur down to watch episodes.

Ernst Pound has come not as a decrepit old man but in uniform; yet it's a disguise of sorts — he's well kempt, shaved, with a shine on his boots. Arthur catches only a few glimpses of him, by the wall, unarmed, his eyes sharp and crazy as he looks for the thrill killer. Kurt Zoller is a caped superhero, with a giant *Z* stitched onto his tunic. Oddest of all is a four-footed ensemble of Stoney as a kangaroo with Dog's head poking out of his pouch and wearing moose antlers, the symbolism of which is unclear.

Arthur is feeling a little odd — not ill in any way, just . . . peculiar. But it's hot in here in this heavy robe, these flattened tin cans. The Tin Woodman of Oz. The exotic nature of the evening, the play and costumery is . . . unsettling.

He asks Al and Zoë to arrange a ride for the Woofers. "I may want to leave early. I'm feeling a little iffy. It's just come on."

"Oh, dear," Zoë says. "Oh, no."

"Oh, no, what?" Arthur asks.

Al says, "I hope you didn't try any of those cookies that were going the rounds. There was more in them than chocolate chip. Stoney had something to do with it, I heard, he and Mookie Schloss. They came out of her oven."

A blast of music ends any hope of continuing this distressing conversation. A cookie laced with marijuana, that's what is causing his growing disorientation.

He decides to get some fresh air. The cannabis is still kicking in; he's not sure if he'll be able to drive, and without a flashlight he can't walk home. For how long will he be stuck in this stoned state?

The snap of cold air gives him sudden relief. There are others outside, talking, laughing, smoking. He senses small alterations of shape and colour. The music is fainter behind those closed doors, but more tuneful.

He sits on a log bench, tries to remember to be happy. *I'm worried now, but I won't be worried long.* The reason he won't be worried long is that a worrisome event has already occurred: he feels utterly stoned.

There stands the evening's most incongruous combo, the four-footed kangaroo, Stoney's hood is down, and his mitts off, as he rolls a cigarette. Dog, still in the pouch, has removed his moose antlers and is sipping from a canned soft drink. When Arthur waves them over, they propel themselves by hopping as one.

Stoney raises his hand as if to stop Arthur's tongue. "Okay, I know you got a gripe, and it's a reasonable one. I want to be frontal about it. I told Mookie them cookies were only for a special list of invitees, and when I seen you scarf one by mistake, I got diverted and then it was too late to warn you."

"How strong is this pot? When shall I be coming out of it?"

"Pot? Naw, I traded the last of the good reefer to your buddy Pomeroy, for some fungi."

"Psilocybin." Arthur pronounces the word slowly, beguiled by its sound, its sibilance.

"Enjoy, man, it's just a little taster — you'd need to polish off at least three of those for the full trip. All you're gonna get is a little peek into the spiritual cosmos. Levels off in a few hours. Enjoy the music. Enjoy the view."

"Jesus will protect you," Dog says.

Brian Pomeroy has by some ethereal means engineered another misadventure for Arthur. He can almost hear him whispering from distant Haida Gwaii: "You're in Zone One, Arturo." Now his voice comes from behind, close and clear: "Good luck, chum, you're knocking on the doors of perception." Arthur turns, expecting to confront Brian and his taunting grin, but there's nobody, just a shadow moving in the darkness.

A voice hallucination? What other alarming mirages will this so-called taster offer up?

Arthur doffs his helmet, and rises, and is relieved that he can find his balance. He could return to Al and Zoë, but he's too self-conscious in this psychotropic state to talk to them or anyone. Maybe he can walk it off. If he can make it to the truck, he can lie down awhile.

Kurt Zoller strolls past to check on his Hummer. Arthur thinks he hears him speaking, another voice memory: *Permission to explore your property, sir.* Arthur follows the caped superhero toward the lot, but pauses by the outdoor toilet. A few of the gunslinging Pieces are yelling to someone inside. This absurd tableau has Arthur smiling. He is shocked that he can find humour in anything right now.

Mighty Mouse and two *Simpsons* characters have joined those trying to communicate with the inmate of the WC, and they're struggling with the door. It finally opens to reveal Nelson Forbish stuck in the narrow compartment, unable to get up. The structure wobbles and tilts as Tildy Sears leads her cowgirls in a mighty tug, and Forbish comes tumbling out, frantically pulling up his thong.

Arthur finds himself laughing outright. These shrooms seem to have a sense of humour. He ought not to fight them. Accept what is. An Aldous Huxley experience. He might even forgive Stoney for the spiked cookie.

He strolls away, the tin cans clanging. He turns to look at the hall, the lights, the cars. No, the scene hasn't morphed into the Roman theatres of Virgil and Cicero, but there's a kind of beauty here. This lovely, quirky island. Its rich cast of characters. All dressed up in their unsubtle costumes.

Arthur has the better costume, a costume of the mind.

The music is muted now as he wanders away from the hall, but still he has a silly urge to dance. A part of him wants to join the merrymakers tending to Forbish; in fact he feels an odd kinship with them, almost a kind of love — even for Zoller over there fondling his beloved Hummer. But what if they make fun of him? No, they won't understand; he's on a different spiritual plane.

When he reaches the edge of the mesa, a ferry appears, the *Trannie*, its lights ablaze, toiling toward Ponsonby Island, its dock twinkling like a star cluster, a galaxy. Far brighter is a fat rising moon that sends a shimmering shaft across the saltchuck. The heavens loom close, an extrasolar quilt of stars.

He is confused about where, in this astronomical vastness, his own body is located. He hears a distant, spooky voice, maybe all-seeing God, some kind of announcement, ominous, prophetic. The voice is familiar, grating. Scotty Phillips! Arthur turns and locates the Community Hall, sees people spilling outside, women lining up at the toilet, men heading for the trees, women dressed as men, men as women. All is weird but all is well. It's Halloween on Garibaldi Island.

Thus oriented, Arthur considers his options for an even better view, settles on Lovers' Leap, three hundred yards away, where there's a 270-degree lookout. He can master this drug experience. He just has to avoid being spooked.

For instance, by one of the cartoon characters hurrying past him: Sideshow Bob, in his rubber mask and canopy of wild red hair, heading for a giant Douglas fir on the escarpment, where he sighs loudly, a ghostly mourn, as he relieves himself in its shadow. Arthur remembers this *Simpsons* character, the bitter, constantly thwarted evil genius.

Zipping up, Sideshow Bob nods to Arthur as he walks past. Two eye slots, a malicious rubber grin. Arthur endures an overwhelming sense of Satan's presence. He checks himself. It's Halloween, for God's sake. That's just one of the locals. Honk Gilmore, maybe, from the height and shape. But he can't get rid of a sense of foreboding, of evil.

A sudden insight: this is what they mean by bad vibes. It's probably a common drug reaction, a psilocybin side effect. He must remember that he is on a drug. The lows come with highs. The world is good. Life is good. *I won't be worried long . . .*

Arthur takes a deep breath of cool night air, and carries on, looking forward to watching a lovely sunrise from Lovers' Leap and wondering why at this pre-dawn hour they are still partying below. His watch says ten-thirty. Time disorientation. Relax. He hears Stoney speak. "All you're gonna get is a little peek into the spiritual cosmos." Arthur looks around. No Stoney. No one.

The narrow, uphill path is lit only by the moon and the distant yard lights of the hall. A dryland forest, firs like towering watchmen over the swirling skirts and tresses of arbutus and oak. They obscure the view until he reaches the wooden bench, with its carved graffiti, a safe ten feet from the rim of the narrow, mossy knoll.

He sits on the bench. He would have a better view of the ferry snuggling into the Ponsonby dock were he to approach the edge. He's not *that* muddled, after all. Actually, he's feeling unusually sharp. His senses are not just working but alive, his mind keen, busy with intriguing notions that demand study but flee. About his role in the cosmos, about the vast good fortune of being alive, when he could be any mass of cells, a rock, a weed, jetsam on the sea.

Yes, this is the peek into the cosmos, the infinite universe, of which he is a part. He's also at its centre, an official observer of the universe from here on planet Earth, and his reign extends from the islands scattered in the Salish Sea to the distant snow-peaked mountains. Zoom to his own little island, to this knoll, to himself, to Arthur Ramsgate Beauchamp. He enjoys an odd, unprecedented sense of worth and well-being.

But here is an unwanted visitor. Arthur makes out Sideshow Bob coming near, grunting as he sits to Arthur's right. Bad vibes again. "Really opens up on you, doesn't it?"

The voice is familiar. It's not Honk Gilmore. "Yes," Arthur says, lamely. "It does."

"I heard they call it Lovers' Leap. Are you a lover, Arthur?"

"Have to go now, sorry." Arthur rises, frightened.

Sideshow Bob stands too. A soft, threatening growl: "Twenty-five years and six months."

Arthur struggles with the math, struggles to clear his brain. Twenty-five years and six months ago: April, 1987.

"I've been waiting for this moment a long time, Mr. Beauchamp."

Arthur is flooded with relief as another notion comes. This is a joke. Arthur is being toyed with, a familiar pattern. "Go away, Brian. I'm not letting you into my head."

"It's a long flight back, so let's do this." He moves in front of

Arthur, blocks his way back down the path. Arthur grabs a rope of his spiky red hair, tries to rip the mask off, expose Pomeroy, expose his callous charade. As he tugs and twists the rubbery mask, he catches the merest glimpse of moonlight glinting on a metal surface, a knife blade, a butcher's knife that is rising to the highest point of its arc and is flashing down.

"Die, you fucker!"

Arthur jerks to the side. Blind within his misaligned disguise, his assailant stabs the air, missing his target by inches. Arthur backs away, the wrong way, toward the edge, as the man pulls off his mask, and that is when Arthur knows for certain, in this ghastly sinister moonlight, that Randolph Skyler is honouring his pledge of brutal revenge.

Skyler keeps darting to left and right, blocking exit routes, backing him toward the lip of the precipice. Arthur is unable to use his voice — terror has engulfed his entire being. But he has managed to draw his weapon, the sickle. He is still a few feet from the abyss as Skyler thrusts again, and he whips the sickle across Skyler's knife arm, slowing its thrust but not stopping it, and the blade penetrates the tin-can body armour with a sharp cold pain.

As Arthur falls backwards, the knife slips out and rattles across his armour onto the ground. He scrambles for it in the moss, but Skyler plucks it away. "I was never impotent! I had to fight them off!"

Arthur is on his knees now and aware of distant laughter and of Scotty on the microphone, something about prizes. He's also aware that he's bleeding from a stomach wound, his groin is wet, his thighs. He's aware, too, that he has crawled almost to the edge of the precipice. Above all, he's aware that Skyler is hovering over him, about to plunge the knife into his back. He knows now that death is inevitable, and he resigns himself to it. His thoughts are on God and the afterlife, the truth of which he will soon know.

There's a shout from behind. "Get down, Arthur! Stay down!"

Arthur turns and sees Ernst Pound emerge from the gloom in

his crisply ironed uniform, running, flailing, weaponless, his arms outstretched. Arthur sees the knife descending. He drops flat into the moss. Ernst dives after him, shielding him, taking the knife in his own back. But then rising, roaring like a lion.

There's a crunch of colliding bodies as he takes Skyler over Lover's Leap.

Ernst's bellow rises triumphantly over Skyler's fading scream. A thud and a rattle of loosened rocks. Silence.

Then, in the distance: "And the prize for best ensemble goes to . . . Somebody better go get Arthur Beauchamp."

SUNDAY, NOVEMBER 11
REMEMBRANCE DAY

With his free hand, Arthur stabs away a teardrop wending its way down between nose and cheek as the Garibaldi Highlanders lead the casket to the grave, mournfully piping "The Battle's O'er." Arthur is one of the lead bearers, and is feeling weak and dizzy, though trying not to show it. He has disobeyed orders to remain in bed.

The Highlanders, vigorously augmented by Kurt Zoller on accordion, make a homelier sound than the lofty, sonorous lamenting of the full RCMP pipe band, which performed at yesterday's salute in Vancouver, at division headquarters. Arthur watched it on television from his hospital bed.

His breakout from Victoria General this morning was smooth and swift, engineered by Reverend Al and a collaborator nurse who unlocked a back door. On showing up here, he was chided by Doc Dooley, who has been keeping a wary eye on him. But Arthur could not live with himself if he missed Ernst Pound's funeral — the island version, here at the graveyard at Mary's Landing.

Locals were astonished that their heroic constable had expressed a solemn wish to be buried on the island he claimed to hate. A will of sorts was found, dated a few weeks ago, a signed, scribbled note. "I have nothing to bequeath, Edwina, but my love for you. Please bury my remains on Garibaldi Island."

They were not divorced yet, so Edwina is formally his widow and heir, though he had no estate to give but a widow's pension. She is here, not with her lover, but with their infant, six weeks old, and she is crying softly in the gentle rain.

With the coffin lowered, Arthur stands aside as Pound's family drop floral remembrances into the grave. A sister, two cousins — that is all, and Edwina. Arthur plucks a flower from a bouquet, and gives a silent prayer as he tosses it in, and others do the same, friends and neighbours, even the boys from the bar who'd taunted Ernst, all looking hangdog and teary.

Arthur walks carefully over to join his friends and family, Al and Zoë, Yoki and Niko, and his unswerving life companion, the Member for Cowichan and the Islands, who has not left his side since rushing to it eleven days ago. His daughter, Deborah, has been here a week. His grandson, Nick, dropped in for a few days from California. Brian Pomeroy is somewhere in this vast throng. Almost the entire island is here. Press from everywhere. Top Mounties. Politicians.

There's to be a reception at the Legion, but Arthur won't make it — his knees are weak from that slow march with the heavy casket and his wound hurts afresh. He welcomes the extended arms of his wife and daughter, who lead him to a bench near the church. Reporters eye him hungrily but none approach; Margaret has already lit into them once, forbidding any interviews.

She ripped into Stoney too, on first arriving, after being filled in on the horrific events and his role in them, his doping of cookies with psilocybin. Stoney has been unable to look Arthur in the eye.

Margaret kisses him. "Let's get you home and stick you in bed."

"A minute more. It's almost over." It would be rude to drive off just as the Highlanders launch into a plaintive version of "Will Ye No Come Back Again?"

Deborah shares some tea from a flask. "Keep telling me you're okay, okay?"

"I'm okay."

Just okay. The mending is slow. There's still pain, especially if he twists, or carries a coffin. The wound was only an inch deep, but the knife penetrated his stomach wall. His armour of flattened cans saved him from a deeper wound. The Tin Man.

There'd been a search party to find the Best Ensemble co-winner, whose parked Fargo was proof he could not be far afield. Apparently Yoki and Niko were the first to find him. He was given emergency aid by a trained medic and a retired nurse. Doc Dooley soon arrived, in pyjamas.

Arthur has no memory of any of that, or of the flight by helicopter to Victoria General. And for several days he had no memory of the events on Lovers' Leap, but eventually reconstructed them from his nightmares.

His one memory, on awaking at about noon the next day in a private ward, was of Stoney telling him it was only a little taster. He was dosed up with morphine but could still sense an aftertaste of psilocybin. Zone Ten, maybe. The never-to-be-repeated last stage.

The mourners begin to disperse. Arthur gets to his feet and strolls off holding hands with his wife and daughter, one on either side. He sings softly: "I asked the judge, 'What's gonna be my fine?' He said, 'Twenty-one years on the Rocky Mountain line.' I'm worried now, but I won't be worried long."

Deborah says again, "Tell me you're okay."

§

Arthur's doting daughter tucks him into the bed she has made on the parlour couch. He finds it hard to get up the stairs to the bedroom, and he gets too anxious when alone.

He asks, "Have you settled on a date?"

Deborah has accepted a marriage proposal from Grant Shanahan, her ocean scientist. She's in love, and it's wondrous to see. Deborah, once his little girl with the green hair, who'd jabber away about all the drippy schoolboys as he drove her to figure skating.

"We're thinking soon. In summer. Maybe January."

"Ocean scientist. You're sure he's not some cold fish?"

She laughs. "He's hot."

She'll return to Melbourne in a few days. Annabelle's disclosures about her formidable sexual history have not been raised during Deborah's stay here. Arthur wants to put them to rest.

He particularly wants to bury the issue of Hubbell Meyerson and his whoring with friends' wives. He doesn't want to talk to Margaret about him, doesn't even want to think about him. A letter from Hubbell, begging forgiveness, was waiting for his return from hospital, and lies crumpled in his wastebasket.

Brian comes from the kitchen with a Ziploc bag of chicken sandwiches, and puts them in his packsack. He is followed by Margaret and the Woofers, bringing more sandwiches, and, for Arthur, a bowl of chicken soup.

Brian zips his pack. Tildy Sears will be coming by soon to take him to the ferry. Moose is on the northern seas again, and Brian spent the night in her Pan-Abode. "I couldn't help it," he said on returning this morning to fetch his gear.

Margaret gives him a hug. "You crazy dope. Have a safe flight."

"I warned him," Brian says, wagging a finger at Arthur. "I don't mean to sound callous and uncaring, but I want that acknowledged with reasonable sincerity, and, if possible, gusto."

"You warned me, Brian. Thank you."

"I let my guard down in the last couple of days. I was fooled, I'll concede that. Everybody was fooled."

Skyler's disappearance went unnoticed for a night and a day. Authorities blame his father, who believed Randolph's story that he met an attractive divorcee who invited him to stay overnight. His dad foolishly covered for him with the police and parole office, unaware that Skyler had booked an overnight flight to the West Coast. He arrived on Garibaldi on Halloween morning in a rented van.

Presumably, he did careful research before buying his costume in Toronto. The Halloween dance was promoted in Garibaldi's online events calendar. The Garibaldian of the Year would be named then. Arthur was high on the list.

"I'll pay you back pronto, Arturo." Brian was pinched, predictably, and needed an "advance" to cover his air fare. "I'll be rolling in it when my screenplay sells." The horror script. Brian claims that recent events have inspired him to spice up the ending.

§

It is evening, dark, and the rains of November have begun, driven by wind, splattering on the upstairs windows. Arthur is lying in his own bed, upstairs, reading the rest of his mail, trying not to think of the discarded letter from Hubbell. Margaret was not mentioned in it, just Annabelle. That was suspicious in itself. Hubbell might at least have wished Arthur continued domestic happiness.

He remembers his vow. Stop worrying. Be happy.

Here's a snivelling note from the author of the scholarly work on Euripides. Arthur's review appeared in the online edition of the *Journal of Ancient Drama*. Arthur's complaint about "lapses into unnecessary euphemism" has generated even more such lapses.

There are dozens of friendlier letters and emails, expressing shock at the attack on Arthur, wishing him speedy recovery and a long life. He lays these notes down as Margaret enters with a mug of tea and his nutritional supplements.

She explains she has winnowed out those that might irritate his stomach. She has been a comforting angel, careful not to chide him, never asking why he'd kept from her the terrible secret of Skyler's threats. When he volunteered the feeble routine explanation, "I didn't want to worry you," she brushed it away.

"Drink more tea. Liquid is good."

She perches on the side of the bed, contemplates him. "I have something I have to tell you, darling."

That sounds ominous. Arthur doesn't want to hear it.

"I need to get it out." Seconds slowly pass. "I had a . . . relationship."

Arthur stiffens, feels a wrench of pain. He sets down his mug, fearing his shaking hands will spill it.

"Please, Margaret, don't tell me."

"I have to get it off my chest. I don't want secrets. I love you."

"Then that's enough." But then he blurts, "Don't tell me it's Hubbell."

Margaret looks shocked. "Oh, God, no! That self-absorbed old lecher? Where would you get such an idea?" She shakes her head in disbelief. "I never got why you were so pally with him."

Arthur listens numbly as she confesses. A social scientist. Frank Chalmers. The name is familiar, maybe important. Yes, he'd seen him onscreen, a TED Talk she'd encouraged him to watch, about climate-change-denial neurosis. Craggy, long-haired, a sense of humour. Probably many other qualities Arthur lacks.

"There were only a couple of times. Well, three. It's over, I told him we had to stop. It was a fling, that's all."

She begins to cry. "I do love you, really, oh God. You're so solid and real and caring and lovely, but . . . I think . . . maybe your constant worrying . . . sometimes it drove me nuts. I just needed a . . . a reprieve, a moment or two with somebody with a sunnier outlook. No, it's not that, not because of you. I was overburdened. I needed some optimism, damn it."

Arthur is hugging her now, she weeping, holding him so tight it hurts.

"It's okay, darling. Everything's fine."

"I'm so sorry."

"Don't worry," he croaks. "Be happy."

AFTERWORD

"Any resemblance to persons living or dead . . ."

Though I practised mainly as a criminal defence counsel, I was on occasion retained by the Attorney-General of British Columbia to prosecute homicide trials, some of which attracted wide public attention.

The trial featured in the opening section of this novel roughly recreates one of them, an alleged thrill killing in Vancouver of a lonely down-and-outer.

The accused was John Wurtz, a bright young man visiting from Toronto. On his journey west, he'd been absorbed in *The First Deadly Sin*, a popular thriller by the late Lawrence Sanders, whose mentally warped serial killer uttered musings like "The murder of a stranger. A crime without motive . . . The act of killing is an act of ultimate love."

Morbidly inspired by such ruminations, Wurtz befriended the victim, a stranger to him, and found himself accused of a copycat murder, his quarry stabbed 56 times with a pair of scissors. The only evidence putting Wurtz at the scene of the crime, a humble West End flat, was a single print on a beer bottle on a window ledge.

The chief Crown witness, Wurtz's travelling companion, had

originally cooperated with the police, but at trial changed his story, supporting Wurtz's alibi. That involved a mysterious third man who'd shown up in the flat, the victim's jealous male lover.

The trial was a difficult one, well defended, but after a strenuous cross-examination of the accused, the jury convicted.

As Wurtz, in handcuffs, was led past the prosecution table to begin his life sentence for first-degree murder, he paused by my chair and audibly whispered, "Some day, Mr. Deverell, I'm going to get you."

This, from the *Vancouver Sun*, is the last I heard of John Wurtz:

> Convicted of stabbing a homosexual playmate to death, John Richard Wurtz is now leading police on another, final run-around.
>
> Dubbed the "thrill killer" back in 1976 for killing the closet Vancouverite homosexual he had picked up while cruising Granville Street, Wurtz, 24, later vanished from a Kingston, Ont., jail.
>
> Now police are puzzled by the mysterious delivery of ashes said to be his remains to his eastern Ontario family from a Florida crematorium.
>
> Or, are they his ashes?
>
> Because there is no body to exhume, positive identification cannot be made.
>
> People who were close to Wurtz are unwilling to confess to police that he is in fact dead. That could open up charges against them of harboring a known criminal.
>
> So, for the time being, police must consider Wurtz, described as a bisexual, alive and the case still open, even though they think he's dead.
>
> "We are reasonably certain that he is dead but we can't say conclusively without the help of others who are obviously reluctant to co-operate without a guarantee that they will not be charged," a Kingston police source says.

Court testimony in Vancouver had shown that Wurtz had talked to a homosexual friend about killing someone just for the thrill of it. He had later returned home with teeth marks on one leg.

Police picked Wurtz's fingerprints from a beer bottle in the dead man's West End apartment.

Rui Flores Romao, 44, a janitor, "had been stabbed at least 56 times" with a pair of scissors.

(*Vancouver Sun*, December 1984)

Incidentally, a truer version of the actual trial, based on a script I wrote, "Death of a Stranger," was broadcast by CBC Radio in its *Scales of Justice* series, produced by the power duo of the late, great Edward Greenspan, QC, and best-selling novelist Guy Gavriel Kay.

William Deverell

Published by ECW Press
2120 Queen Street East, Suite 200, Toronto, Ontario, Canada M4E 1E2
416-694-3348 / info@ecwpress.com

This is a work of fiction. Names, characters, places, and incidents either are the product of the author's imagination or are used fictitiously, and any resemblance to actual persons, living or dead, business establishments, events, or locales is entirely coincidental.

Library and Archives Canada Cataloguing in Publication

Deverell, William, 1937–, author
Sing a worried song : an Authur Beauchamp novel / William Deverell.

Issued in print and electronic formats.
ISBN 978-1-77041-245-3 (BOUND)
978-1-77090-727-0 (PDF)
978-1-77090-728-7 (ePUB)

1. Title.

PS8557.E8775S49 2015   C813'.54   C2014-907592-8   C2014-907593-6

Editor for the press: Dinah Forbes
Cover illustration and design: Natalie Olsen | kisscut design
Printing: Friesens   5   4   3   2   1

The publication of *Sing a Worried Song* has been generously supported by the Canada Council for the Arts, which last year invested $157 million to bring the arts to Canadians throughout the country. We acknowledge the support of the Ontario Arts Council (OAC), an agency of the Government of Ontario, which last year funded 1,793 individual artists and 1,076 organizations in 232 communities across Ontario, for a total of $52.1 million. We also acknowledge the financial support of the Government of Canada through the Canada Book Fund for our publishing activities, and the contribution of the Government of Ontario through the Ontario Book Publishing Tax Credit and the Ontario Media Development Corporation.

Printed and bound in Canada